I0763464

FAR FOREST SCROLLS

Tattered Shred of Eternity

The ground waits in hungry, yet patient and
dispassionate, anticipation of our return.
For written at our birth is the simple truth:
flesh fails. However, hope and almost infinite
possibilities are also born in that moment.
Aspirations and dreams, through sacrifice, can
be attained. The power, and ruination, of life is
its amorphousness. Helplessly thrust into the
world with a bellow,
Shocked at the abruptness of reality outside the
swaddling, murky womb.
The sands of our hourglass start falling before
our first breath.
From the time of consciousness until our play is
writ,
We are the architects, building our lives,
Placing one brick forward at a time,
Brick by brick, day by day,
We construct our life.
Failure knocks down
Most who dream and
Reach for greatness.
Arise and dream anyway.
Each defeat can, if we stand to fight again,
Be the mortar to seal the vector of our life,
Towards the horizon of success, for in the end,
When breath is ripped from our lungs, our silent
scream is swallowed by the void.
So life begins. So it ends.

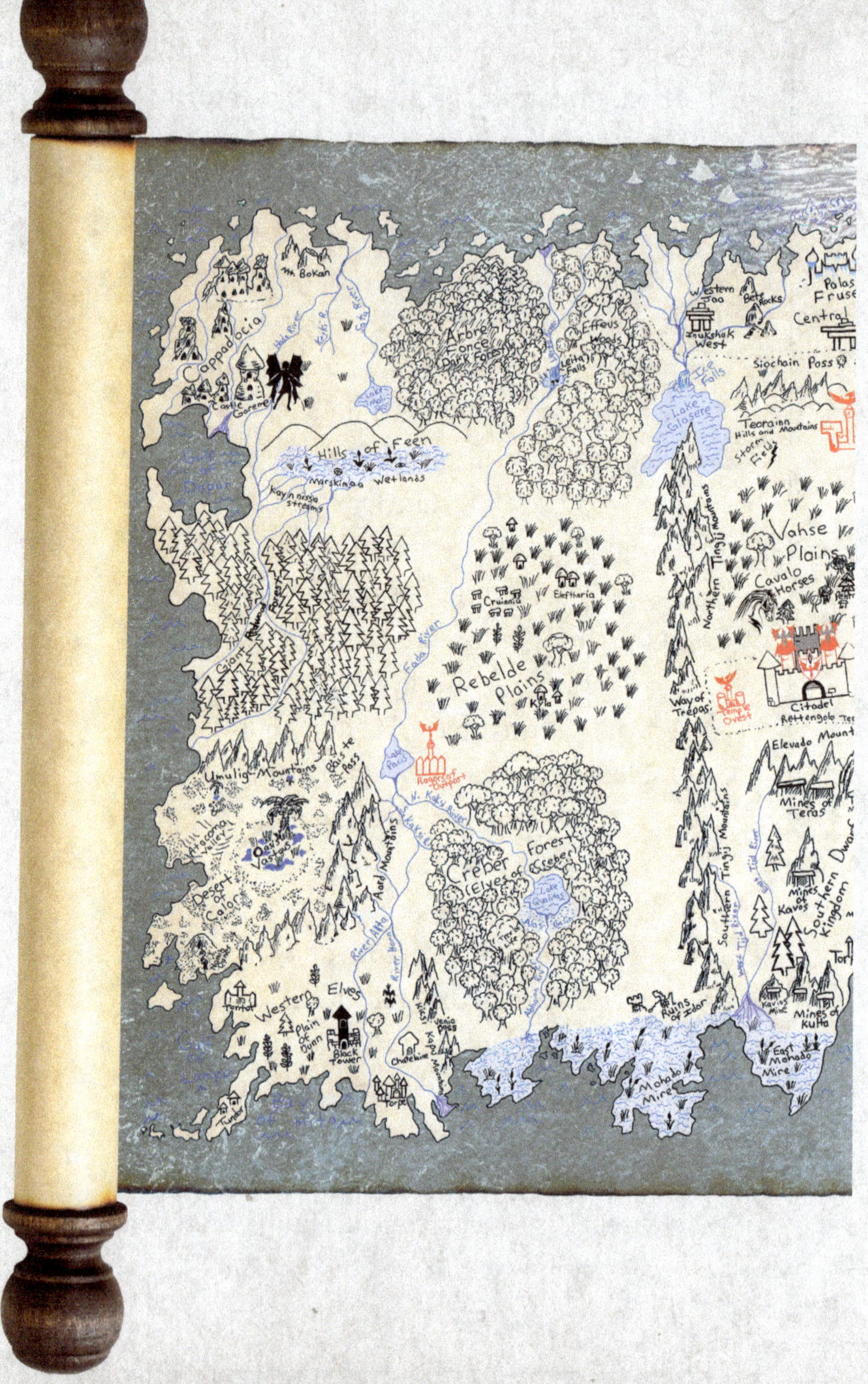

Mt. Bokan
Cappadocia
Castle Goreme
Hada River
Kerki R.
Satu River
Lake Moli
Arbre Fonce
Dark Forest
Hills of Feen
Marskimaa
Wetlands
Kayinnissa streams
Gulf of Dopur
Effeus Woods
Leita Falls
Western Jaa
Bete Rocks
Inukshuk West
Palas Fruse
Central
Siochain Pass
Ice Falls
Lake Glosere
Teorainn
Hills and Mountains
Storm Fields
Northern Tingjii Mountains
Vahse Plains
Cavalo Horses
Cruinniu
Eleftheria
Fada River
Rebelde Plains
Kyla
Way of Trepas
Temple Ovest
Citadel
Rettengolo
Giant Redwood Forest
Umulig Mountains
Baiste Pass
Lake Pacis
Ragors of Outpost
N. Kaky River
S. Kaksie
Atacoma Valley
Oasis Vastous
Aard Mountains
Desert of Calor
Creber (Elves of Creber)
Forest
Lake Qualitas
Mines of Teras
Mines of Kavos
Southern Kingdom
Southern Tingjii Mountains
West Tiid River
East Tiid River
River Alta
River Horn
Western Elves
Plain of Dunn
Black Tower
Chatelaine
Venia Pass
Kapu Mountains
Torpe
Tundor
Gulf of Lampo
Bay of Hitau
Ruins of Idor
Mohado Mire
East Mohado Mire
Mines of Kulta

Eastern Jaa
Nord
Jaa
Inukshuk Mitte
Inukshuk East
Koori Mountains
Northern Dwarves
Kino Mountains
Mount Honoo
Keho Haudella Volcanos
Starten Flower Fields
Amen
Kippe
Ruins of Murbh
Haj
Piscium
Kala
N. Azul River
Taiheart
Glan
Piscium
Pescare
Miksi River
Pallen Lake
Cosan Bridge
Toil Shaor
Haavi
Prolate Channel
Dark Sea
Tallcon Temple
Kisa
Tuikea Mountains
Prolate Islands
Koro Cliffs
River Vita
Ager
Liberum
Azul Delta
Orcite Mountains
Temple Engel
Pluvies Delta
Cliffs of Karst
Dark Sea
Isle of Hirmulisko

FAR FOREST SCROLLS

Tattered Shred of Eternity

BOOK FIVE

For more information visit:
http://farforestscrolls.com

Scrolls from 1000 C.E.
discovered during an archeological dig
in the Far Forest region of England,
the soul of this ancient fantasy tale
is reborn in your mind's eye.

Author: AAAA (Alpha Four) Illustrations: AAAA and Paganus
Scroll translation to English: Radek Novotny PhD Image Restoration:Altier Restoration

LCCN: 2021906304

ISBN (Hardcover, color edition) 978-1-7357528-4-6
ISBN (Paperback, black & white edition) 978-1-7357528-5-3
ISBN (e-book) 978-1-7357528-6-0

Eihwaz comes from the warrior's (Heimdall's) second Aett. This complex rune represents the League's quest, and the perseverance required to see its completion. It also symbolizes the battles ravaging Verngaurd. Even if we live ten thousand lives, all things end. Eihwaz represents rebirth: regardless of what happens to the League, and the wider scope of ravaging battles, the entire world shall be renewed—

It is just a matter of how.

Sentient existence.
A simple bargain swaddled within an absurdly complex reality: Our life is but a Tattered shred of Eternity.
Time rips us forward, demanding our body morph.
Youth crescendos up, age decrescendos down.
That is the compact gift life bequeaths.
We are all endowed but a small ribbon of time, upon which to journey.
To live, to love, to rise…to fall.
How will you spend your time?
How should you fill your days?
Our **minds'** *development, the fortification of our* **spirits**, *the safeguarding of our* **souls**.
Those invaluable possessions, and their fates, are left to our decisions.
How we live decides which part leads. When we rise above base emotions, weaving together our Talents, that is when our tattered shreds, sewn together for each other, blossom into magic.
Each step moves you towards our inescapable destination.
Make sure each stride is teeming with intention.

Table of Contents

Chapter One

The Battle of Liberum: Turnabout is...

Scroll 1: How About a Ride?

“Gimelli, wake up. You’re giving away our position,” Arend said, shaking her.

Sitting up quickly, she headbutted him. “What?”

“You were—” Arend abruptly stopped as Gimelli put up a finger to silence him. He rolled his eyes. *Jumeaux... again.*

As Gimelli talked, now telepathically, Kainen walked over to his Eaglian friend. “How’s your watch?”

“Strangely quiet. I mean, not a single griffin or hippogriff. No whiff of a Proliate patrol either. It’s like they disappeared,” Arend answered.

“How’s the talon and side?”

“Stiff and painful, but better.”

Kainen unfurled the map for Arend, Lontas, and Scelto as Sankari and Bellae slept. "The path through the Way of Trepas is likely not cleared, so how do we get to the Mines of Kavos? Crossing the mire is extremely dangerous to the point of being impractical."

"Are there any smaller paths through the Southern Tingij?" Lontas asked.

"No," Kainen answered simply.

"I don't see how we have much choice," Scelto declared. "We have to risk Trepas. We certainly can't march north again and risk being captured traipsing near Jaa."

"The Proliate are unlikely to have cleared the avalanche, and if we manage to get through, they'll be waiting," Lontas said.

Suddenly, Gimelli emerged, reaching out to hug Scelto. Pleasantly surprised, he pulled her close. He could feel her body shaking and realized she was sobbing. After an awkward silence, she pushed back. "Liberum's under attack." She paused to sniff back tears. "Fifty thousand Proliate plus Magicians, hippogriffs, and griffins."

"Fifty thousand?" Scelto said. "That number's ridiculous. Jumeaux said this?"

"Yes, and asked if we need help. Can Liberum hold out against that many troops?"

"No." The answer came from behind them. It was Bellae, holding Grym and Borb in her hands, wearing a sad expression.

"Bellae?" Lontas questioned.

"We all know it's true. Wanting the answer to be different isn't going to change reality, and saying the truth is not disrespectful. Which way's the quickest?" she asked, the others staring in disbelief. "What? I love Liberum as much as anyone. It just makes fulfilling this prophecy more critical. We have to hope there's some magical answer waiting at the end of this madness."

Bellae had a faraway look. Unbeknownst to the rest of the League, the crystals continually promised wealth and power.

Arend nodded. "I thought of another option. If we skirt south until Pieni Peak—the third mountain north of the mire and the smallest in the entire Tingij range—I can fly you over one at a time. Without Crann…" He stopped, realizing he had picked open a sore wound for Bellae.

"It's okay. Like I said, it's not disrespectful to tell the truth," Bellae said, this time with tears in her eyes. "We need to finish this."

They were headed south towards the blocked Way of Trepas, making good progress along the western edge of the Tingij, when Arend abruptly took off, shooting into the air like an arrow. The rest of the League watched in stunned silence as he disappeared from view.

"Griffins?" Scelto asked.

"I don't think so," Kainen replied. "But, apparently he's feeling better."

After several long moments, three small dots became visible on the horizon. "Take cover until we know for sure that's Arend," Kainen said as they scattered to the side of the mountain.

The three figures zoomed lower until they could make out Arend plus two other Eaglians.

"He's Eitilt, and that's IsGéire," Arend announced once they landed, and the League emerged to introduce themselves.

"We have bad news," IsGéire said.

"We know about Liberum," Arend said.

"I wish that was it," Eitilt replied sadly. His large yellow eyes misted as he avoided looking directly at the young Eaglian. "Arend, your dad, Aquila, was killed in battle."

"What? That can't be!" Arend squawked, his mind filling with visions of his dad's incredible strength and grace. Holding his head in his hands, he began to sob violently. Kainen and Gimelli went over, silently comforting their friend.

"I'm truly sorry," IsGéire finally added. "With the loss of Aquila and General Orel, we're hurting for leadership."

"We'll help you get over the Tingij, but once Liberum falls, the hippogriffs and griffins will join Watchers and Nishi filling the skies, and there are just too few of us left," Eitilt stated.

Arend was still looking down when IsGéire stepped towards Kainen. "There's something you should know."

Kainen took a shaky breath, worried about his own father.

"Creber's under siege."

Kainen took a few mindless steps backwards but said nothing.

"We helped for a while but couldn't stay due to Watchers," IsGéire continued. "So far, it's only the outer forest—no sacred trees have been touched. Rebuilt Ragorsaf is attacking from the north while the Dark Warriors attack from the south."

"Bloody snakes!" Kainen said. His eyes snapped west, towards Creber. He took a deep breath, resisting the urge to run home. *Sacrifice for success,* he thought. *I am the League.*

"You guys are full of great news," Sankari said angrily.

"It's not their fault," Gimelli said. "All our homes are threatened in one way or another."

Arend suddenly stood tall, his miserable eyes wet. "I promised my father I'd see this through to the end and will do so. If you can help us over Pieni Peak, we'd greatly appreciate it."

Eitilt nodded. "The timing's good. We've been granted a brief reprieve because they're attacking Liberum."

It was evening of the next day by the time the three Eaglians carried Kainen, Bellae, Gimelli, Scelto, Sankari, and Lontas over Pieni Peak.

"All right," IsGéire said. "We'll circle around and make sure there are no imminent threats. If you don't see us in the next ten minutes, all's clear."

"Thank you very much," Bellae said. "Have a safe trip back and protect your home."

The two Eaglians nodded kindly before taking to the air.

Kainen unfurled the map. "Let's look at this while they scout."

"Looks like we head straight north to the source of the Western Tijd River, then head east," Lontas said. "Once we cross the Eastern Tijd, we should be close to the Mines of Kavos."

Slowly, with heavy hearts, the League of Truth set off through enemy territory towards an unknown destination.

Scroll 2: Last Gambit

A young squire ran up to Friar holding a top-empty hourglass. "Sir," she squeaked, "the last sand has fallen."

Friar nodded, remembering when the Knights started down the antithetical sapper tunnels, an hourglass had been turned over to mark the timing of their emergence. "Time, as it is want to do, went fast. Alert Constable Rhyfeler and the signalers. It's time for our distraction."

The signal flags quickly alerted the Knights of the need for a diversion, and they ordered smoking logs to be dropped between the real and fake walls.

Soon after, Rhyfeler emerged, standing directly on top of two merlon teeth of the fake wall, with an enchanted Huuto. His yellow robes fluttered as fast as his like-colored hair as he raised his arms. His eyes widened as he screamed, "We are…"

"Knights!" the rest in the castle answered, its force reverberating out.

"Our lives we dedicate to…" Rhyfeler continued as several projectiles zoomed by.

"Wisdom!" the thunderous reply rang out as the cycle continued.

"Each day we live with…"

"Temperance!"

"Our hearts we steel to…"

"Courage!"

"We fight for…"

"Justice!"

"We shall…"

"Never give up!"

"We are…"

"Knights!"

"Now, you all die!" Rhyfeler shouted.

"Morieris!" the Knights howled repeatedly while performing the Knight salute—each Knight thumping their chest twice before raising their right hand with the palm facing backwards and all but the fourth, or heart, finger extended—forming an upright letter *K*. Finally, each brought their hand in a fist to their left shoulder, making a quick slicing motion across their neck.

"That's cute," Lidenskap said. "They think they have a chance to live."

Storlax nodded but shivered as memories of their massive losses outside Trepas stabbed into his mind and doubt inked its way across the fissures of his brain.

As Rhyfeler continued, two elite corps of Knights emerged from secret tunnels on either side and behind the enemy formation. Ritari motioned for the group of flanking sappers he was leading to set up their weapons as Knight Varg commanded the same on the other side. Some were small, mobile versions of the ballista but used Sorea's Sunstar technology and had multiple shooting platforms, which were cranked open. Others used compressed air to launch projectiles. Once those groups of weapons were ready, he motioned for the large platform-based hailstorm weapons, based on Finn's small design—the last weapon he ever used against dragon Hullus.

"So many," a Knight mouthed, motioning to the ocean of Proliate.

Ritari nodded, but under his black panther helmet he grimaced, knowing there was no way for them to beat this many Proliate without help—and no aid was coming.

As the Proliate gazed towards Rhyfeler's continued chanting, the Knights lifted preplaced rectangular boxes out of the ground. They appeared harmless enough, as they were locked onto crisscrossing support legs. The sod that had been planted on top slid off to reveal thousands of diamond-shaped slits now pointing towards the enemy lines. *Thanks Finn,* Ritari thought as they finished preparing the preloaded hailstorm boxes.

"How many of the refill bins should we take out?" a Knight whispered.

Ritari waved his hands at the innumerable Proliate. "All." There were five boxy structures. Each had thousands of spring-loaded projectiles ready to fire. The back half could be removed, and a fresh cassette of ready-to-fire missiles attached.

Once they were set, Ritari gave the silent signal, and they released fifty ballista arrows, each tipped with ceramic pots full of white phosphorous and naphtha. The bolts slammed into several diezmars, trebuchets, and large numbers of Proliate infantry. The inexperienced Ultor Division soldiers, who had either not fought at Trepas or enlisted afterwards, quickly spread the naphtha flames amongst themselves. Panic and fear ripped through both ends of the Proliate army. Flashing explosions continued to send white streaks flowering from each strike.

"Release the colossals," Ritari ordered. As his words finished, compressed air units shot monstrous spears high into the air.

"Discovered," a Knight breathed.

"Oh, you think they noticed that?" another asked sarcastically.

"Reload. Fire at will. The rest of you, unleash Sorea's lightning grenades with Balearic Slings!" Ritari ordered. "Start with the longest. Move to the shortest as they advance."

"We don't have them all unpacked," a Knight complained.

"Well, throw the ones that are!"

The same white phosphorous and naphtha grenades used in the Battle of Trepas were lit in large leather pockets presoaked with water. The specially trained Knights spun their large slings and released. Flying hundreds of yards, the grenades exploded in fire deep within the rear lines of the Proliate. Screams erupted from the revenge-minded warriors of Tallcon.

"Fire the ballistas one more time," Ritari said as thousands of Proliate stormed towards them. "Switch to shorter slings! Hit the ones in front—there's no need to drive them towards us. They've accepted our invitation."

The slingers continued hurling grenades towards the oncoming army as Lidenskap and Storlax emerged, riding in an arc to get behind them with Red Guard cavalry.

"Light up a wall of fire to deter the cavalry," Ritari said.

The slingers complied, and a fire barrier forced a longer path for the horses.

"A few hundred versus fifty thousand?" a Knight said.

"You have your orders," Ritari thundered. "We fight until we can't. Prepare Finn's Diamonds in the massive hailstorms and be ready to reload them instantly. We've trained for—" He paused at the sight of Proliate infantry being magically sped up. "Slingers, keep the cavalry off us! Fire hailstorms at will." *I thought we'd have more time.*

The five rectangular weapons all fired at once, the springs ejecting the diamond-shaped blades, hurtling them forward. Even though the vast majority hit shields or missed, the sheer volume assured deadly hits, especially with the soldiers being magically rushed forward. The Proliate infantry screamed to the Magicians to cease the spell and allow a shield wall as the Knights removed the back of the hailstorm, reloading with a fresh set of ready-to-fire projectiles. The second, third, and fourth rounds of firing from the Knights continued serving up damage.

"Use the green boxes," Ritari ordered. "Be careful not to drop them!"

The Knights unlatched the back half of Finn's Diamond shooters, throwing away the spent cartridge before attaching green ones, with spring-loaded blades soaked with a neurotoxin developed from algae in the Torpen Sea, hellebore, and antiarin. They fired. The Proliate were so close the Knights could hear their breathing, huffing to move under the burden of armor driven by vengeance. The blades ripped into their lines, the proximity amplifying the damage.

"Reload and fire!" Ritari commanded.

Only thirty yards away, the fresh blades resulted in Proliate falling in droves. Enough time had passed that those hit with the poison-soaked blades were succumbing to the effects. Muscle spasms were the first complication, especially prominent in their head and neck regions. Some of the throes were so powerful their helmets were thrown off as they thudded to the ground. Not long after, seizures and involuntary defecation vented across the bloodied soil. The convulsions not only took out the affected soldiers but disrupted the shield wall of those around them. The gaps in their lines were exploited with deadly execution, and throngs of Proliate fell.

"We only have a couple of Finn's Diamonds left," a Knight informed.

"Well, fire them, and how about *now*?" Ritari demanded. "Anyone not slinging or firing the hailstorms, load the compressed air launchers.

Let's see how they enjoy white phosphorous down their throats. We fight and die, but they shall pay dearly for the right."

"The cavalry will be upon us soon!" a Knight slinger warned. "Ritari, head back to Liberum. We'll hold them off and blow the tunnel."

"I shall not leave you, or my post."

"We don't have time to argue. We all agreed on this for you and Varg. It doesn't take a genius to know we're never coming back from this mission," the Knight said, pushing Ritari towards the tunnel entrance. "Our Castle needs its Captain. Defend it well, kill as many of these snakes as you can, and preserve the Knights as long as possible." As the door was closing, the Knight added, "Run. I'll have to burn this entrance soon—they're almost on top of us."

As the shadows danced along the rough-hewn tunnel from his lantern, Ritari hustled as quickly as his large frame would allow. He was a third of the way back to Liberum when the tunnel filled with flames, and his pace quickened. The distal tunnel, closest to the fighting, caved in once the supports weakened under the fire, ensuring the Proliate could not follow. Once at a safe distance, he slowed, then stopped.

The rumble of war roared overhead, vibrating into his armor as he sat, slouching against the shaft's wall. "A complete disaster." The sound echoed with hollow resignation. "Everyone fighting knows how this ends. I'd better get back to an even bigger disaster…my final one."

Scroll 3: By My Knight Hands

"For Tallcon. To Victory!" a lieutenant yelled as the silver-clad Ultor Divisions prepared to storm through a break in what they did not know was the fake wall.

"Why's the moat so shallow?" a Proliate stated, gratitude laced with caution. "It's barely past my ankles." He continued probing the moat's depth with his spear.

"Best to lay the wooden pontoon bridges over it so we can travel faster. It might be deeper in the center, or it could just be lazy Knights cutting corners," the lieutenant replied. After the pre-made bridges were laid down, the Proliate began streaming across.

"There's more water…a second moat after the wall!" a soldier nearing the end of the bridge screamed, belatedly, as the pressure from those behind punched them forward, stripping them of alternatives. Those forced through the sham wall quickly found themselves sinking in the real moat—their heavy armor condemning them to greet the bottom. The weight of the Proliate behind continued serving dozens more to a watery death. The true moat began to turbulently fill with air bubbles and frantic splashing.

"There are two moats!" another soldier repeated over the screams of the drowning. They could see the water, but due to the smoke, not the second wall.

"Hold! Bring forward the reserve pontoons."

With blistering efficiency, the Proliate had a solid area of pontoon bridges spanning from the outer fake wall to the true fortification of Liberum.

The lieutenant moved to the front and quickly through the smoky area to find himself staring at the impressive, and intact, real castle wall painted black. "Bring up ladders!"

"Dowse the burning logs and engage phase one!" Sorea yelled from the rampart.

Knight archers rose up from behind the merlons and unleashed on the Proliate stuck between the two walls, killing them in droves.

"Two!" Sorea commanded. Up on the battlements dozens of ballistae shot out massive spiked balls that were attached to the real castle walls by chains. Once they tensed out their chains, gravity commanded them back to the earth, causing them to swing like murderous pendulums. Soon a web of terror meshed across the Proliate bridges, ripping and tearing at the backs of the enemies' ranks.

"Three!" Sorea screamed, directing two large torsion machines, which had been tucked safely against the real wall, to the desired positions.

When they were aligned correctly, she signaled, and the Knights below pushed forward U-shaped metal tracks that were heaved up onto the battlements before being guided across the moat to the outer fake wall. Once the guide tracks were in place, the machines fired, launching two massive beams with what looked like two enormous sails on their spines. They traveled up through the guide rails and then, as the tethering cords slowed them, the giant joists held at the top of the battlements before tipping, falling to lay across the two walls. The ends of the beams had immense hooks, which scraped across the edge of the outer fake wall, clunking into place.

"Go!" Sorea chided. "Get the tarps off. Archers, continue firing."

"The dimwitted Proliate forgot to send archers to disrupt us," a Knight said. "Plus, they must be resting their griffins and hippogriffs."

Sorea swiveled towards him with a look of disdain. "They did, however, bring fifty thousand soldiers hyped up on revenge."

Several predesignated Knights scurried across the two beams, undoing the canopies covering the four massive, C-shaped blades pointing up to the sky like sails of a ship on either side of the break in the wall. Once finished, chains locking the monumental, bladed weapons pointing up were carefully removed.

"Return!" Sorea yelled, but one of the Knights on the beam stumbled, falling over the edge of the beam, barely managing to clasp the edge by her fingers. Sorea grabbed several nearby Knights before they could scamper to help. "It's too late. Insert levers. Cranking Teams, now! Archers, hold fire. Let the Proliate fill up the kill zone."

The fallen Knight pulled herself up, but the towering metal weapons had already begun to creak and moan ominously. Teams of four brawny Knights came and connected long handles with four indents—each wide enough for two burly hands to crank.

"Start cranking," Sorea ordered.

Several of them gave sideways glances to the Knight out on the beam as loud, groaning whines, which sounded like objections, sprang from the lofty metal towers now beginning to fall. Despite their strength, the Knights on the levers had no chance of slowing the weighty weapons from swinging. The Knight stuck out above the moat attempted to edge around the closest, now moving, metal bar, the heft of which easily bent her backwards, snapping her body and spine over like a twig before juicing her insides, which dripped and drizzled into the moat below.

"Cranking teams, push!" Sorea instructed. "Use the momentum of their fall to keep the blades of death swinging."

The hulking Knights pushed on the lever and kept pressure on it. As the four massive metal blades swung around, crisscrossing just above the bridge full of Proliate warriors, the sharp edges, with help from the weight and momentum, sliced effortlessly through the silver-clad warriors—the force creatively dashing the black walls with cones of artistic red splatter accentuated with fragments of bone and particles of flesh.

"Feel the movement!" Sorea encouraged the Cranking Teams in charge of keeping the blades moving in arcs of death. "Keep this up. I'll return after creating some havoc," she added, moving to reinforce a shorthanded verndari.

One of the hulking Knights was lifted off the walkway by the force of the crank as the weapons began to pendulum the other way. Back and forth the blades arced their destructive, metronomic path. Soon the bottoms were colored red with body parts and entrails fluttering off. Taking advantage of the chaos, archers and the ballistas increased their kill percentage.

There were so many dead the moat was filling up, and the surface coated in bodies and bits. The smoke of revenge obscuring their vision of the reality of what was happening, the Proliate unquestioningly pushed forward, crawling over their dead comrades in a futile attempt to fight their way into castle Liberum but instead finding themselves in a preordained kill zone.

"The last of the Knights' sappers are dead," Storlax said. "Are there any more tunnels?"

"Not sure, but I'm convinced something's wrong. We haven't had one signal from the front-line troops. We need an aerial assessment. The warbirds have had enough rest, and it's time the Magicians get in the fight," Lidenskap implored.

"They'll complain. They're still upset at having to move the diezmars," Storlax added.

"Not my concern," Lidenskap scoffed, signaling the order for their air reconnaissance.

The High Commander nodded but thought, *Did he learn nothing from Trepas?*

Within minutes, hundreds of Magicians riding griffins and hippogriffs streamed into the sky flying in tightly stacked formations. As they glided over Liberum, they unleashed their blue fire orbs. A wave of destruction tore into the Knights on the two walls, sending scorched flesh and battered armor on their own doomed airborne trip.

Prast's face contorted into rage at the deception. After ordering the others to continue attacking, he broke off, returning to Storlax and Lidenskap. "The Knights built a false wall in front of the real one—that's what your siege engines partially destroyed. Your men are currently pouring into a death trap. The space between the outer fake and inner real wall is stained red and blanketed with your dead. I—" Before he could finish, Lidenskap was yelling.

Within a few moments, the Proliate infantry was retreating with discipline.

"As soon as our troops are clear, unleash the diezmars. I want that false wall demolished and then the machines adjusted so the entire front wall of Liberum is reduced to rubble," Lidenskap yelled.

The rest of the Proliate infantry began the eerie chant, "Revenge!"

"I want only a skeleton crew on the walls, Ritari. They've figured out our deceit. Watch out!" Friar added, diving to the side on the battlements just as the blue light from the Magicians tore into several nearby Knights. Warm gyrations of smoke danced up from their sliced bodies.

"Without dragons in the sky, the Magicians are going to cut us to pieces," Ritari said.

"I fear them leaving more than staying," Friar answered.

Before Ritari could question his words, the Magicians were in full retreat. Soon the air force was behind the Proliate lines. The moment they were clear, the diezmars unleashed their wrath. Groups of three concentrated on different sections of the wall. Each one delivered eight precise projectiles to the same spot. The fake outer wall was quickly reduced to piles of debris and dust under the resonant power of twenty-four sequential hits. The sound of the diezmars was as deafening to the ears as it was deadening to their souls and any hope of Knight victory. The only break in firing was when they undertook the gargantuan task of re-aiming the beastly machines to the actual Liberum wall. The Knights were given no chance to rest as the lull saw the skies fill with warbirds.

"Friar, it's just a matter of time before the real wall falls," Ritari stated.

"No!" Friar huffed in frustration. "We didn't kill enough."

Ritari looked down. "Your stratagem was sound for…maybe up to twenty-five thousand attackers, but no amount of planning would allow our castle to survive against fifty thousand, air superiority, and diezmars. So, I ask, your orders?"

"I want everyone who can stand mobilized and armed according to the omnes enim mori plan. Make sure the tutors organize the construction of the barricades to bottleneck the attackers once they're through the walls. They need to start the obstructions in the bailey, angling back to the cemetery—our last stand. Confirm Hephaestus shut down the armory, get his men to set up weapons at strategic points behind each barricade. We'll need them as we displace."

Our last stand. Friar repeated to himself. *So, this is how it ends?* He gazed at the exhausted Knights. *In the end, I failed. The victories at Ovest and Trepas were nothing more than a delaying tactic…perhaps a provocation.*

"You, sergeant!" Friar called.

"Yes, sir," the young man answered wearily.

"Get to Cookie. See if she needs help stocking the cemetery with as much food as she can. Once it's stocked, they should stay there. We'll join them for our last gasp soon enough."

The sergeant grimaced, shaking his head. The idea was too absurd. With the tunnel-flanking movements doing nothing more than

Figure 1: Sorea fights alone on a verndari against hordes of the enemy's air force.

annoying the enemy, and the outer fake wall destroyed, they were all going to die. Now, it was just a question of how many Proliate they could entice to join them. A piercing shriek brought Friar back to the moment. Sorea was the final Knight alive on the last anti-siege tower, or verndari.

Sorea fired a ballista, which tore through the wingpit of a griffin, pinning it like an entomology specimen onto the chest of a hippogriff. As those two creatures plummeted, Sorea did a three-sixty spin, ramming a sword into the beak of a griffin. Leaving the sword embedded, she peppered the bird with several blistering stabs with her forearm tallon weapons before delivering a side kick, sending it over the edge in a nosedive of death. A fireball from a Magician sliced across her back, shredding her leather chest protector and leaving red and blackened skin. She dove, rolled in a somersault, and jumped up on a multi-tiered crossbow weapon. Firing, she instantly killed the griffin and Magician.

"Protect—" Friar was cut off as streams of war birds slammed into the Knights on the wall.

Sorea desperately pumped to pressurize the modified Dragon Flame weapon, like the one she had used against the Western Elves outside Trepas. When she was nearly done, another Magician's fireball zoomed just over her head.

"Nice timing," she said to herself, flipping the end of the Dragon Flame up and into the path of the next fireball. She adjusted so the wick was lit as the flaming sphere shot past her shoulder. With the weapon primed, she released the concoction, including naphtha, incinerating several war birds and their Magician riders.

"There's one Knight left on that monstrosity. Take them out!" Prast screamed.

"We've been trying, but she's—"

"She? She?" Prast repeated. "Wait, I recognize her. Take her down, now!"

Dozens of war birds descended on Sorea's tower. She shot flames in a devastating arc, dispatching ignited beasts to the ground with fire and smoke trailing after their death spiral. Those hit had others take their place as the weapon spewed the last of its flame. Sorea ducked under the nozzle as the talons of a hippogriff scraped across the metal.

She rolled, grabbed a loaded crossbow from a fallen Knight, and shot a griffin between the eyes. Talons scraped across her back vertically, leaving gashes and blood spurting as they crisscrossed burned and unburned flesh. Two hippogriffs slammed into her from opposing sides. She huffed, the air compressed from her lungs. She exploded several quick blows with her tallon blades to the one in front. After dodging a beak snap, she slammed her right tallon up into the chin groove. It instantly collapsed as the one behind dug its talons into her sides. Crossing her arms, her tallons sliced into the scaly legs. As the claws were withdrawn in pain, she jumped, spinning around, her tallon weapon arced, slicing open its carotids. Blood surged, soaking her already painted body. Prast began flying closer as Sorea's enemies shrank upon her.

"Kill the blasphemous female! She's an affront to Tallcon!" Prast said as a griffin was bearing down on her from behind. She sprinted to a large ballista pointing out over the wall, grabbing the crescent-shaped handle used to aim it with her left hand. She leapt off the platform, spinning the ballista around, her body swinging out almost horizontally over the edge of the verndari. Using all her might she reached forward with her right hand and pulled the trigger release. The massive bolt obliterated the griffin's head, dropping it immediately.

Prast continued his rants as momentum carried her around, back upon the verndari. Running forward, slipping on the ice field of body parts and blood, she made it to a roughly formed crate. Scratched on it was *Finn's Toy Box*. She roughly flipped up the lid as the draft of wingbeats closed in around her. Grabbing his hailstorm weapon, the same one used at the Tournament, she held it over her shoulder without looking and fired at where her burned back felt the closest wing beats. As a hippogriff screamed in pain, impaled by Finn's spring-loaded diamond blades, she grabbed the prototype hailstorm weapon. It was clumsier, requiring both hands, but she fired at a griffin howling towards her from the right.

"Can you birdbrains let me find what I'm looking for?" she asked with mock frustration while grabbing Finn's telescoping dagger.

She spun around and unleashed the sharp point, which telescoped out, through the open beak of a griffin on her left. With a flick of her wrist, she retracted it and loosed it several more times before turning back to rummaging. "Got it!" she screamed joyfully. Picking up what she had been searching for, she also grabbed his kama weapon.

"Kill the heathen female!" Prast shouted, moving ever closer as his frustration widened.

Sorea hungrily fed a griffin attacking from her right the blade of Finn's kama, the sharp weapon easily shattering its skull. Leaving the weapon embedded as the bird flipped in death throes, she rotated and quickly began spinning Finn's flying star weapon. She loosed the grappling hook end out with deadly precision, and the rope wrapped around Prast's neck several times before the sharp claws bit into his shoulder. She quickly lashed the rope near the flying star side around a ballista, forming a pulley, and yanked hard.

The Magician was catapulted from the griffin, his crosier falling uselessly to the ground, as Sorea roped him in. As he flopped onto the top, his face was turning blue, and he desperately clutched at the rope around his neck. Sorea slurped the kama weapon out of the dead warbird's head and ran towards the Magician across the garden of blood and bodies that was the surface of the verndari. She ducked under the claws of a diving griffin, rolled, grabbing a spear, and threw it, the tip piercing into its spine. The massive bird fell out of sight, squawking loudly in pain.

In a heartbeat Sorea was up and moving again. Prast had managed to pull the hooks out and unwrapped the cords around his neck. Blood spurted out of the holes from the grappling claws, and his neck was fiery red from the rope. Sliding in blood and entrails, Sorea skidded to him just as he sat up. She straddled him, putting his abdomen in a figure-four leglock from behind. The attacking Magicians hesitated, unwilling to accidentally hit Prast.

Her lips went up to his ear. "I thought Friar told you long ago, out here, in my armor, I am a Knight."

"Your fighting is an affront to Tallcon!" Prast huffed, his muscles atrophied in comparison to the hardened Knight's. "You shall die, foul woman!"

"I have no illusions as to my fate this day," Sorea hissed. "But I can die smiling, knowing I silenced your vile orations by my Knight hands."

Before he could reply, she savagely raked the kama weapon across his neck, showering blood in a violent storm all over her and the already crimson-steeped verndari. She stood up and instantly felt an intense burning on the top of her head, at first believing it was a Magician's fireball. However, the waterfall of blood surging out, instantly covering her exposed skull and torso, belied it was the beak of a griffin slicing her helmetless head. She managed to spin around and slash the neck of the newly attacking griffin with the kama.

Friar, tears draining out his eyes, looked on in silent horror as the back of Sorea's head flopped open to reveal her fractured skull and brain. *I lose a bit of myself with each Knight's death,* he thought. The nearest hippogriff used his razor-sharp talons to rip off the muscle of her left shoulder, the arm slumped into disuse as quickly as it was coated with blood.

Friar could hear Luchar's scream, distorted by his paralyzed face, as Sorea's head was once again under attack by the griffin. Now a large section of her head was missing. The griffin shrieked, its honed beak showing her flesh and bone. Her body slumped and was instantly enveloped by a horde of attacking war birds.

After several flesh-degloving moments, most of the assaulting beasts flew away. One griffin remained. Standing on its back lion paws, it let out a frightful squawk before flinging her stripped, almost skeletal, body over the top of the verndari. After her body tumbled for a short while, a hippogriff swooped in to catch it in its mighty talons. He flipped her limp body, stripped to muscle and bone and partially decapitated head, up in the air before turning and slamming its back horse legs into her falling chest. With a sickening crunch her body ricocheted off the wooden wall before quickly resuming its fall. Blood showered from her injuries as the top of her head fluttered wildly on the rapid descent. With a rude jolt her body crumpled to the earth, flattening as bones shattered before settling into a pool of her own blood.

Friar yelled, "Light up the verndari! Get naphtha up there and get them burning as hot as possible. The smoke will help shield the sky." *Now, a slow retreating fight, ending in death.*

Cookie stood alone in the main kitchen. She had thrown her temper around one last time to clear it out. Only Ri purred anxiously at her feet, unsure and troubled.

With a deep sigh, Cookie took off her chef's hat, laying it on the counter. She found herself unable to remove her hands from the fabric when several drops fell onto the counter. Instinctively she looked up. It took her a few moments to realize the leak was from her own eyes. Her body shook as sadness and loss wracked her soul. It was quite a while before her tears slowed from sheer exhaustion, not from coming to terms with reality.

When she finally managed to pry her fingers from her hat, they ached from squeezing so tightly. Lovingly she ran her hands over the surfaces of the kitchen she knew so well. The cold steel of the pans, the worn, smooth counter, the deeply grooved and scarred cutting boards, the bumpy surface of the well-seasoned cauldron, the soft fur of her tripping partner, Ri the cat. She inhaled the familiar smell of flour, honey, and cooked meat that permeated every crevice. She gazed at the fine mist of dust and food particles dancing through the streams of light.

Shaking her red hair, she took off her apron for the last time and threw it on the floor. She wouldn't need it. She heard enough to know they would all die. She had stocked the cemetery because she was ordered to, not because she thought they would ever have a chance to eat there. Methodically, and with greater care than needed, Cookie blew out the remaining lanterns. *Bellae, luv, I hope you're in a better place.* Turning, she exited her kitchen for the last time.

Scroll 4: This is Totally Normal

"It'll take forever to find something," Sankari whined as the League hid several hundred yards from the Mines of Kavos. "If we get caught, the Southern Dwarves will kill us."

"They build their mines facing south, avoiding direct sunlight shining in, as their large eyes are suited for darkness," Lontas said. "We have to assume that the Daoine Crogall would have wanted this entrance to be hidden before they were killed off."

"So, how does that help us?" Sankari huffed impatiently.

"Remember, the mire lapped around the bottom of the mountain when the Daoine Crogall lived, so the entrance has to be high up. Since the Southern Dwarves hate climbing on the outside, they probably never found the entrance," Lontas said.

"So we're looking for a cave high on the north side?" Gimelli asked.

"I think so. A cemetery *on* the mountain isn't practical, so I think it will be a crevice or cave that leads to a burial chamber," Lontas replied.

"Or, it could be some sort of symbol marking a hidden entrance," Kainen added. "Arend, can you fly to top of the mountain while we find a place to make camp?"

Arend nodded, crouching to take off.

"Wait!" Bellae yelled, grabbing the bag with the crystals. "I'll go to help. That is, if you're feeling well enough."

"Oh, your feeble human eyes will see the opening before an *Eaglian*?" Sankari huffed.

"I feel better," Arend said, ignoring the Fairy. "Plus, two sets of eyes can't hurt." After taking to the air, he looped around, gently grabbing Bellae.

"You could have warned us!" Grym complained from her pocket. Despite the pain and loss, she smiled. There was something freeing about being in the air with the wind rushing by.

"I'm sorry about your father," Bellae called out once her ears popped.

Arend craned his neck to gaze at her. "Thanks. Me too."

"I never knew mine. The only father I knew was Finn," she said. Even uttering his name tore at the scab on her heart, sadness spilling out. "After all of the ridiculous things we've gone through, these crystals had better be the answer to all the world's problems."

Arend began looping around to his right to come at the Mines of Kavos from due north.

"Let's do a few passes," he suggested, scouring the rock face with his amazing eyesight.

"Something's not right there." He pointed. Bellae followed his finger but did not detect anything unusual. "There's a ledge. I'll set you down, then fly around and land. Hold on."

Bellae did not need to be told, desperately clinging to the mountain. Her white knuckles squeezed harder while buffeted by the air from Arend's wings as he landed. "It's okay, Bellae. There's a nice ledge here." Slowly, she released her grip, the blood rushing back into her fingers.

"What do you think these symbols mean?" Arend asked.

"I hadn't noticed," Bellae replied of the series of symbols and shapes in rows carved into an outcropping of rock jutting out at a forty-five-degree angle. Each symbol had a square carved around, framing it. Some of the shapes were short segments of curved lines. A few contained more complex figures.

"Is this some sort of weird writing?" Arend asked.

"No, symbols…I think."

"Look, there's one blank in the corner."

"Does that help?"

"No…not really," Arend responded as they continued staring at the tiled symbols.

"I hate to ask, but can you get Lontas?"

Arend twisted his majestic head. "You don't think we can do it?"

Bellae heard 'we' but understood he had taken it personally. "Not that we couldn't. It's just, you know, he's Lontas." Wordlessly, he left, donating a healthy gust of wind. She reticently tucked herself against the side of the mountain. Time gunged forward until finally Lontas and Arend approached, talking about staying on target.

"You were right, Bellae," Arend whispered once they landed, in a much better mood.

"Definitely not letters. They're lines, shapes, but random," Lontas said, kneeling to peer closer and ramming his knee. Feeling something below the symbols, he twisted to look. "Hey, there's writing under here."

"Should we get the others?" Bellae asked.

"I could get them, but they wouldn't fit comfortably, so just read it."

"Agreed," Lontas said, rubbing his knee.

Bellae began:

"Speak if you be of our line,
Unerring, you must align.
Once said: correctly discover,
The top is but a cover."

Bellae sighed.

"Wait," Lontas said. "Initially, I misheard. It says *of* our line not *on* our line."

"How's that help?" Arend asked.

"At first I was thinking it meant the lines of the symbols, but it means Ainmhi Caint. So Bellae needs to speak…something. Then we discover what we need. Could it be as simple as saying 'correctly' or 'correctly discover' in Ainmhi Caint?"

Bellae nodded, saying, *"Correctly discover,"* in Ainmhi Caint. The top slab glowed white before grudgingly grating downwards.

"Grab it!" Lontas said. "The top slab's a cover."

Arend deftly moved to slow the square of rock's descent.

"There's an exact copy underneath, but it's made of metal," Lontas stated, raking his hand over the lines and symbols.

Arend propped the heavy slab against the mountain and his legs.

"Just like on the cover," Bellae said. "There's a square missing in the upper corner."

"That has to be significant. I wonder if we're supposed to find what's different?" Lontas asked. After several minutes of studying, he breathed out in frustration. "They're identical."

"You sure?" Bellae asked. "It could be small."

"Nope. Same. Let's look at this differently. The main anomaly is the empty space."

"Can I set this down now?" Arend asked, doing so after Lontas nodded. "Hold on. There's writing on the back of the stone slab."

"Whether you sleep or wake, it is the same.
It is a beast none can tame.
Like a spear thrown in an arc, on its way to a mark,
We fly through it as one, and then we are done.

FIGURE it out and you can pass on.
DISFIGURE it means disaster will spawn.
Good luck as you move ***them*** on the groove.
What you seek has already started to move."

"That doesn't make any sense," Bellae said. Grym and Borb peeked out of her pocket, and she read it to them.

"Put us up there so we can see these so-called symbols," Grym demanded.

"Be careful," Bellae replied, setting them down. "I think the part that makes the least sense at first is the most important since 'figure' and 'disfigure' are highlighted."

Lontas nodded. "You're right, especially when combined with this part about 'move on the groove.' I think—"

He was cut off by the mice squeaking loudly.

"Slow down. I can't understand," Bellae declared. "They say the squares move. The mice felt them tilting and noticed the groove in the metal frame holding each symbol."

"The groove of the riddle. We move *them* to make a figure," Lontas said.

Arend's eyes widened. "It's a puzzle, and we have to arrange the squares in the correct order. The empty space is so the pieces can be moved around. That's why this looks funny. These squares are jumbled tiles we arrange into the correct image."

"We should see if they move. Even though they were protected by the slab of stone, they're super old," Lontas suggested. Leaning in, he whispered, "Thanks for asking for me."

"You and me," she mouthed before trying to move one of the figures into the empty slot. She could feel it wobble, but it did not slide. Grym and Borb moved to help, their back legs bracing against the closest tile.

"Maybe—" Arend was interrupted as the square jolted forward, creaking into the previously empty space.

"It works!" Bellae exclaimed. Her joy was short lived as a loud click resounded from under the metal pieces. "Uh oh."

A small rectangular section to the right of puzzle began to vibrate and move outward. *Please not spiders, scorpions, or snakes,* Lontas thought.

A loud grating noise could be heard as if something was stuck. Grym boldly went up to the vibrating section of stone, bouncing on the ledge until a square section fell, sending it, and the mouse, tumbling down. Borb quickly ran over, standing and sniffing into the newly formed opening. Bellae boosted him up so he could study the hole.

"There are chains and gears back there," Borb said.

Arend grabbed the piece. "It says,

Now that you have started,
Move quickly or ALL become departed.
No time to proceed halfhearted.
After your great climb,
Shake off fatigue and grime,
For you have limited time.
If it runs out,
Death will sprout.
A trap your life shall rout."

Bellae's cheeks recast into a deep crimson. "Oops, time limit!"

Arend craned his neck as something caught the corner of his vision. "If you thought it couldn't get worse…two badly injured Eaglians are coming from the east."

"That's horrible!"

"That's not the bad part," Arend said. "There are several hippogriffs and Magicians coming from the north to intercept them."

"Now *that's* horrible," Lontas replied nervously.

"Still not the worst news. There are twenty griffins coming from the west."

Bellae stared at Arend expectantly.

"That's it. Time limit of death, hippogriffs, Magicians, griffins—that's all the bad news."

"Let's figure this out," Bellae announced, but Lontas was already studying.

"I'll hold them off while you keep working," Arend said.

"Are you crazy?" she exclaimed. "We need all the help we can get, and one against that many? You're amazing, but you're just going to die."

"You're the Chosen, and he's Lontas!" Arend scoffed, anxious for battle.

"Killing a few will not make you feel better about your dad, or any of the people we've lost," she said. "Help us."

The young Eaglian looked to the western sky. It was getting dark, and the strip of reddish orange in the sky would soon yield to stars and moons. He reluctantly turned to the symbols.

"It's starting to make sense," Lontas said, pointing. "See these parts? They're wings."

"You're right. If we rearrange those pieces, there'd be a pair of wings!" Bellae said.

Working quickly, they managed to grind the roughly moving squares. Eventually, an image with two wings on the sides took shape. The middle, however, remained a jumble.

"What's supposed to be between the—" Bellae was cut off. Borb and Grym began chittering loudly as a different stone tile fell off, revealing another message.

"You reached halfway.
To keep death at bay,
Work quickly, doing your best,
Or your demise ends the quest.
Time flies—watch yours,
To death, complacency lures."

"That's super helpful," Arend said.

Lontas bent down to silently trace the lines on the tiles in the middle, willing them to help find the image.

"They're getting closer," Arend prompted. "Time's one thing we don't have. Now imminent threats of death? That we have a plenty."

Abruptly, dozens of crossbow bolts zoomed up from previously hidden holes in the rock ledge. The majority were far away, but several were close—one barely missing Bellae's head. She could feel the rush of air as it raced past. Another tore into the skin of Arend's massive shoulder. A good-sized gash opened up, instantly germinating blood. He grimaced, squawking in a twist of surprise and pain. Bellae quickly tied a strip of cloth from her bag around his wound.

"Time's the key," Lontas said.

"How's that?" Arend asked.

"We track time with an hourglass!" Before Lontas finished speaking, he and Bellae started moving pieces, which were finally loosening up.

A griffin's shriek startled them into realizing how close they were.

"Bellae!" Borb said, nervously pawing his tail.

As the last piece slid into place, Bellae scooped up the mice, putting them in her pocket. She could feel the presence of the beasts closing in around them. She turned to see the two determined, but seriously injured, Eaglians streaking to intercept the griffins and hippogriffs having recognized Arend and Bellae.

"Time flies! An hourglass with wings. Great job," Arend congratulated, staring at the picture of an hourglass with a skull surrounded by wings.

"Is something supposed to happen, or...?" she asked.

"It'd better," Arend answered, anxiously gazing backwards. "Down!"

Several Magician fireballs exploded against the mountain just as a loud *crack* sounded below the hourglass figure.

As blinding bright light scalded into the ridge they were standing on, it abruptly gave way. Screaming, they fell under the hourglass figure, landing on a slide. The strip of light behind them was quickly extinguished as a slab of stone slid in front of the passage. They came to a stop. Looking left and right, they could see endless rows of headstones with strange writing upon each one lit up by the bluish light of bioluminescent vines.

"The graveyard of the Dionne Crogall," Lontas said. "I bet—"

The floor suddenly dropped away, and they began a steep slide. Bellae hit her head as the three were immersed in total darkness, continuing to glide downward.

"Ow!" Arend screamed, his wings snagging even after rolling onto his stomach.

The three continued tumbling, loose rock and dust giving way beneath them. Eventually they came to a stop. Mustiness competed with darkness to see which could rule more completely over their senses. Bellae was feeling dizzy from the ride and head blow.

Arend fumbled in the darkness until he found her and Lontas, who had ended up rolling together. "Everyone okay?"

"I think so. Just a little blood. Lontas?" Bellae asked.

"Uh, good, I think."

Arend found her cut and gently put pressure on the superficial wound with the bandage that had been on his arm.

After sitting in the dark for several minutes, Lontas spoke. "We should have brought supplies. We don't have a torch or anything."

"We didn't know this was going to happen," Arend countered, finally removing the bandage from Bellae's head after the bleeding stopped.

Bellae yelled, "Hello!" But only silence greeted them. "Guardian… anyone?"

"Light!" she screamed in Ainmhi Caint, but darkness remained.

"I guess we just sit in the pitch black," Arend said. "Lovely. Out of the path of an arrow, and into the track of a crossbow bolt."

Scroll 5: Not to Deceive, No Reprieve

Friar had never wanted night to fall quicker. All their massive defensive machines, the verndari, were ablaze, sending plumes of smoke into the air, including the one Sorea had died upon. A small bit of good news was that the smoke, as hoped, helped keep the air attacks down.

Ritari staggered forward. "Friar, the barricades are finished according to the death plan's specifications. The tutors have things under control."

The diezmars creaked and moaned, flaunting their ability to destroy, as they ate aggressively at the real castle walls. The howling wind whipped through the enormous machines of war, encouraging them. *As if they need any further motivation,* Friar thought.

"I don't know if the real walls will make it through the night," Ritari said.

"Given the late hour and their wariness of traps, I think they'll save an infantry assault until morning. Let's disrupt their plans a little. Have Lovag direct trebuchet fire at them from the bailey. I want all remaining ballistas arrayed behind the barricade lines to concentrate fire on the bottle necks," Friar stated. "As we displace, they shall bleed for every inch of our home."

"They seem determined," Ritari commented.

"Nothing energizes and motivates quite like revenge. Its outrage can feel as heavy as armor plates. However, its hidden heart is fueled by hate and rarely leaves one satisfied or at peace. In fact, it often manages to tear a hole larger than the original injury. This battle will leave many empty shells of armor, loss in many a family and groups of friends, all harvested brutally."

A new sound pierced the sky, and they froze. Dozens of clay pots whirred through the air before exploding on the ground around them. The vessels that Proliator Temere had discussed with Scelto sent the Knights scurrying, expecting flames or entrails. Neither came. Instead, a fine powder slithered out in serpentine drifts. Before they could ask what it was, their eyes started to sting and their skin to itch. Sanar, one of the healers, sprinted forward with a cloth around his mouth. "I recognize this. It's from the euphorbia plant—a horrible irritant."

"We've discovered that ourselves," Friar said, rubbing his eyes.

"Squires! Form a fire brigade, dousing everyone with water. That should control the spread of the irritant," the healer said. "You Knights, bring up blankets, tarps, anything that can cover the pots. Place heavy rocks around to hold them down."

Friar nodded appreciatively as the healer went off to organize the control teams.

"Ritari, have large barrels of reserve water brought forward to assist in the cleanup. I want to go to my office one last time."

Ritari nodded, setting to work as flaming bundles hurtled over the wall.

Friar sighed, surprised he had dozed off. Outside his office was dark save for occasional Magicians' fireballs or flaming projectiles. Standing up, he examined the gallery of portraits on the wall. Their expressions suddenly appeared judgmental and condemnatory. A cavernous sadness struck, deeper than when the Knights lost the Citadel. *At least we'd been able to move to Liberum. Now, there's nowhere to go, nowhere to run.* Images of children playing, squires learning, and Knights training flashed through his mind. Unwelcome tears started vengefully as he remembered his promise that Liberum would not fall while he lived.

I guess that won't be a problem. I'm sure to die, but not what I meant. He could not shake the feeling he was just a continuance of his father's failure. *I shall oversee the complete collapse of the Knights.*

An angry knock startled Friar. After drying the tears, he yelled, "Come in!"

Ritari burst in, stopping abruptly at Friar's despondent look. His eyes were red and swollen from the irritant, but it was clear his tears grew from something deeper. His grey hair was disheveled, reaching skyward in frantic stretches. "Sir, the Proliate and Magicians are pounding us from in front of the walls and above."

"How's it holding up?"

"Crumbling. The only good news is they'll have to crawl over the false wall, their dead, the debris from the real wall, and both moats. The Magicians and their fireballs are thwarting our attempts to disrupt them. We've concentrated our defense around the trebuchets. The walls are mostly abandoned to the diezmars," Ritari reported.

"How long until dawn?"

"A couple of hours."

"Let's go, then," Friar responded. As he neared the door, he stopped and turned around. "Go ahead. I'll be down in a second."

Slowly he took in the features of his office for what he knew would be the last time. The meetings, the naps, the friendships, the planning, the years of his life that had happened here all bore down on him and combined with the unheard screams of all past Knights and Friars admonishing him to an impossible victory. Shaking his head, he turned to leave. "Sorry to history, to...everyone. There'll be no victory today."

Ritari was waiting at the bottom of the stairs.

"If you're interested, I'm happy to step down and let you take over the Friardom."

Ritari rolled his eyes. "That's not funny."

"We still have one castle left, and I'm sure Veli Pingius would let you take over."

A serious look came over Ritari's face. "Friar, we still have *two* castles left."

Friar smiled. "You are, of course, correct. Let's go see how many hours we can make that a true statement."

As they walked towards Lovag and the trebuchets, chaos exploded on every side. Griffins and hippogriffs were diving up and down all around them. The Magicians riding the griffins were unleashing streams of fire orbs upon the castle bailey, casting grisly shadows of death and the dying. As they neared the trebuchets, a stream of flaming arrows came whirring over the crumbling castle walls.

"Sir!" Lovag cried. "We're getting pounded here. We need to fall back!"

"Where, exactly, would you like to fall back to?" Friar asked.

Lovag shook his head wearily before yelling, "Incoming!" as the area around them exploded with fire orbs. Several smashed into dirt, others erupted on the wood of the trebuchets, and some burst on Knights, engulfing them in pain and fire. Streams of flaming arrows continued whistling over the disintegrating walls as well.

"Sir!" Lovag yelled passionately.

"Son, there's simply nowhere to run. We fight at each position until we can't. I'll stay with you." Friar ran to one of the burning trebuchets. "Get some water up here and wood to brace it. We need to keep them humming for the last few hours of darkness."

The griffins and Magicians had swung around and blasted their position again with the eldur hnottur enchantment. Fire orbs continued erupting all around them.

"Help me load!" Friar yelled despite the flames dancing all around them. A squire came up and began to help. Soon, others joined. "There's nowhere to hide," he said grimly. "Might as well fight!"

As the griffins passed overhead, another stream of flaming arrows rained down on them. The squire who had come to help was peppered with arrows. Two struck Friar, one grazed his leg, and one penetrated at an odd angle on his upper back.

Friar limped over to rip the dead squire's clothes into strips. Lovag rushed over to help remove the arrow and apply two rough pressure dressings.

"It's loaded. Release!" Friar yelled.

Scroll 6: Fun Aquarium?

"Do you think the guardian's dead?" Lontas asked.

"It's possible, but we still have to find a way out," Arend said as they struggled through the darkness to find a door or passageway.

"Definitely nothing close. Let's move forward," Bellae said.

Hand in hand, the three inched forward. *Click!* "Uh-oh," Lontas whispered.

Arend pointed at a faint glow. "Are you seeing that?"

"I see it," Bellae replied, her heart racing as the light slowly intensified, spreading until it stood from ceiling to ground through most of the cave, broken only by beams of rock.

"The glowing part isn't rock," Lontas said, reaching towards the softly glowing wall.

"Is this…glass?" Bellae asked, gingerly stepping towards the luminescent wall and feeling the smooth surface.

"They're like giant containers," Lontas said. "Bubbles are floating behind the glass."

"There's water behind…whatever this is?" Arend asked.

"Looks too thick to be water, but some other liquid," Lontas said, noticing a murkiness.

"These containers must've been created with magic. They'd be impossible to build," Arend said. "The enormous vessels go all the way down on both sides."

They could now make out the dark stone of the tunnel above and below as well as thin, skillfully chiseled sections between the massive canisters.

"Something's in there," Bellae said, pressing her face against the glowing vessel.

"Be careful. We don't know what that stuff is or why it's here," Lontas warned.

"There's definitely something floating. Maybe I can talk to it," Bellae said before yelling in Ainmhi Caint, *"Is someone there?"*

"We should keep moving," Arend whispered, feeling increasingly uncomfortable.

"Let me try again. The guardian could be aquatic." She pressed her face to the glass, calling out. After a moment, they could see something moving forward. *"That's it! Come over."*

"It's definitely heading towards us," Lontas agreed as a shadow grew larger.

Bellae abruptly stumbled backwards as a human head, it's eyes frozen in a wide-eyed look of horror, slammed against the glass. Arend supported her as the man bobbed behind the translucent barrier. His skin was laced with a bluish tone and afflicted with deep, saturated wrinkles. Something made her look behind at the container across the way. Arching around Arend, she let out a muffled whimper as the body of a dead Dwarf floated up to the glass.

"Okay, now what's going on?" Borb asked as he and Grym peaked from her pocket.

"Oh, the part of this trip where we meet floating dead people!" Grym said. *"Lovely."*

"We should get out of here," Bellae muttered.

Nodding, Arend gently helped her move. Bellae closed her eyes but could still mentally see the faces floating around her. Feeling as if she had to move or pass out, she pulled away and sprinted down the terrifying hallway. *There has to be a way out!*

"Bellae! Wait!" Arend screamed.

She was breathing so hard she did not hear the clicks as she ran. Coming to the end of the hallway, she abruptly slammed into solid rock, knocking her backwards. Moving forward again, arms outstretched, fingers working desperately to find a way out from the hallway, she shouted commands in Ainmhi Caint for a door to open. Realizing the hallway behind her was now filling with brighter light, Bellae swiveled.

Arend was standing in stunned silence about halfway down the passageway pocked with dozens of glowing watery tombs.

The light shining through the liquid made watery reflections dance on the dark floor, broken only by gloomy shadows of the corpses bobbing in the strange liquid—their expressions frozen in horror. Lontas had not moved, intensely studying the denizens bobbing lifelessly within the fluid. "It's obviously some preserving fluid," he whispered. "Their clothes tell they're from many different ancient periods and haven't decayed."

Wide-eyed and numb, Bellae shuffled towards Arend. Despite an internal voice telling her to look away, she felt a magnetic, perverse pull to examine the floating Elves, Dwarves, humans, even an Eaglian. An Elf, its eyes and mouth wide open, unexpectedly collided with the glass right next to Bellae. A small current repeatedly pushed his face up against the glass. *Tap...tap...tap.* The lifeless eyes seemed to be sentient in their relentless, unblinking stare.

"Why would someone do this?" Arend asked.

"What happened to them?" Bellae wondered, fearing how they ended up here.

Arend shook his head. "Absolutely no clue. Someone's obviously messing with our heads...and doing a fine job."

Bellae was feeling increasingly claustrophobic as the rippling light of the cave gave the dried blood on her scalp an eerie glow.

Arend hunched down. "Hey, there're symbols carved into the floor."

Lontas was instantly on his hands and knees. "You're right. The floor alternates with plain stone tiles and three repeating symbols."

Bellae took out Grym and Borb. *"All right, friends, we need help."*

"Wow, you take us to the nicest places! Floating dead people in giant glowing lanterns? Fantastic," Grym chittered.

"If we want to get out, we need to figure out these three symbols on the floor," Bellae replied. *"Is there anything underneath? Do you see any trigger mechanisms?"*

The two mice began scurrying back and forth across the floor, moving in and out of the waving light from the containers.

Borb suddenly started spinning in circles. *"Something's different here!"*

Bellae moved to where Borb was whirling, noticing a section of writing. *"Borb, you're awesome!"* She dropped a kiss on the top of his head before reading.

"Three symbols to show,
Beneath waters' glow.
It can cut like a knife and be filled with strife,
The symbol of **Life.**

The world's greatest hunter, eventually crushes all breath,
The symbol of **Death.**

All journey towards it, no matter how nimble,
The **After Death** symbol."

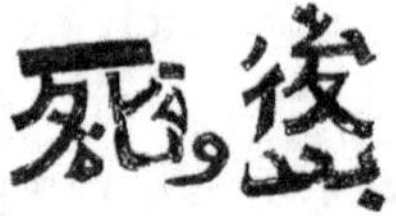

"Each of the three bolded words has a complex symbol next to it—the same ones repeating in the pattern over the rest of the rocky floor," Lontas said.

Arend nodded. "Okay, so we know what the symbols mean but not what to do about it."

"Excuse me, geniuses. A little factoid—you're kneeling on writing," Grym said as Bellae and Lontas scooched backwards.

"Where's my smoochy-smooch and thanks?" Grym asked, sulking off to explore against the wall where the magical glass held an aquarium full of the dead.

Scroll 7: Pay for the Privilege

"Veneficus wants us to *conserve* our crystals," Pitkä, a tall, lanky Magician, the highest-ranking one since Prast died, said to Lidenskap and Storlax. "Our orders were to use magic to seal victory, not create it. It's bad enough we moved the diezmar siege engines intact. Do you have any idea how many mindre crystals we've burned through?"

"He also said *we're* in charge," High Commander Storlax spouted.

General Lidenskap smiled. "Pitkä, you realize we're dealing with Knights that decimated our troops at Ovest and Trepas? Plus, their Allies, the Dark Warriors, are amassing behind us. I would say that makes this attack vulnerable to failure and in need of magic."

"You have your orders, Pitkä. Put up shield walls in front of our troops and diezmars. Their trebuchet fire is killing too many," Storlax said.

"I loathe the Knights, but moving the diezmars intact and fighting an aerial war without ground support—"

"Follow your orders!" Storlax interrupted. With a snort of disgust, Pitkä left.

"Magicians are egotistical maniacs, but they've saved a lot of our men. The Battle of Liberum will be one of the greatest Proliate victories of all time!" Lidenskap stated.

"I still fear Friar and his tricks," Storlax countered.

"His days of leading us around are over. Imagine thinking one victory, born from deception, could win this war? Pathetic. The Knights panic behind their crumbling walls."

Storlax sighed. "Until Friar's head's on a spear, I'll remain cautious."

"Wise," Lidenskap fawned. "Praise Tallcon. I'll excuse myself to prepare for the assault."

As Lidenskap exited, Lovag was briefing Friar on the new magical wall that had appeared to protect the Proliate from their trebuchet shots. He was well past the point of exhaustion, his body littered with bandages covering wounds and burns.

"Lovag, get our cavalry," Friar said. "First light is coming, and we shall wheel and fire on the first troops. Once they're organized, I want you to fall back to the first barricade. I'll see to soaking the trebuchets with naphtha to light our retreat."

As Lovag limped to the stables, Friar assessed the bailey. There were hundreds of dead Knights and squires strewn about. Ghastly shadows danced around them at behest of countless fires. Sorea's verndari were reduced to piles of burned-out ashes. He imagined her charred body ingloriously lying in one of the heaps. *There'll be no reverent funerals for our dead. Soon enough we all join her in the dust.* The ground was scorched from the near-constant bombardment of the Magicians' fire orbs and flaming projectiles. Flaming arrows in the thousands littered the field, the back half peeking out from their earthly grave.

With the Proliate archers and Magicians giving them a break, Friar hobbled to a rare section of partially standing wall. Once on the crumbling rampart, Friar quickly glanced at the field in front of Liberum as thin strips of pink spied over the horizon. His whole body vibrated in tune with each boulder strike. He could see a line of Magicians creating a magical shield preventing their trebuchets from inflicting damage on the well-rested Proliate infantry. Suddenly, a Magician gestured wildly, pointing to the sputtering light on his crosier as another Magician gave a signal and the green wall disappeared. After hustling back down, Friar began working with a few squires and injured Knights to get the functioning trebuchets loaded. "Fire on my command. We must time it perfectly."

After receiving a thumbs up, Friar yelled, "Fire!"

Simultaneously, five trebuchets released large boulders, creaking into action as the protesting, and in some places burning, wood groaned. Over the din of the diezmars they could hear the crashing projectiles and screams of the Proliate. Friar smiled. *We still have some fight left. You shall know the last of our strength and pay dearly for the privilege to take it.*

Scroll 8: Kindly Donating Blood

The Mardin sun had been up for over an hour, and silence settled over the battlefield. The walls of Liberum had been reduced to rubble save for a few broken segments rising ineptly in jagged, mostly toothless, defeat. Friar stood with the rest of the tattered Knight archers and cavalry. Most of them had multiple wounds, and blood red became the predominant distinguishing color for the Knights. *Maybe they'll mistake us for Proliate?* he thought.

The archers stood widely spread out to help negate the attacks by the griffins and Magicians that were sure to come. The Knight cavalry was bunched in front of the first series of barricades. Everything from desks and chairs to doors and beds made up the line of debris designed to bottleneck the Proliate infantry.

Suddenly, a lone scout on the battered remnants of what had been Liberum's wall gave the dreaded signal. The attack was about to commence. He made the motions as if holding reins before raising his hand sequentially into "5-0-0."

"Five hundred hippogriffs?" Ritari scowled. "That must be the entire population of Hirmulisko."

"Archers, ready!" Lovag yelled. "Aim true."

Using the enchanted Huuto shell, Friar spoke, "The time for fancy speeches is long past. They will show no mercy, and neither should you. Hit them with everything you have and make them pay for every inch of our castle. There is no tomorrow. For many of us there isn't even a next hour. To a person we are injured, bleeding, dying, with our backs against the wall, but we know something they don't. Our spirit is unbroken and steady. Let them come!"

There was no cheer in response to his words, only a gritting of teeth and resetting of resolve. To add to their motley appearance, the injured from the infirmary streamed up to the first barricades. A few were placed on chairs with crossbows. A crisp, fluttering sound started as a whisper, but as the hippogriffs drew closer, it grew to a rumbling waterfall. The Knights could hear them chattering to each other with short, high-pitched neighs. As soon as they crested the battered remnants of the walls, the Knight archers loosed. Dozens fell. Undeterred, the hippogriffs streamed forward. They attacked the Knight archers with a vengeance: chewing with their powerful horse jaws, ripping with their sharp front talons, and kicking with their powerful back hooves. Looping around for another pass, they caught sight of the Knight cavalry. Hatred spewed from their eyes as they swerved towards them.

"Cavalry, break into groups of twenty. Wheel and fire!" Friar screamed.

The cavalry began to separate, and a few even managed to fire their bows. However, the hippogriffs were already on them. A brutal battle ensued as the two sides clashed. Many of the Knights were thrown off as their horses pinned back their ears and bucked up to paw at the attackers. A loud horn blast from the Proliate startled everyone.

"They're killing us. Why are the hippogriffs retreating?" Lovag asked.

"Something worse is coming," Ritari said.

"Continue forming up in groups of twenty and spread out," Friar ordered. "If griffins or hippogriffs return, restart wheel and fire teams, retreating as necessary. If ground troops come next, then take position en masse and give them a taste of misery."

"Dragons!" Lovag yelled.

Filled with hope, Friar rotated to see a stream of green Vioma dragons flying towards them. A loud cheer rose up from the Knights.

"Yes!" Luchar roared. Sick of waiting for the ground battle to begin, he had positioned himself at one of the first set of barricades.

Friar staggered back. His leg was throbbing where the arrow had skimmed it. "The beautiful sight of dragons makes everything hurt less."

"Did an Eaglian get through?" Ritari asked.

"Must have," Friar said. "For the first time since the Proliate showed up, a ray of optimism lights the dark despair broiling within me."

Ritari looked at him uncertainly. "Wasn't expecting poetry. If the dragons clear the skies, we can use the cover to make the Proliate pay dearly."

Friar swiveled his head. "Make them pay? Dear Ritari, we can win this day." He turned and yelled, "Clear an area for them to land! Let's give them a Knight welcome!"

His weary Knights responded by bellowing fierce cries. Looking around, he could see relief digging its way across their faces.

"Look at their numbers. They must have sent them all!" Ritari exclaimed.

The dragons were thirty yards away when the cry of, "Spraks!" rang out. Friar turned to see the lizard beasts sneaking over the piles of rubble and dead. Their stone-grey bodies were coated with fierce scales, highlighted by shimmering wings with yellow and red circles mimicking angry eyes as they fluttered menacingly.

"Archers, fall back!" Friar ordered. "Let the Vioma dragons handle the spraks."

The archers were just reaching the first barricade when the dragons suddenly shifted course from the spraks and descended towards the Knights.

"What the..." Ritari murmured. His words trailed off as the dragons shimmered, transforming into griffins.

"The Southern Dwarves disguised the griffins as dragons. Fire!" Friar said.

The griffins wasted no time, battering the Knight archers and cavalry, who were in perfect position to die: bunched and completely caught off guard. They were quickly shredded and killed. The griffins started tossing body parts from the dead Knights and their mounts over the barricade. Friar stood in stunned silence as the griffins tortured and mutilated at will.

"You heard your orders! Fire!" Ritari yelled. "Anyone with a bow or crossbow, fire now. Try and get the griffins away from them."

"I guess the dragons aren't coming," a squire said dejectedly.

"I think not," Friar answered, sensing the morale deflating around him. "But we shall fight all the same."

Luchar let his small axe and good shoulder slump, feeling exhausted and weak. His infirmity and injuries had chipped away at his faulty belief of invincibility.

Friar turned to his humbled Knight, taken aback by his most courageous warrior's appearance. With a suppressed tear teetering on his eyelids he said, "We fight! Now we fight for true victory—the triumph over self and terror. Against all odds we fight and make them pay for invading our sacred land. To beat us they shall have to donate a healthy dose of their blood."

The griffins were quickly joined by hippogriffs, which had returned. A blood bath of the cavalry ensued. The Knight cavalry was outnumbered, outmuscled, and clustered together after making space in anticipation of the dragons landing. The flying creatures attacked lustfully. Soon the blood-stained ground was littered with chunks of flesh from horse and rider.

"What can we do?" Ritari asked Friar.

"If we leave the cover of the barricades, we'll suffer the same fate. We can't compete, especially with so many archers and cavalry dead. Plus, you know...giant lizards."

Scroll 9: If You Step on Them, It Will Come

"Find the one to solve ***the last riddle***.
Step only on that one's middle.
Start where you began,
Go as fast as you can.

If you are correct, then *slosh*,
In death you wash.
If you are incorrect, then *bam*,
Life-taking arrows will slam."

"Is it me, or do both of those options seem particularly bad?" Arend asked.

"Definitely seems wrong," Bellae whimpered.

"A lot of things about this are ridiculous," Arend said.

"This stupid quest is testing our mantra of eat, sleep, repeat," Grym squeaked.

"At least we're not eating dead guy eye goo!" Borb added, shivering at recollections of the battle in the Dark Woods.

"Not eating dead guy eye goo," Grym said, observing the floating dead, *"yet!"*

Lontas was engrossed in rereading the passage. "We have three symbols representing life, death, and after death, but where's the riddle we need to answer?"

"We walked past these words, so let's go back to the start, where we weren't looking for words," Bellae said, moving back she got down on all fours. "There's writing!" Brushing off some dust, she used the ghostly light to read.

"You need to wash in ________.
You can only do that if you answer the question in ________.
The answer ***you need find*** is the one no being alive can answer,
But often guides their actions. What happens ________?"

"The first one's idiotic. You need to wash in blank? Just nonsensical," Arend said.

"The previous writing mentioned washing in death, but let's start from the bottom—the one we *have* to get, and the easiest. Only After Death fits grammatically," Bellae said, hunger, thirst, the disorienting presence of the floating bodies teaming up to make her lightheaded.

"You're right!" Arend perked up a bit.

"Let's see how that sounds," Bellae suggested. "You need to wash in *death*...if you answer in *life*, and what happens *after death*?"

"All right, we have to carefully step on the 'After Death' symbols," Lontas stated. "Are we worrying about the whole if we're correct, wash in death thing?"

She shook her head. "We're locked in a cave with floating dead, and our two options are a death wash or being shot with arrows. So…a regular day on this quest."

Bellae let her head rest on Lontas' shoulder as she fought the dread welling within. After a deep breath, she straightened. "Complaining won't help. I'll go, then Lontas, finally Arend."

She stepped on the first 'After Death' symbol. A faint whining noise came from under the stone, and it rumbled slightly. The design started to glow blue while the water in the first two chambers radiated red.

"Is this good?" Bellae whispered.

"No arrows is good," Arend said. "Why are you whispering?"

"It makes me feel better."

"We must have stepped on some of them before. Why didn't they light up?" Arend said.

"The first one's off to the side, and it must be the order you step on them," Lontas said.

Each time she stepped on the 'After Death' figure, it glowed blue, and as they progressed down the cavern, sometimes the light within the tanks turned red.

"The symbols are starting to blur together," Bellae said, her cloak drenched in sweat. "Although it's only been probably twenty minutes, it seems like hours."

"We have to be close," Lontas said. "All of the liquid is glowing red." As he finished, several corpses plunked up against the glass, the floor sparkling in crimson reflections.

"It's hard to see, but I'm pretty sure there's only one 'After Death' symbol left." She paused, anxious to escape the corridor but keen to avoid the seemingly grisly outcomes waiting. A *click* rang through the tunnel as the last panel glowed blue.

"I really hate clicks," Arend commented as they awaited the inevitable consequence.

Within a few seconds, the red liquid inside each chamber began to spin. The water became more turbulent, rotating faster and faster, sending the corpses mindlessly, and violently, thumping against the glass.

"Please tell me a door's going to open," Arend pleaded.

"That's not happening," Lontas said. "I think we know what wash in death means."

The whir from the spinning grew, highlighted by pounding as the bodies smashed the containers. Lontas moved towards the side, placing his hand on the smooth surface. "Hey, it's heating up." As his words finished, small cracks began to breed along the glass. Each thumping crash of a corpse created rupturing fissures zigzagging in frenetic bolts.

Lontas backed up to Arend as lighting cracks dominated the surface. Streams of liquid began spraying angrily into the tunnel. Bellae sprinted to Arend, burying her head in his chest. Just as he wrapped his wings around her and Lontas, the corridor exploded. Glass from every container blasted into the hallway, engulfing it in tiny shards needling all over Arend. His back became a lacework of fine cuts as he grimaced in pain.

The liquid from the chambers flooded into the cavern in a deluge. With alarming speed the room began to fill. Taking a wide stance, Arend struggled to stay upright in the churning water. His talons scraped against the rocky floor as he fought against the surging liquid. They clung together, watching the surface level soar.

Bellae used her free hand to push away a large section of fractured glass. Instantly replacing it was the corpse of a dead Elf—his frozen eyes directly opposite hers as they butted heads. She screamed, shoving the body away.

Scroll 10: Dogs, Meet Poisonous Lizards

The stench of death continued to intensify into the unbearable range, summoning hordes of flies to the shredded flesh. The griffins and hippogriffs hadn't just killed the Knights' archers, cavalry, and horses—they had fragmented and disemboweled them. The dead, and their tattered remains, littered the once-pristine bailey of Liberum. Now, one hundred of the dreaded twenty-foot-long spraks lined up inside their walls with their fearsome sail-like appendages spread out and quivering—resembling hundreds of daunting eyes staring down the Knights.

"Bring up the war hounds," Friar ordered.

Ritari quickly ran over. "They can't stand up against the spraks."

"Neither can we," Friar answered simply. "Our only hope is to slow them down…uh?"

He was rendered speechless by the sight of General Lidenskap strolling up in front of the spraks who were pulling ferociously on their chains. Joining him was Master Magician Pitkä, who magically enhanced the general's voice.

"Anyone surrendering now will be killed painlessly. If you continue to fight, we promise to make your death slow and painful." Lidenskap motioned with his hands at the puzzle pieces of flesh that once had been their comrades.

"Friar, may I answer him?" Ritari asked.

"Oh, please do," Friar said. "After the ruse by the Proliate, our morale is at rock bottom."

Ritari thought about saying turnabout is fair play but decided against it. Before the ballistae could fire, dozens of Knights sprinted from behind the barricades.

"Get back, you bloody cowards!" Luchar screamed, waving his small, but lethal, axe.

"Ah, a few sage souls. You've chosen wisely," Lidenskap announced. The spraks moved forward, making a passageway for them to get to the general.

"That's it. Come to a genial death," Lidenskap soothed before yelling a command.

With a ferocious growl, the spraks descended upon the Knights, running between them, ripping and clawing. Their razor-sharp teeth sliced through armor, flesh, and bone. Their wing-like projections flittered hungrily as they killed and feasted.

"Ah, looks like the spraks were hungry. My fault," Lidenskap announced. "The next group that surrenders will be killed humanely... trust me."

"Anyone else stupid enough to go?" Luchar bellowed, hitting his manica with his axe. "Bring it on, pansies!"

"So be it," the general said ominously.

With a slight wave of his hands the spraks lumbered in awkward but menacing torques toward the Knights' barricades. Their halting swing gait might have looked comical if not for their thickly armored scales, ferocious teeth, and terrifying red sails.

"Ballistae, ready!" Lovag yelled as they neared.

The massive spraks clambered with surprising grace over the barricades.

"Fire!" Lovag screamed, pushing away a healer trying to staunch his wounds.

The ragtag medley of different-sized ballistae fired their bolts. While several managed hits, few did real damage. Any injured spraks were immediately set upon by the beasts around them as the distant barks of war hounds howled behind them.

"Guess, they don't like weakness," Lovag said, gawking at the site of spraks feasting on spraks. Grey scales, blood, and flesh shot out of the frenzy.

"They're moving again!" Ritari yelled as several arrows and bolts barely fazed the massive lizards now refocused on them.

"Release the dogs!" Friar commanded. "They shall provide cover while we fall back to the next barricade!"

Boman, the dog trainer who perpetually spared with Bellae, froze. His throat stuck with emotions coated in regret at his perpetually harsh treatment of the war hounds as he stared at the massive lizards and his dogs' certain death. The war dogs, sensing battle, were whining and howling anxiously at the smell of the vile spraks toddling closer to the displacing Knights.

Ritari yelled, "These dogs wear armor, and like all Knights of Liberum they have the privilege and the honor to fight and die this day."

Wiping a fetal tear, Boman yelled, "Attack!" Each utterance grew in resonance with his resignation as hundreds of war dogs burst through retreating Knights and squires towards the spraks. Among them was Fochmhar, the one Bellae faced during the squire battles, and Canities, the dog in red armor that humiliated Lontas. Even the largest war hounds looked ludicrously small nearing the spraks. The spraks hissed, their long jaws thrown open to show intimidating teeth dripping with poisonous saliva.

"Lovag," Friar said. His Knight nodded, realizing the spraks' attention was on the dogs.

After yelling orders, Lovag and a group of Knights quickly winched back the ballista levers. "Pick your targets. I want three ballistae going for the same sprak. Their scales are tougher than we thought." Once loaded, they unleashed a dozen ballistae. Four spraks fell. One unfortunate sprak had two ballista bolts hit it from opposite sides. The first one severed its spine while the second one ripped off its head. Blood and poison splattered as several nearby spraks dove in to feast on their fallen.

"Reload!" Lovag yelled as ten spraks charged the Knights manning the ballistae. Lovag managed to put two arrows into the eyes of one of them. Blinded, it ran with maddening fury. Veering to its right, it slammed into another sprak, and the two started fighting. Within a few moments, fifteen of the spraks were busy fighting each other or feasting on the recently injured. The distraction was enough for the Knights to get off another round of shots. The massive bolts ripped into the spraks, sending many of them rolling end over end in writhing pain.

Friar, hearing the dogs retreating, ran back before reaching the second line of barricades. "Boman, there's no retreat."

"But most Knights got safely—" Boman started.

"There's no safe place in Liberum. Every living creature not associated with the Proliate shall die this day. It's only the order and timing that needs to be worked out."

Friar moved back to a second barricade, watching helplessly. *No way can those dogs survive the spraks.* Boman began yelling orders, and the snarling war hounds went back on the attack. Using their claws and teeth, the spraks easily repelled the assault. Yelps of pain joined a field littered with flayed open armor, stained red with blood, peeled back to reveal entrails and gore from the dead and dying dogs discarded by the massive creatures. Some of the spraks began feasting on the dogs, gulping them down in large chunks. Those dogs with their skin punctured had the beasts' toxin burning through their bodies, causing them to thrash about until eventually succumbing to the poison.

Boman continued screaming commands with tears streaming down his face. Changing tactics, he began directing packs of dogs to attack individual spraks in waves from different sides. Several had jumped on one sprak's back, biting and tearing with vengeful payback. Both larger sails of the sprak were ripped off, and it let out a harsh cry that startled the air.

Nearby spraks rushed towards their embattled companion. They tore into the dogs, ripping and shredding mercilessly. Heads, internal organs, entire halves of dogs began to fly around the bailey. The spraks quickly turned on the injured lizard, devouring him remorselessly. With the spraks busy fighting, or eating, each other, Lovag was able to get two more rounds of the ballistae fired.

"How many of those lizard things do they have?" a Knight asked.

Lovag shook his head as a loud war cry went up behind the first barricade, and over ten thousand Proliate Ultor warriors, with more streaming in, made their way inside the rubble that had once been the walls of Liberum. Several of the sprak trainers moved forward and began directing the beasts. The remaining forty spraks formed a line, howling before moving forward.

"Lovag, get your Knights back, now!" Friar yelled as four spraks bolted towards them. They easily splintered the ballistae and started tearing the Knights to shreds. Initially, it seemed Lovag might make it. However, the spraks made such short work of the others, they were now barreling after him.

"Boman! Move your hounds to protect Lovag!" Friar ordered.

As Friar looked up, he saw the last of the dogs being mutilated. Boman did not attempt to run. He drew his sword and charged at the massive beasts. They quickly surrounded him. A volcanic spray of flesh and blood shot out of the middle of their feeding frenzy as Lovag helped a gravely injured Knight towards the second barricade.

"He'll never make it on his own," Luchar wheezed.

"Come back!" Friar yelled as the heavily armored Knight shuffled between a small opening in the second barricade after his old friend. His large manica shielded his ineffective left side while he anxiously twirled the axe with his right hand.

"Stay, Luchar!" Lovag shouted, giving an anxious look to the quickly gaining sprak.

"For one last time, I've got your back," Luchar said as Lovag and an injured Knight staggered past. "Kill the beasts who kill me…if you can."

"Looks like a hobbling sow coming to face our spraks," a Proliate yelled.

"Pig to the slaughter," another added. "First, they let women fight. Now cripples?"

Luchar seethed. *I'm going to kill that fool.*

"Wake up!" Friar shouted to Luchar, who looked up to see just how close the advancing monsters were.

"Get back with us," Lovag pleaded.

Luchar shook his head. "It's been my honor to fight with you, brother."

The closest spraks decelerated, unsure what to make of the solitary warrior. In the bright morning sun, Luchar's new armor glistened ferociously, the reflection dancing in blinking flares within the creature's yellow eyes.

Suddenly, Luchar shot forward. His axe whizzed down and stuck right in between the closest sprak's eyes. The creature's body twitched violently, the now-spasming brain cleaved. After struggling unsuccessfully to get his axe out of the sprak's head, Luchar began to back up. Another sprak lunged, and Luchar raised his reinforced manica. The sprak's jaws clamped down and squeezed with such force, it started to crush into his arm. Screaming, he grabbed his dagger and slammed it into the beast's eyes. He twisted it before stabbing the beast repeatedly in a fit of rage. Soon, he was surrounded by spraks, and the Knights completely lost sight of him.

A blur of five figures burst past the barricade, sprinting towards the hope of where Luchar subsisted. As the spraks wrestled with one another for the right to kill him, he released Hephaestus' surprise. "Eat this!" Luchar wailed, pulling a cord with his good hand, releasing a hidden blade up through his manica. It skewered the closest sprak through his jaw and up into his brain. He instantly fell as the others, understanding he was still a danger, began to chomp down on him with their massive jaws. Using the last of his strength, he began to roll before heaving his reinforced manica in front of their massive fangs.

"I hope Hephaestus' work holds up long enough for me to kill you all!" he yelled—his dagger repeatedly stabbing, blood and fluid flowing over him.

"It's the newly minted Tilkeri Knights," Friar said, surprised at their action and still wary of the former bullies who seemed to put tormenting Lontas on even field with breathing on the ladder of necessity. Rhyfeler blurred past. "Where are you going?"

"Freshly birthed Knights shall not outshine the constable of Liberum!" Rhyfeler yelled, his yellow surcoat flowing behind as he ran.

Lovag shouted, "Bring forward the toten bows for cover if they can get to Luchar."

As the enormous bows were rushed forward, one of the bowmen spun Lovag around. "Sir, these massive missiles are meant to be fired at a great distance, not close quarters."

"Regular bows aren't meant to be fired at giant lizards either, and, I might add, we're not meant to fight for our very lives against them, but here we are. Set up your bow and shut up."

Tilkeri Knights Tiron and Stratto had long, powerful spears and rammed them into two spraks' heads. Alta, Tempaus, and Saccade jumped over the two creatures squirming in death throes and brought powerful sword strikes down on the next three. The beasts were caught off guard, having focused on the solitary Knight. Tiron ripped Luchar's axe out of a now-dead sprak and threw it to him. Luchar dropped his dagger and caught it with his working right hand and in one fluid motion rammed it into the snout of one of the spraks trying to break through his armor. His fortified manica and chest plate were crushed, decorated with teeth marks, saliva, and yellow-green venom.

Alta rushed to help Luchar up as the other four hacked at the reeling beasts, but it took several tries to steady him enough to stand.

"I'm fine!" Luchar howled, but was clearly not as he tottered precariously, the world spinning violently.

"Get him back to our line!" Friar yelled.

Alta began moving him towards the next barricade as the other four battled while retreating against the regrouping sprak.

"You can run but not hide, my bacon-wrapped-Knight," a Proliate standing just behind the spraks yelled. "Just delaying the inevitable."

As the spraks moved after the Tilkeri Knights, Rhyfeler appeared, two swords spinning in a silver blur. "Get him to safety, boys."

As the first sprak lunged, the sword in Rhyfeler's left hand raked across the beast's right eye, while his second sword punctured through the jaw open in a screech and up into the brain. Just as he turned to his right, the spraks encircled him. He crossed the swords around the beast's neck, nearly decapitating it, but was now surrounded. Even as he donated flesh to them, he managed to bring his two swords down on top of one's head. Falling to his knees, he watched the life drain from the sprak just before his was released. Yellow, the color he was known for, now converted to orange at the behest of healthy volumes of blood.

"Load!" Lovag commanded to the dozens of toten bows now in place. Each one was operated by a Knight laying on his back, his feet in circular stirrups at the front of the twelve-foot-long bows. Only a select few Knights were tall, and strong, enough to pull back on the string while laying down to allow the massive missile to be placed. An area of the barricade had been thinned, and Luchar was unceremoniously dragged over before the area was re-fortified.

"I could have scaled it!" he protested, but under his helmet his sweating face flushed with a mix of embarrassment and uneasiness at his frailty and exhaustion.

"Leave it to you to survive an attack by a mob of sprak," Friar said, trying to hide his concern at the infirmity of his once-powerful Knight.

"They were more worried about fighting each other than me," Luchar said. "They didn't know how tough this fortified armor is."

"They're coming!" Tiron said, scrambling over the barricade with the other Tilkeri.

"Rhyfeler?" Friar asked.

Tiron shook his head.

"Everyone behind the toten bows," Lovag said before addressing the bowman. "Fire at the first sign of anything cresting that barricade."

High Commander Storlax had joined Lidenskap just outside the first barricade as the spraks advanced upon the second. "When are you sending in our troops? They grow restless."

"Soon, but with food shortages, we have too many spraks," Lidenskap said. "This thins them out and keeps our men fresh. Scouts have seen heavy troop movements of Dark Warriors on the coast. This battle is but an appetizer, the main fight is yet to come."

Scroll 11: Wash Yourself...in Death

As the Elf's corpse flowed away, another dead body immediately struck Bellae. Letting go of Arend, she managed to push it away, but in doing so the swirling water separated them, and she was quickly sucked into the increasingly turbulent liquid gushing into the hallway from the shattered containers. Lontas, trying to stabilize Arend, reached for Bellae as she flowed past. He lost his base and was tossed into the frothing liquid. Bellae was thrown into the side of the cave, pain biting into her shoulder. She desperately pulled out Grym and Borb, placing them on her shoulder before securing the bag with the crystals. *"Hold on!"*

"Oh really?" Grym said. *"You're saying don't go for a swim in the torrential liquid infested with dead people?"*

The water rose so quickly Bellae and Lontas were paddling to stay afloat, constantly pushing away from the jagged rock and fighting off churning dead bodies. The sickly red light shining down from the chambers cast ominous, waterlogged shadows across the cavern. A loud rumble reverberated, and the substance began sloshing even more violently.

"Bellae, I can't do this!" Arend yelled after pushing himself up to the surface.

"How can we help?" she asked.

Before he could respond, his drenched wings pulled him under. They anxiously waited. Finally, Arend surfaced, gasping for air, struggling against the weight of his wings.

"Arend!" Bellae screamed, fury coalescing with fear. *You can't die!* she thought, just as the red lights flickered. The flashing cycle sped up, creating a haunting strobe effect highlighting her mice's desperate scuttling on her shoulder, Lontas wrestling with the water, and the terror radiating from Arend's eyes when they appeared at increasingly irregular intervals.

Bellae could see the strain clinging to Arend's face as he struggled up. She thought he might say something. Instead, he nodded before descending into the turbulent water—an acknowledgement of their friendship and acceptance he was going to die. *He's not coming back up,* she thought, her arms and legs burning from fighting the raging liquid.

"We're approaching the ceiling," Bellae said as Grym and Borb shivered with exhaustion, their paws digging into her cloak. Her head surged against the top of the cave with a violent wave. Fresh blood eagerly ejected from under her fleeing scab.

"What are we going to do?" Grym whimpered.

Bellae never answered as the liquid reached the ceiling and she was sucked under. Her cheeks puffed up as she desperately tried to hold her breath. She could see Arend limply whirling in the current at the bottom of the cavern along with a sea of dead bodies. *Washing in death? This's dying with the dead,* she thought. White lights began flashing in front of her eyes, adding to the surreal underwater scene. Grym and Borb lost their grip, swirling out of sight. Panic and fear exploded within as a blindingly bright light shone from above.

A rough hand grabbed Grym, who was floating above her, his legs moving in a blur of effort against the current. Borb was nowhere to be seen, and Bellae used the last of her strength to swim towards the white light. As she neared, the hand dunked again, grabbing her by the cloak and wrenching her up with incredible strength. Her body thrashed through the air before being set on the edge of a circular hole at the top of the flooded cavern. Her lungs ravenously devoured the air. After a few gasping breaths, she stammered to the blurry figure in front of her, "Did...you get...the other mouse?"

"No, just one rodent," a deep male voice replied. "You the Chosen One, finally?"

She nodded as he added gruffly, "Another one?" at a hand rising out of the frothing water. Coughing and sputtering, Lontas was wrenched up and manhandled to the ground.

Realizing she could no longer feel Borb and despite her air hunger, Bellae set the bag of crystals down and dove back into the water. Searching desperately, she saw Arend. It took all her strength to pull him up through the liquid, now only occasionally lit by fluttering red light. When her head poked through, she could hear the man's voice chastising her before reaching down and pulling Arend up. "I've got the winged man. Now get up here!" he commanded angrily.

"One...more," she said, diving again.

The red light trembled as her eyes darted. She abruptly found herself face to face with a bloated Dwarf. His gritty beard scraped across her face, and she wrenched it away. *"Borb!"* she screamed, the sound swallowed by the liquid along with a stream of bubbles vaulting upwards.

There! she thought. Optimism surged, but briefly, obliterated as her mind screamed at the site of Borb's body pirouetting lifelessly in the water. She desperately swam forward, grabbing him before frantically shooting towards the hole in the ceiling, pushing through the dead bodies, which were now impatiently congregating there thanks to the eddy. After gently setting Borb down, she pulled herself up despite the deceased slamming into her. Lontas came over to help but suddenly backed up as the strange man neared. Bellae ignored them, hovering over Borb as Grym squeaked wildly, skittering in circles around his dead friend.

"I know. I'm sorry," Bellae repeated, crying and reaching out for Grym. He avoided her hand and continued screeching angrily.

"This spectacle, for a dead mouse?" the man said.

Bellae rotated, looking up to truly see him for the first time. Her tears stopped, jaw dropped as she stared at a Daoine Crogall. Despite hearing about these creatures, seeing the crocodile man in person was jolting. Although humanoid, he had the head of a crocodile and fierce, green-hued scales covering all of his body except his lower forearm and human hands. He wore a leather chest plate and cloth pants complete with a double belt that held two swords.

"Have you lost the ability to speak?" he asked, flashing fearsome-looking teeth lining his long snout. His gold and black eyes were set on the top of a massive head lined with spikes.

Silently, Bellae looked to Lontas, who maintained his slack-jawed expression.

"Ah, I understand. Not expecting someone so handsome?"

"Arend?" Bellae said after recovering from the shock, surveying the large and impeccably clean cavern with detailed carvings on tan walls. Seeing no other creatures, she went straight for Arend, who was on the other side of the opening of the seething liquid.

"Don't worry about that…eagle thing," the Daoine Crogall said, placing a heavy stone over the opening. "You're all we need for the mission. My name's Fiacla, by the by."

Bellae ignored him as Lontas ran to Arend, both still dripping wet. Rolling him on his stomach, they began pounding on his back. They felt a twinge of guilt seeing the innumerable small cuts he had sustained, protecting them when the containers exploded. After repeating this several times, Arend sputtered and coughed, the nasty liquid came out as Bellae quickly moved to Borb's lifeless body. She could feel panic in Grym but nothing from Borb as she alternated patting his back and pushing on his stomach.

Use the power to save him! the crystals hummed. She could feel the pulsing capability radiating from them. A rumble of energy shivered through her body, calling with alluring temptation. Premonitions of danger if she succumbed to their influence flashed across her mind.

After ten minutes, and several comments by the Daoine Crogall, Lontas finally said, "It's enough, Bellae. You've done more than enough."

Figure 2: After washing in death, the League are greeted by guardian Fiacla.

Bellae shook his arm off out of frustration more than anger. *Not another one,* she thought.

Grym began squeaking loudly, looking angrily at Bellae. She cuddled him tightly before leaning against Lontas. He gently put his hand on her shoulder while keeping his eyes on the crocodile man. Arend was still on the other side of the opening, looking exhausted and occasionally succumbing to fits of retched coughing. Bellae moaned not just in sadness but enraged with the crystals' accusatory chatter, chiding her for letting another friend die.

"It's so weird not feeling him," Bellae said. "We've been together so long. It's like part of me is missing." She squeezed tears out angrily, furious at the sacrifices the quest demanded.

Scroll 12: Enoughkill? Or Overkill?

"Tilkeri," Friar said, "get Luchar back a few barricades to let him rest." He preventatively held up his hand. "I know you can still fight. We'll be displacing to join you soon enough."

"Fire!" Lovag called out as spraks slurped over the barricade, only to be riddled with projectiles as the toten bows released.

"Although those massive arrows did not perform well outside Trepas, they're doing exceedingly more damage than I expected against the spraks," Friar said admiringly.

Lovag nodded. "Totens, reload!"

"They're easier to move, reload, and aim than ballistae," Friar added. "We've found our way to kill them."

"Let's get him to a healing station," Tiron said, heavily supporting the struggling Luchar away from the second barricade.

The strength seemed to be going out of Luchar's right side, and his paralyzed left felt icy and numb. *I'm out of shape and nearly defenseless,* he thought, exhaustion weighing him down physically and mentally. *I didn't think I would decondition this fast.*

"Did one bite you?" Tempaus asked, wondering if that was why he was weak.

"I don't…think…so," he huffed, struggling to hop away from the front lines.

Moving between houses, Tiron yelled, "Healer Sanar! We have one for you."

"I was just going back to a healing station to resupply." Sanar could not help gawking at the pitiful sight of Luchar. "Alright, looking at how damaged that armor is, we need to get him to a healing center. I'll need you to help me get him there."

Before Luchar could falsely protest he was fine, a massive round of Proliate attack horns rang out and a wave of Proliate stormed the second bulwark.

Calls for help blasted from the barricade they had just left, "Infantry!"

"Breach!" a panicked shout rang out. "Proliate have breached the second barricade!"

"We have to hold them a little longer before displacing!" Friar yelled. The drums beat a call for able bodies to the second barricade.

"That's our signal," Alta said.

"Get in there, Luchar. That house has a strong door. Barricade yourself in," Tiron said. "Sanar, do what you can. We'll try to hold them off."

The healer was about to object about his lack of supplies when Stratto gruffly pushed him into the house, saying, "See to him. We have to go right now!"

The hobbling Luchar was helped in as Tiron continued, "We'll try to counterattack. Hopefully we can retake the second barricade and give you some time. If so, we'll come back and pick you up as we redeploy."

"I guess…you guys aren't as horrible as I thought," Luchar said.

Sanar smiled. "Hey, that's his way of saying thanks." The healer closed the door, sliding the paltry wooden lock as the Tilkeri headed back to the second fortification. After helping Luchar to the ground, the healer began moving anything he could find to barricade the door and windows, starting with the table as Luchar tried to catch his breath, his weakness battling against the crushed armor. As Sanar continued to create the only possible, if not inept, obstacle, Luchar began to breathe faster, louder, his armor suddenly feeling more like a tomb than protection.

"I got you," the healer said, rushing over and removing his helmet. "Woah! Your chest plate is mashed, looks like by spraks."

"Yeah, I wanted to see how it felt so I volunteered to let several bite me," Luchar seethed. "Super fun. Highly recommend."

"Alright, alright, I know it wasn't on purpose, but I honestly didn't know their jaws were powerful enough to crush Hephaestus' reinforced manica. Your arm guard and chest plate are trashed. This all needs to come off."

Panic leached into Luchar's mind at the stifling feeling in his lungs. "It feels like several spraks are sitting *on* my chest."

"Mangled and crumpled armor has a way of feeling oppressive, in my experience."

"This house isn't big enough for both of us to be sarcastic," Luchar said.

"Gotcha. Sorry," Sanar replied, "the crushed armor has to feel confining."

As his breathing continued to quicken, Luchar said, "Actually, it's more claustrophobic to be trapped in a broken body, half of which can barely move. The smashed armor you can remove, but I am forever ensnared within this damaged body, without hope of escape."

Sanar paused, staring at his words. "Well, the armor, at least, I can help with," he said while deftly removing the mangled manica before moving to the compressed chest plate. "One thing they don't teach while training to be a healer, but you learn on the job, is how to remove damaged armor. There, take slow, deep breaths."

Once the armor was off, the healer stared at the salient atrophy of Luchar's paralyzed side, suffering under the lack of innervation from his damaged brain. Luchar looked down self-consciously at his wasted left side. His hand on that side curled into an inept, contracted claw. "I know. It's embarrassing for me too," the proud Knight said, slowly trying to calm the suffocating alarm blaring from his mind and air-hungry lungs as his dented, and stippled by sprak teeth, armor clattered into silence on the floor. Once it came to rest, the only movement was that of blood refugees and gore from those Luchar had killed migrating to the floor. *I shall never wear armor again,* he thought, the notion not helping his oppressive anxiety.

"My strength," Luchar said, glaring at his withered left side, "has failed me."

"Strength, beauty, and life itself are all inevitably lost by all who borrow them. They are not something ever really owned. They are but brief gifts bestowed in varying degrees to all who draw breath. It is the cost of living, of existing, of growing older."

Luchar nodded. "I understand the concept, but my power was relinquished sooner than it should have been from ageing."

"That's true," Sanar said. "My healers bag's empty, the price of battle this bloody."

"Doesn't matter," Luchar huffed. "No need to tend to the wounds of the dead."

"We're not dead yet."

"In definition only. In all practical purposes, we are."

"Breathing better?" Sanar asked, wiping the drool that was pooling on Luchar's paralyzed right face before returning to barricade duty.

Luchar nodded but leaned heavily against the cold bricks of the fireplace. "Don't think we're getting out of this one, brother," he slurred as exhaustion entwined with his facial paralysis to fight his words.

The healer closed his eyes and nodded briefly before pushing a bookshelf over against a window. It joined every other piece of furniture the room had to offer. "Won't help much, but…" Sanar's face fell as his voice trailed off.

Luchar looked at the fickle, if not outright backstabbing, muscle mass he had worked so hard to build that had traitorously fled. "When you're young, your mind never lets you imagine a day when you could get old or frail. I never expected to be this weak."

"Youth has a way of shrouding the truth of many things, including the stark reality that awaits us all…old age…death. Even though we see the truth all around us, the juvenile mind has a way of denying the path so undeniably laid out before us," Sanar said, sitting down next to the increasingly tachypneic Knight. *He likely has blood filling his lungs,* the healer thought.

"Can I let you in on a little secret?" Luchar asked but did not wait for Sanar to reply. "I've always been terrified. Every second, every single day, every single battle."

Sanar's eyes shot open, completely taken aback by the normally constantly enraged, often to the point of being mean-spirited, Knight.

"The secret? The concealed truth to my wrath? Fear. Most of my life is rage born of dread. One day, when I was a young squire, I had been beaten down and bullied. After they left, then and there, I decided to be through with being afraid, and from those ashes grew anger. Whenever I started to panic, I just made myself pretend to be irate."

The two could hear the battle getting closer, the Proliate having overrun the second barricade.

"Displace!" Tiron yelled. "Any of Liberum that can hear us, displace now!"

Sanar made a move to rise then looked to Luchar's sagging body along with his quick, ragged breaths and flashed an inept smile of acceptance before sitting back down.

Several Proliate who had broken through the second barricade and its defenders howled in anger, and then Tiron screamed as blood splattered against the part of a window still visible. It formed a blurry red halo around the bookshelf. Stratto suddenly gurgled. After a thud against the side of the house, his last wheezing breath joined the shrieks of the dying.

"Go house by house, door to door. Kill everyone!" one yelled.

"Push them back!" Knight Alto screamed, and the battle outside intensified. "We have to kill them and get back to the second barricade and the rest of our forces." The clanging and squishing sounds moved away.

Luchar continued, "Eventually fury just became who I was, and then, at some point, I wasn't pretending, or afraid, anymore. Rage took over, becoming my baseline, and I found myself always angry. Couldn't turn it off."

"I have to admit, most of us were intimidated by your radiating anger. I must ask, why tell me this? Why now?" Sanar asked.

Luchar looked down, hints of tears lining up along his eyelids to take in the view. "Leave it," he said, using his good right arm to stop the healer's hand from wiping his chin. "The drool just keeps coming. I know a lot of people thought I was a jerk, but some mental armor, once fortified, cannot be taken off even when you might wish it with all your heart. I guess I wanted at least one person to know before I die. Rage became an expectation from others and, as time went on, it not only became easier for me to wear—it became my standard."

Sanar nodded. "Emotions are funny things. They can transform our priorities and how we view the world. Feelings, passions...they shape and guide us. The angry man lives in an angry world. The happy person, Gimelli comes to mind, lives in a happy world. I wish we had more time to talk. This Luchar, the one opening up to me now, is someone I want to know better."

"Unfortunately, our time together is almost done." Taking a halting deep breath, Luchar added, "I will miss training, fighting, laughing, bleeding with all my fellow Knights. I'll miss the battles. The small daily ones where your spirit lifts a tired body to keep going. The big ones standing against a massive army."

Tears pulled themselves over Sanar's eyelids, as if trying to escape the coming fate. "There's a lot I'll miss too." They could hear streams of displacing Knights running past.

"It's Tiron and Stratto!" Tilkeri Knight Saccade said. "Nooo!" His scream held fury and despair at their dead bodies. "Luchar, and all in earshot, displace right now! The second line is completely overrun," he yelled, pounding on the door while Tempaus and Alta battled for time.

"Stay and fight!" Alta implored several retreating Knights.

"We have our orders. Displace!" one replied.

"In the end..." Luchar started, and stopped, remembering his talk with Dwarf Abhac outside the Storten Flower fields so long ago on the way to the Tournament. "What did I tell him?" Luchar asked, coughing loudly, blood oozing out of his nose and splattering out of his mouth in an arcing, but doomed, flight.

"Hmm?" Sanar asked.

"Long ago I told Abhac, 'In the end, it is the effort given in battle, and the honor with which we fought that will echo on forever.'" Luchar halfheartedly chuckled.

Sanar tilted his head, confused.

"From a considerable distance, 'the end' sounds fabulously heroic, until the finish has abruptly, and unwelcomely, arrived, that is.

Then it just sounds terrifying, and all too soon. I guess that's the fallacy all warriors live with. We all wear blinders to the truth of life as a combatant—death is just around the corner. The warriors' deception."

"Deception?"

"The self-delusion that someone else will be the one to die, and I'll survive."

The footfalls of displacing Knights went silent, broken only by the thuds of the last three Tilkeri falling. Sanar tensed as a loud pounding on the door alerted them—the Proliate had found them. The two men looked at each other—a flash of fear, a splash of resignation, all surrounded in complete comprehension that "the end" had arrived and was about to crash down around them.

Boom!

The forceful ramming of the door made the table and shelves shudder anxiously in their feeble, ill-fated role as a barricade.

Boom!

The two men nodded as the vibrations grew increasingly wrathful.

"No one's coming to help," Sanar stated, hope, an incompetent and thin veil over the staggering reality, fading.

Boom!

"No. No, they're not."

"But we're coming!" a Proliator said in a singsong voice.

"Help me up, and hand me my axe," Luchar demanded.

Boom!

"You're in no shape—"

Luchar smirked. "No shape to what? Die? We both know there's no choice in the dying part, but the how? I'll go out on my feet, swinging. Death in battle was always the last act in the play of this warrior's life. It's as good a way to go out as any and certainly beats rotting in infirmary hell as drool soils the front of your shirt and your battered brain dims into shambles broken only by infrequent, muddled memories. Let me die on my feet, even if as a broken man."

"No."

"No?"

"I'll help you die on your feet as a proud Knight, standing together, shoulder to shoulder, with his friend."

Luchar slid on his helmet, blocking the tears. "Yes. That will do."

Sanar nodded, struggling to help the feeble Luchar rise. Weak from blood loss, he could barely grip his axe, but pure untainted will forbade him from dropping it. His uncovered left arm looked as fragile and infirm as his whole body felt.

"Don't pick up a weapon, healer. They may let you live."

Sanar nodded but knew it would not make a difference.

The splintering sound grew louder with each reverberating hit. Luchar turned. "I fought for good…right? I used my power to honor the Knight's code? To help the weak?"

Sanar returned his visored gaze. "A singer sings. A chef cooks. A healer cures. A warrior fights. However, a soldier *can* choose their cause and the principles for which they give battle. You, brother, fought with wisdom, courage, temperance, and justice."

"That's all any Knight can ask for," Luchar replied. Overcoming a catch in his voice, he continued, "I could have done better with the whole temperance thing."

Smiling, Sanar gently patted his sweat-soaked aketon padding. "You did enough, Luchar. What you did was enough."

Luchar nodded while looking doubtful under his helmet, but circumstances dictated his life would end and his past self and actions would have to stand on their own with no further additions. *Blood-splattered memories haunt my sleep and obscure my concentration,* he thought. *Now, before things get worse, is as good as any to die.*

A final boom was followed by wood splitting in an angry creak as the door obliterated. The table against it flew backwards, dispatching all the other smaller furniture, which skittered away in doomed screeches. Their moaning caroming finally came to a stop in tipped-over disarray. A dozen hardened Proliate warriors thrust through the fragmented door, streaming through the clutter, into the room.

"It's the pig from earlier. Looks like we have work to do before killing you," one hissed.

"Fine, kill me, but Sanar? He's a healer. You—"

Luchar did not have a chance to finish as a Proliator spear bisected the healer's face. Luchar barely flinched during the blood shower as Sanar crumpled to the ground. Luchar growled, calling on his last reserve of vitality, and lunged with his axe knocking the closest spear upwards before slashing down. Fatigue and weakness conspired, and his blade missed the closest Proliator by several inches before seven spears skewered into his body and neck, one blow knocking off his helmet. Before his body hit the floor, they had retracted and plunged their spear tips into his flesh for a second round, this time impaling his face.

A third round of thrusts, their minds covered in the red mist of revenge.

Luchar's body jerked several times as his last breath whimpered out.

Another, and…

…another. His lifeless body lurched and jumped with each cycle of contemptuous blows as they skewered his already eviscerated corpse. His blood drenched the floor, the flood of his lifeblood easily overtaking the relatively small pool of Sanar's.

The closest Proliator grabbed Luchar's axe and chopped savagely until the Knight's head rolled away, no longer obligated to his body. Scraps of his broken-down manica and smashed chest plate were the only traces of the once-proud Knight. They looked like broken shards of bones swimming in an ocean of blood and entrails.

"Overkill much?" one of the Proliate laughed.

"I really don't ever want to see that guy again, like ever."

"Pretty sure mission accomplished there," another said.

General Lidenskap appeared in the doorway and nodded in satisfaction. "He was responsible for many of our dead. Now move on, warriors of Tallcon! Eat your anger! Consume the painful memories of our friends and comrades dying! Let its righteousness feed our bodies, nourishing us into battle rage and sweet revenge."

"Revenge!" stung through the death and annihilation still clinging in the air.

Scroll 13: Strive For...

"Borb's buried," Arend said, pausing to cough, heaving up more of the fluid and mucous into a bucket Fiacla had given him. "We did our best to be respectful to our friend."

"Yeah, sorry," Lontas added. "Borb was loyal, and he and Grym really helped."

Bellae nodded, rubbing her red eyes—sore from the combined abuse of treading and paddling in the horrifying liquid and sobbing. She continued rubbing Grym's back. The two talked for a while before she put him in her pocket.

"Seems like he's calmed down a bit?" Lontas said.

Bellae nodded. "They've been together since birth. It's hard, especially him dying that way," she said, glaring at the fearsome Daoine Crogall.

Fiacla, Lontas, Arend, Bellae, and Grym were in front of a fire within the hewn cave. The flames danced off the tan rocks and highlighted the magnificent relief carvings adorning it.

"I was just telling your friend Arend here about Stralande," Fiacla said. "I received word from the Kirvella dragons that he died and you would be coming to see me—if you survived. Did you know, Bellae, Stralande was at your birth?"

"What?" Bellae questioned. "Stralande acted like we hadn't met. He lied?"

"He'd never met the you of the day you remember," Fiacla said contemptuously. "I assume you'd agree you've changed a great deal from the day of your birth?"

"That seems like an excuse," Arend said.

"Does it?" the Daoine Crogall uttered. "We are constantly flowing beings, shaped by the windswept landscape that is the ups and downs of time, our experiences, our lives. The good, the bad, the horrible, the joyous all mold, shape us. We're never the same moment to moment."

Bellae looked at a gleaming bead of saliva hanging from one of his fangs. While he picked at his dagger-like teeth, she couldn't help questioning everything Stralande told her, especially the bits when they were alone.

"Wait, I thought no part of the prophecy knew about any other?" Lontas asked.

Fiacla nodded his massive jaw, which, given the length, projected as awkward. "There was some redundancy for us, as we possess no magic. As to what you endured or what you've left, I've no idea. Magical creatures can fend for themselves. I'm a simple mortal and glad you showed up when you did, as there are but three Daoine Crogall eggs left. Since we only live for a hundred years or so, that means the prophecy would be out of luck in some three hundred years.

"Of course, it was the Southern Dwarves who tricked and killed most of my kind. Three of my ancestors happened to be with the Kirvella dragons, working on setting up an education system. Luckily the Dwarves didn't find our storage area of eggs. They did murder all within one class of our nursery—ones about to be hatched." Fiacla took a sullen breath before handing Bellae, Lontas, and Arend a hot drink. "This is karkadé—a kind of tea.

"Right after the genocide, my remaining ancestors decided we'd keep the intact eggs and hatch them one at a time until the prophecy was complete. Our eggs don't mature unless you keep them warm for months."

"So there's been one Daoine Crogall here for thousands of years?" Arend asked.

"Much longer, actually."

"Your eggs last that long?" Lontas questioned.

"They don't go bad if that's what you're asking. When we approach ninety, we hatch one. The Kirvella check on us every so often—several times finding the guardian dead before hatching a youngling. So they raised one themselves, teaching them what they needed to know. Millenia ago there was talk of hatching them all to repopulate my species, but we wouldn't survive once the Southern Dwarves found out. They are a virus upon our sacred home."

The drink Fiacla had given them was thick and sludgy, but the warmth beckoned them to drink greedily. Bellae, thinking of the dragons and their fire pits to hatch babies, asked, "How do you warm the eggs?"

"In here," Fiacla said, lifting his leather shirt and stretching a pouch from his belly. "Both women and men of the Daoine Crogall can incubate eggs."

"How did the Kirvella manage it if they don't have pouches?" Lontas asked.

"Ah, very astute. They created one from wool and discarded dragon scales."

"How do you keep the Southern Dwarves from finding this place?" Bellae asked.

"Greed weighs down their intellect. Avarice corrupts their bodies from the inside out. Like all the self-indulgent, they fixate on worthless things they view as 'riches,' and it becomes a bottomless addiction—never satisfied. They continuously need more—too much is not sufficient. Their arrogance in thinking they destroyed us and their fixation on the riches below means they never saw the need to search for this place," Fiacla replied.

Whatever was in the drink had Arend feeling better by his second cup. "What's with that liquid and the dead bodies?"

"It was not my design. However, perhaps, you should've guessed that the Life and Death–Time crystals were not going to just hand themselves over to you. The hallway of eternal rest was a glimpse into death and its dead sense of humor!" At this Fiacla started laughing, which came out in rumbling, growling snorts. When he saw their humorless looks, he stopped. "Yes, well, sorry about your rodent companion. Now, I want to show you something."

He motioned for them to follow. They walked down the cavern, noticing the scenes of his people and their history in relief, carved with expert skill, eventually stopping at a line of tall wooden screen dividers. "We Daoine Crogall have been working on this for millennia—one at a time, slowly adding more." Groaning with effort, he pushed back large dividers to reveal a wall covered in beautiful paintings. It was evident by the age and brightness of the colors and variation of styles splattered in different sections that many contrasting artists had worked on the gigantic mural.

"This is amazing," Lontas said, his eyes bouncing between the various sections, each one representing a different story or moral.

Fiacla sighed. "I'm not saying art is the greatest struggle, but I will say artists fight under the enormous weight of dreams tangled with ideas of countless projects whispering their siren songs. Even with great effort, time and circumstance conspire against our aspirations, which are often torn and cut on the rocks of reality and tripped up amongst the thorns of obligation."

The League members swiveled to stare after his words.

"The hallway gave you a glimpse of death. These paintings force into your soul a breath of life. Everyone eventually knows death, but few take the little time they have to know life."

Bellae continued looking at him, wondering what he thought of his life, cooped up in a cavern. "This is stunningly beautiful."

"Thank you. I don't know which ancestor started it, but all living after added their touch. The center shows the first of our kin—Sobek—emerging from the Dark Water of nothingness. He had the courage to climb out from the murky, but comfortable, shade into the light. He created order in a world of chaos, dividing the land between the high and low, mountains and valleys, wet and dry, lakes and rivers and solid ground, hot and cold, water and fire. He created the world—saving our sacred place, this mountain, as his, and later our, home."

"What do you call this place?" Lontas asked.

"This is Fayyūm."

"I'm sorry for what the Southern Dwarves did to you," Bellae said, thinking of the Ainmhi Caint and their destruction.

"Despair has the parasitic quality of draining joy. Our culture always looks on the positives." Fiacla pointed to the paintings. "What some could complain is a prison, being stuck alone in this cavern as an isolated guardian, we took as a chance to study, read, and create.

Although, some days, I admit I fight the urge to bellow at the notion my kind will never again walk the world Sobek created. Apathy and willful ignorance are the greatest strains weighing down the success of all creatures. Greed and covetousness, that control those living below who killed my kind, are the most serious threats to peace."

Arend pointed to the top of the mural. "What does that mean?"

Lontas eagerly answered, "Nitimur in vetitum means we strive for the forbidden. An interesting motto."

"Indeed," Fiacla said. "It could mean we have an innate need to taste that which is forbidden or evil. Perhaps it should convey that we strive for knowledge, to know the cold darkness, however uncomfortable it may be. Looking into the abyss, we leave parts of ourselves within. Greed blinds consequences. Pride and arrogance blur compassion. Sadness strangles happiness. Anger overcomes joy. Jealousy spreads over gratitude. Hate blocks love. Fear defeats curiosity and aspiration. Darkness and death strive to strip joy of our time in the light.

"In the end, we all lose. Tragedy and darkness ultimately win. Live with flair anyway. Strive for forbidden knowledge, hidden within the workings of the universe. What we fight for is infinitely more important than the critical way we wage battle. Fight for what is right, not just for you but virtuous, fair—that which brings light and knowledge to the world." He turned to Bellae. "Make sure you choose wisely for that which you are fighting." Fiacla rumbled a chuckle as they gazed at the juxtaposition of sage words sprouting from his ferocious form. "A lesson: do not judge a mind, heart, or soul by its covering." He flicked his finger against his savage teeth.

Arend shuddered into another coughing fit, moving away to hack up more liquid.

"Ah, well, perhaps more karkadé tea, then rest."

Scroll 14: No, No. It's a Massacre.

"At least the spraks are dead," Ritari said through the smoke generated by burning buildings down other paths. He, Friar, Lovag, Varg, and a cadre of Knights receded through one of the twisting veins that wasn't on fire to one in the third series of barricades.

"Yes, the second displacement did not go well, thanks to those creatures," Friar said, his cloak splattered with remnants of dead Proliate.

"I have to hand it to the Tilkeri—they gave us time," Lovag said.

Friar nodded, regret that they would never grow into the Knights he knew they could become pulling down on his soul. Friar could see fires all around them, beacons publicizing their failures according to the omnes enim mori plan, which, along with various barricades, served to funnel the attackers down predetermined, narrow, defensible streets and alleys.

"Sir, we have Acus launchers ready," Varg said. The leader of the Ulven squad looked rough. There was a makeshift bandage around his neck, stained red with blood, and he looked pale in between his salt and pepper beard.

"Ah, our guests should appreciate that welcome from Sorea," Friar said, smiling externally but haunted by her brutal death. "Thanks for saving my hide as we displaced."

Varg nodded. "For a super-old man, you write well with your sword. However, I imagine you kill many more with sheer boredom."

"Fair enough," Friar said, the response tempered by their predicament and exhaustion. As the Proliate approached their barricade, he shouted, "Unleash the Acus!"

Varg stomped on the massive firing button. Nothing happened. He repeatedly trampled on it without effect as the enemy surged forward.

Lovag scrambled up the barricade onto a nearby roof, tracing the pneumatic tube from the button Varg was continually thumping to a series of large wooden boxes facing down upon the street. The Proliate were ten feet away when he found the loose connection. He could feel the air whooshing out with each stomp. As soon as he attached the disconnected ends, tens of thousands of small needles exploded out of the boxes lining the roofs. The two-inch projectiles slammed into the Proliate and wriggled their way into any weakness or break in armor. The Proliate screamed and swatted the air in desperation at the immensely painful hive of stings littering their bodies. As Lovag returned to congratulations, a messenger approached Friar.

"Sir, you need to see someone outside the cemetery," the Knight said breathlessly.

"I'll not leave the front line—ever evolving that it is. We'll displace there soon enough, or have them come to me."

"Sir, it's a mortally wounded Eaglian with a vital message only for your ears. The healers say if we move him, he'll die."

"Join me," Friar said, looking at Ritari and Lovag. "The rest of you, stand strong. Until we return, Varg's in command."

As they made their way through the unnaturally quiet tutor houses, Friar got a chill knowing the Proliate would raze every building and kill everyone living within the walls. With winter coming and food in short supply, there was no room for more mouths to feed even if their revenge-tainted minds would have allowed it. Approaching the cemetery, the messenger stopped and motioned for them to do the same.

Pulling a cart of supplies, Cookie, having lingered too long in the kitchen, ran into a group of displacing healers who looked like they could use their own services—their clothes blood dyed and flesh splattered with scorch marks from Magicians' spells.

"Where are we?" a healer asked, lost in the smoke of burning buildings.

"At least the smoke's so thick the griffins and hippogriffs are keeping away," another said as screaming intermittently popped up from around the castle.

"That last shout was close."

The ragged front line of house-to-house fighting down the predetermined lanes was constantly progressing, but the overall trajectory was the Knights losing ground. Cookie looked up, realizing she had not been paying attention to where she was going. Fires pocked the horizon of the once-pristine castle, sending plumes of congealing black smoke across the sky—marking the rapid advance of the overwhelming number of Proliate.

A healer nodded to Cookie. "I'm lost, everything looks different. Maybe—"

"Maybe you can stay silent and let us kill you," a Proliate replied as a squad materialized in front of them.

"Please, we're healers, trained to alleviate wounds, not cause them. Let—"

He was cut off by several spear thrusts curtly slicing into his body. "Heal yourself of those wounds, why don't ya?" the soldier said as the others laughed.

They greedily looked to Cookie, who was still heedlessly walking forward. With tears rolling out, the turning of her cart's wheels finally stopped and the clattering of pans silenced as she stood still in front of the Proliate. "Ya wudn't kill a lady, wud ya?"

The Proliate laughed. "Why? Have you seen one?" He casually walked up to her when, with blistering speed and surprising strength, Cookie used a large iron pan to dent his helmet. His eyes rolled back in his head before he collapsed.

A spear sliced into her arm, and she dropped the pan, stumbling backwards. Another spear pierced her abdomen, and she cried out, doubling over in pain. Her personal scream was lost in the shrieking sea of death around her as the other healers were brutally terminated. Seeing her incapacity, the Proliate warriors circled around.

“Feeling tough, are we?” one taunted. “Think a pan can stop us?”

“Stopped him, shur’nuff,” she said, trying to smile, but her face was overwhelmed by the pain and fear in her normally rebellious eyes. She grabbed another pan from her cart and ineptly tried to parry several feigned spear sorties. She knew they were toying with her, and after several minutes, the pan, becoming onerous with her blood loss, finally dropped. A dozen Proliate closed in, thrusting their spears. Most sliced through her torso, but one slammed through her midface. Her body instantly dropped into the hungry pool of blood beneath her, already devouring and assimilating the new supply of crimson spewing from her lifeless body.

A loud clink suddenly exploded. The Proliate turned to see one of theirs dropping to the ground and Hephaestus standing over them, withdrawing his version of a war hammer from the soldier’s head. He stood in patchy armor, his massive beard scruffing out from under his helmet. The blood and brain still dribbled from the massive beak projecting from his hammer. Spinning it around with an immense, singed forearm, he showered the gore off from the tip of his weapon.

With prodigious skill he quickly brought the spiked war hammer in an underhand arc up to the closest soldier’s groin. The Proliate fell in a fetal heap, hissing a silent scream, the pain too intense to let any other sound escape.

“*Now* I see a lady,” Hephaestus said, but he did not have time to withdraw the still protruding hammer. Without a shield, he was quickly eviscerated by the others.

“Come, boy, we have a battle to get to!” Ritari moaned. “Lead us to the Eaglian.”

“Battle? You mean *slaughter*? You have about as much chance of surviving this as a solitary ant against a stampede of trompe,” the Knight said.

"Wait a second," Lovag said. "I don't recognize you. What squad are you with?"

Before he could answer, Ritari had his sword at the man's throat. Lovag moved to take the strange Knight's weapon. "What the..." Lovag said as his hand passed through the sword.

Suddenly, the Knight began to shimmer and shrink before their eyes, his armor turning into a white robe. When the man stopped shrinking, the form of a short, plump Dwarf stood before them. "I'm Fresler. There's no Eaglian. Do you think one could get through the swarm of hippogriffs and griffins circling overhead? I hate to break your delusion, but this isn't the Battle *for* Liberum, it's the Massacre *at* Liberum. You're all going to die."

"Kill him and let's get back to the fight," Ritari said.

"Wait!" the Dwarf squeaked. "I'm from...what used to be the Rebelde Plains. I was on patrol when one of the Northern Dwarves saw the smoke. He dropped me off, saying I was to get Friar and Ritari. However, we have room to take Lovag as well."

"You're sadly mistaken, Fresler. I'll never leave," Friar stated solemnly. "I promised Liberum would not fall while I live. We're not fools, we know the cause is lost, but we shall fight to the end and die together."

"How noble. Did you practice that speech? There can be no Knight victory here, only a bath of blood and pain."

Friar scoffed, thinking of his speech with Bellae before the Tournament. "Actions inspired by hopes of glory or fortune result in false prizes that quickly decompose. That's something I once told our youngest squire. I added that you should move through life as if every one of your actions will echo forever. We were talking about victory of the world versus true victory. We have no delusions of a triumph you or the world would understand. However, we shall fight beside our brothers and sisters with all our ability, all of our strength—and that shall have to be enough. Your lack of understanding of our Knight's Code, and its inherent honor and beauty, does not change the conviction in our hearts. This shall be our victory."

Fresler rolled his eyes.

"Please, feel free to stay here and fight with us, Dwarf, unlike your comrades at the battle of Trepas," Ritari said angrily. "But we three are going to fight and die here."

"How righteous of you. Just wait," the Dwarf said impassively, looking up. "You must see something first. Ritari, stay. Lovag, here. Friar, there… Perfect. Now, look there. See it?" he said, moving next to Lovag and pointing above the cemetery.

Flabbergasted at his actions, the three stared incredulously.

"What exactly are—" Ritari started before a massive wind gust hit them. As they turned, something clamped around their torsos, and he and Friar were suddenly lifted in the air. A moment later, Lovag and Fresler joined them airborne, zooming over the cemetery. The infirm and children of the castle looked in horror as their leaders and a Dwarf magically flew above.

"Listen up down there," someone unseen stated. "You're being carried by exhausted Vioma dragons hidden by prestidigitation. If you keep fighting, we'll drop your wiggly butts."

Ritari stopped. "Abhac, is that you?"

"Yeah, now be quiet. You can fall and die, or you can live to fight another day. Griffins to the north! Dissolve them now!" Abhac commanded. The Dwarves skilled in prestidigitation riding on the dragons made them disappear just as they were crossing the wall of Liberum.

Friar twisted his head around to see, with tear-obscured vison, the enemy drop the boarding planks and start to stream across into the lightly defended cemetery, easily overwhelming the Knights there.

"Take me back! I can't leave…" Friar's words trailed off as he saw the numbers of warriors arrayed against them, their anger and rageful desire for revenge radiating off like glinting sunlight. He could not help but gasp. There, outside the wall bordering the cemetery across the River Vita, where Finn and the squires had once fished for a monster, stood thousands of troops. The soldiers were a mosaic of Ager, Piscinian, and Southern Dwarf troops pushing more siege engines to the wall. By the looks of them, they too were out for vengeance: retaliation not just for Ovest and Trepas but for the horrors the Dark Warriors had inflicted upon their countries. Strategically, it made no sense to waste the resources to storm that isolated section of the castle, as the bridge could be cut and your army trapped in a cemetery. *But not if revenge and death are your only concerns,* Friar thought.

"No offense," Abhac called out. "That's not a battle. It's a mass execution."

"You should have sent dragons to fight with us!" Ritari said angrily.

"Just because you have a large army surrounding you, doesn't mean we don't. We're surrounded by Dark Warriors, wyvern, Watchers, and did not know of your predicament. Our patrol happened to see the massive fires. If we'd flown back home, by the time we got there, the Kirvella Council and King Abernan signed off on an attack, we mobilized our forces, and returned, you'd all be dead."

Visions mercilessly streamed through Friar's mind: his father Isa, the loss of Cumhacht to the Proliate who defiled its visage into the Citadel, the loss and concessions the Knights made after the Battle of Petturi when the Southern Dwarves betrayed them to the Dark Warriors, to Trepas, the libraries lost, the Knights killed, the villagers massacred, the dragon at the Tournament debasing Finn's body.

Once clear, they were no longer hidden, and ropes flew down. The deft Air Ridire warriors slid down and attached harnesses to them, which were used to pull the reluctant travelers up. Friar and Ritari had been lifted by the claws of the same dragon and sat numbly while being strapped into the wooden carriage.

It was only when a large, blood-stained hand fell on his shoulder, Friar realized he was sobbing. His eyes closed as ruthless visions continued past. Ritari spoke naught, as there was nothing to be said. The wind rushed angrily over them as the dragons flew, their strength powerless to blow away the desperate heartache. The screams of those huddling in the cemetery were still echoing in their ears as they headed north, to Mount Honoo.

Chapter Two

Time For a Bath in What?

Scroll 1: Gluttony of: Faces, Vertices, Edges

Bellae woke from spasmodic sleep due to force-fed visions of those close to her dying: Crann being mauled, Borb drowning, Finn spurting blood.

"It's okay. I'm with you, whatever happens," Lontas said.

Whispers from the crystals swirled within, and she closed her eyes tightly to fight against them and looming tears. Arend convulsed awake with fitful choking, rasping up more of the liquid that nearly drowned him, the thick fluid retching into his ever-present bucket.

The Daione Crogall added more wood to the fire. "Well, I don't know if we shall sleep any longer." The others kept their eyes closed and blankets above them. "It's almost morning."

"How can you tell?" Lontas asked groggily.

"Ah, I have a series of...hourglasses..." Fiacla's words trailed off as if he was embarrassed at the word. "...to track the hours marching across the day and time's continual striving across our lifetimes."

"What was that liquid?" Lontas asked, watching Arend's body shudder under another wheezing fit—a prattling within his lungs. "The bodies looked ancient, yet preserved."

"Ah, keen eye," Fiacla said. "The Ainmhi Caint experimented with preservation liquids. When they started to be wiped out, the Kirvella took over and developed a series of unique liquids. That fluid is conserving. Later I shall introduce you to another liquid."

There was a dejected expression in Fiacla's eyes, and Bellae flashed the others a worried look. *Haven't we been through enough?* she wondered, but, after her experiences on this quest, the answer was a resounding no.

"Well, if you wish to rest, I'll see to breakfast."

It seemed to Bellae she had just closed her eyes when Lontas appeared, gently shaking her shoulders. She sat up to the smell of something delicious permeating the cavern.

"You look better," she said to Arend.

He nodded, wordlessly continuing to eat from a bowl like the one Fiacla handed her.

"It's full of vicuña, a camelid creature that roams the mountain, and pīti, a red root vegetable that grows up here," Fiacla said.

"How do you catch animals if you don't leave?" Lontas wondered.

"I have traps sporadically placed around the mountain that are accessible via tunnels and a few gardens. I use small holes and mirrors to bathe my crops in the sun's light."

When they finished eating, Fiacla sighed heavily as if preparing for a gruesome task.

"Can't you just give us the scroll?" Arend appealed.

Fiacla scrunched his eyes. "The point of the riddles and trials is they must be earned."

"Stralande told me the Chosen One was a made-up title about the first one to speak Ainmhi Caint." Bellae pointed to herself. "A choice of one. I didn't 'earn' that deplorable title."

Fiacla growled ominously. "Nature endowed your gift. It could have landed on anyone but chose you. Of the trials you have completed, were any handed to you?"

"Not even close."

"Well then, you've earned them and merited this journey. Speaking of which…" His voice trailed away as he spun around, walking up to a heavy, burnished door that had remained closed their entire visit. A carving above the door read: ΑΓΕΩΜΕΤΡΗΤΟΣ ΜΗΔΕΙΣ ΕΙΣΙΤΩ.

"Let no one ignorant of geometry enter here," Lontas translated.

Fiacla nodded. "On the other side of this door is your next test. I did not design it and cannot change it." As they approached the door, it began to glow blue and oscillate. "Alright, to start you must say unlock in Ainmhi Caint."

Bellae stepped forward. *"Unlock!"*

Loud mechanisms grumbled behind the door before it stopped vibrating and the glow faded. Fiacla pushed the door open before wordlessly grabbing a torch and holding it out.

Lontas cautiously took it, the light revealing a claustrophobically small hallway leading to another door. Fiacla pointed, and after moving down the path, they came to a new door.

Lontas said, "It has four square sections missing."

"There are four cubes that look the right size sticking out from the bottom of the door," Bellae said. "Maybe we remove them and fill the empty parts to open the door?"

"They don't come out," Lontas said after handing the torch to Arend and trying to remove the four cubes stuck within the door.

"There's a fifth cube on a pole going across the middle of the door," Bellae said. "Plus there's writing on the door just above."

"Look, this fifth one slides." Lontas demonstrated before reading.

"To release the others on your route,
Find me everywhere within and without.
I am pure gold but do not sparkle.
Although priceless and top hierarchal.

Worthless to some, I have no weight.
Find me to open the gate:
Taller plus smaller divided by taller is identical to
longer divided by shorter.
Answer wrong? Arrows pierce—a quest thwarter."

"What's the symbol on the cubes?" Arend asked. "It looks like a snake eating its tail."

"It's an ouroboros symbol and represents the eternal cycle of destruction, or rebirth, depending on how you look at it," Lontas answered. "Life, death, rebirth. Some think of it as destruction and regeneration."

"That makes sense for the Life-Death–Time crystals," Arend said, staring at the figures with heads of dragons and snake bodies in perfect circles, their tails in their mouths.

"There are numbers below the sliding fifth cube," Bellae said, running her hand down the numbers, most of which were extremely long decimals. "They start with 0 and end with 2.61803398874989485."

Arend sighed. "Ridiculous, unsparkly, weightless gold thingy with taller-smaller-taller than something momentous or adventurous?"

"It's eaaa…" Lontas' voice trailed off, choosing not to say easy. "It's asking for the golden section or golden ratio. It's a pattern occurring in nature. There is one ratio that divides a straight line into segments so that the shorter section is to the longer one at the same ratio as the longer section is to the entire line segment. They've made it easy for us because if the shorter section is 1, the longer will be 1.61803398874989485."

Bellae looked to Arend with an "I told you so" expression, and he nodded.

"So," Lontas continued, "we just slide the top cube into the golden ratio. Since the entire thing is 2.618, etcetera, we therefore know the shorter is 1 and the longer is 1.618." He moved the cube to the correct spot and pushed. The four cubes below dropped forward onto the floor.

Bellae bent down. "They all have an ouroboros on the front, but with different words underneath the snake thingy and the backs have distinctive geometric shapes."

Lontas took each one in turn. "This one says vita, which means life, with an octahedron or eight-sided shape behind it. The mors, death, has a tetrahedron or four-sided pyramid on the back. Post mortem, after death, has dodecahedron—twelve-sided shape. Finally, tempus, or time, has an icosahedron or twenty-sided shape."

"There are sets of writing on the sides of the hallway," Arend said. "They don't have titles that match anything you just said, but they have numbers separated by dashes above them."

"There are single numbers below these blank cube spaces in the door. We must find a way to place the correct cube in the right spot... like four keys. That must be why the backs are different," Bellae said, leaning in to look at the four open sections in the door. "They are the perfect size for the blocks that fell out. We just need to figure out which goes where."

"So each of the riddles have three numbers above that relate to the number of faces, vertices, or points, and edges of one of the Platonic solids. There are four of the five represented behind each cube," Lontas said.

"Platonic solids?" Bellae ventured.

"They are five shapes that possess perfect symmetry, meaning every face is exactly the same as every other in not just size but shape and position relative to every other face. Take the death cube, mors. It has a tetrahedron on its back, which means it has four faces, four points, and six edges. That is the 4-4-6 above the riddle. What's interesting is that means they've already told us where they go."

"How?" Arend asked.

"Below the cubed-out spaces in the door are the total degrees if you were to add up all the angles of the shape. So the mors, death, with a tetrahedron in the back, would go in the spot labeled 720°. For a tetrahedron each angle of each face is 60°, so three angles of sixty on each face is 180° per side. Multiply that by the four sides, and you have 720°."

"So we could just put them in without looking at the riddles?" Bellae asked. "We could feel past this tattered black cloth hanging over the openings and feel which one went where."

Fiacla growled, "That would be unwise. You would lose your hand to a spiked trap."

"Okay...we should read them," Lontas said. "Remember the answer is zero thing in the desert? We shouldn't be too hasty."

"The first set of writing has 20-dash-12-dash-30 above it," Bellae said.

"We would assume then," Lontas said, "that it is the icosahedron with twenty faces, twelve points, and thirty edges, and therefore, this cube that says tempus, or time, would go into the slot with 3600° below it, as that is the total of all the angles in degrees."

"Like you said, let's double check," Bellae said before reading.

"Without arms, I creep. Without legs, I sprint.
Without wings, I fly.
No one can buy or acquire more, no matter what they try.
I am gift without instructions,
Cannot be returned and am impervious to seductions.
Wealth does not interest me.
I kill kings and destroy castles even if they plea."

"Definitely time," Lontas said, sliding in the tempus cube with the icosahedron on its back into the cube-shaped space above the 3600°.

A loud clanking noise sounded within the metal door, but Fiacla growled. "Perhaps, a wise quester might figure all of them out and read *all* that is written before proceeding?"

Bellae smiled appreciatively. "Thanks. The other guardians were... not helpful."

Fiacla nodded, but his eyes flinched downward. "I know what awaits on the other side."

"Alright," Lontas said, "we solve each puzzle and just set it in front of the correct slot."

"The slot that *appears* correct," Fiacla corrected.

Lontas nodded. "Righto. The second riddle has 4-4-6 above it—tetrahedron/death cube."

"Below it," Bellae read:

Tattered Shred of Eternity

"Without weapons I am always victorious.
The fastest creature cannot outrun me, that's vainglorious.
No hiding place can deter my success.
I make the rules, finding each egress.
You could sooner shake off your shadow than me from your case.
No matter what deeds or heroic actions, everyone ends up
in my embrace."

"Death has a tetrahedron and fits everything the words say. So I'll put the death cube in front of the 720° open space, the sum of all the degrees of its angles."

"I'll read the third one, 12-20-30 above it," Arend said.

"That's the dodecahedron," Lontas said, "twelve faces, twenty points, thirty edges."

Arend nodded, continuing:

"Most desire to understand,
A few seek to know me before the final drop of sand.
Many fight tenaciously to avoid going through my door.
Once encountered none can recount the tale anymore.
Many pontificate, but only those who can no longer reflect,
Could truly inform of my appearance and effect."

"A dodecahedron is the shape on the back of the after death cube, and the riddle seems to be talking about what comes after death. I'll put this cube in front of the space with 6480°, the sum of all the angles of the dodecahedron," Lontas said.

"The last one has 8-6-12 on top," Bellae informed.

"A gift never requested,
Given to all, but the measure not equally vested.
The first and last of me are similar—full of need.
You begin with all of it, but a small seed.
You end with knowledge expanding,
And greater understanding.

But no matter what sought,
All are left with naught."

"Sounds like life. At birth we have our whole life, 'begin with all of it,' and we know more when we die but have no aliveness left," Arend said. "Do the sides and faces match up?"

"Definitely, the life cube has an octahedron with eight faces, six vertices, and twelve edges," Lontas said. "I'll put that one in front of the matching sum of the angles, 1440°."

Bellae swiveled. "Hey, there's one last riddle!

So now you have them complete.
But were your actions too fleet?
If not, switch the two that some would trade again to start,
Beware, a second round may be bitter and tart.
Starting again means no guarantees at all,
You begin so weak as to not crawl.
Avoid ire despite the situation being dire,
Change fire for air, air for fire!"

"Avoid ire?" Arend said. "Then stop giving us ridiculous puzzles! Trade again to start? Who would want to be too week to even crawl?"

Lontas smiled. "What they're saying is they want us to switch two cubes. The 'second round' they mention is another chance at life. Being born again means we're babies—too weak to crawl. So we switch life for death."

"Why not after death for time?" Arend asked.

"Well," Lontas said, "from just the top part, it would be hard to say. However, the bottom part solidifies the answer—pun intended. Each of the five Platonic solids has an associated element. Life, the octahedron, has air. Death, the tetrahedron, is fire. After death is ether—the dodecahedron, and time is water—the icosahedron. Just for completeness sake, the one they didn't use is a hexahedron—that's earth. Here, let me just draw everything out for you."

Tattered Shred of Eternity

Tetrahedron
Fire-Death

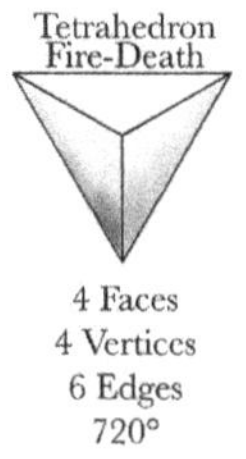

4 Faces
4 Vertices
6 Edges
720°

Octahedron
Air-Life

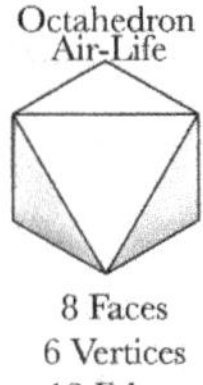

8 Faces
6 Vertices
12 Edges
1440°

Hexahedron
Earth

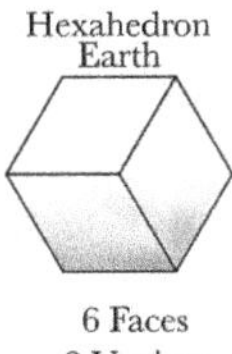

6 Faces
8 Vertices
12 Edges
2160°

Icosahedron
Water-Time

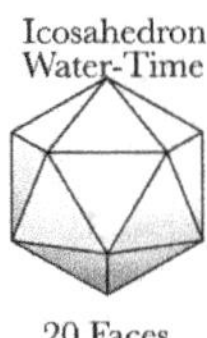

20 Faces
12 Vertices
30 Edges
3600°

Dodecahedron
Ether-After Death

12 Faces
20 Vertices
30 Edges
6480°

Bellae put her hand on Arend's shoulder. He resisted the urge to scream, frustrated at the riddles and annoyed he did not know more. "Yeah, I know, the guy who broke into the library."

Scroll 2: I've Heard of Watching Your Time, But...

Lontas switched around the life and death cubes before inserting the remaining three into their correct positions. The sound of weary gears began grinding in exhausted, spasmodic spurts.

"Back up," Fiacla said as they squeezed by his massive frame. The door clicked, as if gears were misfiring. Fiacla slammed one of his enormous webbed and clawed feet against the door. It vibrated before the clunking mechanisms began purring. "Move out of the hallway."

With that he opened the door, coughing at the rush of stale air. He rambled down the hallway, pushing them out. "Let me get more torches while the air circulates a bit."

Bellae rubbed Grym while they waited. Once Fiacla gave the signal, they followed him into an enormous cavern dominated by an unusual, gargantuan structure.

"What the...?" Lontas said, craning his neck up as his jaw dropped.

Arend looked protectively toward Bellae, trying to imagine what she would have to do with such a complex construction.

"Isn't it amazing?" Fiacla asked, pointing to an enormous hourglass rising from the cavern floor to near the ceiling, looking ridiculously out of place. The top, bottom, and three support beams were all made of metal. The hourglass itself appeared to be empty except for one curious object sitting in the bottom half. A flimsy-looking rope ladder hung outside the mountainous design. The rest of the cavern was quite dull, lacking carvings or paintings, just roughly hewn rock, dug out high enough to allow the massive shape to rise.

"You need to climb the ladder, Bellae," Fiacla stated, turning serene.

"She goes, I go," Lontas said.

"She's not climbing until you explain this...monstrosity," Arend added.

Fiacla shook his head. "Not possible for anyone else to go or me to explain further. If you want the next crystals, she goes...alone."

"Is that a...desk at the bottom of the giant hourglass?" Arend wondered.

"I cannot say more until you complete my last request. So, please, climb the ladder."

Bellae handed Lontas the bag with the crystals before heading to the ladder. Arend put his talon on the bottom to steady it. Once she reached the top, she noted a circular door and four massive tubes running from the cavern's ceiling above into the top of the hourglass.

"What are these tubes—"

She was cut off by Fiacla below, chastising Arend, who had started to fly. "This is only for her! Bellae, pull up the rope ladder and lower it down the hole in the top of the hourglass."

Lontas and Arend looked at each other, feeling increasingly agitated as Bellae heaved open a groaning circular door on the top. Grym peeked out but silently slid back into her pocket. Slowly she pulled up the rope ladder, struggling with the weight before lowering it into the round opening. With a *twang* it drooped down just above the desk, rattling around the narrow section in the middle before coming to an unsettled, quivering rest.

"Climb down," Fiacla said, putting a hand up to silence questions.

Bellae carefully descended, going slowly through the narrow throat of the hourglass. Eventually she reached out with her foot for the wooden desk before lowering herself to the floor and longingly gazing at the contents of the desk. Unbeknownst to her, Fiacla had gone over to the far wall and pushed a rock with the death symbol.

A loud groan made Bellae look up to see the ladder fall and a circular door slam shut as clear liquid began dumping over her, spurting through the tubes from the ceiling. She ran to the side, looking questioningly at Fiacla as the liquid waterfalled over the desk.

"The entire hourglass is going to fill up!" Fiacla shouted over the gushing liquid. Bellae's eyes widened in terror. "There's no escape, except through completing the challenge."

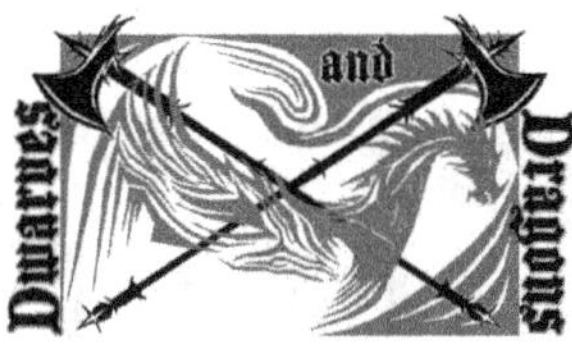

Scroll 3: Too Late

Friar sat up quickly, sweat dripping from his forehead at the images of the infirm and children of Liberum being brutally murdered by Confederate troops. *Thousands of years of history erased in a heartbeat.* He visualized the squires on the eve of becoming a Knight meandering through lonely gravestones in a crowded graveyard, searching for a quote that would strike a chord. Their souls knew what their strong bodies and young minds did not allow into consciousness: they were just a blink away from joining those underground.

I should have stayed and died, he thought grimly, shuddering to think about what they did to his office, its paintings, weapons, and trophies. Now, several days later, he sat in a small barren room, unfurnished save for a cot that was way too short for him but perfect for the Northern Dwarves who lived there.

"Friar!" a voice cried out.

Calling for someone to "come in" when the "door" was a curtain seemed foolish, but he said it anyway.

"Sir, we have news. Come to the Council of Kirvella dragons!" a young Dwarf proclaimed excitedly. "Ritari and Lovag will join us."

Friar felt deep remorse jumbled with shame as he walked down the hallway Bellae and the other League members had so long ago, showing up in the Council's chambers with nothing but two warriors. *The Knights are finished,* he thought gloomily.

"Welcome," a blue-clad Vasama Dwarf greeted. "Please hurry."

Friar followed him through the antechamber, glancing at the statue of Pugnatex, the famous Saatana Dragon. He was shoved, more than shown, into the Council's stone chamber. Ritari and Lovag were both looking better. The Kirvella dragon healers had done wonders.

"Friar," King Abernan said as many of the blue dragon Council members nodded.

Sarskil pointed to the last open seat at the table. Friar felt sheepish taking it, as there were many Kirvella standing around the table. There was a large map of Verngaurd spread out on the table. Dark lines representing Dark Warrior controlled territory had been drawn up and down the eastern seaboard. Only Toil Shaor and parts of Piscium were left white. Friar was taken aback to see Liberum supposedly under Dark Warrior control.

"That's why you're here," King Abernan said somberly. "After you were flown out of Liberum, the Proliate army crushed the rest of the Knights, and the cowardly men of Ager, the Piscinians, and the Southern Dwarves killed the rest. I've heard tell they had quite the pile of plunder to take back to their own homes. That is, until the Dark Warriors slammed into the rear lines, decimating two-thirds of the Proliate forces."

"They killed over thirty thousand of the Proliate troops?" Friar asked, stunned.

"Likely," Pistis answered. He rubbed the blue scales around his ear.

"How big was the Dark Warrior army?" Ritari asked incredulously.

"Two…hundred…thousand," Abernan stated. Exaggerated gasps and grumbling echoed through the chamber.

"Impossible!" Friar shouted.

"You might think so, but you'd be wrong" King Abernan said. "The other Confederates and around fifteen thousand Proliate escaped because of their air power. They created a small wedge for those troops to squeeze through. I bet there was hell to pay when the Dark Warrior commanders reported that to the White Wizard."

There was stunned silence in the room. If there really was an army of Dark Warriors that size in Verngaurd, it was all over, other than the wait.

"It seems," Contatto, a Kirvella dragon, said, "that we walked right into the Dark Warriors' trap, weakening our armies, becoming easy prey, even if they didn't have an army of two hundred thousand."

"The armies of the Alliance are shattered. I doubt we could even put a respectable army in the field," King Abernan stated. "The Rebelde Plains are totally destroyed. Creber is under siege right now, and I doubt they could leave. The Proliate are harassing them from the north with soldiers from rebuilt Ragorsaf. Dark Warriors are burning their woods from the south."

"Have they reached the sacred forest?" Friar asked, feeling sick to his stomach imagining the normally serene woods being terrorized by fire.

"We've heard nothing. Air travel has become restricted with Watchers and wyvern from Ifrean. The Knights have one castle with five thousand troops. However, Toil Shaor is surrounded by Dark Warriors. Our own troops have taken a beating from the constant assaults."

A sense of dread and humiliation washed over Friar. *I'm no better than my father. Our family will forever be known as the ones responsible for the collapse of the Knights.* He looked down under the depressing thought that their world would be destroyed so completely that perhaps no one would even remember the Knights at all.

"Can the Proliate and their Confederacy stop the Dark Warriors?" Chiffre asked. "Do they have the numbers to pull off another victory like they did decades ago?"

Abernan sighed. "The Western Elves and Southern Dwarves don't have many good warriors left but they could throw out a few. Ager has refugees at the Citadel, but all of Ager is completely overrun. As for Piscium, they're fighting fiercely house to house and would be unlikely to leave."

"What of Jaa and the Proliate themselves?" Lovag asked.

"Jaa's female warriors were almost completely smashed, courtesy of the Battle of Trepas. They have all their male warriors, but they're responsible for the defense of their homeland and do not leave their borders."

A spear of regret pierced Friar's heart. *I'm just a pawn for the White Wizard,* he thought. Images of all the dead from the Battles of Ovest and Trepas sped through his mind.

"In terms of the Proliate…it's hard to say. We know their best troops were destroyed at Ovest and Trepas. Now, with another thirty thousand down…who knows?" the King of the Northern Dwarves said.

"We must unite with them," Friar said to a chorus of groans.

"There have been too many egregious injuries from both sides to have that happen. It's simply too late," Abernan scoffed.

"What choice do we have?" Lovag asked.

"I'm not sure what the Magicians have left. Friar and his Knights can speak firsthand about the significant role they played in the crushing defeat of Liberum. The rumor is that they used so many mindre crystals moving their diezmar siege engines and fighting that they're almost out. What that means for their combat effectiveness…I can't say," Contatto declared.

Friar took in a deep breath at the plague of war spreading its evil across their lands.

Scroll 4: Let's Just Breathe

"You're killing her!" Lontas said, pounding on the glass.

"I'm doing nothing," Fiacla said, "but following the instructions of her ancestors. The liquid is from the storm fields north of the Vahse Plains. The Kirvella dragons say it's a blend of substances that don't normally mix called PFC. They said something about an old horse burial grounds and a meteor that hit with a yellow-green gas. Anyway, those things were charged with electricity from the storms, and it turned into a pond of breathable liquid."

"I can breathe this water stuff?" Bellae asked.

"It's not water. But, yes...for a while," Fiacla said.

"You mean perfluorocarbon," Lontas said, gazing at the liquid rising surprisingly fast.

"That's correct," Fiacla said.

Lontas flushed with anger. "But perfluorocarbons have too much density!"

"What does that mean?" Arend asked, glaring at Fiacla.

"PFCs can carry oxygen and get rid of CO2, but there are problems with breathing it, including its density. Barometers measure pressure, and water is in the order of eight hundred times denser than air, and PFCs are twice the density of water. It would take a ton of effort to move the PFCs in and out of her lungs. It's not possible."

Fiacla sighed. "I believe it's magically altered to be more breathable."

"You believe?" Arend said angrily.

"You realize how old this is?" Fiacla turned to Bellae. "You'll be totally under this liquid in a short while. You *will* be able to breathe, but only for about twenty minutes, then the oxygen trapped in the liquid runs out. Read what's written on the table and follow the instructions. The other thing is the lights are going to go out when the liquid hits the top of the hourglass."

"She has to do it in the dark?" Lontas said incredulously.

"Either let her out or I break the glass," Arend said.

"If you do, your quest is over. The crystals and your next scroll will be dropped down a secret tunnel and flooded with magma. If you try to cheat, you'll doom the prophecy to fail."

"Like I care more about the prophecy than her!" Lontas said defiantly.

"Ridiculous, but interesting," Fiacla said. "Bellae, once you're submerged, take slow, steady breaths. It will feel uncomfortable the entire time."

Bellae couldn't help crying. The liquid was above her knees. *Either way it'll be over soon*, she thought.

"What are you doing?" Grym asked angrily. *"Crann, Borb, and Finn."* Her eyes snapped to her mouse friend.

"They would be ashamed of us if we quit!" he chastised. *"If we don't finish this, they died for nothing."* Bellae took a deep breath before kissing his head.

"What do we have to do?" Grym asked. Bellae recounted everything Fiacla told her and then found writing carved into the table.

"Make no mistake,
Your **life** is at stake.
Study well the symbol below.
It disappears when the liquid stops its flow.

As darkness settles on the tabletop.
Hidden pieces will appear with a pop.
Make them into the shape of **time**,
Then fit it in the lock after up you climb.

Get it right, and you are free,
The scroll and crystals you shall see.
Get it wrong,
In liquid **death,** you belong."

Bellae read it to Grym before adding, *"This symbol is labeled 'Time.' Looks like we have to take some pieces that are going to appear and make them look like this."*

الوقت

"A secret compartment!" Grym squeaked, running in circles. *"I smell something…rust, and there's an edge in the table with a hollow center. I can tell the difference when I run."*

"The 'pop' must be a compartment opening, giving us the pieces needed to make the time symbol. Let's memorize this shape. Once the pieces are together, it acts like a key for a 'lock.'"

Bellae kept running her hands over the symbol. When the water was to her chin, she stood on the table and waited as the thick, syrupy liquid continued rising.

"Are you sure we can breathe this?" Grym asked from her shoulder.

"That's what he said."

"I tend not to trust creatures with teeth larger than my head," Grym said.

Bellae smiled. *"I'm so glad you're here. You, Borb, and Crann got me this far."*

Before she could say more, the water moved over her chin. Standing on her tiptoes, she took another breath before stepping off the table and pulling herself down. Still holding her breath, she glanced to see Arend's beak pressed up against the glass, his eyes wide with terror. Lontas' hands were outstretched. The burning in her lungs was growing as Arend pounded on the glass. Fiacla was yelling at him, but Bellae could not make out the muffled words.

Oxygen deprived and unable to wait any longer, she sucked in the breathable liquid. Immediately, it felt like she was breathing fire as it flooded her lungs. She could sense the fluid sidling down the treelike pattern of her airways. As the weighty liquid cascaded in, panic tightened around her. *I'm going to drown!* It wasn't until her head hit the side of the glass she realized she was thrashing about. Every time she tried to breathe in, her muscles ached. It felt like a vice was closing around her chest. To assist her respiratory muscles, she threw back her head and raised both arms.

"She's dying!" Arend yelled. "Get her out."

"You don't catch on, do you? Break the glass, *you* die. If she fails to get out, *you* die."

Bellae was floating at the bottom of the hourglass, clutching her throat and using her entire body to exchange oxygen in her lungs. Horror and confusion swirled within. Breathing the liquid felt foreign and painful. She couldn't seem to pull in enough oxygen. The cold liquid enveloping her was making her hands and feet numb and she couldn't help swallowing some of it causing her stomach to bulge and bloat. A burst of energy flowed through the room as the torches magically went out, plunging the entire room into startling darkness.

"Time starts now. She has twenty minutes to save…all of us," Fiacla stated in a tone too calm for the meaning.

"This is unfair," Arend said.

Fiacla sighed. "Our perception of fairness does not change reality."

Arend sat down against the glass, trying to send Bellae positive thoughts.

Total darkness blanketed Bellae. The burning in her lungs and fatigue in her body bid her to float where she was and relax, but it was impossible to stay calm when each breath required her to heave her chest and use abdominal muscles to force the liquid in and out. An image of Finn flickered in front of her, and she imagined hearing him, "Hey, my hands are holding you, and my spirit will always be by your side."

It was enough to get her moving. She felt the edge of the table, but the symbol was gone. Groping along the top of the table, she smiled, her hand touching wet fur. His front paws pushed her finger towards the left. Eventually, she felt cold metal. She fumbled until she had three pieces in her hands. The far right piece was easy, but the next two were harder, both having a similar number of loops.

"Fiacla, how much time does she have left?" Arend asked. After no response, he yelled, "Running away in the dark? You coward!"

Grym was using his front paws to help fit the pieces together. After several minutes of work, they finally snapped them into place. Bellae grabbed Grym and the metal time symbol before swimming up through the desperate blackness. Despite her hands reaching out, her head bonked on the edge of the glass. Once she got through the bottleneck, she sat on the edge of the upper bowl of the hourglass. Her lungs were burning even more, and she knew the oxygen was running low as her respiratory muscles shrieked in agony from pushing the liquid in and out.

Eventually she stood. Pushing with her legs, she fought through the thick liquid towards the top of the hourglass. There was a small metal bar hanging down from the ceiling, and she grabbed it with an exhausted arm. Her other hand searched the metal for a keyhole that could fit the recently assembled figure. *Come on!* she thought, feeling Grym crawling up her cloak. Scooping him up, she put him on her head.

Arend could hear noises high in the hourglass. "I'm going up." Despite the complete darkness, he flew towards the top. Feeling with his talons, they screeched along the glass, managing to stay close before landing on top. He sat on the cool metal and felt around, locating the tubes that had brought the horrible breathable fluid. Eventually he discovered a handle and an outline of a hatch. He yanked, but it did not budge.

Bellae could hear a scraping sound as Arend's talons dragged above. She could also feel the vibration as he jerked on the lid. *Arend!* she thought gratefully, but was starting to feel lightheaded, her fingers finding no keyholes.

"What do we do?" she tried yelling to Grym.

He moved toward her ear, muttering weakly, *"Lay it against the door."*

That's it! she thought. She had been so intent on finding a keyhole she hadn't stopped to think about the ridges. She touched along the metal outline, matching the symbol of time. *Click.*

Upon hearing the sound, Arend immediately ripped the lid up. It flew open so forcefully he couldn't stop it from smashing down, blasting out loudly, metal slamming against metal. Arend instantly reached into the sticky liquid. It clung to his arm as his hand thrashed wildly for her. Finally, his fingers closed around her limp arm. Pulling her up, he closed the hatch and gently laid her motionless body down.

"Fiacla! She's done it. Turn on the bloody lights!" Arend yelled fiercely.

With no answer, he turned Bellae on her stomach. Putting his large, feathered ear on her back, he could hear faint, raspy breathing. He began smacking her between the shoulder blades. Her eyes shot open, and she retched violently, expelling liquid out of her twitching lungs. Her tired, quivering respiratory muscles ached in protest, heaving to expel the sludge. There was another surge of energy, and the lights snapped on as Bellae tried to sit but instead vomited more liquid. Air hunger ravaged her mind, panic forcing her to flail around. Her ears felt clogged, and all she could hear was intense ringing. Each wheezing cough conjured up more fluid. Over and over she whooped to get the substance out, but it never seemed enough.

"It's okay now," Arend said.

Despite his reassurance, alarm bells exploded across her mind. Arend tried to support her, but his grasp felt claustrophobic, and she pushed him. With the size difference, her mass lost, and her slippery robe aquaplaned sideways, tumbling off the hourglass. Arend immediately sprang up. Swooping down, he managed to grab her and spread out his wings to slow them just before she hit the floor. His talons flipped her to his arms, his well-muscled legs absorbing the fall.

As soon as he set her down, Bellae resumed coughing and gaging, rolling around as fear broiled within. "Get...Grym," she gasped between hacking.

Arend flew, hearing her croaking out fluid repeatedly. He grabbed Grym and was about to fly down again when he saw the lid to a secret compartment crack ajar. Carefully he opened it. Sitting there were two glowing crystals and a scroll. Bellae was still alternating between coughing up liquid and vomiting. Lontas tried to help, but even his presence felt suffocating. Spasms fired pain signals all over her chest as the intercostal muscles convulsed to expel the liquid despite cramping and quivering with exhaustion. Lontas began pounding her back. He helped her move away from the growing puddle of liquid she wretched up. He could feel the contracting muscles heaving to deport the fluid clinging to her airways. Everything burned or ached, and her lungs felt like they were inflamed as blue hypoxia encircled her lips.

Arend landed with Grym, who seemed much better off. Lontas nodded concernedly to Bellae, whose breathing was still pocked with audible wheezing between coughing fits. She was on all fours, struggling to stint open her lungs and force the liquid out. After what seemed like hours, her fits started to ebb, her eyes fluttering with exhaustion.

"Do you think you can lay down and rest?" Lontas asked.

Nodding, she grabbed Grym and put her head on Lontas' leg. She was soon asleep, her breathing harsh and congested with phlegm.

"I searched. There's no way out," Arend said.

For the next several hours, Bellae alternated between restless sleep and suffering through agonizing coughing fits.

"You did great, Bellae. I wouldn't have made it," Arend said when she finally sat up. "How're you feeling?"

"My lungs feel scorched, and I'm so tired."

"Hope you didn't miss me," Fiacla commented, startling them.

"Where the blasted were you?" Arend asked angrily.

"Getting food," he said.

Arend's anger quelled when Fiacla brought in roasted meat and vegetables.

"How do we get out of here, Fiacla?" Lontas asked.

"Finish eating, and I'll show you." Fiacla took a huge chunk of meat in his teeth, raised his head up, and shook it side to side until the meat fell back into his esophagus.

"Gimelli's likely going crazy missing you," Arend commented.

"I wish she came, but love having you, my brothers," Bellae replied.

Fiacla scoffed. "You're clearly not related—impossible."

"What?" Arend said. "You'd better look again. The resemblance is amazing!"

Bellae gave Arend and Lontas a hug. "I couldn't have done it without my big brothers."

Fiacla rolled his eyes. Lontas smiled through his worry at her grating breathing. When they embraced, he could feel a rattle in her chest, and she spasmed into another coughing fit, bringing up more vile slop.

Scroll 5: Wyverns?

"Is he expecting you, Fino?" a Proliate guard seethed outside Veneficus' office.

"No," the sallow Magician replied. "However, I have news from the East."

"Go ahead," the guard grunted.

Fino hesitated due to how temperamental Veneficus had been. "Is he meeting with Jumeaux?" The guard nodded. *The former squire's becoming too influential.* "I'll give them a few minutes," Fino said.

"Do you mean the school may close?" Jumeaux asked within.

"It's possible. Initially we'll thin our ranks in stages, to avoid panic and mayhem," Veneficus answered. "Once the Macht Crystals are returned we'll restart the Academy of Magic. I need to be kept up to date with the League's activities."

"Of course. Bellae, Lontas, and Arend went off to explore one of the mountains and haven't returned. Gimelli is freaking out. What will happen to those let go from the Academy?"

"Don't worry about them. You're invaluable. If things continue to go poorly and our staggered cuts do not work, we'll head to a top-secret place with a select group of Magicians. We are surrounded, our backs against the wall with dwindling mindre crystals. The Battle of Liberum was a disaster. Lidenskap disobeyed orders—draining three-fourths of our mindre crystals. Stay on Gimelli, as it's essential we get the Macht Crystals." Veneficus suddenly stood. Walking to the door, he whipped it open. "Did you need something?"

Fino's dark eyes widened in surprise. "I…I wanted to give you some time with the boy before interrupting."

Veneficus sighed. "Come in."

Fino nervously strode in, standing anxiously beside Jumeaux.

"I assume there's a reason for your visit?"

Fino nodded. "Horrible news. After the Knights were crushed at Liberum, a large force of Dark Warriors fell upon our troops." Veneficus sat down heavily as Fino continued. "Two hundred thousand Dark Warriors! Our Magician force, the griffins, and hippogriffs were able to help around fifteen thousand Proliate troops escape, but they were harassed all the way back to the Citadel. Our air power had to fight wyverns."

"Wyverns?" Veneficus said. "Just when we start to control the air, they show up.

"The news is worse, Supreme Master," Fino continued. "They captured all the remaining mindre crystals left over from the battle."

"What!" Veneficus thundered. A bead of sweat oozed onto his forehead. He quickly wiped it away. "Things are more desperate than I imagined. Jumeaux, head to your room. Alert me if there's any news from your sister."

After Jumeaux left, Fino sat. "What do we do?"

"We start expelling people from the Academy immediately. I'm not sure of the exact timing, but to avoid a riot we shall do it slowly. Those remaining after each thinning dare not speak out. Eventually, an inner circle of Magicians, plus Jumeaux, will depart."

"Leave the Citadel?"

"We're in a fight for our very survival. We must get the Macht Crystals soon. Once we have them and recharge the mindre, we'll expand our ranks again. A thousand Magicians with enough magic for one enchantment are not as effective as ten who can cast a hundred."

"Jumeaux comes with us?"

"Until we get the Power Crystals, he's our only link to Bellae through his sister."

"Why not blast Bellae and finish the prophecy, guaranteeing we get them?"

"Never underestimate the Ainmhi Caint. There are traps and barriers designed to capture impostors. No, only a traitorous animal talker can finish this race."

"I know the backstabbing Ainmhi Caint say they stole the Power Crystals to protect us from some 'evil,' but what happens when she finds them all?" Fino asked.

"Every creature with a hint of magic will smell their power when reunited. We bide our time until Bellae has them, then we get them back at *any* cost," Veneficus said ominously.

Fino smiled, itching to pay back the upstart squires who tricked him outside Creber.

"The previous battles have been a prelude. The real war for Verngaurd is about to start."

Scroll 6: A Spoonful of Honey Makes the Concoction...

"Still febrile?" Arend asked days later after returning through a hidden entrance with the supplies Fiacla requested.

Lontas nodded, dabbing Bellae's forehead with a rag.

"I know the Ainmhi Caint were trying to prevent the crystals from falling into the wrong hands but...too much." Fiacla said. "Most Ainmhi Caint thought the future would be more kind and would use this power for good, and, therefore, they hid the crystals. Others wished them destroyed. The optimists won and spread the crystals around the globe, protecting them until the prophecy. Maybe the crystals will bring about a magical age full of improvements. Even so, it's hard to imagine such trials, especially for those so young, as necessary."

Lontas nodded, feeling guilty for blaming the Daoine Crogall. He had stayed up for several nights with Bellae, helping her heal. "This will help her pneumonia?"

"Yes," Fiacla answered. "Thanks to Arend, we have the needed ingredients."

Lontas watched carefully as he mixed garlic, onion, elderberry, ginger, purple coneflower, and green tea into a boiling concoction with other ingredients known only to him. The smell was as pungent as Lontas' skepticism.

"Now spoonfuls of honey help it go down—with the bonus of assisting her fighting the infection," Fiacla said, mixing his fabrication.

Arend took and handed the cup to Lontas before gently propping up Bellae with well-practiced efficiency. Together they got her to finish the drink despite her incoherent rambling.

"What else can we do?" Arend asked, laying her on a cot next to the fire.

"Wait," Fiacla said.

Several days later, Bellae's fever finally broke, but she looked peaked with dark circles under her eyes and was still beholden to coughing fits.

"At least she's not bringing up that blasted liquid anymore," Fiacla said optimistically.

"Do you feel up to getting the crystals and next scroll?" Arend asked.

"To be honest, if I never see another prophecy scroll, I'd be very happy."

Arend craned his neck awkwardly. *I can't tell her I'm tired as well.*

Bellae gave him a smile, but it slumped, weighted with exhaustion. "Let's get them."

Feeling wobbly, Lontas and Arend helped Bellae up before moving through the narrow hallway to the giant cavern and its massive hourglass.

"What will you do with this 'thing' now?" Lontas asked.

Fiacla's massive shoulders slumped, burdened by sadness. "Once you leave, this room will be destroyed. I'm not sure what to do with the unhatched eggs. Maybe I'll incubate them all and have a party, a last hurrah for the Daoine Crogall."

Arend flew up and around before grabbing her. Once at the top of the hourglass, Bellae took a deep breath before grabbing the crystals. She was instantly transported to a black, star-studded night. Suddenly a single coin came spinning frenetically towards her from the darkness. *"Existence is but two sides of the same rotating coin. The first, Life, is the gift. The other, Death, is the reminder that your Time is limited. So make the most of, and enjoy, your stage,"* a voice said. The rotations of the silver coin slowed. *"People talk about the courage to die, but what about the courage to live?"* The coin turned on its side, thin edge towards her, as a newborn appeared floating above. *"Life is THE greatest gift, not asked for, bestowed."* Tree roots sprouted around the child while a trunk dashed down, towards the top of the coin. At the same time, support legs and rounded glass germinated from the bottom of the expanding piece of currency. *"There is no saving your bounded Time. Participate zealously. Make the most of each second, minute, hour, day, week, month, year, for it shall end when it shall end whether you valued your Life's entrustment as the gift it is or saw it as a burden. Your Life has the purpose you choose. Be passionate, love, create, enjoy, leave the world better than you found it. Remember your Time has meaning based only upon what you treasure."*

The coin had transformed to a large hourglass with the tree of life, complete with hands and burning stars, bursting through the top, morphing into the black sands of time as the newborn grew, crawling down the tree's trunk, ageing as each trickle of sand fell. *"Death, unbiased, unprejudiced, even-handedly harvests each generation, one life at a time with an eye on what shall come. Mortals like to anthropomorphize death, but its deeds are written in life's birth. Death is but a reflection of Life, which ravenously demands change on a species level."*

Figure 3: Bellae sees the tree of existence creating a life and watches it move through its tethered time as the sands of the hourglass fall, eventually releasing a personification of death.

The roots of the tree of life turned into ash, dissolving, as did the trunk, branches, and fiery hands. The residue fell, joining the black sands until they ran out and a skeletal figure, robed in black, burst through the bottom of the hourglass. *"Whether great or small, all of our gifted tomorrows blur into threadbare yesterdays, drop-drop-drop, until eventually the sands of time run out and Death's grip escorts us out."*

Shaking her head, Bellae looked to Arend, who was grabbing the scroll. She put the new crystals in her bag. As they went back to sit by the fire, Fiacla bolted the large door.

"I can't believe my part in the prophecy is fulfilled. The Daoine Crogall who raised me said each of us are at once convinced it will never happen while secretly believing it will be us who completes our responsibility. Know you're welcome to stay and let Bellae rest. Perhaps I can show you our library?"

Lontas stood so fast his feet rose a bit off the cavern. "Library? Yes! She definitely needs more time to recover."

"I guess we'll wait to check out the next scroll?" Arend said to the retreating backs of Lontas and Fiacla.

Bellae rolled on her cot to face the fire, smiling despite the burning in her lungs.

Scroll 7: Stupid is as Stupid as Stupid is

Friar carefully lowered himself from the dragon Soma via the wobbling rope ladder, surprised when Pumilus followed him.

"We don't have a lot of time," Abhac called down from the restless dragon. When they did not respond, the green glad Northern Dwarf deftly slid down the rope ladder.

"Show off," the redheaded Pumilus said.

"It's called practice," Abhac replied. "Now if King Abernan could not talk you out of this foolhardy plan, I won't try. While I wish you luck, it's too dangerous for us to stay here even with this former Southern Dwarfs' prestidigitation shielding us."

"I understand," Friar replied. "Believe me, I hold no delusions about my chances for success. However, if I don't try, all of Verngaurd will fall."

"I've known you a long time, Friar," Pumilus said. "If I'm being honest—"

"Being honest for a change? That would be nice," Friar interjected.

"How impolite! As I was saying, you've done some incredibly foolish things in the past, but this little 'idea' of yours is frankly the stupidest thing I've ever heard of in my entire life. Your brainless idea cannot succeed, like zero percent chance of success—you're going to die."

"I appreciate the vote of confidence and inspirational talk."

"I'm not done. Not only are you going to meet your end—you're going to die a slow and painful death after a long and labyrinthine maze of torture."

"I think I'm beginning to understand your feelings on this mission," Friar said, the words stirring the dust of his own doubts.

"Wow! Quite the inducement there," Abhac said, scanning the area outside the Citadel for signs of Proliate, griffins, or hippogriffs as Soma stomped nervously, craning his neck left and right, his ragged ear wagging pathetically.

"We need to go…now!" an Aer Ridire above yelled.

"I'm sure I'll never see you again," Pumilus said. "Good luck being tortured and killed."

"Give it a rest, red," Abhac said. "In case you survive, we, including this bundle of sunshine, will come to this spot weekly until Stor-Manen's next full moon. Then you're on your own." He roughly pushed the prestidigitating Dwarf up the ladder. Once they were on the wooden platform, the dragon disappeared. Friar moved backwards but was still almost knocked over by the forceful gust from the dragon's wings. He shuddered, feeling starkly bare and isolated outside his former, now foreign, home. *It hasn't been my home for many lifetimes.*

As the fluttering wingbeats faded, Friar thought about screaming for them to return, doubting this would end favorably. *Alone, unarmed, behind enemy lines. What could go wrong?* He began walking towards the

Citadel, eventually joining a desperate looking group of refugees fleeing the chaos in the countryside thanks to increasing Dark Warrior attacks. He wormed his way into the center of the group, putting his head down to avoid the prying eyes of the scattered guards now lining the path to the Citadel. *I don't want to be killed before I get in the gate.*

As they finally approached the barbican, Friar let himself fall back, not wanting the group he traveled with to come under suspicion. *Him,* Friar thought, seeing a Magician and walking towards them. "Please, I wish to be taken to Storlax or Lidenskap."

The Magician scoffed, about to laugh before recognizing Friar. He quickly jammed the wooden end of his crosier into Friar's abdomen, doubling him over. Friar fell into a fetal position as blows from the Magician and nearby Proliate reigned down. After some time, he was roughly lifted up by armored hands while his were secured behind his back. A foul-smelling sack was forcibly thrust upon his head. He was violently picked up and thrown into the back of a wagon. Sightless, he could feel the cart begin to move. The squeaking and grating of the wheels was highlighted by shouts of the Proliate ordering their path clear. Occasional revengeful jabs slammed into his body until finally the wagon came to a stop.

With the pungent bag still over his head he was forcibly led into a building. After several changes in direction, jingling keys turning locks, moving through unseen doorways, he stumbled down several flights of stairs, the guards roughly holding his bruising arms. Groans and screams of others echoed around him.

"I'm guessing you're not taking me to—" Friar huffed as a hard blow to his side brought him to his knees.

"Up, scum!" a guard said, guiding him through a veiled maze of corridors and doors.

Occasionally he would hear sobbing or a warning from other guests as he passed dungeon cells. The humidity was building, and the floor became damp and rough. He was abruptly forced into a sharp right turn and guided up against a wall. His hands were untied only to have them chained, outstretched, to the wall. Finally, his hood was removed.

"Ah, thanks for giving me the best room of the inn," Friar said. "This is lovely. The mold, the rats, dripping water, the smell of shite? Amazing."

Wordlessly the Proliate rammed his fist into Friar's side—a small crack harkening a rib fracture. The chains kept him from collapsing as he gasped, his shoulders aching.

"Make yourself comfortable," the guard said. "You're here…until we kill you."

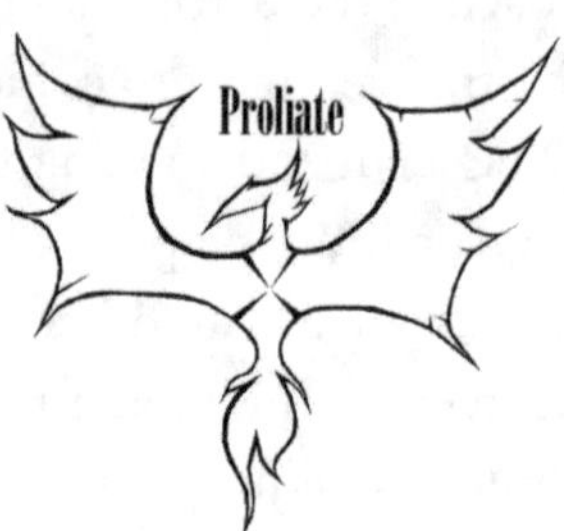

Scroll 8: You Say Torture…I Say Torment

After what seemed like days being chained, save for foul water and brief breaks to use a now overflowing bucket, the cell door creaked open angrily. Storlax stormed into the dungeon, looking out of place in his glimmering red armor, his eyes showering Friar with disgust as he gazed up and down the chained leader. "You will admit your treachery—understand this as a foregone conclusion."

"Is it?" Friar interrupted, his mouth parched. "I should think, if you've already decided my guilt, then there's no need for the pesky truth to get in the way."

"Your actions decided your guilt. I just desire to hear you admit it."

"I will not lie, if that's what you want."

Storlax scoffed. "What I want is for you to stop lying, just for a surprising twist! Every fabric of my being says I should immediately kill you. However, there's something you must do first—admit your sins either with or without torture and magic."

"We all have sins and regret, and I, having lived a long life, have a wealth of both. How much time do you have for me to recount them? Where should I begin? As a child? A teen? If, however, you want me to admit to working with the Dark Warriors, plotting against Verngaurd, or killing innocent villagers, then I cannot, as I did not. We were all deceived, brother."

"I am not, nor have I ever been, your brother. Your death is inevitable. Your guilt? A foregone conclusion. However, the paths before you are divergent. It can be over quickly if you admit your wrongdoing here and now and I relieve your head from your body—quick, painless, and, I think, you shall find atonement in the honesty. The second route, well..." Storlax turned away, as if examining the molding decay on the damp grey walls. "...sometimes one needs pain to purify away moral decay, and that trail will be long, arduous, and indescribably painful."

"Could you try to describe it?"

Storlax whipped his head around to stare at Friar, confusion bleeding into his rage.

"You say it's 'indescribably painful,' but please, try to express exactly what will happen. I would like to know my options before making a decision. Specificity, a good practice, I should think, for all conversations."

Storlax smiled. "Arrogant to the bitter end. Pain, suffering, torment, and torture. Is that a good enough description?"

"You're a shrewd negotiator, really selling both options with equal vigor. But I wonder, is there, perhaps, a third option without drama and theatrical rantings where we actually talk?"

"How did the White Wizard spare you from Liberum? I was there—all died! His black magic rescued your decaying body and soul."

Friar looked down in sadness. "It was *not* the White Wizard."

Storlax shook his head before moving to wheel away.

"Wait, I freely admit to being fooled by the Dark Warriors and White Wizard and to letting myself be manipulated. For that I'm truly sorry. That said, you too were exploited. Remember, it was you that declared war upon the Knights. I came to allow us to move beyond the past and let bygones be bygones."

"I won't be letting anything go by, including my fury. I shall not let any painful memories be gone. You, however, shall be saying bye to bones and blood. A 'bye-bones' instead of bygones—I hope that's alright? Considering the eternity pushing behind me and that to arise in front of my existence I, being a reasonable man, won't hold my raging grudge against you for all time…just for the rest of my mortal being."

Friar looked down dejectedly.

"Did you think you could waltz in here and jester your way out of this?"

"I was hoping, with both of us on the brink of extinction and Verngaurd about to be overrun, that I could reason with you. I have not done the things you accuse me of."

"Were you not the architect of Ovest? Of Trepas?" Storlax's smile arched upwards across his face before rotating away from Friar. "Then it's decided. Bring in the Magicians for his purification." As they entered, Storlax nodded to each one. "Clerics of Tallcon, do what you must until this leech and stain upon Verngaurd admits his treachery and deceit. Use whatever, and however much, magic you need!"

"Sir, you know of our shortage. Perhaps—"

Storlax, his eyebrows soaring in anger, raised up on his toes into the face of the questioning Magician. "Use…what…you…must! I shall have my confession!"

Scroll 9: That's Just Crazy!

"All right, seriously. How long are you planning on hugging?" Sankari grumped when the League of Truth was finally reunited and had recounted their tale.

"Sorry again about Borb," Gimelli sympathized, ignoring Sankari.

"Before we read the next scroll, I want to show you this," Bellae said after Gimelli's embrace, carefully laying out the first three pairs of crystals next to each other in the cave. "The first two, the Seeing Crystals (Perception-Deception), glow red. The Strength Crystals

(Power-Weakness) glow orange and yellow. The Time Crystals (Life-Death) glow green."

"What does it mean?" Lontas asked.

Everyone turned to Kainen. "Not sure. We'll have to wait and see," he said, shrugging his shoulders. *I don't have all the answers.* As Bellae put the Macht Crystals away, Kainen read.

"The **Time** Crystals you did acquire.
Yet this is not the moment to retire.
Two sets of crystals remain.
Expect to experience more pain.
To continue **Life**, you held your breath.
Briefly, you have to wait on **Death**.

Sacrifice crystals are set four.
To find them, you'll need to pull oar.
Love is one side—**Hate** the other.

The chosen decides who dies, yourself or another?"

"Whoa! Whoa," Gimelli interrupted. "Someone dies?"

Kainen reread the passage. "Looks like Bellae has a decision to make."

"That's seriously crazy! These trials are bad enough, but now she is supposed to decide who dies?" Gimelli ranted as all eyes turned to Bellae.

"Why doesn't Kainen finish reading," Arend said.

"With each decision in life there is a cost.
Something gained, something lost.
Love is about giving more than receiving.
Hate bleeds heartache on the hater—no deceiving.

Sail towards the beginning sun.
Towards despair, not fun.
The ocean waves you need call home,
As over the seas you roam.

Unravel what we did **TWIST**.
Beware, maps of this place are oft missed.
The land there, few have seen.
Head to **IF NEAR!**
Specifically go where she **IS O SLEUTH.**
There, seek truth, both righteous and vile.

Next, get **FOO**d in **PIN CAVE.**
Once there, your destination is plain.
Find the Lion's Mane.
One with no teeth, hair, or brain.

Behind the Lion with no roar,
Find your next chore.
Don't just stare at the Evil Eye.
Jump in the cenote, for one must die.

Dive down, just don't drown.
Head north, through the stalagmite crown.
Rise up and breathe, for your test.
Sacrifice, Love, Hate—choose the best."

"I'm the first to admit these have been annoying, but this…is about to drive me insane!" Sankari fluttered, tears starting from her eyes. *I want to go home!* she screamed in her mind, flying in circles before dropping into Gimelli's lap. Surprised, Gimelli managed to catch her and give her a hug. Tired, hungry, and riled, the League sat in awkward silence as Sankari sobbed.

As her tears slowed, Lontas spoke. "There are two things I notice. First, the bolded words after twist don't make sense or rhyme."

"Tell us what you're thinking," Gimelli encouraged.

"Twist, of course, can mean more than rotate or swivel. It can mean to distort, change, or garble," Lontas said. "Twist is telling us the other bolded words are garbled. Look at the first, 'If near.' Doesn't that seem suspiciously close to the name of a place? Especially one that would fit the things they say about it?"

"Couldn't be," Arend said, letting out a squawk.

Kainen stood and walked out of the shallow cave.

"Wait? What?" Gimelli asked, still holding Sankari.

"Ifrean," Scelto whispered. "'If near' uses the same letters.

"It also fits in terms of rhyming," Lontas added. "Seen–Ifrean."

"There's no way we're going to that realm of psychos," Sankari asserted.

"Is this possible?" Scelto asked as Kainen came back in, taking deep breaths.

"No idea. Remember, even the guardians don't know where we're going next."

"This line doesn't make sense," Sankari commented, still perched on Gimelli's lap. "'Specifically go where she is o sleuth.' That should read 'where she is *a* sleuth."

"I don't think so," Lontas said. Sankari shot him a disapproving look, but he continued, "I think it's the name of the location within Ifrean."

"Why are we even discussing this?" Gimelli asked sharply. "Going there's impossible. First, there's war. Second, they're completely insane! Lastly, we have no way to get there!"

Scelto put his arm around Gimelli. She turned around and put her head into his chest while he spoke. "It does seem impossible."

"Did the Ainmhi Caint know how psychotic the Dark Warriors were when they wrote this?" Arend asked.

"Hard to tell. It was so long ago. Obviously, if they hid a pair of crystals there, they had to know something about them," Kainen replied. "We can ask the Piscinians. They sail."

"They're fiercely proud and clannish, and unlikely to give anyone from outside their country a ride under the best of circumstances. With the war? It seems unworkable," Arend added. Lontas had cleaned his back, but it itched despite using the laak-htua salve.

"Mariners trade between Ifrean and Verngaurd and use Haavi as a port. The Piscinians tolerate them because they made a deal to never attack a ship coming to or from Haavi's tower. We could try there," Lontas suggested.

"Mariners?" Arend challenged. "You mean pirates!"

"I didn't say it was a great option, but it might be our only one," Lontas replied.

"The first thing we need to do is get a map of Ifrean. If Lontas is correct and we need to unscramble the ridiculous bolded phrases, then we're stuck without one. We can't organize letters into cities we don't know," Kainen said.

"Agreed," Arend said. "Where can we get a map of Ifrean?"

"We should try Piscium," Lontas suggested. "The Citadel libraries have been ravaged by the Proliate."

"Sorry, Bellae," Gimelli said. "I promised not to question or leave the prophecy. So if we need to go to Ifrean, then we go. Look how far we've come already."

Scroll 10: Survey Says...

When the dungeon door slammed, Friar startled awake. *How many days of torture, I wonder?* He could feel the dried blood, seemingly as exhausted as he was, having run out of energy to keep flowing, instead turning a gloomy black and clinging to his deeply fatigued and bruised body and face. He had fallen forward, tensing the chains. His shoulders sent lightning strikes of pain to his mind while his hands and fingers screamed for blood flow in aching tingles.

Several new Magicians entered. Two looked maliciously eager, the third looked close to retching. The two enthusiastic ones began fervently kicking Friar.

After several moments, they stopped.

"Not asking questions today?" Friar said, spitting freshly roused blood.

"Why bother? You'll just lie," Lidenskap said, moving into the cell. "I can see you're enjoying our hospitality. The makeover of your external is going well. Eventually, with enough physical purification, we shall reach your rotten spiritual core. I wonder, why do you continue lying? Confess something! Admit one thing. Perhaps...that portals to Ifrean do not exist!"

"You believe, fanatically I might add, in a phoenix god that will give you a forever afterlife but not in magic portals seen by dozens of witnesses? With that kind of reasoning power, I guess maybe it was a mistake to come."

"You dare to compare your lies to the all-powerful Tallcon?" Lidenskap said. "Perhaps another day of ripening purification will change your deception."

When he left, one of the Magicians came forward, lustily holding up Friar's chin so he had to look him in the eyes. "Before we're done this day, you shall sing any song in the chord we ask to make this stop." His crosier lit up, accentuating the shadows of his slender face. Chanting, Friar's cloak magically disappeared. "Let's get rid of that. It makes it harder to do this," he said, raking the crystal across Friar's body in vicious slashing motions.

Friar's screams turned into harsh, gurgling cries as the pain evaporated his breath.

"You see, we don't waste magic if I just scrape the crystal across your skin."

Friar's skin sizzled, and spittle bobbed from his quivering lips as he shuddered in agony.

"If it's too much pain, just nod your head," the Magician said. "Did you have a deal with the Dark Warriors? Did you make a pact with the White Wizard?"

Friar kept his head down, lurching with each slash of the crystal against a new part of his skin. He remained silent.

"Did you destroy villages to create havoc in Verngaurd in the name of the White Wizard? In the name of power?" He was asking questions so fast there was no way Friar could answer, just jolt at the inflicted pain.

"Ease up, Huono," the young, queasy-looking Magician said, moving forward. His brown skin had beads of sweat popping up. His head was shaved except for a ponytail running down his back. "You don't want to kill him."

"We do, actually, want him to die," Magician Huono said before chanting a healing spell.

Friar sighed as the skewering pain crisscrossing his body slowly eased.

"Oh, you shouldn't be happy," the grey-haired Huono said. "You know the cycle of pain is just starting. Setting down his crosier, he grabbed what appeared to be modified blacksmith's pincers. "This little guy has a few add-ons to help me do this." He opened the handles before clamping the c-shaped ends upon Friar's fingernail. "If these tongs can twist metal, I think they should be able to…yep, works." Friar groaned in pain at the loss of his fingernail.

"You're not going to ask him questions before pulling them out?" the young Magician asked after several more rounds.

"Why, Venlig? He's not going to answer. Are you?" Huono asked rhetorically before moving to Friar's other hand. "He's had plenty of chances to answer the call for truth. There now. You won't have to trim those pesky nails…you're welcome."

Friar's head slouched, weak from the torture and lack of food.

"Now," Huono said, "the fun begins."

Scroll II: He's Back!

Everyone but the night watch, Kainen, was fast asleep until Gimelli woke everyone with a scream. With memories of her death sickness, Scelto rushed over to find her eyes normal. "I have horrible news," she said. "Jumeaux just told me the Proliate reduced Liberum to rubble."

Lontas sighed, thinking of all the books and knowledge undoubtedly destroyed. Bellae couldn't help thinking of Cookie, Friar, the Pantteri Knights, and all her animal friends.

"Ritari? Friar?" Scelto asked.

"He didn't know, but he told me that the Academy of Magic might be closing."

"The entire Academy of Magic, closing?" Arend uttered.

"Apparently they're almost out of mindre crystals. Something about attacking Liberum ran them down. That's not the most incredible thing," Gimelli said. "The Dark Warriors came in after the Proliate destroyed Liberum and annihilated them."

"I would guess the Dark Warriors now control almost everything east of the River Vita. We'll have to travel at night, securing a place to hide out during the day," Kainen said.

"Don't be mad, but I told Jumeaux our situation," Gimelli said.

"We can't trust him!" Scelto chided. "We—"

"It's okay," Bellae interrupted. "Will he help?"

"He's going to talk to Veneficus when he gets a chance, but things are crazy over there with the mindre shortage," Gimelli answered.

"We have to be careful with Veneficus," Arend advised.

"The bigger question is how do we stop him, or the White Wizard, from taking them once we collect the last two crystal pairs?" Lontas asked. "Everyone, I mean *everyone*, will try to take the Macht Crystals. Whoever controls them controls the destiny of the world."

Silence replied to the unanswerable question. Eventually, Arend spoke, "The prophecy is careful not to get more than one step ahead. We won't find out how it ends, until it ends."

"You know Veneficus needs them big and bad," Lontas said. "But the Ainmhi Caint started this whole thing off by stealing them from him. So would we give them to him? The White Wizard has people looking for the crystals too. What about Tacet-Vand, the Wizard?"

"We're getting ahead of ourselves," Scelto said. "Let's take Veneficus' help, for now. As we get closer to the last pair of crystals, I think we need to be careful."

"Let's concentrate on getting the fourth pair by whatever means we can, then the fifth," Kainen said. "I have to believe the prophecy will tell us what to do. I mean, finishing this quest saves Verngaurd, right? So they won't just cut us off with no guidance."

"Shh!" Bellae said suddenly, feeling Grym tense in her pocket as they scoured the dark. Their meager fire was quickly put out, and they inched to the mouth of the cave.

"What is that?" Sankari whispered as faraway voices called out.

"They're definitely getting closer," Kainen said. "Bellae, Gimelli, Scelto, Lontas, and Sankari, head north along the Tingij. Arend and I will find out what's going on. If it's the Southern Dwarves, we'll delay them."

"We stick together," Bellae said, terrified to lose anyone else.

"If we leave quietly now, we could make it," Scelto added.

"Okay, but at the first sign of trouble, Arend and I go towards it, you guys head north," Kainen instructed, his kama weapon out and ready.

After packing up, they continued north. Stor-Manen, the largest of the thirteen moons, was out, helping light their way as they stayed close to the mountains for cover. Suddenly, they heard a bellowing roar with a strange vibratory element, startling them to stop.

"What makes that noise?" Kainen whispered just as a Southern Dwarf came hurtling over a bush, crashing down in front of them. The Dwarf, his head completely ripped off, rolled several times before coming to a pitiful, blood-soaking halt—his neck generously donating red to the ground while his normally pristine armor was grimy and dented.

"Finally found you," a voice called out.

Kainen motioned for them to head north, but Bellae grabbed him. "Fiacla! Over here."

"Are you crazy?" Scelto whispered.

"That's the guardian. If he wanted to kill me, he would have already," she replied.

"It sounds like he tried," Gimelli warned before startling as the Daoine Crogall sauntered forward. He was using his human hands to pick springy blood vessels out of his massive teeth. His chest plate was sprinkled with blood while both swords and sheaths dripped gore lavishly.

"Ah, I see you met my Southern Dwarf friend here," Fiacla said. "Anyway, I haven't been off that mountain much, but that doesn't dim my hatred for them."

"Are there more Dwarves after us?" Kainen asked.

"Oh, yeah, but don't worry. I've got your backs once I give you this," Fiacla said, handing Bellae a scroll, the outside now carrying bloody fingerprints.

"Thank you."

"You're most welcome. You youngsters run along," Fiacla said after a loud commotion from the south. "Payback's mine." The Daoine Crogall set off with speed into the bushes. The same loud, resounding roar echoed out.

"Now we run," Kainen said.

They could hear the Dwarves screaming for the first fifteen minutes of the journey. Kainen finally held up a hand to stop when they had run into silence. "We should have enough distance between us. Bellae, let's see the scroll he gave you." As he unrolled it, a series of gasps went through the League as dawn was starting to wake up over the Droite Mountains.

Scroll 12: Pound of Flesh

Friar woke up abruptly, water being poured down his throat. He sputtered, trying to swallow the advancing clean water without choking as thirst beckoned him to drink lustily.

"Hurry and drink," Magician Venlig said, the concern in his voice surprising Friar. With only one working eye—the other had swollen shut—the image of the young cleric was blurry.

The dryness caking his esophagus crackled with relief. Friar could feel the cool water flowing down into his stomach and intestine and realized he likely had a fever. When he finally had enough, he said, "I welcome this, thank you."

"I've been sent as a last hope to get you to confess."

"I'll gladly confess my transgressions, but betraying Verngaurd was never one of them."

"I've been watching the proceedings," Venlig said. "As a new cleric I have plenty of magic left in my crosier, so I've been spying on you."

"By proceedings I assume you mean torture?"

Venlig nodded. "Something's off in the world of magic, and back when they were asking questions, I sensed you were telling the truth. Now I'll know for sure. The other Magicians Storlax and Lidenskap picked are zealots. The truth enchantment does draw a large amount of magic, so maybe that's why they just inflicted pain, or maybe they're just sadistically heartless."

The cleric raised up his crosier, the mindre crystal glowed, and he chanted. As he finished, Friar saw a light emerge and wrap itself around his head. He could feel it piercing his skull before running down the crevices of his brain and squeezing tightly.

"Tell the truth, or the pain will be…intense," Venlig warned, flipping over his ponytail. "Did you make a pact with the White Wizard?"

"No! Never!" Friar replied.

Over the next twenty minutes, Venlig asked questions relating to the invasion, village massacres, and undermining the realms of Verngaurd. As he was finishing, Storlax burst in.

"I should have sent you in first," Storlax said. "I assume you were successful?"

"I discovered the truth. Whether you will find the results successful, I do not know."

"Cleric, cease with your prattle and tell me, do we have our confession?"

"He's still under the truth enchantment," Venlig said, nodding to Friar.

As Storlax stood over him, the broken Friar Pallium somehow managed to look up. "Kill me, torture me more, then kill me, but leave knowing the truth—we were manipulated. If either of us, or anyone in Verngaurd, has hope for tomorrow, we must finally come together."

Rage stormed behind his eyes as Storlax drew his sword. Friar put his arm out as far as the chains would allow. "If killing me brings peace to your heart, then kill me. But I beg you, reach out to the remaining Knights and command them as you will to help rid Verngaurd of the scourge of Dark Warriors."

Storlax lowered his sword as the light around Friar's head stayed white.

"He speaks the truth," Venlig said. "You, more than anyone, know I despise him and the Knights, as my sister from Jaa was killed at Trepas. However, as a servant of Tallcon, I'm also a vassal of the truth, and this man, what's left of him, is telling just that."

"Lies, glossy and shiny, slip and slide out with greasy ease. Deceit stains our inner being and is the easiest of skills to develop, but using it distorts your very soul," Friar said, his chin falling to his chest. His head, and the world, were spinning. "The sad truth is even without magic, it is just as easy to believe a lie as it is the truth, and perhaps it's even easier."

He looked up into Storlax's eyes. "I swear to you I have done nothing, ever, to hurt Verngaurd. I plotted against you because I had visions that war with the Proliate and her allies was coming, not out of malice. We were all made to play the role of jesters by the White Wizard, who has been plotting this revenge for fifty years. While we arrogantly enjoyed our prosperity, he was busy scheming vengeance—a civil war born from deceit."

The light around his head remained white as he continued, "Now, let us take the fragments and shreds of what remains of our strength and finally stand up, as one, against the evil polluting our lands. We may not have the strength to do much, but we shall do it together, whatever the outcome. We may not be able to win, but we will fight, as one."

Venlig released his spell. "I cannot risk any more of my magic, but rest assured it has been the better part of half an hour, and he has never once lied. I take no pleasure in saying what he speaks is genuine."

Storlax sheathed his sword, looked up, and sighed. "In hindsight, we have both taken our pound of flesh from the other, no doubt there. You struck at Trepas, and we cut ours out at Liberum. Perhaps, if we are to survive, and that is quite questionable, we must fight our true enemy, and do it side by side. For now, leave him here. I shall speak to Lidenskap."

Although still in his dank cell, Friar had been cleaned up and given a new cloak. Healers had attended to him several times a day, and he had been given something resembling food. Lidenskap strode through the cell, a mix of emotions swirling around him, and Friar could tell he was struggling to speak. So, Friar went first. "I regret that we find ourselves here. If only we could go back to the Tournament and change…everything. It's my own fault for succumbing to the visions I was force fed, as if they had guaranteed our battles. There is more I should have done. There are more questions I should have asked, and for my role in how we got here, I am truly sorry. I got too caught up in how to win, how to strike hard and inflict as much pain as possible, without thinking about the consequences." Thoughts of his father, Isa, and all that had been lost flashed in his mind. *Did his defeats blind me? Did fear instead of reason guide me?*

"General," Friar continued out loud, "I ask your forgiveness for allowing myself to be led astray and offer you all remaining Knights to fight against the evil invaders. If taking my life helps solidify this last alliance of Verngaurd against the Dark Warriors, take it."

"You would sacrifice yourself and offer up your remaining Knights?" Lidenskap asked.

Friar looked through an eye simultaneously sunken from hunger and swollen from abuse. "It's not for anyone alive that we fight or a specific castle or realm we defend. We battle for the very ideals of freedom, self-determination, and the concept of responsibility and responsible leadership. If darkness takes over our lands, we are dooming generations to live under evil.

"My heart is crowded, ripe with regret and second thoughts of my role in how we got here. I berated Falciss for wanting some glorified ideal of a warrior's death and throwing his troops into a lost cause. But did I do anything different?"

Lidenskap paused, seemingly examining the floor. "How did we get here? How were we deceived so thoroughly?"

"A better question is, how do we dig ourselves out together?" Friar said. "What of the Knights left at Toil Shaor?"

"The Dark Warriors attacking them and Piscium have left to strike at Temple Aon Intinn. It is surrounded with an enormous force, one hundred and fifty thousand strong."

"If we combine all of our forces, we have a slim chance," Friar said. "I keep telling myself our last castle is simply stone and mortar. They shall advance here to the Citadel, which will be our rallying point for all armies except the warriors I have in mind for surprises."

Blowing out a slow deep breath, the general paused, remembering what Friar's previous surprises had cost his people.

As if he could read his thoughts Friar said, "I understand your hesitation. Again, I accept blame and if taking my life makes you trust my ideas for a counteroffensive, I freely give it."

Lidenskap glared at Friar. "There is blame enough to go around, and we were all manipulated. I initially had visions we should come together, then ones that we had to destroy you. I fear they too were from the White Wizard, like yours. If we could get back all the troops already killed, we would have a much greater chance of success."

Friar nodded as images of fallen warriors raced through his mind including Finn, Luchar, and Sorea. "Sometimes the greatest sword strike is the one avoided. Occasionally the greatest victories are the ones occurring without bloodshed."

"We let pride and zeal outstrip our intellect," Lidenskap said, imagining his lost Proliate.

"If one strips away pride, you often find emaciated self-righteousness quivering in a dark corner, hiding its frailty by propping up a fraudulent, boisterous exterior."

Lidenskap nodded. "I find it impossible to believe we're in this situation, the injustice…"

"Justice is often strangled by revenge. Righteousness is often overshadowed by haughty arrogance. The truth is often eclipsed by opinion or desire," Friar added.

Lidenskap seemed deep in thought. "Such wickedness that stirs in man."

Friar released a weighted smile. "The frightening thought is not the evil notions stirring the black gloom of our own hearts. The terrifying reality that makes blood run cold and hope flee is that such ideas, and much worse, stir within the souls of us all. What defines us, decides our value, elucidates our character, is how we handle such notions."

"So...here we are."

"True enough. Here we are. The past is decided, but the future is truly open and waiting. Whatever happened, however it came about, we must move forward."

"What did you have in mind?"

Friar stood up gingerly. Despite the healers, he still ached all over and was weak from the days of starvation. He adjusted the bandage around his swollen eye. "We need to hit them hard with every scrap of power Verngaurd can muster. The one advantage we have is the enemy still thinks we're fractured. Perhaps," Friar moved his hands, bandages covering the missing fingernails, around the musty, grim cell, "we could continue this discussion elsewhere."

Scroll 13: Help me?

As Jumeaux entered the cafeteria, the mood matched the lighting, low and somber. The normally full and magically lit dining hall suffered under scattered candelabra and torches, flickering a pale, austere light while less than half the normal students and staff ate.

Chy nodded to Jumeaux as he sat down before tilting his head at Kaveri, encouraging him to ask what he did not wish to.

"So, how deep will the downsizing go?" Kaveri asked.

"Just look," Chy said, waving his meaty hand around. "There's hardly anybody here. Where'd they go?"

"I really don't know," Jumeaux answered, willing the sweat threatening to pop out on his forehead to stay hidden.

"I heard they were thrown out on the street," Kaveri said.

Chy fought the urge to cry. "I don't want to be homeless and hungry again. You don't know anything?"

Jumeaux shook his head, heeding the warning from Veneficus.

Chy and Kaveri froze at a distant, methodical thumping sound that Jumeaux did not, at first, recognize. The rhythmic plodding grew louder but stayed in perfect tune. It was when the red-armored soldiers marched into the room that the former squire realized what was happening.

"You going to help me, Jumeaux?" Chy asked while screams and protests exploded around the room as the Proliate began forcibly removing students from the dining hall.

"By order of Veneficus and by the power of Tallcon, we have the honor of welcoming some of you to the Proliate army. May you fight and die with honor."

Dozens of soldiers continued grabbing the biggest and strongest. As they drug out the forcibly conscripted, more Proliate poured in as well as several Valo lights.

"This one's big. Get this guy!" a Valo said, as many students stared in wonder at the lights that Jumeaux knew too well.

Another Valo floated to Chy. "Wow, wow, look at this grain-fed beast! Here ya' go, red soldier guys! Get this heaping hunk of muscles!"

"Don't worry. You're big enough to survive…at least for a bit!" another light added.

"Yeah, say high to the Dark Warriors for us!"

"Help me, Jumeaux! Help me!" Chy said louder and louder as a group of six soldiers surrounded him. Chy banged hard on the table. "Help me!"

Kaveri made a move to stand up.

"You volunteering, boy?" a soldier asked.

"That wimpy dude? Not this round at least," a Valo chided as Kaveri sat back down. "Don't even think about taking our bestest buddy Jumeaux either," the light added with a wink.

"Come on, Jar-moo, help me!" Chy yelled. "Tell him, Kaveri! Tell him!"

"Tell me what?" Jumeaux asked.

Kaveri shook his head.

A gruff Proliate stepped forward. "Get up, boy. Come follow the way of truth as our brother. You have the honor of fighting for Tallcon, and there are two ways out: death in battle and, unlikely, dying from old age."

Chy had tears streaming down his face.

"Maybe I can fix this when we recover the Macht Crystals! I'll come back to get you!" Jumeaux said.

"Well, I guess theoretically you could dig him up after the Dark Warriors slice and dice him," a Valo chided.

When he did not stand, two soldiers grabbed Chy's wrists while others ripped him off the bench. "Up, big guy."

Chy screamed, slamming the two holding his wrists together. His yell turned to howls of pain as body blows from soldiers started raining down. In spite of their armor and training, the massive Chy was fighting possessed. He elbowed one in the face, even with his helmet. The soldier dropped, but more soldiers rushed to the upstart student. Chy's robe was ripped in several places, and a soldier kneed him in the face. His nose gushed blood, redness flooding his midface as he dropped. A dozen warriors surrounded him, kicking and hitting. By the time he stopped fighting, a pool of blood had formed beneath his swollen and reddened face.

"Just sit there, tough guy," a Valo said to Kaveri, who was glaring at the soldiers. "Trust me, you wouldn't last long."

"Thanks for stepping up there," Kaveri chided Jumeaux as the moaning Chy was dragged from the cafeteria with half of the students who had been eating.

"Who's going to run the supply warehouses?" a voice boomed.

"Gretten?" Jumeaux asked, remembering the brusque man who had given him his first robes in the basement of the Academy.

Several blows shocked Gretten's ribs to the sound of cracks. He wheezed in pain as they continued carrying him by his thickly muscled shoulders—primitive legs dangling ineptly.

"I need my arm walking sticks!" Gretten pleaded. "You can't do this to me!"

"Throw out the trash!" a Valo sneered. "Into the gutter, dirty man!"

"Are they really going to throw him out into the street?" Jumeaux asked.

"What do you think?" Kaveri asked angrily. "They're cleaning house. I heard those who already left, the bottom half of the students and the sickly, were tossed out with nothing."

"There's got to be something I can do," Jumeaux begged to the Valo.

"Not unless you have the Macht Crystals hiding under your skivvies," one answered.

"Wait," Jumeaux said to the floating lights. "We have to do something!"

"We're all ears...actually all faces, but you get my point," a Valo said.

"Kaveri, let's toss some ideas around."

"Hope they're soft," a Valo replied.

"What?"

"I hope your ideas are soft. We don't want you to poke your eye out on a sharp idea if you are going to be reckless tossing them around." The Valo chuckled maliciously before floating out of the room, following the cries and screams of the new, unwilling, Proliate soldiers.

"I've lost my appetite," Kaveri said, getting up to leave.

Scroll 14: *As Expected*/ They Seem Nice

"Well, I have to admit I'm flabbergasted you live," Pumilus confessed, hands on hips.

"It's great to see you too, my friend," Friar replied, each breath hurting as he limped towards the magically shielded dragon, one eye and the ends of his fingers still bandaged.

"Looks like they treated you as well as expected," Pumilus said, pointing to the now yellowish-brown bruises decorating his face and head.

"I'll cut them to pieces!" Abhac seethed, walking out of the prestidigitation shade.

"I appreciate the sentiment. I do," Friar said. "However, right now our very survival depends on building bridges and fighting the true enemy, the Dark Warriors. Speaking of which, we head to the frosty north!"

"You don't mean Jaa?" Pumilus sighed.

"I do indeed."

The formerly energized dragon rider shook his head as Pumilus put voice to his concerns. "You realize they detest you, me, the Northern Dwarves? The only reception we shall receive is pain and death."

"You recognize that you prognosticated something similar about the Proliate?"

"Your luck will run out eventually," Pumilus said.

"Oh, of that I am cognizant, but I do not think it runs out today. If we just stand around, we'll be obliterated. So we might as well try."

"I was about to say Pumilus is right, this is supremely foolish, but I thought that about the Citadel and Jaa," Abhac said as they flew south a week later.

Pumilus suddenly bent over, dry retching.

"Don't you throw up on my dragon!" Abhac said as the redheaded Dwarf released a noxious stream of intestinal vapors.

"My stomach was emptied long ago, but the agony and cramping remain," Pumilus said.

"Permission to hurl this twirler off?" one of the Aer Ridire manning a crossbow asked.

Pumilus scoffed. "First, 'hurl' isn't the smartest word to 'throw around' to a Dwarf full of nausea. Second, the term twirler is derogatory. It takes tons of training and time to skillfully *wield* the loitsia sticks, which, by the way, are keeping you hidden from wyvern, griffins, Watchers, and hippogriffs. I blame the former squire Scelto."

"What?" Friar asked.

"Princess Hamaza said he absolutely loved and guzzled down massive amounts of that Torahammas milk they drink up north. I swear that stuff is eighty-percent poison! I fear my stomach will never recover," Pumilus said.

"Then, twirler, why did you drink a large glass right before we left?" Abhac asked.

"I thought it would be rude to do otherwise, and I did not wish to offend the princess."

"I imagine Scelto endured a similar situation," Friar said. "Ah, we approach the island."

"I'm sticking to my previous predictions, despite your insane good fortune to date," Pumilus said, strapped into the dragon Soma. "The Isle of Hirmulisko? There's a reason the creatures on that giant rock were put there. They're vicious and bloodthirsty."

"That generalization seems an overreaction," Friar countered.

"What is that?" Pumilus asked, pointing to a figure on the shore.

"That, my Dwarf friend, is a centaur," Friar replied.

"Isn't it bad enough you almost killed us all in Jaa—now you want us to die in the Isle of Crazy Beasts?" Pumilus inquired.

"We just had to tread water for a bit in Jaa. It wasn't—"

"It was FREEZING!" Pumilus interrupted. "Plus, it was not, not, *not* for a 'bit'!"

"Hey, they agreed to our plan. We need all of Verngaurd for the coming battle."

"What's our play here, Friar?" a nervous Air Ridire Dwarf asked.

"Pumilus keeps you invisible while you let me down far away from that centaur on the beach. I shall disembark while you take off and circle above, keeping hidden."

"Do you want us to come collect bits of you when it rips you to pieces or just leave you to rot? We could bury your shredded strips in the sultry sand if it doesn't eat you," Pumilus said.

Friar did not reply but watched as the northern edge of the Isle of Hirmulisko slowly drew near. There was a narrow beach complete with repetitively lapping water and dense forest lands behind. Off in the distance to the west were hone-tipped mountains. He had removed the bandage over his eye, but the wind was making it tear up, and his vision was blurry, so he closed it. His broken ribs were mostly healed, and he examined his fingernails, which were growing in nicely. He used their healing tips to trace the innumerable wounds scarring across his body.

As they were descending, a streak of brown and blue zoomed past.

"What the?" Abhac asked. "How does it see us?"

Before anyone could answer, a falcon zoomed by again.

"I think they know we're coming," Friar said as the dragon landed. He quickly scurried down the wobbling rope ladder before moving away and kneeling in anticipation of the wind gusts from the still-hidden dragon.

Once the flurry of wing beats receded, Friar stood up, raising a hand to wave at the centaur further down the beach. Friar froze as a stunning blue falcon alighted on his raised upper arm. Its blue eyes stared into Friar as it turned its mostly brown plumed head that was littered with blue feathers. Its neck was white, and the sturdy wings were highlighted with blue streaks.

"Hello," Friar said timidly, unsure of the bird's intentions. "Was that you greeting us?"

The falcon pushed his beak forward as if encouraging him to walk towards the centaur.

"Alright, that's as good a plan as any," Friar said, moving as fast as the sand allowed, his raised shoulder already aching.

"You can stop there," the massive centaur said. "I haven't charged and killed you because Gorm seems to like you."

On cue the bird used his intimidating beak to gently peck at Friar's neck.

"Gorm is a magnificent blue falcon. My name's Friar Pallium, head of…the remaining few Knights."

"How did you arrive here, and do you not know humans are forbidden from this isle under penalty of death?"

"I came by dragon, and I apologize for arriving like this, but the matter is urgent, and I would love the chance to talk with you."

"You knowingly break the decree of this land, then wish to talk?" the centaur asked. He had a series of horns jutting out from the top of his human head and cheeks. His thick hair swung down his back, turning into a mane before joining his horse body. His human torso had

Figure 4: The blue falcon Gorm welcomes Friar to the Isle of Hirmulisko.

patches of thick brown fur, the same color as the horse body carrying him towards Friar. "Human fear and weakness drove us from the mainland. Now we stay here, and you stay there."

"I understand…uhm, your name?"

The centaur twisted his head, his eyes flashing indignation. "I'm Cruba."

"Cruba, I apologize again. However, hordes of invaders are about to overrun all of Verngaurd. Once they finish on the mainland, they'll surely come here. It's absolutely imperative for all of our futures that we defeat them."

"Will the Magicians be there?" the fierce creature asked cautiously. Friar was taken aback at the thought someone so fierce could be afraid. "Magicians are brutal, and they said we would suffer if we returned."

Friar nodded, remembering his own torture. "Some will fight with us, not against, but it will be far too few. Most will selfishly hoard the little magic they have left."

"We would fight other humans?"

"From across the Dark Sea, yes. However, they will certainly bring creatures from Ifrean as well. Minotaurs, unicorns, maybe Stymphalian birds."

Cruba began aggressively stomping forward, leaning in while snorting angrily. Gorm flew off Friar's shoulder as he took a step backwards.

"I'm sorry if I offended—"

"Unicorns will once again invade?"

"Likely, given the creatures already brought against us. You said invade again?"

The tight rage on his face relaxed a bit. "Humans have short memories, being born with no innatism, no memory of your past. When centaurs are born, the past speaks to us. Generations bleed their experiences and knowledge into us. Humans wish only to take and consume. It is your greatest weakness to the world and significant strength against others in attempting to satisfy your ravenous yearnings. The unicorns came many eons ago when we still roamed our true home on the mainland. I think it best if you kill each other and then, perhaps, we can return home." Cruba turned to leave but stopped as hundreds of centaurs emerged from the tree line. "I will alert our council of elders to your request. You should leave now."

Disappointed, Friar turned and signaled the magically hidden dragon, hoping they could see his aggressive waving. "Thank you for your time, Cruba. I enjoyed meeting you."

Cruba nodded before galloping towards the tree line. He did not make it far, as a large cast of blue falcons arrived, many landing on Cruba forcing him to stop.

"We shall watch the comings and goings on the mainland," Cruba said, startling Friar.

Rotating back towards the tree line, Friar nodded. "That's all I can ask. You seem to have a special relationship with the falcons."

"All of us have at least one, and they will be how we keep watch upon the mainland. The forests of this island are infested with pryfyn—parasitic bugs that have flowing hair matching ours. The blue falcons sense them by their temperature and remove them from our bodies."

"I see," Friar said, thinking of the reikas boring bugs of the Forest of Creber, suddenly noticing the band of centaurs had silently descended from the forest.

Cruba abruptly, and deferentially, spoke in a braying language Friar did not understand. He conversed for several moments with someone unseen.

After bowing humbly, Cruba spun around, facing Friar. "This is Kentauri, our patriarch."

As the senior centaur approached, his brown fur and mane appeared faded, having been replaced with grey, and there was a slight catch in his gait, as if hampered by arthritis.

"It's an honor to meet you, and I apologize again…"

Friar stopped at the elderly centaur's hand for silence. He took a few more hobbling steps forward. "You audaciously come here, demanding us to fight for you?" Kentauri asked.

"No," Friar said. "I humbly hope you might consider it." For the first time Friar noticed a humongous centaur, his long black hair melding into the inky fur of his body. His horns were much larger than the others, and his head shivered as he snorted aggressively. He circled behind Friar as he told Kentauri of the Dark Warriors and the coming battle.

"This is Sabots. He's Kantauri's personal guard," Cruba said when Friar finished.

Friar nodded an unreciprocated greeting.

"Let them try and come to take our land!" the massive Sabots said.

The elderly centaur held up a hand to his bodyguard and said, "The Magicians banished certain beings, including us, they deemed 'dangerous.' Then, years ago, they stormed in and stole all but the young and elderly of the hippogriffs. Not that we have love of them, but they too were banished here. The agreement was you creatures stay there and we stay here. You broke this agreement and ripped them away."

"You have not been treated fairly, of that there's no doubt," Friar said.

"Since the Magicians banished our use of weapons when we were outlawed to this island, do you expect us to fight with our hands, or perhaps foul words?" Kentauri sneered.

"Would you like weapons?" Friar asked, trying not to let his excitement break through.

"Weapons would be nice. If we help you win this coming conflict, could we return to the mainland, our native pastures, when this is over?"

"It would certainly be open for this discussion."

"I am glad you did not promise yes," Kentauri said. "Human promises, while often blustery and bold, hold the weight of a soft breeze."

A dragon was revealed down the beach, released from the prestidigitation shielding.

"Could we take some measurements for armor and optimal weapon length?"

Kentauri nodded, and Friar signaled to several of the Aer Ridire who cautiously dismounted the wooden carriage and made their way towards them.

"Could you please take measurements for armor and weapons of our friends?" Friar asked the skeptical Dwarves.

Their faces drew tense as the tree line released thousands of other centaurs.

"Maybe we could take a few representative ones?" Friar said, smiling between the wrathful centaurs and cautious Dwarves. *Perhaps a glimmer of hope,* Friar thought, looking west as the last of the setting suns smeared red caution against his optimism across the horizon.

Scroll 15: New Friends Die Hard

"What are you talking about?" High Commander Storlax asked Veneficus within the Proliate headquarters at the Citadel.

"You can't leave!" Lidenskap declared angrily.

"Ah, that's funny, coming from you!" Veneficus thundered. "I told you to conserve magic for *dire* circumstances, and what did you do? You used it repeatedly to spare your troops. Do you have any idea how many mindre crystals we lost over the last few months? We simply don't have enough crystals to keep the Academy going."

"Are you all leaving?" Storlax asked.

"All Master Clerics will remain to keep your temples running, some Magicians will elect to stay with you, and the rest will leave, forced to find their own way."

"Are you going to look for the Macht Crystals?" Storlax asked.

"I will assist the Chosen One in the search for them. When the girl has all five sets, I can guarantee they *will* end up in my hands. Then, it will be time to recover our great land."

"What do you expect us to do for air power?" Lidenskap challenged.

"Some Magicians will stay to help control the hippogriffs. I cannot guarantee how long their crystals will hold out, but they should help against wyverns." Veneficus turned to leave. Before reaching the door, he turned. "You realize without Macht Crystals there's little I can do."

"Where will you go? How will we contact you?" Storlax asked.

"I'll be watching events closely," he replied before walking out.

Lidenskap sat down, staring at Storlax. "You look like I feel—exhausted and dejected."

Neither of them had recovered from their beating by the Dark Warriors at Liberum. To have a startling victory turned into overwhelming defeat so quickly was disheartening.

"How can we fight the Dark Warriors with so few of our own?" Storlax asked. "Plus, now we lose the Magicians?"

Finished packing, Jumeaux thought, glad to be going with Veneficus but deeply saddened that the awe-inspiring Academy of Magic was closing. *Not that there are many left.*

A harsh knock on the door startled him. "Come in!"

"Hey, you heard…" Kaveri froze, seeing the packed bag. "What's going on, *friend*?"

Jumeaux could see the hurt and disappointment in Kaveri's eyes.

"Leaving, buddy?" There was an ominous quality in his tone.

A little taken aback, Jumeaux tensed, unsure of what to say.

"I asked you a question. You going somewhere?"

"Ven-Veneficus commanded me to go with him," Jumeaux finally answered.

"Is that right?" Kaveri said. "Were you planning on telling me?"

"He told me not to."

"I thought we were friends. Abandonment is how you repay me?"

"Attention!" a voice boomed, seemingly from the walls. "This is Supreme Master Veneficus. I have grave and troubling news. Due to the near exhaustion of the mindre crystals and widespread war ravaging Verngaurd, the Academy of Magic is, effective immediately, officially closed. You have one hour to vacate the premises or suffer the consequences."

A muffled roar of disapproval echoed around the Academy from the few remaining.

"All functions at the Academy will be immediately shut down. Master Clerics will be assigned to a Proliate Temple. The rest must promptly leave," Veneficus continued as another clamor sped through the stunned Academy. "A small group of Magicians will join me on a special quest to save magic in our world. Thank you for your hard work and service. Good luck!" Veneficus finished as boos echoed around the hallways.

Jumeaux clutched his bag anxiously. Suddenly, his friend's robes disappeared. Kaveri was left in ill-fitting, dirty, and ripped pale blue and yellow clothes worn in Piscium.

"These are like the crappy clothes I walked in here with. The pig can't even let us keep our robes?" Kaveri said, tears welling in his eyes.

After a moment, he continued ominously, "You want to know what Chy wanted me to tell you? Veneficus promised he would take care of us if we pretended to like you. You wet-nosed, scrawny, and annoying—" Kaveri rushed at Jumeaux, his hands out menacingly. Jumeaux cringed and ducked just as the white light of a transporter spell began to consume him.

When he opened his eyes, Jumeaux found himself in a room with a dozen other Magicians talking in animated voices. He only recognized Fino, who nodded at him. Jumeaux retreated to the corner and sat on his bag. *Veneficus made them be my friends! I should have known this was too good to be true.* The thought of their betrayal was so cold, jagged, and hard to swallow it seemed to rip up his insides as he digested it. Closing his eyes, he looked down to hide the tears. Suddenly, and quite unexpectedly, he thought of his sisters and Liberum. Even more surprising, he found himself grieving over Liberum's destruction.

"It's okay, boy," Fino said. "One day we shall regain our glory and return. Veneficus himself told me he's been through worse and recovered."

"Yes, sir."

"There is nothing wrong with crying. We've lost a great deal. However, we shall, one day, regain our strength," Fino added.

Chapter Three
The Mariner

Scroll 1: Return of...

"You're close?" Gimelli said before putting up her finger for them to be quiet. *"We understand how crazy things have been for you. Thanks for coming."*

Kainen suddenly shouted, "Griffins! Arend, griffins!"

"Wait!" Gimelli bellowed. "It's Jumeaux coming to help. Remember they've saved us once already and he's my brother."

"Arend?" Alarm bells were ringing in Kainen's head, but he knew they could use help—the skies were littered with griffins, hippogriffs, Watchers, and wyverns.

"We don't have any choice," Lontas finally said, "we've barely made any progress East.

Arend nodded but stared angrily at the approaching griffins.

"Everyone be nice," Gimelli reminded as Jumeaux and the sickly looking Magician Fino dismounted their griffins. There were five riderless griffins set in a protective ring around them—all baring fearsome beaks at Arend.

"Nice robes," Gimelli said as she ran to hug her brother, who was wearing yellow robes with the blue stars of an Adjutant and carrying his own crosier. As the twins hugged, the mindre crystal adorning its top glowed a soft blue.

"Interesting," Fino commented.

"I just got these," Jumeaux said, his facial expression glowing with pride.

"Congratulations," Bellae said sincerely. As she hugged her brother, the bag with the crystals touched his crosier, which began to vibrate while glowing brilliant blue.

Bellae quickly backed away. Fino looked hungrily from Jumeaux to the satchel Bellae was carrying, the pulsating power whispering in his mind.

"Very interesting," the Magician commented. "That bag you're holding is supposed to shield the power of the Macht Crystals, but obviously it's not perfect." Fino grasped Jumeaux's crosier. "I can feel you transferred power to his mindre crystal. Only when all five pairs are together should power be transferred and then exclusively within the sacred pedestal."

As Fino rambled, Jumeaux sweated. Veneficus had instructed, *"Avoid talking about the crystals. We're in the trust-building phase. Once they have them all, we set upon them."*

"This is Fino, one of Supreme Master Veneficus' most trusted advisors," Jumeaux said loudly, interrupting his ill-advised speech.

"We've met," Gimelli said caustically, remembering when she was separated from Bellae outside Creber.

Bellae carefully set down the bag of crystals and went to re-hug Jumeaux. She whispered, "Thanks for coming. It's nice to have you back. You look handsome in those robes."

Jumeaux blushed, nodding appreciatively as Lontas and Scelto awkwardly shook forearms with him.

"So, what now?" Scelto wondered.

"Let's figure out where you need to go. Then I'll take you to a mariner that owes Veneficus a favor. He'll get you to Ifrean," Jumeaux explained. "We'll magically shield the griffins as they fly out to sea, then up the Proliate channel south of Haavi where we'll walk into the city. Veneficus sent the mariner a magical message, so he's expecting us."

"Are mariners trustworthy?" Gimelli asked.

"Mariners are the only long-distance seafarers, and this one will not double cross Veneficus," Fino said. "Some parts of Piscium are under their control, others are ruled by the Dark Warriors. Haavi, the mariners base, is about half and half in terms of dominance."

"We brought food." Using his crosier, Jumeaux moved several sacks from satchels on one of the griffins to under the tree. "Thanks for the power up, Bellae."

"Nice trick," Scelto said, patting Jumeaux on the back.

Jumeaux bristled, thinking he was making fun of him. "It's no trick!"

Scelto nodded kindly. "I know. I can tell you're good."

He only respects my power, Jumeaux thought.

The League ate and drank greedily while Fino and Jumeaux watched.

Jumeaux, seeing Grym eating from Bellae's hand, joked, "Still have your rats!"

"Not funny!" Scelto growled.

"It's okay," Bellae said. "He doesn't know. Borb died helping me get the last crystals."

Serves him right for pooping in my bed, Jumeaux thought. A sudden pang of sadness rang in his heart, surprising him. *Why am I sad at the thought there's no Liberum?*

"You look good, Jumeaux," Gimelli said after she had beaten back hunger. "But I think the yellow robes might be a tad much for Haavi."

"Forvandling!" Jumeaux shouted, then whispered another chant, causing his robes to morph to a dark brown.

"That's handy," Gimelli said, impressed.

"Should we head out?" Fino queried anxiously. "I have to get back to... Veneficus."

Arend flew independently while Sankari and Gimelli shared one griffin. The rest of the League (Kainen, Bellae, Scelto, and Lontas) all had their own. Together, with Grym, they flew out to the sea while being shielded. After stopping briefly on a small island off the coast, they headed north through the Proliate channel. Far to their left, the Piscinian peninsula was taking a pounding from the harsh sea as the moons beckoned the water to leap at their gravitational call. Surging white frothy waves lurched, sending finger sprays of water stretching up towards the travelers. When the griffins finally touched down south of Haavi, it was deep into the night. The winds had made the flight exhausting, and the League greedily searched for shelter.

"There! A cave," Jumeaux exclaimed, striding confidently up to the opening. "Clarus lux walls!" he shouted, the sides exploding in light.

Several fia asteikko bolted out towards the League, frightened by the sudden light.

Kainen and Gimelli quickly put two arrows into the largest as the other animals scampered off into the night.

"Nice shots!" Lontas said.

"Don't sell yourself short, Lontas," Jumeaux smirked. "If you'd been closer and fallen, you'd have tripped one and it would have hit its head and been knocked out by a rock."

Lontas blushed but stood his ground. "I don't fall much...anymore."

Jumeaux paused, gauging his old squire mate. *There's something different about him, a confidence and ease in his stride that wasn't there before.*

"Thanks, but maybe tone down the light. We want to stay concealed," Gimelli injected.

"Of course," he said, whispering an enchantment to dull the light.

Eventually Arend found enough wood to make a fire to cook the fia asteikko.

"You're pretty handy with that thing," Lontas commented.

"Thanks," Jumeaux said. The two stared at each other, still trying to figure out their relationship. So much had happened, they had morphed into entirely different people.

Silently, Kainen unrolled two scrolls—the one Bellae had earned conquering the last trial, and a map of Ifrean Fiacla provided. "Everyone, ready?" Despite their fatigue, they nodded. Bellae had insisted, over Scelto and Arend's protests, that Jumeaux and Fino be allowed to stay.

Kainen read, emphasizing the important lines,

"Unravel what we did **TWIST**…
Head to **IF NEAR!**
Specifically go where she **IS O SLEUTH**.
Next, get **FOO**d in **PIN CAVE**."

"Are they all this…ridiculous?" Jumeaux questioned.

"Pretty much." Bellae sighed, grabbing her brother's arm and squeezing lovingly. He smiled, resisting the urge to recoil from her touch.

"So we figured out the 'twist' is telling us the capitalized, darkened letters are scrambled—Ifrean from 'if near,'" Kainen explained. "With this map we can work on the next two starting with, "is o sleuth."

"There aren't many to look at," Scelto said.

"You should be grateful for what you have," Fino said caustically. "The White Wizard's fanatical, ruling by terror. He wants to restrict movement for his own people and make it difficult for invaders."

"It's not a city, but South Isle works. Both have nine letters," Lontas said excitedly, carefully writing both words in the sand, matching up the letters.

"Well done," Kainen said. "So we head to Ifrean, South Isle. Next we're looking to unscramble 'food in pin cave,' and it should rhyme with plain."

"You just use the letters, 'foo-pin-cave,'" Jumeaux commented. "Those are the only ones capitalized and darkened."

"Good point," Lontas said, his voice full of joy at the challenge. "We're looking for a word or words with ten letters."

"On the South Isle, only Cove of Pain fits," Kainen noted.

Lontas quickly wrote out both. "The letters match!"

"The next part's almost too easy," Gimelli added. "Lion's Mane Rock has to be the 'Lion with no roar' the scroll talks about, but, I'm not sure about the next part."

They argued through dinner over possible solutions before deciding to sleep on it.

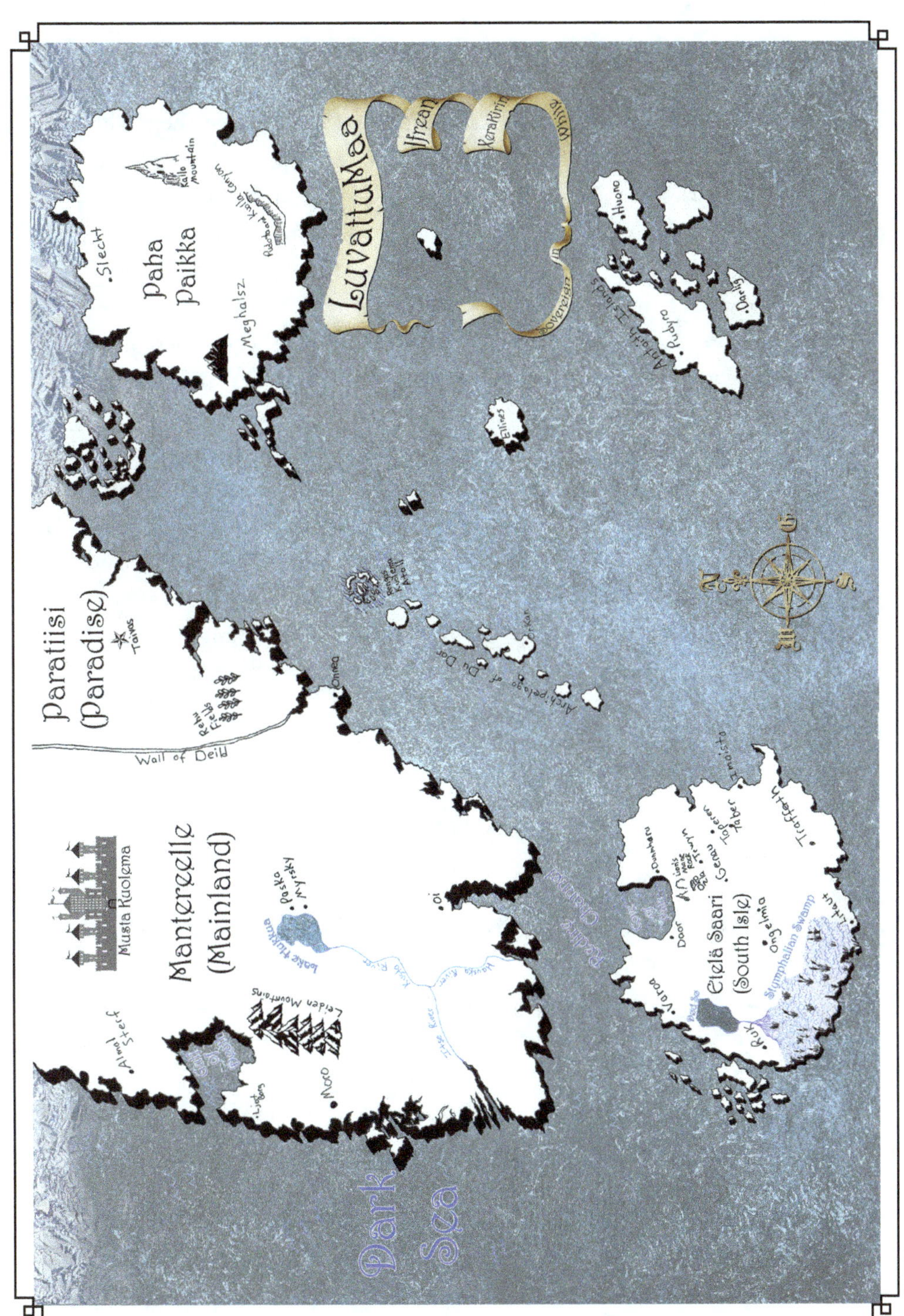

Figure 5: Map of Ifrean

"Fino, what's this part here past the Wall of Deild called Paradise?" Jumeaux asked.

"No one knows, dear boy. As I said, most people live their whole lives never seeing a map of Ifrean, much less visiting."

"Tomorrow we head to Haavi and the mariner Mor-Leider," Jumeaux added.

"Isn't there anyone besides a pirate who can help?" Gimelli asked.

"We don't really have a choice. Plus, he's sanctioned."

"What exactly does a 'sanctioned' pirate mean?" Scelto asked.

"It means he's partially employed by the White Wizard," Lontas answered. "The White Wizard sanctions a small percentage of ships. In exchange for being allowed to trade goods across the Dark Sea, sanctioned mariners agree to carry his troops or do raids on cities that need retribution. They also get to attack any non-sanctioned ships and take their cargo."

"Basically, they have special status from the White Wizard," Jumeaux added. "Without his approval their chances of survival going to Ifrean are near zero. Plus, if he double-crosses Veneficus, he'll pay."

"Let's get some sleep. Tomorrow? We meet a sanctioned pirate," Kainen said, rolling his eyes.

Scroll 2: Truce Without Complete Mending

"You really are magnificent," Bellae said, sitting out near the griffins, scratching their thick manes. *"Better to spend time with you than flip around not sleeping."*

"How long have you been up?" Jumeaux asked, emerging from the cave as the first kiss of sunrise rose, the sky blushing auburn at the affection.

"About an hour," she replied as they sat down together in the rocky sand. "Thanks again for helping. I can't imagine getting there without you."

"No problem. I couldn't sleep either after getting up so early at the Academy of Magic."

"I can't believe how good you've become. You have an amazing gift."

"Thanks. Hopefully it'll reopen when things calm down and..." He paused, leaving out they needed to steal the crystals Bellae was collecting. "...yeah, when things slow down. It really was amazing. Lots of good...things." He was about to say good friends, but knew those he treasured had been counterfeit, merely following Veneficus' orders.

"We missed you. It's nice to be back together." Bellae rested her head on his shoulder.

Jumeaux flinched. Too many throbbing memories of Liberum flooded back. His mind had always painted them pessimistically. He was having trouble knowing how to feel and reconciling his recollections with the loving welcome his sisters were giving him.

"It's okay, Jumeaux. I'm your sister." *In all the ways that matter*, she thought while laying her head back on his shoulder. The two sat and enjoyed the waves crashing against the shore, each breaker sending misting plumes dashing excitedly, sometimes frantically, into the air.

"It's beautiful, isn't it?" Bellae commented. Even if Jumeaux had seen her tears, he would not understand their source, but they were flowing down her cheeks all the same. She struggled to keep the quiver out of her voice. With each spray she could see the faces of her dead friends mixing with glimpses of a future that was coming all too quickly.

"It's stunning." Jumeaux paused before adding, "Sorry about Crann and Borb."

Bellae snuggled in closer, mostly to hide the fast-flowing tears. She could feel him stiffen behind the hard shield he constructed around his heart but refused to back away.

Later that morning, Jumeaux and Lontas found themselves inside the cave on their own. Lontas' eyes drifted up furtively at his former nemesis, but he kept his head down.

"What?" Jumeaux asked. "Are you whispering something?"

"I was just saying you might want to apologize."

"I could say the same for you!" After a pause, Jumeaux loudly added, "Stop mumbling!"

"Just because my words are soft doesn't mean my mind isn't screaming or my thoughts aren't important. Being boisterous doesn't make you correct." Small tears surfed over Lontas' cheeks. "My brain's always churning, continuously thinking. I constantly see every possible negative outcome in every situation. Those scenarios feel real, making my heart race while leaving me constantly terrified. You, and your bullying, made Liberum infinitely worse."

Jumeaux paused, thinking of his perceived betrayal by the squires and the actual ones of those he thought of as true friends at the Academy. A small chisel of doubt hammered cracks into his self-righteous certainty that he, in fact, had been the victim. "Yeah, I kind of get it."

"Just because I'm not athletic and fall, or fell, all the time, doesn't mean I wanted to, and it certainly doesn't mean that bullying isn't torment. Don't mistake my humility for lack of confidence, my lack of a response for an absence of intelligence, my paucity of retribution for a shortage of rage, or my quietude for a sparseness of internal emotion."

Jumeaux's eyes scrunched in recognition, seeming, for the first time, to see a true reflection of himself and his past actions. "I know you might not believe this, but I've learned to appreciate and understand what you're saying. I'm starting to see I acted like a jerk some…maybe most, of the time. That doesn't mean I haven't learned, been force fed really, a load of humility. Just because I never said I was sorry doesn't mean I'm not regretful."

The two stood silently staring, each uncertain what this exchange meant, or what their relationship was now. There was such a cavernous debt of charitableness that the words, while a beginning, were not nearly enough to buy back the freedom of forgiveness and friendship.

"I'm leaving!" Fino called, rescuing them from delving deeper into their emotional, history-laden rift.

"Safe journey," Jumeaux said, emerging from the cave as Fino ascended a griffin.

"To you as well. I shall leave one griffin for you to join us at our stronghold when your mission's complete. Good luck and don't fail." With a stern nod, Fino took flight.

"So, what's the plan, Jumeaux?" Scelto asked.

"Veneficus helped me prepare cover stories. As we weave our way to meet the mariner, unfortunately, we'll cross between territories controlled by Dark Warriors and Piscinians, because the only accessible gates are the south and north. All others are barricaded."

"Where do we start?" Lontas asked.

"The Dark-Warrior-controlled southern gate," Jumeaux replied.

After making ready, the group climbed off the beach via a steep embankment. They stealthily moved between gnarly trees and sturdy bushes up to a small knoll.

Laying on their stomachs, they peered upon the walled city. A large ornate tower dominated the skyline beyond the tan walls. Several fires were visible, pockmarks within the otherwise surprisingly large and splendid city.

"The southern gates to Haavi," Jumeaux said as the others shivered at the sight of Dark Warriors loitering outside. Their shoddy armor and undisciplined ranks brought back memories from the battle outside the Forest of Creber.

"Can't you fly us to the spot in the city where we need to go?" Scelto asked.

"Absolutely not," Jumeaux said. "Any place with Dark Warriors will have Watchers and Nishi patrolling the skies with a magical net of detection, so even if shielded, we'd be discovered. Piscinians will view anything flying as hostile." Standing up, he said, "Naamiointi!" He then whispered, and the wood of his crosier crawled up and over his mindre crystal, transforming it into an ordinary-looking walking stick. "Okay, which one is going with Bellae?"

"Wait, what? What are you talking about?" Gimelli asked anxiously.

"I already told you. Mor-Leider will take Bellae and one other."

"Whoa! You never said anything about that!" Scelto said angrily. "We're *all* going."

"Kainen and Arend need to leave right now! An Eaglian and an Elf in Piscium? Are you crazy? They're going to stand out, and if they go, we all die."

"Can't you magically shield them?" Scelto asked.

"Not for the time required. With the battle lines constantly moving, I'm not sure how long we'll be there," Jumeaux said. "Also, a bigger group is more suspicious. Finally, as I said, the mariner will only take two."

Scelto was about to protest, but Kainen put his hand up. "He's right. There's no way all of us should go. That place is crawling with an alternating mix of Piscinian soldiers and Dark Warriors, and neither have any love of Eaglians or Elves. As much as I hate it, he's right."

"Why didn't you mention this before?" Gimelli asked.

"Sorry, thought I did," Jumeaux replied. "You do realize how difficult it was to find a mariner that would agree to carry you?"

"We'll head back to the cave and wait. I don't see any other choice," Arend said.

Gimelli's eyes widened with apprehension. "No! We stick together. Look what happened last time. Bellae almost died!"

The others continued to argue, but Jumeaux was blocking them out. The painful betrayal of those he thought were his friends sometimes created a fog in his mind, making it hard to concentrate as he bitterly relived the duplicity. *How could I have been so stupid?*

"Jumeaux. Jumeaux!" Gimelli said, shaking his shoulder. "I'll go with her."

"It can't be Arend, Kainen, or you," Jumeaux answered.

"Wait, why?" Gimelli asked defensively.

"Women are bad luck on ships according to the mariner. Bellae is questionable, but since she's younger, he agreed to take her," Jumeaux answered.

"I'll go," Lontas volunteered immediately. Bellae nodded and squeezed her friend's hand.

"Why did you ask if there's not really a choice?" Gimelli asked.

"I could fit in a bag, if Lontas would carry me," Sankari offered.

"That could be risky," Jumeaux commented.

"It would make me feel better," Bellae said. "She's helped out several times with riddles. Then we'd have four members of the League." When the others gave her questioning looks, she added, "Me, Lontas, Sankari, and Grym."

"Listen, sis," Jumeaux threatened after Gimelli continued to protest. "I can leave and you figure your own way, or you meet Mor-Leider and he gets four of you to Ifrean. This is the best Veneficus can do."

"How long's the journey?" Scelto asked.

Jumeaux shrugged. "Maybe six months?"

Glaring at her brother, Gimelli gave Bellae a long hug. "We'll be in the cave. Come back as quickly as possible."

"We're going to wait *a year* in a cave?" Scelto asked.

"We'll wait as long as we need to," Gimelli replied icily.

"That's not what I meant," Scelto said, still feeling raw no one suggested he go.

After their goodbyes, Jumeaux added dirt to their clothes. "So we look destitute."

Once he was done, Bellae, Lontas, and Jumeaux began walking towards the city gate. Bellae carried Grym and the bag with the crystals. Lontas heaved a satchel with Sankari.

"Avoid eye contact. Look dejected," Jumeaux whispered as they walked down the hill.

Nearing the gate, they could see several Dark Warriors milling outside. Unlike the Knights or Proliate, there was no order to their armor or movements.

"You rats lost?" one asked, twitching in his rusted brown armor. His helmet was as broken down as his rotten yellow teeth. His odor preceded him, winding its way up their nostrils.

"I said, you lost?" he repeated. "Or do you only understand brainless fish-speak?"

"No to both, sir," Jumeaux answered. "We live in a small fishing hut south of here. Our father needs new netting. He sent us to fetch some."

"Got money?"

"A little, but he told me it should be enough," Jumeaux replied.

"Did he tell you about the toll?" the guard asked.

Jumeaux withdrew an anemic-looking money pouch and handed him two coins. The Dark Warriors laughed viciously.

"That's not enough to stop us from just killing ya much less paying for entrance!"

Jumeaux sighed deeply before handing him a few more coins. "I probably won't have enough for the netting now."

"And why would we care? How long you staying?"

"One or two days. Our uncle lives here. We'll stay with him," Jumeaux answered. Bellae and Lontas kept their eyes down, listening to Jumeaux calmly lie through his teeth.

"I better see you runts within *two* days! Also, if you're caught begging, we'll skin and eat ya. Remember not to venture into any of the dangerous sections controlled by the bloodthirsty Piscinians! Soon we'll control all of this rubbish heap. Open the gates, you lazy gits!"

The three started walking towards the entrance. Suddenly, one of the guards grabbed Bellae's arm. "Get over here." She gasped at the roughness of his hands.

"Clean my toenails, would ya?" he hissed, while taking off one of his tattered boots. "Look at this baby!" he cried, pointing to the twisted, thick, yellow abomination that surged in triumphant deformity off the top of his great toe.

Bellae gasped in horror at the sight of his filthy toenails sticking through a sock so shredded it hardly seemed worth the effort to wear them.

"Sorry, but we must meet our uncle," Jumeaux said, quickly pulling her into Haavi.

"On the way out then!" the guard cackled.

Relief swept over them as the gate closed. Inside the walls, they were greeted by burned-out and destroyed buildings. A few rotting corpses wearing Piscinian armor ungraciously served as banquets for swarming herds of carnivorous insects and insults to their nostrils. Several dangled from ropes with handwritten warnings about resistance to Dark Warrior rule.

"The Piscinians put up quite the fight," Jumeaux commented as they scanned the structures while the acid smell of death lewdly assaulted their nares.

"Good job back there," Lontas whispered.

Jumeaux shot him a look. *He used to make fun of me,* Jumeaux thought but stopped as a stream of memories flooded back. *Was it the other way around? Did I make his life miserable?*

Lontas smiled before asking, "Okay, where now?"

"A pub called the Dark Sail," Jumeaux said. "Veneficus made me memorize the layout."

As they moved deeper into the city, the buildings and houses were less damaged. Still, there was a palpable tension. Many store signs had been defaced by the Dark Warriors, replaced with crude symbols or words. The country's beloved colors, light blue and yellow, were consistently vandalized with a white hat and staff—the symbol of the White Wizard.

Bellae unexpectedly stopped and grabbed Jumeaux's arm. "There's a group of Dark Warriors harassing a Piscinian family twenty feet ahead. They look like serious trouble."

"I've got this," Jumeaux said with a look of determination. Chanting softly, a blurring shield encased them. "Look down. Say nothing. Avoid touching anyone."

Slowly, they walked forward, drifting left, away from the abusive Dark Warriors. One of them slapped the man. "So, let's review. How do you address us?"

"Mighty rulers of Dark Warrior territory," the man said, clasping the welt on his face.

"First, doesn't sound convincing," the Dark Warrior replied. "Second, our homeland is LuvattuMaa—not Dark Warrior territory, not Ifrean. Third, we're not 'Dark Warriors' but mighty Vartija! I don't want to hear any of the filthy names made up by you lying mongrels!"

"Please, let us go," the woman pleaded as the soldiers laughed.

"Get moving," Jumeaux whispered to Bellae, who had stopped.

"Wait!" one of the Dark Warriors said. "I heard something?"

Bellae stared at the hatred and loathing. *What are we trying to save?* a part of her wondered. *How can we ever stop all the evil in the world?*

"Do you see something?" another asked. "Like it's there, but not?"

Jumeaux frantically waved her to follow as several Dark Warriors moved towards her.

"Yeah, something's there!" one growled as Bellae remained frozen.

"Is this some trick of the evil Blue Wizard? Imagine our reward for killing him!"

Bellae's heart raced, breathing quickened as Grym panicked in her pocket as they closed in on her shrouded form. Lontas grabbed her and pulled. "Run!" he breathed.

Jumeaux sprinted behind them, his cloaking spell shimmering enough to give them away.

"After them!" a Dark Warrior screamed.

Jumeaux's incantation fizzled completely as they ran to keep ahead of the soldiers. A blur of terrified Piscinians scurried out of the way as they rushed forward.

"Now what?" Lontas huffed as Sankari screamed angrily at the rough ride.

"Follow me!" Jumeaux said, cutting right, leading them around a large group of children, then cutting left down an alley.

They ran through foul-smelling mud to find there was no exit, greeted instead by a solid wall. Jumeaux began chanting, creating the impression of a wooden fence in front of them. They tried to calm their breathing as the dozen warriors streamed past.

Scroll 3: Glad to See You?

Pre-sunrise the next morning, Bellae, Lontas, Jumeaux, Sankari, and Grym emerged from behind their makeshift tent of alley debris.

Bellae stretched her sore back as Jumeaux said, "Let's head to a small Piscinian section, then we cross over into another Dark-Warrior-controlled area."

"Do I have to go back in the bag?" Sankari lamented. "I'm regretting coming."

"You may be *the* difference," Lontas added as Sankari reluctantly clambered into the bag.

They carefully made their way through a maze of streets until coming to an impromptu barricade. Several Dark Warriors were asleep in front of a ten-foot-tall mess of trash, furniture, and scraps of wood piled and packed together to form a disorderly, but sturdy, wall.

"How do we get to the Piscinian side? All the roads and buildings along the border are blocked or boarded up," Lontas asked.

"I know a way," Jumeaux said, leading them over several streets before coming upon a boarded-up fishery littered with graffiti from the Dark Warriors.

"Are those the kids from yesterday?" a growling voice wailed.

"This will have to do," Jumeaux said, running up to the building. He chanted, and the barricading timber instantly dissolved as more and more Dark Warriors began shouting. After another incantation, the door swung open. Stepping through into the pitch-black room, their eyes and noses stung from the pungent fishy odor along with a deep, scaring mustiness.

"Did they forget to clean this place, I don't know, for like a hundred years?" Lontas asked, holding his nose.

"You know this is Piscium, right? Lots of fishing, lots of fish," Jumeaux said as he magically sealed the door before illuminating their way up to the second floor.

"What are we going to do up here?" Lontas asked.

"You're going to stand there. I'll be opening these shutters," Jumeaux said. When he finished, he looked out briefly before abruptly jumping.

Bellae screamed as she and Lontas ran to the opening in time to see Jumeaux magically lowering himself to the ground. He quickly placed his finger to his mouth and pointed to his right. As they looked left out the window, they could see the back side of the rubbish heap serving as a street barricade and hear yelling from the Dark Warriors side. A few exhausted Piscinian warriors snapped to attention and turned to face the impromptu border between the part of the city they controlled and that ruled by their enemy.

"Wait, does he want us to jump?" Lontas asked just as loud banging on the door to the fishery was joined by shouting from the Dark Warriors trying to break in.

"Now would be good!" Jumeaux said as loudly as he dared.

Bellae and Lontas could hear the Dark Warriors breaking into the building through the windows and decaying walls with axes.

"Wait, what's this about jumping?" Sankari yelled from inside the bag. "I'm delicate—" Clasping hands, Bellae and Lontas nodded before wordlessly jumping. They sighed with relief as a magical force gently slowed them to the ground.

A few Piscinian guards came running over from the barricade.

"Rope," Lontas whispered.

Nodding, Jumeaux quickly summoned a coiled rope so they would not think magic was used to lower them.

"What are you kids doing?" a Piscinian guard asked, arriving with several others, all looking fierce in their armor.

"Our home used to be in south Haavi, and we were looking for our parents. Some Dark Warriors found and chased us," Jumeaux answered.

"You used that rope? I don't—" the guard was interrupted by several Dark Warriors appearing at the windows, sending spears hailing down.

"Get out of here," a Piscinian shouted as Suoli warriors arrived, creating a shield wall.

Jumeaux pulled on Bellae, and they sprinted down a narrow backstreet. A spear landed just in front of them. Jumeaux abruptly rotated and chanted, "Orbis proteger contego!"

A shield formed around them just as several spears bounced off. Jumeaux stopped the shield and hauled them left down a side street.

"The Piscinians saw that spell and think we're with the White Wizard!" Bellae said.

"I know. Keep running!" Jumeaux huffed as the Piscinians raised alarms.

"No need to worry about me in here!" Sankari screeched, her voice jostling as her body flipped within the bag. "I love being scrambled like an egg and never wanted to fly again, so feel free to keep destroying my wings!"

"Sorry!" Lontas said as they continued sprinting.

After several more turns, Jumeaux stopped. "Hold up!" He chanted until they all looked like they were wearing either pale blue or bright yellow cloaks of Piscium.

"This isn't inconspicuous," Lontas said, holding out his yellow cloak.

"Everyone moving within Piscinian-held territory has to wear their colors or risk being killed. It's probably why those guards ran over to us," Jumeaux said just as a few Haavi residents meandered by, all, as Jumeaux predicted, wearing the same colors.

"A little warning about having to jump would have helped," Lontas said.

"I have a rough map in my head, but lots of things look different because of war and vandalism. I'm doing the best I can, but we'll have to make things up as we go."

When it was clear, Sankari stretched her wings and flew around a bit, muttering obscenities. "I can't get back in," she said, her lips quivering, as dawn began waking up the city.

Jumeaux said, "Everyone in Haavi is on edge, seeing you might set them off. Most people aren't familiar with Fairies."

"Try this," Lontas said, grabbing a piece of broken wood. "If I place this across the bag, it should provide a little space and protect your amazing wings, at least a bit."

"Soldiers!" Bellae said.

"In, quick," Lontas hissed as a squad of Piscinian warriors approached.

Taking a deep breath, she grudgingly entered the bag, bracing the wood in front of her.

"There are soldiers everywhere," Jumeaux said, noting the Piscinian guards bore many battle scars and scorch marks. "We need to get out of here before they try to conscript us."

Lontas whimpered as the rotten and burnt wood they were huddling on creaked and moaned precariously. "This does not seem safe."

Jumeaux hesitated to hurl the insult about Lontas percolating within him, the weight of his own betrayal at the Academy pushing it down. The treachery greatly undermined his confidence. "We need to wait until it's totally dark before flying down."

"It looks clear," Lontas said.

"I know how it looks, but when we reenter Dark Warrior territory, if we're spotted, we'll be killed. There's no justice system, no judge to plead with—just death. We wait."

Sankari clung to Bellae as they huddled in the corner of the top floor of a war-torn building. Most of the roof was gone, and massive holes littered every floor. The remaining boards groaned while precariously holding together. The Fairy squealed as the damaged floor shifted beneath. The faster the current whipped, the slower the third sun Pheobus seemed to perform its slow-motion plunge towards the horizon.

Several loud shouts had Jumeaux jumping up. "I'm going to check that out. It came from the Piscinian side." After chanting, he disappeared. Several agonizing moments squeezed by before he rematerialized. "The Piscinians are going on the offensive at the closest barricade. One said they're going to retake the section we'll be traveling to. We move now."

Jumeaux transformed them out of Piscinian colors before moving to the edge. A group of Dark Warriors were sprinting to their left towards one of the innumerable street barricades serving as territorial markers. Without warning, Jumeaux created a magic shield around them, chanting until they floated to the ground, once again, in Dark-Warrior-controlled territory.

"Hey!" a voice called out, startling them.

"Quick, in the bag," Lontas said to Sankari as a Dark Warrior sprinted towards them.

Jumeaux stepped forward confidently. "I have news from the Sovereign in White."

The Dark Warrior's look changed to one of confusion, unsure of what to make of the three children. "I saw you flying."

"All things are possible with the help of Troldmanden," Jumeaux answered as Bellae and Lontas exchanged looks of confusion. "We just infiltrated the fish-scum territory and need to inform you of an imminent attack at the closest barricade. Not one inch of ground must be lost."

The Dark Warrior looked up to the top of the building they just flew down from, processing the information. Sensing his concern, Jumeaux spoke preemptively, "You've been warned. I suggest you see to the defense of that barricade."

Nodding, the warrior ran off, shouting warnings to summon reserves.

"Most from Ifrean call him the Sovereign in White or Troldmanden," Jumeaux said in answer to their unspoken question.

"You just doomed the Piscinian attack to fail!" Lontas said.

"It'll be easier for us if there's *not* a battle raging around us while trying to find the meeting place. Plus, the mariner's under the protection of the White Wizard."

Jumeaux spent several minutes getting his bearings as Dark Warrior troops sprinted towards the barricade's defense. As darkness continued falling, he wordlessly led them down a series of streets and alleyways. Scattered torches were lit along the way, but most buildings and houses were dark as the inhabitants huddled in hiding.

"Against the wall," Jumeaux hissed, slamming his back to the closest building.

He pointed as a stream of Watchers and Nishi flew overhead. Several Nishi stopped, looking in their direction. Bellae could hear the crystals whispering and actively fought to silence them, closing her eyes tightly. Lontas readied his forearm talismans just before the Piscinian attack on the barricade began, and they flew off.

"That was close," Lontas said as they resumed jogging.

After weaving through more streets and alleys, Jumeaux stopped, silently pointing to a building across the road. A sign out front had once said, "Dark Sail Pub and Eatery." The Dark Warriors had used whitewash to write over it, "Dark Warriors, Scrub our Feetery."

"Move now!" Jumeaux said, taking off, the others forced to follow. The former squires rushed through the door of the pub just as a gang of Dark Warriors ambled down the street. Entering, they were engulfed in darkness equal to that outside in the inky night. A few feeble candles were unapologetically flinging pale light around the wood-paneled room. It was hard to tell if the walls were naturally dark or simply covered in layers of unkept grime.

There was crimson splatter, pasted on during preceding brawls, and gashing scars from weapon slashes littering the walls. Although the gloom prohibited seeing them, their ears could hear skittering from emboldened rats.

"Touching or consuming anything in here would be ill-advised," Jumeaux said, grabbing Lontas' arm before he could touch a scarily unidentifiable globule condemned to harden and glimmer against the blemished wall.

Lontas nodded, noticing signs. *Protected by the Sovereign in White. Killing and maiming allowed, but do not destroy the building. Officially Sanctioned Mariners Preferred.*

Taking a few cautious steps, they could make out a rough-looking man behind the bar aggressively picking at his armpit. His full beard did little to cover his vacant expression. His arms lay bare save for ridiculous amounts of dark hair wooling its way around. His generous belly was pushing hostilely against a soiled shirt. There were dozens of people scattered at various rustic tables. They were obviously not native Piscinians or Dark Warriors and glowered at the newcomers from beneath tricorn hats with three sides turned up and long woolen coats.

Jumeaux guided Lontas and Bellae towards a table in the back where a man was sitting by himself. Unlike the others, a red cloth was visible underneath his black tricorn. His arms were crossed upon a portly belly. The hint of grey beard flowed unkept upon his chest.

The three stopped a couple feet away. Jumeaux gave the others a questioning look. When they shrugged, he said, "Excuse me, I saw the red cloth. Are you Mor-Leider? Vene…"

Jumeaux did not get to finish as the mariner instantly sprang up, his two swords inches from Jumeaux and Lontas. The blades were only two feet long but were heavily weighted.

"Uhm," Jumeaux murmured apprehensively, "we were sent by Ven—"

Again, he was interrupted. This time the mariner pocked his sword into Jumeaux's nose. There was sufficient pressure to make his skin dimple. While keeping his swords in their faces, he leaned close. "We don't say names such as those in this establishment, or any other place for that matter. You follow?" he asked in a gravelly voice.

Jumeaux started to nod, but the sword prevented it. "Uh-huh," he burbled.

"Well, then. Good. I'm glad you're a parrot that can learn. I had this scraggly crew member once that didn't acquire knowledge well," the mariner added, putting his swords in his belt. With a loud huff, as if it was hard work, he sat down. "I had to dispatch his earthly form, you see. For time yet to come, hear this, make the same fault three times, I'll extinguish you."

The children glanced at each other as he smiled genially.

"Ah, my manners. Sit down, wretched children—all children be wretched creatures by my accounts. You can summon me with the tag of Mor-Leider."

They instantly sat around the table, all wondering if that meant his name was actually Mor-Leider or if it was just a moniker.

"So, you're interested in a glamorous excursion across the sea?"

"Actually, just these two," Jumeaux answered. "I'm here to introduce you. I need to return to the person whose name I shouldn't say."

Mor-Leider smiled. "I do love parrot sprogs that grasp the situation at hand. I'd hate to fit you with a casket so late in the evening. So, you two will accompany me on our luxurious sojourn. I hope you don't mind tight spaces. As stowaways—"

"But—" Jumeaux interrupted.

Again, Mor-Leider's sword flashed out. "Interrupting a mariner's a nice occupation, but only for fellers wanting to try my skill and method of skinning firsthand. You can consider this cautionary warning number one on this topic."

"Sorry, sir," Jumeaux whimpered.

Just then a tiny, beady-eyed man, bending aggressively forward due to a severe hunch in his back, hopped through the door to several loud jeers.

"Is that…Trelos?" Bellae asked of the crouched figure hoping between the tables, his hands out. They could not make out what he was saying, but it was not well received.

"The one who made the Nishi bracelets?" Lontas said. "Oh yeah, that's him. Looks like he's begging. Everyone's being so mean."

"Focus," Jumeaux whispered. "We have business."

As Trelos shambled towards a nearby table, a rough-looking man did not even give him a chance to talk, instead kicking Trelos, hard. The diminutive man spun around, his frail body striking roughly against their table. His narrow face produced a projecting nose, and his eyes jutted out so far the whites were visible, encompassing the entirety of his black irises.

"Watch it, freak!" the mariner said callously.

Trelos' bug eyes glistened with a tired, resigned sadness thanks to a lifetime of abuse. A look of recognition sprung onto his face upon seeing Bellae. "A kind soul," he whispered while hopping his bent and twisted body over to her. "Rare that is, and not just these days, but any."

Scroll 4: Don't Push My Brain

As Trelos leaned in close, Bellae could smell odor born from lack of hygiene as he whispered, "Only the weak of will, gelid of heart, and those cowardly of spirit feel the need to bully by peacocking their so-called 'physical' strength. A parting, fleeting gift."

"You'll get no charity here, misfit! Begone!" Mor-Leider gruffed.

Still leaning close to Bellae, Trelos said, "Adding mead to small-minded, insecure beings only serves to diminish their already lacking intellect and vacant sympathy. Instead, drink my words, swallow the lesson, digest its benefit."

"Hello, Trelos. I didn't think I'd see you again," Bellae said tentatively.

"You make predictions on whether or not you'll see people again? How odd."

"I'm...not sure," Bellae said tentatively.

Trelos rolled his prominent eyes before standing as tall as his curved back would allow. "Are you, in fact, the Chosen?"

Bellae remembered what Stralande had told her about the construct of the "Chosen" as a way to obtain and keep loyalty from the League. *I don't want to get into that.* "I am, Trelos."

"You are Trelos?" he huffed. "I see you're just as dim-witted, kind soul or not! You're *not* Trelos." Pointing to his dirty brown robe he said, "Me, Trelos," and then poking her arm, "you, squire Bellae! Wow, a few too many drops on the old noggin as a youngling I guess."

Bellae could not help chuckling despite the offense. "No, I meant, I am—as in answering the question. Not, I am Trelos."

"What're you doing here?" Lontas asked.

"Ah, well, Emperor Fanga summoned me to help for his Nishi problem. Then with the whole 'invasion thing,' he lost sight of the need for specter protection. Now, I'm trapped." Trelos paused as if thinking deeply. "On my way into this den of nescient delinquency I thought I saw a couple of stinging insects buzzing around, but I wasn't sure."

"Okay, and so?" Jumeaux said, anxious to finish their business with the mariner.

"It made me wonder, two bees or not two bees? That is the question."

"What are you on about?" the mariner asked, obviously agitated.

"I don't know, but it seems important," Trelos replied, looking up to the ceiling as if contemplating something profound. Abruptly Trelos stopped his deliberation and scampered to Jumeaux, sticking his nose unsuitably close to his armpit, inhaling deeply. "I smell treachery and rejection! Betrayal eats at your heart, chopping with a dull spoon in a slow, agonizing demise."

Jumeaux blushed. "Definitely not!"

"A skunk smells like a skunk whether you want to admit it or not," Trelos said.

Jumeaux recalled the spurn from his false friends at the Academy. *How does he know that from sniffing?* "You need to depart, twisted man."

"I concur!" the mariner agreed.

"You swindle pooches?" Trelos gasped, his wiry arms flinging to his chest in horror.

"What?" Mor-Leider replied angrily.

"You said you 'con curs.' That's a horrible profession, but to admit it so freely? Worse."

"He said *concur*, to agree, not con curs," Jumeaux said.

Bellae grabbed Trelos' hand. "Do you want something to drink?"

Trelos looked taken aback at the kindness. "Speaking of drinks, there's a ravenous creature that eats everything it comes into contact with. However, if it drinks, it dies."

"Easy. Fire!" Jumeaux said. "'Drinking' water puts out fire."

Trelos seemed annoyed. "Immodest could really become I'm modest with work. Even though it's a measly one apostrophe and single space from immodest to I'm modest, it can be a long and arduous journey for some. However, with determined effort towards self-improvement you could transform, metaphorically, into a being with an apostrophe and a space."

"Someone with an apostrophe and a space is good?" Jumeaux asked, genuinely confused.

"You're a lost cause, boy," Trelos mumbled, moving misguidedly closer to Jumeaux.

"Man, why are you—" Jumeaux started.

"It's fine!" Lontas interjected, remembering sniffing had something to do with Trelos' perceived "safety."

"Take a seat," the mariner said angrily, kicking an empty one towards Trelos, growing anxious at the attention they were drawing.

"Oh, well, thanks, but I already have enough chairs. Also, it would look odd, me carrying a chair down war-torn streets. Finally, I'm sure you do not own this establishment, and therefore do not have the authority to tell me to *take* this seat."

"I meant *sit down*! We're trying to keep a low profile," the mariner replied.

"Then why are you telling me to steal chairs? I would advise against blatant theft if you do not want to draw attention. Or, or, do you mean you're about to hunch down in your seat, so as to make it so your 'profile is low,' as in less visible? You really must speak clearly and concisely for any conversation to continue with someone of my superior intellect. My suspicion is you have drunk too much ale on dry land and large amounts of salt water at sea!"

"Not that this conversation hasn't been sublime, but—" the mariner started.

"What would happen," Trelos interrupted, "if we travel *above* the fruit?"

Jumeaux chuckled at the absurdity while Mor-Leider brandished his swords, again.

"All I'm saying," Trelos responded defensively, "is that if sub-the-lime is marvelous, would going above the green, citrusy fruit perhaps over-lime or above-lime, be better or worse?"

Mor-Leider pounded on the table, drawing the attention of the patrons. "Enough!"

Jumeaux whispered, "We need to be careful. There could be spies."

"Don't you be needing to turn in my crooked friend?" Mor-Lieder asked.

Trelos looked genuinely shocked. "I suppose you'd like that? Soon enough all of us will be wearing a thick blanket of earth as we tuck ourselves into decay and mind numbness."

"I meant to sleep, not die, ya fool."

Ignoring him, Trelos began inappropriately sniffing Bellae's arm. "How are my Nishi guards working?" After lifting her sleeve, he gasped. "It's beaten up and…is this dried blood?"

"We've been through a lot but asked for none of it," Bellae replied. "We haven't seen them much lately."

Trelos' eyes wobbled back and forth, and his breath quickened. "Not good."

"What do you mean?"

"The White One will never give up on the crystals. Therefore, they're waiting for you to finish, and then…" The former squires jumped as he slammed his hand against the table. "…smash you like a bug and steal them! That's the only explanation."

The pirate's sword was instantly at the squirming Trelos' neck. "Hit the table and spill a bit of my drink again, and I take your head."

As the blade was removed, Trelos muttered, "Value drink over life, how novel. You're not the first to have your mind twisted by the fetters of toxic tonic." He shuffle-hopped closer to Bellae before whispering, "Those who are loud and obnoxious are often trying to drown out their own thoughts, usually regret and insecurity. Perhaps, if they act like big enough jesters, keep moving, keep shouting, they won't have to evaluate their own life." Trelos' proptotic eyes suddenly whirled. "We are all just living in our own dream."

"You can't live in a dream," Lontas said.

"Without dreaming we cannot live," Trelos answered. "Boy, some things live only in dreams. Perhaps we, all of us here, are dreaming now, and reality is when we sleep. Maybe both are absolute hallucinations. In the long stream of eternity our existence is but a trifling. So, mariner, tell me how you'll get these children to Ifrean?"

"How do you know this? I don't give secrets away to a perfect stranger."

"I'm flattered you think I'm 'perfect,' but it's oxymoronic to call someone 'perfect' and 'stranger.' As, if you don't know them, you could not accurately predict their status on a perfection scale. Anyway, 'perfection' as an attainment is likely impossible for any being. To circle the squished rectangle into a square back to your original, obtusely triangular question, you come to mariners when in need of smuggling goods or people. Seeing no goods, it's children who need passage."

Mor-Leider rubbed his temples. "This fool pushes my brain aggressively into agony."

Scroll 5: Battle of Abhainn: Kama, Meet Face

"Ailante!" a Varna, defender of the forest, called out. The aged leader of the Elves of Creber turned to see him gliding anxiously through the forest.

"What is it?"

"Sir, the Proliate have stopped attacking our forest to the north stating an alliance has been forged between Friar and the Proliate. However, they are moving south at speed."

"Can we trust this?" another ruling-class Archerian asked.

"We have no choice," Ailante replied. "We can't continue to battle on two fronts, and the Dark Warriors are closing in on the sacred forest. Divert all available Varna south, but keep a keen watch on all sides."

"I'll see to it," Kempe said, jumping into a nearby tree before scampering away.

"Ailante, are you sure you want to be this close to the action?" an Elf asked the next day.

"I won't miss this, even if it costs my life. The Dark Warriors have been methodically burning our outer ring of Creber trees on either side of the Abhainn River. With their total disregard for life, they're making progress despite heavy losses from our Elven arrows."

"They're now only a few rings of trees away from our sacred forests," a Varna said.

"Our Elven brothers and sisters whose arbor breith birth trees are closest are already feeling heat and pain as their roots suffer under the encroaching scorched earth," Ailante replied.

Kempe growled. "Even though we've killed fifty thousand, the Dark Warriors still have a force of over twenty-five thousand within the horseshoe shaped section of burned ground around the river. They continue leaving garrisons along the river to prevent us from using water to put out the fires."

"Lead troops streaming in from the Proliate front around to their rear and see if you can slow them down from behind," Ailante said as Kempe sprinted off.

"They don't ever seem to sleep," a Varna said.

Ailante nodded. "Then, until they all die, neither shall we."

"Commander Koketti, behind us!" one of the Dark Warriors called to his superior.

Their commander wore a bright yellow cloak with a purple belt holding various weapons, including a sword and axe. He looked up to see a force of over five thousand Elves of Creber behind them. "We fight savagely to die well, or the White Wizard will have his retribution."

"Should we pull back the brigade in charge of starting the fire and form up?"

"No. You lead ten thousand of our troops and form up here. Do not attack. When they charge, fight ferociously, delaying your death as long as possible. The Sovereign in White commanded we burn their sacred forest. We must torch some birth trees. I'll lead the rest and pierce as deeply as possible," Commander Koketti answered.

"It's an honor to die!" the Dark Warrior answered. "Paradise!"

The commander tipped his hat. "Die with honor for your family." He looked with pride at his troops. They had managed to cut deeply into the outer ring of trees serving as a buffer for the arbor breith despite ferocious fighting. He thought of his family as he kicked up blackened soot sitting on top of the normally fertile forest. *The Sovereign in White should be pleased.*

A short while later, ten thousand Dark Warriors formed up lines facing south. Standing against them were five thousand Elves of Creber. Another fifteen thousand Dark Warriors, led by Commander Koketti, were facing the intact forest. The northern-facing troops had divided into four sections—half on either side of the River Abhainn. The front two groups consisted of five thousand infantry. The rear two were fire spreaders with two and a half thousand in each section.

Ailante sighed, the pain from the forest around him nearly blinding his Elfin vision. "Their front two sections facing us are suicide troops, recklessly throwing themselves forward."

"They fight as fiercely as any army we have ever faced," an Elf warrior said.

Ailante nodded. "We must fight our way through them to get to their fire brigades armed with flaming arrows and torches. Their sole purpose is to start fires within our sacred forest. They obviously learned from our battle with the Proliate at Blodskogur Woods. We can't fight from trees razed to the ground."

"Remember who and what we are fighting for!" Koketti yelled to those facing towards the sacred forest. "To die!"

At his command, the forward two sections recklessly charged towards the forest. The first several lines were instantly obliterated by the heavy arrows of the Elves. Undaunted, the waves of Dark Warriors screamed in fury as they advanced. The scorched earth sent up puffs of black soot as they strode forward. Their straight lines formed into a spear tip as they charged. The fire brigade sections released their flaming arrows, pulling additional Elves to water duty.

"Signal Kempe to attack from the rear!" Ailante bellowed as fire and ash spread everywhere, the air clogged with burdensome smoke. "Unleash our Special Forces and tell them to focus on the fire spreaders!"

"There's our signal. We must fight through to the archers! For our Forest, for our families!" Kempe said.

The five thousand Elves of Creber under Kempe's command descended on the Dark Warriors' rearguard. Most of the Elves had their kama weapons out. With its bladelike beak, the kama was a deadly weapon, especially against the lightly armored Dark Warriors. With their sacred forest about to be burned, the Elves fought ferociously. Kempe was in the front and quickly accumulated six kills. His kama slammed into the face of a Dark Warrior for his seventh. The beak bit deeply into the man's face, exploding it in blood and fractures. The splatter soaked Kempe's face—the red of his enemy dominating his body save his brown and green eyes.

The tip of his kama slammed into another Dark Warrior's cervical spine and lodged in between two vertebra. Just then, two Dark Warriors with swords attacked from his right. Releasing his stuck kama, Kempe grabbed his nunchaku and quickly knocked the closest sword away. His nunchaku arced around and shattered the attacker's sword hand. He then swung it upwards, fracturing the attacker's forearm.

Kempe grabbed the falling sword before briskly swinging it up, injecting it into the man's face. With Kempe's stout frame and the Dark Warrior's momentum, the blade easily shaved through both sides of his skull—releasing brain and flesh out the back side of his head.

Suddenly, the Elves broke through the Dark Warriors' line. Instantly, it felt like a trap. "We haven't killed enough to be through to the fire spreaders! Hold! Archers to the front!" Kempe yelled, but too late. Over half of the Dark Warrior rearguard had hung back and nocked their arrows, which they now unleashed.

Kempe dove down and lifted one of the corpses on the ground as an impromptu shield. Since the forest normally acted as their screen, the Elves felt exposed and vulnerable.

"Archers, return fire!" Kempe howled as he stood and slowly advanced using two Dark Warrior corpses as arrow cushions. Hundreds of Elves fell, but given their tough, bark-like skin, many sustained only superficial wounds. Screams of the mighty Elven long arrows shrieked overhead. Volley after volley wailed, the Elves' skill and speed overwhelming the enemy.

Scroll 6: All I'm Saying is, You Die

"You think the White Wizard's waiting for us to finish before killing us?" Lontas asked.

"Oh, definitely," Trelos answered. "It's not the worst way to go. For most the patterned banality of everyday life slowly melts time, speeding our lives along a blur of routine rushing by faster and faster in an imperceptible, but inevitable, wheel of decay. Only the extraordinary wake up their spirits and minds to truly see the power of the moment, here and now.

"You mortals fear death because you will be deprived of the universe. Your baseline mistake is that you think the universe has any concern for you. It cared not for your entrance, cares not for your life, and certainly couldn't care less about your passing out of it."

"Are you…not mortal?" Jumeaux asked cautiously.

Trelos huffed. "Of course, I am! I just accept it. That doesn't mean I ever stop toiling for knowledge unlike a sluggish sloth! Do you wish to succeed or fail?"

"Uh, succeed?" Lontas ventured.

"Wrong!" Trelos seethed. "Those of idle nature who do not seek the truth will always succeed. Those who search for verity within the universe will always fail no matter how hard they struggle, as we shall die before we get there. However, that does not mean we shouldn't fight! We can never know all the secrets of the universe, as it is too vast, too many unknowables. An example of failure as victory is a life seeking truth, and an example of triumph as losing is apathetic idleness."

"I have no idea what's happening here, but I strongly feel I should kill this rat!" Mor-Leider said, taking a deep swig from his tankard.

"Does knowing you live in a prisoner's box change your actions?" Trelos asked, ignoring the mariner while getting inappropriately close and sniffing Lontas.

"I'm really not sure where you're going with this," Lontas said, arching back.

Trelos huffed. "Each life is but a small nook to dwell. We have such a narrow space within which to operate. That box, our time here, cannot be expanded, only accepted."

Lontas looked at Bellae.

"Why do you look to the girl?" Trelos wondered. "Does she think for you?"

"No, but…"

"No butt? That must make defecation exceedingly difficult," Trelos said, genuinely concerned. "Does it come back out your mouth then? Ooh, or some other orifice?" The odd man struggled to stand on his chair, looking in Lontas' ears, but quickly seemed to tire of that and his previous line of conversation. "Who sees better, a blind man or one with sight?"

Lontas resisted looking at Bellae again. "One…with sight?"

Trelos huffed. "A blind man can obviously see more. They don't see race, color, affliction, or creed and 'see' more through their other senses than those who rely on the crutch of sight. Don't you agree that ears speak louder than words?"

"Ears…speak…louder?" Bellae stumbled, completely confused.

"My dear, listening and being attentive speak more to caring than blathering, of course!"

"That's actually pretty—" Lontas started but was cut off by Trelos.

"Who writes history, do you think?"

"Historians!" Lontas answered lustily.

Trelos snorted. "History is written by those who bow to the party line of the victors—the ones providing the bloody ink won in brutal battles, needless to say."

"If I give you money, will you please, please leave?" Jumeaux asked.

"He could be a danger to your mission. Death seems the best answer and the quickest relief to his pain, and ours," the mariner said.

"You're a freak and a loser!" a patron yelled. "What are you doing with him, captain?"

Mor-Leider growled while Jumeaux blushed, ashamed of the negative attention. "Doesn't it bother you, them constantly making fun of you?"

Trelos looked at Jumeaux as if he were the one to be pitied. "I shall answer your foolishness with a tale. That 'man' offered to pay me to clear rubble from his dwelling. I worked hard for days, but when I approached him for payment, he beat me and threw me into the mud."

"That's horrible!" Bellae protested, finding it hard to imagine anyone wearing their life scars more prominently than Trelos. Or, perhaps, the way he was formed combined with others' shallow perceptions, dooming him to suffer the scars in the first place.

Trelos put his shuddering hand on hers while projecting a look of kindness. His expression soured as he swiveled back to Jumeaux. "Who, would you say, is in the wrong? The dishonest man who did not pay, or the one who worked hard through physical pain you do not fathom? Are you saying honest, hard work is wrong and dishonesty is right?

"Is it the one born different that is at fault, or those who do not know me, cannot see beyond those measly external factors and hurl feeble insults born from their own unseen, but clearly infirm, minds? True victory, true honor, is not necessarily what society would label it as. The reality underneath, that is where true triumph reigns. Perhaps you blame me, as if I had a choice in my construction? Or, maybe, would you see the corruption of the words hurled as insults—a moment on their treacherous lips but a lifetime of veiled mental scars for me?

"Let me tell a truth. We enter and leave our existence with only our soul. Nothing else is truly ours." Trelos poked Jumeaux's skin before pinching and pulling on it. "This...fallaciously adored but fabulously flawed flesh is but an infinitesimally transient receptacle for your soul. Across the ages people have called the true self soul, while others: character, individuality, essential self, etcetera. Whatever the nomenclature, it is born from your actions and colored by how you treat others." Falling silent, Trelos held out his hand towards Jumeaux, who pulled out his coin purse and gave him several coins. Trelos looked back and forth from his hand and the money bag. Jumeaux kept adding more until finally Trelos nodded and turned to leave but quickly hopped back. "You're going to die. Despite this monumental travesty to you, it is but a minuscule afterthought for me. I shall carry on." He shuffled out the door to scores of jeers.

"His brain be missing more than a few ribs from the vessel's hull," the mariner said.

"I don't know," Lontas said. "If you really dive into some of the things he says, they're quite profound." He looked back to the others to see looks of horror.

Mor-Leider shook his head. "Now, you parrots are too scrawny to be of much use, and we're in possession of sufficient cabin mates so, occurrences forming as they have, you hide in the hold—that there's the bottom of the ship. You'll have plenty of rats for company."

Lontas swallowed hard while Bellae gently patted the increasingly quiet Grym.

"So, where exactly are you hoping to depart upon LuvattuMaa?" Mor-Leider asked.

"Wait, what's that?" Bellae asked.

"LuvattuMaa is what you call Ifrean," he replied. "You do know it's massive with multiple land masses, innumerable islands, and countless archipelago formations?"

"They need to reach the South Isle, Cove of Pain," Jumeaux answered.

"Luck seems to be blowing the sails. My ship goes by there, and I can stop in the Cove without suspicion," Mor-Leider announced.

"Could you help us figure out exactly where we're heading?" Bellae asked.

Mor-Leider smiled. "We'll have plenty of occasion to discuss the details later. Right now there's issues needing my attention. Do you have the agreed-upon money?"

The question startled Lontas and Bellae, but Jumeaux expected it. "Here's half. I'll give you the rest in the morning when they board the ship."

Mor-Leider smiled. "I accept your terms. This here fine establishment has a room for you. But they, unlike my trusting soul, will need you to pay them in full. I'll see you on the wharf, at first sunup." Walking away, he looked back. "Your first Dark Sea crossing is always the worst. Enjoy your last day on land. It's a wee bit choppy where we be sailing."

Scroll 7: That Explains...

"Something bit me!" Jumeaux howled.

"Grym's with me. It's not him," Bellae said sleepily.

"You shouldn't complain," Sankari chirped. "I spent the last couple of days in *a bag* being crushed, jostled, humiliated, demeaned, and other words my scrambled brain can't recall."

"This is unacceptable. The bugs here are bigger than your rat," Jumeaux complained.

"Who knew a pub renamed Scrub our Feetery would have less than sparkling clean rooms?" Lontas said.

"The stables at Liberum…were cleaner," Jumeaux added, another jolt of unexpected sadness at the memories.

"We've been sleeping on the ground. This isn't too bad," Lontas said.

"You mean it hasn't been all fun and games since we parted?" Jumeaux asked.

"We've had some rough spots," Lontas answered.

"Like what?" Jumeaux asked defensively.

"Ever hear of lihumari?" Lontas asked, explaining his run-in with the flesh-eating log.

"I heard about carnivorous logs, but I thought they were kidding. Oh, Lontas, leave it to you to sit on that thing," Jumeaux said, suddenly laughing.

"It's not that funny!" Lontas replied.

"I wasn't laughing at that. Remember the green slop story?" Jumeaux said.

"No, but definitely interested," Lontas said, perking up.

Jumeaux proceeded to tell of his adventure in the infirmary with green slop and patient Crassus with his snackable belly button goo.

"I can't believe you never told us that story," Lontas proclaimed.

"You really didn't know?" Jumeaux questioned.

"How could we?"

Jumeaux remembered his anger, convinced they were making fun of him because of his misadventure. Painfully sharp images of Kaveri telling him they were forced to be his friends besieged his mind. His shifting perception opened a small crack in his heart.

"I'm sorry that happened. If some dead guy latched on to me, I think I would freak out. Plus, Crassus sounds crazy." Lontas suddenly paused.

Even in the darkness Jumeaux could see the sad expression on his face. "What is it?"

"I was thinking Crassus is dead. I shouldn't speak badly of him. Goodnight, Jumeaux."

After several minutes, Lontas started laughing, and Jumeaux followed.

"What now?" Bellae asked.

"Sorry. I can't get the image of Crassus in his small orderly outfit slopping in the green gunk they serve as food," Lontas replied.

"It's funny *now.* It wasn't then, especially with Necare's corpse attacking me."

In the pitch-black room, with all the stress of the world swirling around her, Bellae gently petted Grym's black fur. There were too many wounds and too much to think about to laugh.

Scroll 8: Day One: Claustro-Meet-Phobia

"About time you display yourselves!" Mor-Leider said angrily the next morning. "Mariners aren't known as prompt risers. However, we wake up, orienting ourselves with respect to shoving off time!"

"Sorry, sir," Jumeaux said. "I'll walk you guys into the ship then take off."

"Let me transfer you to the hold, parrots," he said gruffly.

"Sir, why call us parrots?" Bellae asked.

Lontas and Jumeaux held their breath, waiting for Mor-Leider's swords to come out. They didn't. Instead, he flashed a smile, surprising his stiff beard into creasing. "Because the young of our race are of no higher quality than a parrot. Sure, I can educate you into saying a few words, but you don't know their true meaning. You haven't had your teeth long enough to bite into life to savor, appreciate it, and spit out its true meaning."

"We've seen quite a bit, actually," Bellae said defiantly. Lontas and Jumeaux cringed again, holding their breath while Mor-Leider gazed fiercely. Bellae stared back, unblinkingly.

To their surprise Mor-Leider smiled again. "I can see you might have discerned more than your fair share of difficulty...at least for your lack of elderliness. Now move!"

"Do you think he knows parrots don't have teeth?" Lontas whispered to Jumeaux.

"Not the best analogy," Jumeaux said, surprised to find himself enjoying their company.

The three followed him across a wooden gangway onto the large ship. It had three sizable masts with square sails on them, the larger mainsails on the bottom and smaller topsails above. In the front there were three triangular foresails or jibs.

"This beauty bears the title Amathia," he said, looking at them expectantly. He scoffed at their blank expressions. "You've been informed of nereids? Sea nymphs?" Instead of explaining further he sneered, walking on, mumbling, "Parrots."

Pausing on the gangway, the mariner took off his hat. For the first time they could see the tangled mess of scarcely washed hair blundering out from under his red headscarf. Bowing his head, he said, "It is extremely hard to see the grandeur all around us, and all that we have in the present while one covetously looks abroad. May we be thankful for nature's gifts and trials. May the gods guide us on our journey and protect us on the route." Taking a considerable breath, he stepped onto the ship while replacing his hat. His face crumpled in disappointment as the three former squires ambled onto the boat. "Show some respect to this here girl. The sea teaches many lessons. Number one is humility. Number two is always turn into an approaching storm, facing it head on. A tempest that has you in its sights will arrive regardless of whether you wish it.

"Anyway, this is the quarter deck, the captain's quarters is that way, below the poop deck—where the wheel of the ship belongs. Let's head down through the berth deck to the hold. It was loaded with supplies yesterday. I included two empty crates just for you two to enjoy the voyage," Mor-Leider said with a sly grin, grabbing a sickly looking lantern.

"Where's the crew?" Jumeaux asked.

"I took on a new crew, and they're currently getting the 'secret' story about the hold being haunted and how they should try to avoid going down there. It's just a ruse to keep them occupied while I sneak ya down and slow traffic to the hold. See this bell?" Mor-Leider asked as they walked down rickety steps ripe with soft rot. "My First Mate be telling them to keep the ghosts away, ring the bell before entering…thus givin' ya some time to hide."

Lontas could feel Sankari wiggling angrily at the idea of going from bag to crate. As they descended further into the bowels of the ship, the darkness became more complete. The mariner pointed to two crates at the back of the ship. The lantern barely cast enough light to see them behind stacked crates and tied-down barrels.

"At least three times a day someone, likely the quartermaster or sailing master, will come down to get supplies," he said.

Jumeaux clumsily gave Mor-Leider the rest of the money. The pirate felt its weight and nodded before securing it inside his coat.

"I guess…goodbye," Jumeaux said. "Gimelli will tell me of your return." His eyes darted down as he thought, *So we can come steal the crystals.* "Let me know if you need more help."

Bellae gave him a hug. "It's nice to see you, big brother. I missed you. Thanks again for helping. I won't *ever* forget it. I always knew you loved us. It's just nice to see you prove it."

She stepped back and looked into his eyes. Jumeaux struggled to maintain eye contact, wondering what emotions were swirling. *Was it love? Was it guilt knowing Veneficus' plan for the crystals?* Either way, he knew he had to lock them up before returning to the Magician stronghold. If the White Wizard was always watching, so was Veneficus. Despite his fear, the nagging idea that Veneficus was using him like Bellae, Kaveri, and Chy kept bubbling up.

"One last thing," Jumeaux said. "Clarus lux eternus!" he said, pointing his crosier at a compass withdrawn from his pocket. The compass immediately started to glow with white light.

"An agreeable skill to have, for a parrot," Mor-Leider remarked, obviously impressed.

Jumeaux handed the glowing compass to Bellae and looked at his crosier apprehensively. "The eternal light enchantment took a lot of power. Anyway, good luck." He nodded to Lontas.

"Wait," Bellae said. She quickly gave him a hug with the bag of Macht Crystals out in front. Just as when they first met, Jumeaux's crosier soaked up some of their power.

"Thanks."

Bellae paused, eyes staring ahead. *Yes, use our power. Feel our potent strength. Only you can save the world. Take what's yours,* the crystals haunted in her mind.

"Bellae?" Jumeaux uttered. "I said thanks."

"Of course. Love you, big brother," Bellae called out, coming back to the present as he rotated to leave, waving but not turning around.

"That's a handy little device you got there," Mor-Leider said. "I'll be returning once the ship and open waves have a chance to reacquaint. There are two buckets in the corner for your 'business.' Make sure you keep the lids securely tied down. If you spoil food, I'll personally kill you. We'll remove your waste once per day."

Before he could leave, Bellae waltzed up to him and held out her forearm. Smiling, he took it. "Thank you for helping us," she said sincerely.

Shaking his head, Mor-Leider left them in the dark hold. Their enchanted compass was now the only light. Sankari flew around a few times before joining Bellae in her incredibly uncomfortable and cramped crate. Mor-Leider had rigged the lid with a rope so they could seal themselves in. Even with the tops off and holes drilled around, the air quickly grew stale. Their knees were jammed into their chests, and there was no room to stretch out.

Lontas sighed, feeling claustrophobic. In the gloominess time seemed to sludge forward. Even moored to the harbor, they could feel the rocking of the waves—the rhythmic movement of the boat seeming to toss them in little circles, as if playing gentle catch with the giant ship. *A small sample of what's to come,* Bellae thought. She suddenly, and aggressively, squeezed her mouth closed as Lontas retched.

Scroll 9: Day Four: Sea Stomach

"I don't think—" Lontas didn't finish, spewing in the extra bucket Mor-Leider brought down for their prolific, incessant vomiting. "I didn't know you could have cold and hot sweats at the same time. Plus, the dizziness and headache bonuses are awesome. I—" *Blargh.*

"It does feel like the world's turned upside down," Bellae added, holding onto the sides of her crate as the boat pitched and yawed side to side while also heaving nearly vertical as it fought the seemingly never-ending waves. The initial gentle sway of the boat had given way to erratic and harsh movements, sometimes lifting them out of their crates. Voices from above could be heard as those manning the ship fought against the storm.

"There's water leaking in," Lontas said before putting his head back over the bucket.

She wanted to say something comforting but felt too sick. Sankari had decided to sleep through the rough seas and was resting in the crate. Suddenly, the hatch opened.

"They didn't ring the bell, in the box," Bellae whispered. Frantically she reached for the lid, gently keeping the sleeping Sankari on her lap.

Grabbing the rope, she quickly pulled the lid on top of her, slipping the compass in her pocket. Sankari stirred, and Bellae put her finger to her mouth for silence. She closed her eyes to help fight the dizziness sloshing in her skull and near-constant nausea jostling within.

Bellae tried to slow her breathing while her brain begged, screamed, for the motion to stop. Breathing in the stale air of the confined space did not help. Despite her best efforts, panic tightened its grip. Her lungs screamed, imploring for more air. The minute space within the crate seemed to be warping smaller. Frightened, she began to desperately push against the sides of the crate as her heart bounded within her chest. Sweat crowded out on her skin, drenching her back and forehead, as the trapped feeling intensified. She couldn't tell if Lontas had made it into his box as the footsteps grew louder. Part of her wanted to be found and end the agony. The boots stopped next to the crate. Someone fumbled with her lid before the cover flipped off as light from a lantern pierced her eyes.

"You parrots look like you crawled into your graves," Mor-Leider said. "I've a need for you to squawk where I'm supposed to drop you."

"Can we do that another time?" Bellae asked, scrambling out of the crate. She hastily lunged for the vomit bucket to make a deposit.

Scroll 10: Battle of Abhainn: Red-Burns-Green/Red-Surprise

"Follow me!" Kempe yelled. Many of the Elves copied his example, grabbing a fallen body as an impromptu shield.

The Dark Warriors had time to unleash one more round of arrows. Despite the reduced number of archers, given the closer distance, hundreds more Elves fell.

Kempe signaled with his arm then shouted, "Down!" The advancing Elves all dove to the ground as arrows from their Elven brothers behind whizzed overhead. After the Elven arrows sunk deep into the remaining Dark Warriors, Kempe stood up to lead the others in a charge. Most had switched to long wooden staffs.

A sickening symphony of cracks echoed through the blackened field as the tough poles of the Elves broke jaws and facial bones. The ferocity of the Elf attack surprised even the fanatical Dark Warriors, who were forced to stumble backwards.

Ripples in the flowing Abhainn River abruptly exploded as hundreds of Elves burst out of the water. The Special Forces swim squad was sent to get behind the fire spreaders and stop them from burning the sacred forest. However, the rearguard of the Dark Warriors was being pushed back so ferociously the Elven swimmers found themselves forced to fight them. Despite their small numbers, the fact that they fell upon the rear of the Dark Warrior line made their effect devastating. The Elven flanks folded around the crumbling rearguard of Dark Warriors, and they were soon completely annihilated.

As the last of the rearguard fell, several Watchers appeared on either side of them. Kempe directed the archers to fire repeatedly, keeping the desiccated creatures busy deflecting arrows. He then signaled to the trees behind each set of the flying creatures just as more came.

The newly arrived Watchers took up position behind their companions, using them as shields against arrows, and began attacking the Elves. Bolts of lightning obliterated into the Elves, a black line crackling down, splitting their bodies as they collapsed in crumpled heaps. Next, several Elves were raised up until they were floating dozens of feet off the ground. The Watchers made a fist followed by a wringing motion while chanting, and the Elven bodies were magically mangled backwards, bones cracking ferociously. White shards of fractured long bones broke through their tough skin as they were bent backwards upon themselves before falling into shattered, misshapen clumps—blood oozing and body fluids slurping onto blackened earth.

Multiple Nishi, chanting foul obscenities, rushed into the Elven lines, brushing their hands through their heads, causing them to shiver and pause.

In the center of the forest, near the Edelia Arbor Breith, several Watchers appeared intent on scorching the sacred birth tree of Creber. They laughed manically, preparing to burn the humongous tree. Suddenly, like at Finn's funeral, the sand-like caith began undulating violently and glowing an ominous green. Several Prete pulled back the congealed top layer in preparation.

The distracted Watchers suddenly found themselves under attack from all sides as previously hidden Elves appeared all around them, jumping in waves from the sacred trees' branches. Several held onto arms of the Watchers as the others drove in the kama weapons over and over again while falling. Blue magic and blood erupted from their dehydrated bodies. When they slammed into the ground, many of the Elves were injured or knocked unconscious but were replaced by new Elven defenders sprinting forward. The Watchers were weakened, but still conscious, while the Elves roughly hauled them to the rapidly and ravenously billowing caith.

"Did you not think we would protect our Edelia Arbor Breith?" a female Elf said angrily before kicking the Watchers into the undulating caith. "Burning our forest and fighting us on open ground is one thing. Taking us on within our trees is another entirely." The Watchers screams continued for several minutes before finally gurgling into silence.

"Return to your positions!" an elderly Archerian yelled after directing the caith covering replaced. "We expect more attacks. Every leaf of our sacred forest shall be defended!"

Back at the river the protected Watchers alternated between lightning strikes and body-crunching compressions. Elves surged out of the unburnt forest edge, rushing towards them. The first rows had bows, which fired in repeated blurs. The back line of Watchers, now under assault themselves, stopped their attacks, turning to focus on blocking the shower of arrows.

The second group of Elves rushing from the forest wielded long wooden staffs and ran in groups of three. The first line attempted to strike the Watchers with long poles. The second rushed forward, stamping down, then bracing V-shaped wooden blocs with circular indents that could rotate on a thick dowel. Once set, they chanted, and the final group of sprinting Elves jammed their staffs into the blocks—the circular ends fitting perfectly within the notches—using them to pole vault upwards. Once flying through the air, they released the staff, seamlessly grabbing two kama weapons, brutally flailing them towards the Watchers.

Several found their mark. Other aerial Elves were killed by the Watchers, but the arrows were flying again as more and more Elves rushed across the burnt forest floor. Some were elderly, some youths, and soon their numbers overwhelmed the Watchers. As the last one died, Varna came and used their kama weapons to hack at them until the magic bleeding and blood hemorrhaging into the soil stopped flowing. The Nishi, realizing their plight, disappeared.

"Despite their heavy losses, the fire spreaders are moving dangerously close to the first arbor breith trees!" Ailante screamed on the other side of the battle as the suicidal Dark Warriors continued pushing forward, sacrificing themselves to Elven arrows to allow fire spreaders a chance to get closer to the sacred trees.

Kempe yelled, "Stop the fire spreaders!" while charging ahead with his pole staff towards the rear of the Dark Warrior lines made up of archers with flaming arrows.

"They're about to hit our sacred trees! Loose!"

From all around the heavy Elven arrows showered down in waves. Despite suffering massive losses, the Dark Warriors continued moving closer to the arbor breith trees.

"All Elves, leave the safety of our trees! Attack!" Ailante commanded in a panic, burning trees all around him. "We must save the sacred forest at any cost!"

Elves of all ages rushed out from the trees, the warriors firing one last arrow before switching to close-combat weapons.

Overwhelmingly outnumbered and completely surrounded, the Dark Warriors were quickly cut down. The violence of the Elves defending their homeland easily matched that of the slowly dying Dark Warriors.

Commander Koketti's hat was long gone, as was almost his entire force. His cloak was torn and laden with blood. Only a handful of Dark Warriors remained, completely encircled. He could not see if any sacred trees were burning, but he had to hope at least one was. *The White Wizard's always watching. This effort has to be enough for my family.* He didn't have time to think on it longer. Three Elves were bearing down on him. He quickly threw a dagger. It flew straight and true, piercing into the first Elf's eye. The soft brown and green eyeball burst apart in searing pain. His head whipped backwards as he crumpled to the ground.

Koketti quickly grabbed a sword from a fallen warrior and dove towards the two remaining Elves. Out of the corner of his eye he could see his fellow Dark Warriors falling all around him. With a savage blow he brought his sword sweeping around in a rapid arc. With a last-second surge of strength he imbedded his blade into the closest Elf's pole staff and threw his sword—the blade's weight effectively disabling the staff. Koketti jumped on the Elf. Using his teeth and fingernails, he tried to claw and bite at the Elf. While he did manage to draw blood in several places, overall, the Elf's skin was too thick for any of the gouges to be serious wounds.

Even as a dozen Elves fell upon him, Koketti continued to claw and fight, eventually biting down on an Elf's neck. Kempe arrived. With his bare hands he grabbed Koketti's head from above. His right wrapped around the top of Koketti's forehead, his fingers digging into eyes which were vainly squeezed tightly. Blood quickly began to ooze from them as Kempe's other hand clamped onto the commander's jaw. With a sharp backwards motion, he dislodged Koketti's teeth from the Elf's neck. Koketti was whipped backwards by the force of Kempe's movement. Kempe swiftly picked up the raging Dark Warrior and slammed his back onto his knee. With a sharp exhale, Koketti wheezed a scream as his back snapped. Again, another *crack.* Paralyzed from his waist down, he was roughly thrown by Kempe.

"Thank you, thank you," the commander gasped, a fountain of blood spurting out of his mouth faster than it fled his gouged eyes.

Wordlessly, the Elves repeatedly skewered him with their sharp kama beaks. When Koketti's last breath croaked out, Kempe spoke, "They're insane to a level that hurts my head."

"Good job, Kempe, and to all," Ailante said, emerging from the tree line.

Suddenly, one of the Elven warriors, Saemt Eldi, fell to his knees. "Pain!" The word morphed into a shriek.

"His arbor breith is on the border between the sacred and standard trees. A spark from a burning tree must have started his birth tree on fire," Ailante said as the suffering of it threw Saemt Eldi into writhing agony.

"To the arbor breith!" Ailante shouted. "Put out that fire!"

The Elves rushed down the banks of the river to put out the sacred tree on fire, the inhabitants providing buckets and any container that could hold water.

Ailante turned to Kempe. "While he will not die from his tree burning, the pain he's experiencing is unbearable."

Kempe nodded before turning to the few thousand warriors who stayed. "See to the dead. Prepare our fallen for a proper offering to the Edelia Arbor Breith. Pile their warriors high. We shall burn them. In the morning, we till this soil, preparing it for replanting."

"Sir, you need to see at this," an Elf scout said, anxiously motioning them to follow.

Concerned there were more Dark Warriors, Kempe and the Varna around him sprinted south. As they breathlessly neared the edge of burnt ground that used to be their outer ring of trees, five thousand Proliate formed up in squads.

"Inform Ailante of our betrayal by Ragorsaf. The Proliate merely wanted to attack with the Dark Warriors," Kempe told the scout. "The rest of you form up lines."

As the Elves moved forward, the Proliate put down their shields and began taking spiked wooden logs and shovels from wagons. Wordlessly, they began erecting a palisade facing away from the Elves, sealing off the burned section of forest.

"Stand down. Stay here," Kempe ordered as a Proliate commander marched forward.

"Kempe. I recognize you from the Tournament," the Proliate announced. "We have orders to build a barricade to help defend against future Dark Warrior attacks until your forest regrows. Your assistance would be appreciated but is not required. This wood is from our personal supply, not from your forest."

Without waiting for a reply, the Proliate marched back to his men and began helping.

Kempe shook his head. "Who would have guessed?"

Later Ailante caught up, running as fast as his aged legs would allow. It took him a few moments to realize what was happening. "Finally, some good news. I never thought I'd see Proliate fighting with us. Although it's devastating to lose any, we lost only one Abor Breith despite the savagery of seventy-five thousand Dark Warriors. Our outer ring shall recover."

Kempe nodded. "All shall be restored."

Scroll II: Week Four: Drivel and Sea Legs

"At least we're not throwing up as much, and there's more room to walk around," Lontas said, stretching his legs.

"More room because the food stuffs are dwindling as fast as the repulsive rats proliferate," Sankari stated, fluttering angrily. "Why are you feeding them?"

"First, they're my friends," Bellae replied. "Secondly, if I feed them, they'll stay out of the crates and barrels, so no rat pellets in the food we eat."

"Yeah, that makes sense!" Sankari sarcasmed, mumbling insults at the rats.

"Just me!" Mor-Leider yelled from the stairs as Bellae shooed the rats into the shadows. "Look at you parrots, not squawking out the lining of your stomachs!"

"Hello, Captain," Bellae said.

"You appear to be growing sea legs. That's a hard fact to conceive, given how ailingly green your skin was shining previously."

Bellae nodded but was feeling exhausted. The intermittent rough seas and near-constant barrage of messages leaking from the crystals were wearing her thin.

"Might try smiling, missy. You follow?" the mariner said. "Deep thoughts and chasmic worry transform the skin of youth into cavernous wrinkles. Just look." He pointed to the deep furrows highlighting his creased brow. "It seems to this salty mariner, they that pushed you out into the world on this quest did so before you were ripe."

Bellae nodded and sucked in air deeply in an attempt to stop the tears from falling.

"When do we land and get out of this prison?" Sankari said, fluttering in a frenzy.

"I don't control the time it takes in crossing, and you're lucky I let you stay aboard, stowaway! That said, you raise an interesting point. 'Prison' is truly defined by perspective. Being forced to be somewhere and compelled to do certain things a specific way is a type of prison—perhaps worse than one with bars surrounding a small cell."

Sankari wobbled her head sarcastically. "If we can put useless philosophy aside for a bit, what sort of dangers will we be facing when we land?"

"When we land in LuvattuMaa, Troldmanden, the White Wizard, will know. There are the regular Vartija, Dark Warriors to you, and then the horde of the deranged."

"What horde?" Lontas asked.

"A new branch of soldiers for his army—complete psychopaths."

"The regular soldiers weren't intense enough?" Bellae asked, shivering at their ferocity outside Creber.

Sankari flapped closer to the mariner, eyeing him suspiciously. "If the White Wizard knows all, sees all, then why does he allow you to voyage there?"

"He isn't the sort to admit it, but LuvattuMaa needs trade, and we are the only ones who can provide it," the mariner said, pride leaking into his expression.

"Aren't you afraid of *him*, of sailing to Ifrean with all the Dark Warriors?" Lontas asked.

"We come into the world naked and isolated. We leave the world unescorted and alone, doomed to spoil to rotting flesh. What can happen to you during the in-between time that could possibly arouse fear?"

"Why do you do it?" Lontas asked. "Trade with Ifrean?"

The mariner laughed. "Out of the goodness of my heart. Is that what you care to hear?"

"Greed casts dark shadows, tangling innocence and choking compassion," Lontas said.

Bellae shot her head towards Lontas. "Did you just make that up?"

Lontas wobbled his head. "I've been thinking on it.

"That be a self-righteous load of excrement," the mariner said.

"You better not lead us into a trap," Sankari said, flittering close to his sun-beaten face.

The mariner scowled. "People wish for an immortal life but are served an immortal death. I'm in no rush to find mine. It's true enough, I've dispatched more than my fair share of lives, but have been paid handsomely to get you to LuvattuMaa and back, and I shall do so. Mariners without a code, delivering what they are paid to, soon find a painful death." *Troldmanden is also paying me, so no way will I betray both Wizards,* the mariner thought, a smile dribbling out from behind his beard at the satisfaction of a double payday.

"I'm sure he's not going to trick us," Bellae said, gently grabbing the Fairy's hand even though she was absolutely not sure of his motives. *There's nothing we can do. At this point, we can't exactly jump off and swim back,* she thought. "How'd you become a mariner?"

"From the time we are tiny parrots, we all bow down to something, whether literal or figurative. On the land it tends to be money, greed, drink, power, some deity. Out here on the ocean? We bow down to the power of nature. The power of the sea is a humbling master. We tiny mortals skim across the surface, begging to get to our destination armed only with our frail skills and the mighty array of stars above.

"Find what you love, and do it while you still have time to sail, for there's no way to go back and there are no second chances. We are all fettered by the chains of the flesh and its never-ending, monotonous list of needs. That said, no harm in enjoying some pleasures before time forces you to throw off the body and return your gift to the earth."

"The sailor tames the ocean, the farmer domesticates the land, the warrior overcomes the body, healers treat disease, but the wise amongst us, no matter our calling, strive for knowledge and deal with our mind," Lontas said. He looked up to see everyone staring at him. "Sorry?"

"Read the deck you be sailing on, parrot!" the mariner said.

"I think your words surprised philosopher Lontas, that's all," Bellae said.

The mariner looked up, as if he could see through the deck above. "The mates sailing under me expect me to act a specific way, say certain things. Although I'm a mariner because I love the sea, I thought I might talk about something else. Anyway, here be your treat. A lime a week keeps teeth in cheek." He tossed a lime to Bellae. "Share that amongst yourselves if you want to be able to chew with gnashers by the time we arrive."

"What was that drivel?" Sankari said after the mariner left. "Do you fancy yourself a bard or something?"

"I-I-I thought it was relevant. I—" Lontas started.

"Don't care," Sankari said. "I don't trust him, and we need to get as much information from him as possible, so keep your poetry gobbledygook to yourself."

Scroll 12: Month Four: Born Day + Wisdom

Bellae awoke to Grym's screeching in a nightmare. *"It's okay,"* she said, stroking his fur.

"Who you talking to, deary?" Mor-Leider asked, startling Bellae.

"Myself."

He nodded unconvincingly as Lontas pushed the lid off his crate, pale with bags under his eyes. "The bad news is our lime tree died. However, we have something to save those teeth."

Despite being able to keep things down, they felt weak and dehydrated from lack of exercise and the rough journey. "Wash the salted pork down with this," he said, handing them small flasks. "That beauty of a drink is a combination of grapes and limes that keeps you from turning yellow and having your teeth fall out."

Grimacing, the three finished their portions of the sour beverage.

"Not a great born day present," Lontas said, looking at the marks on the inside of his crate measuring the days.

"It's your parrot day of birth?" the mariner asked.

Lontas blushed. "Well, actually, both of ours."

Mor-Leider shook his head in confusion as Sankari bristled with a scowl.

"Happy born day to us both!" Bellae said, hugging her friend. She whispered, "I'm so grateful your parents dropped you off at Liberum and you're with me on this journey. I couldn't do this without you. Nine and twelve? Hard to believe."

"Two born days away from Liberum," Lontas whispered, wiping away tears.

"Wait, wait, wait," Sankari said, her temper flaring. "How's that possible?"

Lontas looked down. "Most kids are left with the Knights without details. Everyone not born in the castle to, say, tutors or Knights takes the same born day. Who would want to know a trivial detail like their exact day of birth when you can share it with the other outcasts?"

"That's plain stupid," Sankari said, her wing speed increasing.

"For those of us who don't know, it's nice to celebrate with others," Lontas said.

"Cookie always made huge deserts," Bellae said, choking on the last words as she thought of Liberum's destruction and imagined her death.

Lontas nodded. "We had some good days. Do you remember that picnic after the Squire Battle? Despite the dogs, it was awesome. At the time, I didn't realize how great that day was."

"I remember, and yes, that was a pretty good day," Bellae said, wiping away the tears.

"The familiar, even if infinitely special, can become corrupt in our minds, spoiled into the ordinary, and lose its luster," the mariner said, looking down. "At least until it's gone, then, paradoxically, you tend to finally appreciate its worth."

"You're not at all like I thought you would be," Lontas said.

The mariner scoffed angrily. "You seem smarter than that. Don't go judging a person by clothes or occupation. It's easy, but often erroneous. Life itself is a terminal illness, an ailment none can escape. The best we can do as we skim along the ocean of our lives is learn.

"I was wild in my youth, prone to giving into desires' false glow. I fruitlessly watered its insatiable thirst with drink, I engorged my stomach on fine food to find its hunger unappeasable. I sought the company of strangers only to discover even in a crowd one can feel exhaustedly alone. Each morning, I'd wake to feel the same desires just as strong. That's the sorrowful tale that needs be spread more thickly. Desire can never genuinely be satisfied—it always, unfailingly, demands more. It took many mistakes to realize lustful acts leave you empty, while deeds of action satisfy your soul."

"Friar used to say," Bellae added, "helping someone, doing what's right, reading a book, acts of kindness, they all leave you with an accomplishment that can't be taken away."

Mor-Leider nodded. "Sometimes, being told something's not enough to grasp its significance. I was a murderer, thief, brigand, outlaw, and have many regrets. The mental remorse blisters like sun-poisoning, as with well-worn repetition I replay them. Paradoxically, it is out here, fighting the frothing waves with my ship, my memories being tossed to and fro, that I find peace and calm. Sometimes a foolish mind needs to survive the mistakes, feel the burn of repercussions before understanding. Hearing can be an infinite number of leagues apart from truly listening. It's experience that opens up the ears and shaves some ignorance off our hearts."

"You've lived through a lot," Lontas said, trying to keep him talking.

"The truly brave live a hundred lives, gloriously rising from each defeat like a phoenix, learning, adapting, audaciously fighting on. The death of our former self, the one who lost, the one who fell, the one rejected, the one succumbing to defeat, is wiser, profiting with a broader perspective. Every time we dust ourselves off and rise, we are born into a vision of greater understanding and wisdom. Those fettered with ignorance believe the opposite—that is, cowards who die many times before their final death. That is the blindness of the luxurious, born affluent, spawned into opulence, and swaddled in empathetic illiteracy. It is precisely those protected by prosperity and insulated by monetary arrogance that die but once, not the valiant.

"Take that risk for your dream. Fight for your aspirations. If you fall, get up, wearing the scars of defeat like victory beads. Keep fighting until you succeed. Create despite the storm. Sing joyfully in the rain. Howl to the moon against the darkness."

Scroll 13: Next Battle Up

"It's been months and nothing! Still no word yet?" Veneficus asked Jumeaux.

"Nothing about Bellae," Jumeaux replied.

Veneficus' eyes widened. "You should have insisted Gimelli go with Bellae! Without her to keep an eye on Bellae we could lose everything!"

"Yeah, kid," a Valo berated, throwing woeful light against the tan cave walls that served as the Magician stronghold. In reality, it was simply an elaborate web of dug-out rooms and halls high in the Tingij mountains. "You're as thick and cowardly yellow as Piscinian mustard!"

Veneficus chuckled as the other Valo circled around the chum of his wounded ego.

"What's in your skull?" another asked. "I'll tell you—moldy bread and rancid tallow!"

"Wait, does this kid even know we *need* those power crystals?"

Jumeaux glared at the floating lights. "The mariner—"

"Oh boy, kid. You're not going to give some lame excuse, are you?" a Valo interrupted.

"Well, I didn't make the rule that Gimelli couldn't go," Jumeaux replied.

"Hopefully the last set is not also in Ifrean," Veneficus said.

"Oh, I didn't think of that," Jumeaux replied, dew drops of sweat reflecting his tension.

"No, no, you didn't think," a Valo said. "You might try it, bright eyes."

"Tell Gimelli not to hurry," another added. "These rustic accommodations are just fantastic, and I think I speak for all of us here, lovely and a place we want to stay long term."

"Gimelli did tell me raids by Dark Warriors have drastically decreased since their defeat at Abhainn, so that's good," Jumeaux added, ignoring the Valo who floated around aimlessly. Gargoyle Irvikuva, seemingly depressed in their squalid cave, never awoke.

"Is it good news?" Veneficus asked. "I think it's, in fact, very bad, meaning they're preparing for a massive assault." The Supreme Master paused, staring at Jumeaux. "Is there anything else I need to know from when you met your sister."

"I don't think so," Jumeaux said timidly while aggressively wiping the perspiration from his forehead. Veneficus had been prone to increasingly violent outbursts.

"May I see your crosier?" Veneficus asked. Jumeaux shakily handed it over, self-consciously putting his hands behind his back to hide their quiver.

Veneficus quietly chanted. The crystal glowed a brilliant blue. "Interesting. It appears, to me, your mindre crystal has been recharged. How do you suppose that happened?"

"Yeah, apparently you don't even know when your crystal was charged?" a Valo chastised. "Like we're going to believe that load of manure!"

"I'm so sorry. I forgot about when Bellae gave me a hug and the crystals were in a bag in front—power went into my crosier," Jumeaux groveled, carefully studying the Supreme Master for any sign of anger, but he only seemed deep in thought.

Veneficus struggled to comprehend. Despite being away from the Macht Crystals for so long, he knew what Jumeaux described should be impossible. *The Macht Crystals shouldn't transfer magic unless all five pairs are together in the ancient pedestal. Still, everything's going to plan. I've been through this before.* "How many pairs of crystals did she have at the time?"

"Three."

"Which ones?"

"I'm not sure what you mean."

"Each pair has a name and power source. Did you find out which ones she already has?"

Jumeaux racked his brain to remember what the scroll had said. "I think they had just gotten the time crystals…maybe it said something about life and death?"

Veneficus nodded approvingly. "I caution you to tell me everything next time. The smallest detail often makes the difference between victory and defeat."

Jumeaux nodded vigorously as a stout Magician entered the section of the cave where they were talking. "Excuse me, sir. We have news of the Dark Warriors."

"Well…?" Veneficus asked expectantly.

"They're laying siege to Temples on the Proliate Islands, including Balia and Bars K. The biggest concern is the massive force attacking Temple Aon Intinn. They're skipping the Northern Dwarves and leaving the Citadel alone. Is that good news?"

"I'm not sure we have any news that would qualify as good at the moment," Veneficus said. "You may both go. However, inform me of any changes. Jumeaux, make sure you keep in contact with your sister. I need to know every detail."

Scroll 14: Month Six: Unexpected Empathy

"We're within reach of land, parrots," Mor-Leider said. "The trip here's dependent on the brisk trade winds. The return will be nicer, mostly powered by the currents flowing east to west."

"I can't handle doing this again," Sankari said—her spunk forfeited to the waves.

"We're a day or so away from greeting the Redire Channel. You raised the point of a riddle? This would be the hour to show me."

Bellae removed the prophecy scroll and read it, making sure to keep the crystals hidden.

"I grew from a baby in Genau," Mor-Leider said with a softness born of painful memories.

"Wait, you're from Ifrean?" Sankari asked, anxiety over the mariner's motives growing.

"Yes. I escaped the fate of the Dark Warriors you're so hasty to judge. My father was a mariner, and my mother from Genau. Anyway, what you're trying to obtain is more easily recognized as a sinkhole. Your gaze should wander to the area labeled, 'Oka Zla.' As an inexperienced parrot, I played at that there sinkhole. My mother hid me from the Vartija, giving me to my father and a life on the seas before they took me for training."

"What happened to her?" Lontas asked.

Breathing in through his nose deeply, he fought his emotions. "Torture and death awaited her, but she never gave up my father. Otherwise, he would have died as well. Enough dwelling in the dust of memories. Oka Zla is the title for what we call the evil eye—a sinkhole."

"Of course," Lontas said, remembering the very end of the riddle. "When it says, 'dive down,' it must mean jump into the water and swim north into an underwater cave!"

"You'd be well served to be watchful. There are plenty of sharp rocks," Mor-Leider warned. "I have cause to visit Dunmharu. I'll sneak you parrots off, and you can make your way to the eye. You'll have two weeks to finish your business and get back to the cove. If you fail to make the boat before it departs, you'll have to wait over a year. You follow?"

Bellae, Lontas, and Sankari exchanged looks of horror.

"Can we expect to run into Dark Warriors?" Bellae asked.

"Vartija fight because they have no choice. You're quick to judge but do not fathom what path led them to where they stand. It's only secondary to the mandate of the White Wizard they engage in war. All movement is severely restricted by his henchman, the XeraKirin." Mor-Leider paused, seeing their looks of confusion. "Nasty creatures you call Watchers. Therefore, it's in your best heed that you move all meticulous-like to avoid capture. You shouldn't be of an opinion the White Wizard doesn't know all about you."

"Trelos was correct. We're going to die in Ifrean," Sankari said.

"The White Wizard's acquainted with the notion Bellae's the one going after the Power Crystals," Mor-Leider said, salivating at his double payday.

"Soon everyone's going to be after us." Lontas sighed. "What happens if the White Wizard shows up and wants Bellae and the crystals now?"

"As a pirate, I like gambling with everything but my own being," Mor-Leider answered.

Bellae and Lontas exchanged a glance, knowing he would give them up in a heartbeat.

"You don't realize how wonderful you have it. Life in Ifrean's a nightmare," Mor-Leider said. "The Wizard rules with absolute authority and terror. You won't be seeing schools or healers. I hide my library from everyone. He confines Ifreaneans into little box worlds where the whole of your life is controlled. At his whim soldiers can remove your wife, husband, children."

"That's horrible!" Bellae said.

"Wait, you have a library?" Lontas asked. "On the way back, can I borrow some books?"

"I knew there was a reason I could talk to you differently," Mor-Leider said.

"Why do his soldiers fight for him so...crazy?" Bellae asked.

"The Wizard knows if he pierces flesh, bodies cry out in pain, but we are only left with a physical reminder of the encounter. He goes after something much harsher when he tortures our children and wives. He knows our soul is ripped when family suffers. It bleeds a deeper pain, more hurtful than bodily harm. Souls that suffer enough damage don't scar. They perish," Mor-Leider said solemnly. "If they die for his will, acting according to his teachings, then their families are offered a place in Paradise. They say the land beyond the Wall of Deild is of unparalleled beauty and abundance. Once you go, you never come back. If you're caught trespassing in Paradise, you and your whole family are killed."

"That's why they fight so fiercely? For family?" Bellae said.

Mor-Leider nodded. "Dying on the battlefield is the only sure way to provide your family a place in Paradise and get them out of the work camps."

"Work camps?" Sankari asked.

"When Ifrean parrots reach the age of seven, a certain percentage are torn from their family—boys to military, girls to work camps. They are coerced into building projects, irrigation systems...things like that. The soldiers force the young ones to live together, in cramped dorms. The only hope you have of reuniting with family is if you or one of your kin manage to perform something miraculous enough to make it to Paradise," Mor-Leider said.

"What could the White Wizard truly want?" Bellae asked.

Mor-Leider scoffed. "What do all leaders yearn for? More power to feed his unceasing cravings and over-blown ego, of course. This code set forth by the Wizard will spread across Verngaurd, and you will suffer the same fate."

Bellae and Lontas looked at each other in horror while Sankari shook her head angrily.

"Well, I can't be caught sitting around with stowaways. I best head topside," Mor-Leider announced. With a curt nod, he left.

"The White Wizard has to be the 'evil' the prophecy is protecting against," Sankari said gloomily. "I don't think I could bear it if Cappadocia fell to him."

Sankari flew off to be by herself, and Bellae moved close to Lontas. "How horrible! I never thought I'd feel sorry for the Ifreaneans."

"Whatever happens, *no way* can the White Wizard get the Macht Crystals."

Bellae nodded. The future was slowly taking shape in her mind. The one thing she knew for sure—they had to succeed.

Scroll 15: Ankle Biters

"Time for you parrots to proceed off ship," Mor-Leider announced.

The remnants of the League stiffly followed him up the stairs. As the door was pushed back, the light of two suns pounded upon them, stinging their eyes. Stumbling in the blinding bright, they staggered onto the main deck. The fresh air, with a hint of salt, seemed like the most beautiful gift ever received.

"Put yourselves into the rowboat. This cabin boy will lower us down," Mor-Leider said.

"Hello," Bellae said, squinting.

"You don't need to discourse with him," Mor-Leider grumbled before growling, "Down!" Once lowered, Mor-Leider handed the oars to Lontas. "Parrots row. Captains don't."

"I'm super tired," Lontas complained after rowing for a while.

"Let me take over," Bellae said as Lontas started moving slower and slower. Sankari hovered on the edge of the boat, enjoying the softly rippling water as the boat glided through.

"The only thing worse than a captain rowing is a parrot girl," the mariner said, gruffly changing places with Lontas. "Plus, I'd like to make it back to the ship before darkness settles."

"You find yourselves upon the South Isle. Once the boys unload our trade for the port of Dunmharu, we have three other stops. Then, we sweep the ship of rats and acquire fresh supplies. Directly ahead is Lion's Mane Rock. You'll find a path right between the mountain and the giant stone. Once through, angle west before following that horrifying poem," Mor-Leider said.

Standing on the peach-colored sand, the League could see one unimpressive mountain, more like a friendless peaked hill. To the east sat an unusual scarlet rock. The top was rounded and smooth. The sides looked like vertical waves, rolling in and out all around its circumference. The front had a few protuberances, somewhat resembling a lion's face. As they walked on the sand, they wobbled. Their equilibrium, used to the swaying motion of the sea, was unstable.

"Legend declares Lion's Mane Rock used to have a peak like the neighboring mountain. However, the White Wizard dropped so many bad children onto it that, over time, it became smooth and red," Mor-Leider replied, looking longingly back at the lapping waves.

"That's ridiculously horrible," Bellae said before noticing his backwards stare. "You really love the water."

The mariner grunted. "The obvious need not be elucidated, parrot. Water supports our boat but can also drown you. As with many things dispensed by nature, it is at once extremely selective yet indiscriminate in its gifts and punishments."

Lontas scrunched his nose. "Actually, it's the displacement of water that creates an upward force on the boat. This buoyant force works against the disposition of weight—density times volume—and gravity trying to push it into the water. You must also take into—"

"Boy," the mariner interrupted. "Sometimes a gift is just a gift and does need not be dissected. Sometimes it's enough to just see the beauty of it."

Sankari's head bobbled side to side. "Thank you! Exactly what I've been saying!"

"All I'm observing is that buoyant force equals the weight of displaced liquid. So—"

"That's great, but probably enough. Thanks, Lontas," Bellae said. He blushed a little, unsure how such interesting and practical facts could be so easily disregarded.

"Here," Mor-Leider said gruffly, handing Lontas a bulging white sack. "It should help you regain your strength. I'll be here in two weeks. I'll wait about an hour. If you aren't here, be on the lookout for me in a year or so, if you survive."

"Oh, you'll wait an hour?" Sankari howled. "How generous! Plus, if we don't make it, we can try to survive in loony land for a year? Wow! Great!"

"We'll be here," Bellae said, quickly stepping forward to embrace him.

He did not reciprocate, thinking, *I'm doing this for a double payday.* Out loud he added, "Mariners don't find a need to hug."

"How'll you get back?" Sankari asked.

"Uh...the boat, of course, you overgrown butterfly!"

"What about the captains don't row stuff?" the Fairy said, wagging her head side to side.

Mor-Leider scoffed before trekking to the boat. "Don't forget, two weeks or else!"

"I'm sorry, but that red rock seriously looks like blood," Sankari said after heading to the base of the mountain, sitting down to rest against the black rock.

Their muscles ached, wasted from lack of use on the journey. Opening the sack, they found skins filled with morsen as well as dried meat and cheese. Watching the soft waves of the cove and eating in the sunshine complete with a warm breeze on their faces felt like paradise. Bellae shared some food with Grym. When finished, they passed between the cherry-colored rock and inky mountain. Leaving the sandy water's edge, the scenery abruptly opened into a giant field of monotonous grey stones.

"That's a...whole lot of rocks!" Sankari said of the dreariness stretching out like an ocean of stone. The only break in the slate-colored world was the variation in height from pebble to boulder and the consequential shadows leaning and arching back in uncomfortable-looking crescents as the silhouettes dodged and evaded the suns' light at various angles.

"Do you know where we go?" Lontas asked.

"Of course. I know Ifrean super, super well and have seen thousands of sinkholes and am extremely familiar with how to find them," Sankari said scornfully.

"Sankari's back," Bellae whispered as Lontas rolled his eyes. She could sense something. *What am I feeling?* "Mor-Leider said to head west but he means southwest based on the map."

Sankari fluttered in that direction as a current of wind howled into their backs, gentle encouragement to move inland. Bellae's hair wrapped around her face, and she shivered despite the three suns beating down remorselessly.

Sensing she was traveling alone, Sankari flew back. "Since, you know, you can't fly, probs best if you start walking. If you're waiting for me to circle around and carry you? In case you didn't notice, flying mule-boy with a beak isn't here to haul your sorry butts!"

"Flying mule-boy?" Lontas said, suppressing a laugh. "We're coming," he added at Sankari's glowering look.

"Watch your ankles," Bellae said.

"You can't help turning them a bit," Lontas said, wading into the sea of stones.

"Pick up your feet, klutzes!" Sankari yelled, fluttering in their faces.

"We're twisting our ankles," Bellae said as loud scraping sounds echoed around them.

Sankari blushed. "I heard that before but thought it was coming from you guys."

A shudder ran through Bellae as they froze, gazing around the ashen field. She tried to suppress the whispers of the crystals murmuring pallid warnings and fragrant promises as she sensed sentient beings all around.

"We really have no idea what we're walking into," Lontas said.

"Or *flying* into, you wingless divvy!" Sankari said, spinning wildly as the scrapping sounds intensified. "I see movement!"

Out of the corners of their eyes they caught glimpses and shadows of motion rising up from the ground all around them.

"What exactly is moving?" Lontas breathed.

"How precisely would you expect us to know?" Sankari hissed.

Bellae squealed, jumping backwards as a small rock moved. "The rocks, they're alive!"

The top half of the nearest stone broke apart, stiffly separating with a harsh scraping sound and shower of dust. The upper dome of the rock divided, and below the narrow opening created was a small face with mischievous almond-shaped eyes. There were no visible ears or nose, but slowly a sharp beaked mouth with fangs became visible. As it stood up, two arms and two legs emerged from the sides of the stone. Rounded feet ended in three squat toes. Instead of fingers, one hand sprouted two roughly hewn pincers while the other had three sharp-edged black blades—the first non-grey color of the rock creature.

"What are these…things?" Sankari huffed, flying higher.

They had been so fixated on the one reshaping in front they failed to notice the hundreds of others transforming. Some were only six inches tall, others were quite large, up to three feet in height. Loud grinding and harsh grating resonated around them as the rock creatures clambered to surround them. Lontas screamed as one slashed his leg. Crimson blood lashed between his shredded pants courtesy of the black blades serving as fingers. The gashed skin carelessly propelled blood, maroon dilating outwards as it soaked the surrounding cloth.

"There are thousands surrounding us and no way out!" Sankari lamented, flying higher.

"Stop!" Bellae yelled without effect. *"Stop!"* she tried in Ainmhi Caint.

The stone creatures ground to a halt, looking around in amazement.

"Food!" the one closest said. *"We must consume."*

"Please don't eat us," Bellae said.

"So hungry!" it replied.

"Fronds and blades!" another added.

That phrase struck a chord, and soon they were all chanting, *"Fronds and blades!"*

"Well, that's not creepy!" Sankari said, fluttering above the fray.

"Does what they're chanting involve eating us?" Lontas asked, carefully stepping around the moving stones circling them. "Ow!" he screeched. "One pinched me. Ow! More and more are squeezing and cutting!"

A green streak suddenly flew towards them. In its wake fertile moss spread like emerald fire behind its flight path, sprouting on both inanimate and moving stone alike. As the flying creature neared, they could make out a distinctive green face, soiled with a look scrunched in concentration. Instead of hair, green blades and roving vines flattened behind the creature by the speed of flight. The ten-inch creature had four gracefully thin wings flittering wildly. Various shades of verdant growth feathered from most of its body. Their flight path became erratic, and the amount of moss spreading out on the rocks behind began to sputter.

Figure 6: After a rude welcome, a flying creature made of quivering greenery arrives.

The rock creatures, forgetting about the League, were whipped into a frenzy, aggressively assaulting the growth created by the flying creature. They began slamming into one another, fighting towards the newly created sage mass.

"That green thing's heading for us," Sankari said, drawing her peccary-tusk sword.

"Wait," Bellae said, unsure what she was sensing from the flying creature.

Several feet from them, their wings sputtered. Bellae stepped forward and caught the creature. Its green eyelids fluttered over black eyes before closing. "Please wake up."

"The rock monsters are leaving to get the moss," Lontas said, dodging as they surged forward in pursuit of the growth that had sprouted behind the flying creature.

An all-out brawl ensued as the rock creatures fought for the sprouting growth. Using their blade-like fingers, they ravenously scraped the moss into their voraciously chomping mouths.

"They're eating that green muck!" Lontas commented.

"Brilliant. Now I see why they say you're so smart," Sankari raged, moving towards the writhing green being in Bellae's arms.

"Don't poke her," Bellae defended.

"We should kill it before it stirs!"

"Please wake up," Bellae tried in Ainmhi Caint.

Something in those words made the creature rouse, eyelids parting to reveal green sparkling flecks within an ebony surface. "Move out of these rocks, if you want to live. My name's Viridi. The stone pixies will not be distracted for long, and I don't have the strength to create more moss right now."

"Stone pixies?" Sankari said. "Then what are you, a crass grass loser?"

"Sankari!" Bellae said as the din from the feasting stone pixies began to die down.

"Follow me if you want to live," Viridi said, flying to the west before veering south to avoid the mass of ravenous stone creatures.

Bellae and Lontas immediately followed, ignoring the aching pain in their perpetually twisting ankles as Sankari reluctantly joined the pursuit.

"It's hard to avoid the stone things," Bellae commented.

I'm not trying to, Lontas thought, kicking them with his bleeding and bruising legs.

"Get to the wall," Viridi said. "We'll—" Her voice was cut off as several larger stone pixies jumped to slash at her.

"Fronds and blades!" they chanted. *"More!"*

Up ahead there was a smooth, five-foot-tall wall of yellow rock. No weed or bit of green grew in their cracks, all picked clean by the stone pixies. As they drew closer, the number of stone creatures in front thinned while the swarm chasing grew. Viridi and Sankari reached the wall. As Lontas arrived, he cupped his hands and pushed Bellae up onto the wall. Stradling it, she reached back as Lontas jumped, grabbing his elbow and shoulder, she tugged to help him. They clambered over the barrier, falling several feet onto soft flowers and grass. They could hear the stone pixies banging on the wall, feeling increasingly violent vibrations as more arrived.

"This was built to keep those nasty stone pixies in their place. Otherwise, they'd ravage the entire countryside," Viridi said. "We should move away from the wall. I need to find a place to recharge my growing ability and catch up on some beauty sleep."

"Oh, sweetie," Sankari huffed, "there's not enough time before the end of the world, much less your life, to make a difference on the 'beauty' front!"

"Why are you so vile, and what even are you? Flying brown manure?" Viridi said, glowering the Fairy up and down.

"I'm a Fairy of Cappadocia, the most beautiful place in the world, and whaaat are you?"

"A Pasture Pixie," Viridi said but looked down self-consciously as the blades and vines growing as hair and over her body shivered.

"How can she speak *our* common tongue?" Sankari asked.

Anger mingled with sadness across Viridi's face. "I speak your language because I was captured by a mariner and forced to travel back and forth across the sea many times. When I escaped, I was an outcast since I had been exposed to human customs. I can never fly home."

"How horrible! I'm so sorry," Bellae said. "Can I carry you as a thanks for saving us?"

"Saving us?" Sankari blared. "She riled those stones up and almost got us killed!"

"She saved us," Lontas said, rubbing around the innumerable cuts of his lower legs. "I'm guessing the stone things eat vegetation?"

"That's correct. Every so often a big storm with high tide floods the area and brings loads of sargassum. In between time they can go dormant for extended periods," Viridi answered. "But when something wakes them up, they need to feed or they'll kill."

"Sargassum is the free-floating seaweed we rowed through," Lontas answered. "It's interesting because it never attaches to the sea floor and—"

"Actually, not interesting," Sankari interrupted. "Just what do you eat? Rocks?"

Instead of answering, Viridi shot forward several strands of her vine-like hair. They extended out far, snatching a flying insect out of the sky. The strands recoiled and lips spiraled back to reveal sharpened black teeth moving up and down at absurd speed. The bug was instantly chipped into small pieces as Viridi swallowed contentedly.

"Gross, you eat bugs?" Sankari retched.

"Yeah, you're welcome," Viridi said, before leading them down a hill to a large tree. Seemingly hundreds of trunk sections dove up from the center. The larger branches sprouted a series of supports along their length that dove down into the ground, looking like trunks in their own right, to root for more nutrients. The enormous canopy was a giant circle of green leaves. Each of them found a safe cradle born of trunks and branches to lie down.

Scroll 16: I Can Count—There Are Three!

"Wow," Bellae said, waking up to find they had slept until deep into the night.

"Be quiet," Viridi said, fluttering anxiously. "Other Pasture Pixies are out in force. We, well, they, are nocturnal. Thanks to being banished, I'm forced to hunt in the day."

Bellae woke Lontas, and the two crawled out on a horizontal branch to gaze upon the field. Glowing bugs twinkled in such numbers they blended seamlessly into the clear, star-studded night.

"Ooh! Shooting stars!" Sankari gushed as several streaks of white light, complete with illuminated orange tails, filled the ebony horizon.

"Interesting fact, they're not, in reality, 'stars' at all. They're meteors entering our air-breathing sphere from a differently aerated space beyond. Some ancients believed they were portentous bringers of good, or bad, luck. If made of ice, they're called comets based on the archaic belief that they are 'heads with long hair.' One can kind of see that, but in the Athenaeum I read accounts of meteors hitting the ground. They're actually rocks from space. There—"

Lontas abruptly stopped as Sankari's peccary sword poked into his forehead. "Can we enjoy this without a lecture?"

"You have serious issues, brown thing," Viridi scoffed.

Lontas sighed gratefully as the Fairy turned her pique upon the Pixie. "At least the stone pixies have gone dormant," Lontas said. "That scraping and banging was annoying."

"Speaking of which, let's clean and dress your wounds," Bellae said. "Is there water around here?"

"We must wait until morning," Viridi said cautiously. "Pasture Pixies can be dangerous when they're angry and in large numbers."

"Okay, fine," Bellae said quickly before Sankari could offer a rude reply.

After cleaning everyone's wounds and breakfast of roots and berries, they walked until well past midday.

"If you tell me where you want to go, I can help," Viridi said.

"No!" Sankari said, glaring at Bellae and Lontas. "She shouldn't be allowed to come, but we're *not* telling her where we're going. I'm the only true member of the League—"

"League?" Viridi questioned.

"Another trick to get more information out of me!" Sankari replied.

"You brought it up!" Viridi said as Lontas raised his arm.

"Don't say it!" Sankari huffed.

"Sorry, with the deconditioning of being stuffed in crates for months and sore ankles, I need a break," Lontas said.

Bellae nodded, and they sat down in a large grass field.

Viridi abruptly flew upwards in alarm. It took several moments before the others heard a rumbling noise. Soon they could see a herd of four-legged, hooved animals fleeing across the plain. In front and on the sides were sheep-like animals with five horns while those in the middle were polled. Their fur was brown except on their chests, which were covered in black fur.

"Those are fimm-sau, horned sheep," Viridi said worriedly.

"Are they dangerous?"

"No. I'm worried about what they're running from."

"The ones in back are bloodied," Lontas said as the mass of animals roared past.

"Really?" Sankari said. "Never would have noticed the red splatters or gashing wounds."

"Oh no, oh no!" Viridi desperately looked around. "There's a large boulder about twenty yards to the east. Come quickly. Move or die!"

Something in her voice made them follow despite Sankari's protests. Bellae and Lontas eventually scrambled to the top of the rock, joining the Fairy and Pixie.

"Stay absolutely still, and hope it moves on," Viridi whispered, pointing to an enormous, extremely muscular black horse creeping through the field of tall grass.

"A tricorn horse?" Lontas breathed.

"It's a Cyrn-du," Viridi whispered. "Unicorn."

Lontas made an exaggerated motion of counting with his fingers while pointing. "One-two-three horns. Uni-means one. They're tricorns."

A large swirling horn sat on top of the horse's forehead while two fearsome, hooked horns sprouted from the sides of its head. Purple eyes shone with intensity above menacing fangs and below three insect-like appendages. Two antenna projections, one green and one a series of purplish hues, sat above a green feather-like protuberance. Hard scales sat in clusters down its nose and along its sides.

"Those aren't horns on the sides of its head," the Pasture Pixie said, shivering. "There's no more brutal creature in the world. They make the Stymphalian birds seem warm and cuddly."

Suddenly, the Cyrn-du reared up and let out a resonant roar, sounding more like a Southern Dwarf horn than an animal. Sankari covered her ears as the sound blasted outwards.

"What's it doing?" Lontas asked.

"Letting everyone know it's ready to fight," Viridi answered. "It must smell a threat."

"I think we should push the grassy menace off the edge and run. Let the tri-uni-sin-doo-doo thing eat her while we escape," Sankari said, glaring at the Pixie.

Viridi shook her head as the unicorn continued to march forward, its eyes darting for quarry only it could sense.

"As it moves closer, you'll see what you thought were horns on the side of its head are actually connected to tremendously muscular shoulders by spiked arms," Viridi said.

A series of bleating screeches punched the air as motion exploded all around the unicorn. Six brown creatures burst out of their hidden crouch in the grass. Two massive horns arched backwards off the tops of their heads while three sprouted from the tops of their snouts. The largest horn was red, matching their eyes. The front half looked like a beaked ibex with two front hooved legs while the back half was that of a large bird complete with wings and talons.

"What are they?" Sankari asked as the creatures continued shrieking.

"Ibexadharc," Viridi answered. "They usually surround the Stymphalian Swamp, and those two groups of vile creatures take turns eating each other, but something decreased the numbers of Stymphalian birds, forcing the Ibexadharc to expand out."

Three of the Ibexadharc took to the skies with mighty wing flaps while the other three performed a fluttering run towards the unicorn. As those in the air descended to attack the muscular horse from above, the Cyrn-du slashed with its spiked arms, which moved with lightning speed away from their tucked-in position next to its face. For the first time the League could clearly make out that while the horse had four standard hooved legs, it also had two jointed arms layered with sharp spikes that it kept tucked in by the sides of its head.

The Cyrn-du turned to those attacking on the ground. Its left barbed arm slashed at the closest Ibexadharc in an arc so fast it blurred. The black streak was quickly joined by a stream of spurting blood from the neck of the closest winged creature.

A second Ibexadharc charged with the massive red horn pointing menacingly forward. The unicorn swiftly moved to the side while chomping down on the top of the charging beast's head. The Cyrn-du's powerful jaws gashed into the skull as both its bladed arms stabbed into the Ibexadharc's lifeless body. With a violent twisting motion, the unicorn ripped the Ibexadharc's massive horn with such force it detached. Continuing his rotation, the unicorn slammed the disconnected red horn, complete with the top part of the skull raining blood, into the beakish snout of a third Ibexadharc. One of the three that had taken to the skies was diving straight for the unicorn. At the last moment, the Cyrn-du whirled around and brought both horned arms forward, easily decapitating the Ibexadharc.

"Ooh, super gross," Sankari said as blood burst out in a strobing red fan shape.

"Shhhhh!" Viridi admonished, shrinking against the rock. "If it sees us, we die."

The two remaining Ibexadharc circled above, gauging their odds, occasionally taking turns diving towards the massive horse but always pulling up. After several passes, the Cyrn-du jumped with spectacular power, catching the front hoof of one of the Ibexadharc with its spiked arms. The unicorn was scratched deeply several times by the creature's back talons, but as the horse landed, it repeatedly slammed the Ibexadharc against the ground, transforming it into a lifeless skin, fur,

Figure 7: A Cyrn-du battles a group of Ibexadharc.

and feather receptacle for a broken and bloodied medley. After giving a look of challenge to the last circling Ibexadharc, the unicorn proceeded to devour the battered creature.

"That's…aggressive eating," Lontas breathed as the Cyrn-du tore massive chunks of the dead creature complete with bits of flesh and blood being dispatched in considerable arcs.

Bellae closed her eyes. Pain radiating from the creatures prodded her stomach towards vomiting, and her head was pounding. *Please stop,* she begged the crystals.

Yes, we can make this stop. Just agree to take our power. You must be the one to control us if the world is to survive! Why do you resist the inevitable? You must take control.

Bellae covered her ears despite the voices being internal and shouted back in her mind. *There will be no controlling you!*

Na Cearcaill and its cycle of death can end if you relent!

"Better settle in and rest," Viridi said on their rocky ledge. "Cyrn-du eat a ton, and we can't go anywhere until it leaves."

Hidden in the distance, several Nishi watched hungrily, enjoying the blood bath and craving to torture their young prey. "We can't abuse her even a little?" one asked.

"We observe until the wretch collects the crystals, then she gets torn limb from limb."

"But slowly?"

"But slowly."

Scroll 17: Magic Potion Does What?

"Viridi was just talking to someone. She's a spy!" Sankari tantrumed the next day.

"She saved us twice already," Lontas said. "Bellae, you want to weigh in?"

Bellae's faraway focus slowly came back. "I think we should trust her…for now."

"She just happens to show up when we arrive and need her?" Sankari said before continuing to protest, but Bellae went back to battling the inner voices. She could feel Lontas shaking her arm but just wanted the voices silenced. *Three down, two to go,* she thought, wondering how much longer she could handle the near-constant prattling.

"It's okay to head out now. I scouted around, and other than the mess of flesh and splatters of blood left by the Cyrn-du, no sign of anything that wants to kill us," Viridi said.

Bellae restrained Sankari. "You can come, but we can't trust you with more than that."

A look of hurt flashed amongst the waving greenery around Viridi's face. "I just want to help. It's not like I have anywhere to be, or anyone to go home to."

Sankari sneered as Bellae gently squeezed the Pixie's hand. "Lontas, lead the way."

They avoided the blood-steeped land complete with rotting scraps and fleshy bits of hairy debris left from the unicorn's grotesque feast. Their nostrils were treated to the acid smell of death with a hefty dose of excitedly buzzing insects grubbing indulgently.

Bellae abruptly stopped, closing her eyes to concentrate. *What am I feeling?*

"What is it, Bellae?" Lontas asked.

"Something's wrong. I can sense something…" Her voice trailed off as the crystals within the bag began to pulse.

"Over here," Viridi whispered as they made their way to a small grove of trees. Peering through the other side, they could see several Dark Warriors surrounding a lone human male wearing the long kilt and suspenders with the collar of the Watchers.

"That guy doesn't look like a Watcher," Sankari said. "He looks human."

"Watcher?" Viridi wondered.

"Yeah, flaky psychopaths with four wings and magic," the Fairy said.

"Oh, XeraKirin. He doesn't now, but he will," Viridi replied.

"What does that mean?"

Viridi took a deep breath, blowing it out slowly as if the words to come would be painful. "Eons ago, legend says a group of animal talkers betrayed their kind and came here to live in LuvattuMaa, Ifrean to you, and follow Troldmanden—the White Wizard. Apparently they disagreed with their brethren who had a plan to steal some all-powerful crystals."

At this Lontas, Sankari, and Bellae exchanged anxious looks.

"Anyway, Troldmanden crushed up some lesser magical crystals they brought with them and made an elixir of that stuff with the promise of ultimate power and eternal life. A decent number of the immigrant animal talkers drank from the concoction. Most died. Those who survived morphed into XeraKirin, or Watchers as you say."

Bellae felt guilty about her ancestors—both the ones who double-crossed Veneficus and set up this quest, and the ones who apparently betrayed Verngaurd and came here.

"Legend is some animal talkers wanted a 'cleansing' cycle of purification while the majority of their brethren didn't," Viridi said. "I've heard tales about it—sounds bad."

"Na Cearcaill," Lontas breathed.

"That's it," Viridi said, her greenery vibrating anxiously. "Never-ending cycle of death."

"Blasted Ainmhi Caint! All of this is you and your ancestors' fault!" Sankari said angrily.

"That's unfair," Lontas defended. "Bellae didn't have anything to do with stuff thousands and thousands of years ago and certainly didn't choose any of this."

While Sankari continued to rant, Bellae squeezed his hand and closed her eyes, fighting against the sickly-sweet promises of power from the crystals. Their phrases crashed against the script of contrition about her ancestors. *Were they good or bad? Heroes of villains? They stole from Veneficus and put the world in danger. But the ones who went against the makers of this quest collaborated with the horrible White Wizard. Can they both be wrong? Both right?* Her eyes snapped open as a portal abruptly opened, and the White Wizard casually stepped through.

"There are spies all around Ifrean, looking for animal talkers or those with any hint of magic," Viridi said. "Once discovered, they go through testing and if they have the gift, the White Wizard 'lets' them drink the elixir and become a XeraKirin. By 'let' I mean they do or they, and their entire family, die in horrible agony. Troldmanden is saying these crystals were recovered after the great victory over the red scum at Castle Liberum."

The White Wizard took a vial out of his long leather overcoat and handed it to the man who drank with greedy certainty. The Dark Warriors stepped back while the White Wizard rubbed his scruffy beard. His eyes suddenly flashed up, and Bellae swore he was staring directly at her even though they were hidden within the shade of trees.

"He's looking right at us!" Lontas said, his voice twitching.

"I'm sure he can't see us. Watch. Sometimes they explode, blue magic and red blood splattering out as their flesh is annihilated. However, sometimes they—" Viridi was cut off by the man falling harshly backwards to the ground. "Do that."

His body began thrashing violently, at first in broad, swinging motions, but soon the shaking evolved into tight vibrations. The pitiless quivering started to blur as he began a horrific, inhuman scream that resonated out, quivering in tune with his shuddering. Some of the Dark Warriors laughed while the White Wizard smiled.

"Why are there just men Watchers, er... XeraKirin?" Lontas asked.

Viridi looked at him as if it were obvious. "I thought you'd know."

"How, exactly, would we know?" Sankari said.

"Well, the Ainmhi Caint are from Verngaurd, and Bellae's obviously one of them," Viridi answered as Lontas restrained Sankari. "Anyway, every female who drinks the elixir impressively blows up. Like, anyone in a hundred-foot radius gets splattered! It's super cool."

In response to their looks of horror the Pixie said, "What? It's not like I had anything to do with it. Troldmanden occasionally tries to turn a female, but they go boom! Some think women animal talkers are too weak. Others," she looked at Bellae, "believe it means they are infinitely more powerful than the men. Okay, now the Dark Warriors are saying this one will live, and they wish he would have exploded. See, even they like to see people blow up."

"Sometimes they speak in the common tongue of Verngaurd," Lontas said.

Viridi nodded. "Every human here learns both languages. Troldmanden demands it for when they conquer Verngaurd."

"No way will they beat us!" Lontas said, but even as the words sweated from his mouth, a tinge of doubt amalgamated with panic at the possibility.

Viridi looked at him as if he were dense. "I heard rumors you're killing off the best of your soldiers on your own?"

Bellae nodded.

"I'm not sure you realize quite how large Troldmanden's armies are."

"Turn the wretch over," the White Wizard said. "Prepare him for the gift of flight!"

The Dark Warriors picked up long wooden tools covered in leather that were a cross between a shovel and pitchfork. They strenuously worked to flip him over, his violent thrashings frenziedly working against them. Once tipped onto his stomach, the White Wizard added a few drops of magical liquid to his back and chanted. The man's entire body exploded in blue flames. His back began to morph into something horrific. Bulging projections began punching upwards in fits of flesh-stretching pain. His terrifying scream mutated into a bawling shriek.

As the nubbins violently grew from his back, his skin turned into a dusty, black coal that covered him head to toe. The murky powder seemed to solidify just as the four wings took shape—stopping the quivering and howls of pain. The White Wizard walked to the statue-like body, then abruptly began kicking it. Each blow sent a cloud of black dust showering out in tune with a muffled whimper. Soon the Dark Warriors crowded around, joining in the brutal strikes.

"There's always pain when one transforms," the White Wizard shouted, turning towards the trees where the League huddled.

"Okay, we're out of here," Sankari said, tugging on Lontas and Bellae.

Just then, a harsh gurgling sound was followed by a shriek, sending the Dark Warriors scattering away. The newly forged Watcher rose and aggressively fluttered his four wings. Any remaining black dust shivered away, revealing the desert-like brown skin interrupted only by rivers of flowing blue magic.

"Move, now!" Sankari said just as the Watcher turned, hissing at them.

The blue coursing through gullies within his desiccated skin flowed up into his eyes, leaving scorched darker brown gulches within his parched and sandy skin. As the others ran, Bellae could hear the Wizard's voice in her head. *See you when this is over! You shall suffer a death worse than any before, and I shall have my crystals.* Lontas grabbed Bellae and pulled her backwards. After fleeing for a long time, they huffed to a stop.

"I have no idea where we are," Lontas said.

"What a shocker," Sankari hissed. "We haven't known where we are, much less where we're going, since the rock rats attacked us."

"Viridi, would you please help?" Bellae asked as Sankari's face flushed with anger.

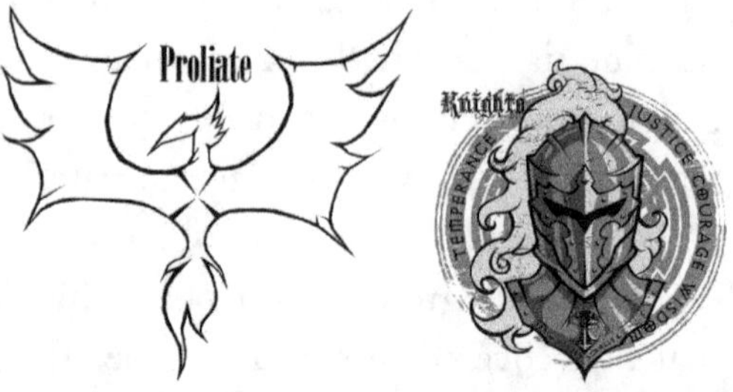

Scroll 18: They Shall Remember

"Welcome, Veli Pingius!" Friar cheerfully greeted the Knights from Toil Shaor as they entered the Citadel, having been shielded with prestidigitation by the Southern Dwarves.

The normally jovial Veli grunted. "We just abandoned our last castle. Doesn't seem like the time to be chipper."

"On the contrary," Friar answered. "All of Verngaurd is finally coming together to fight the oppression of the White Wizard and the Dark Warriors. I think there's no better time to be optimistic. The future looks brighter now than when we were here for the Tournament. After being blinded by their deceit, all the inhabitants of Verngaurd finally see the treachery of the White Wizard. We're no longer being led around."

When Pingius did not answer, Friar asked, "Did you have any losses?"

"Thankfully, none," Pingius said. "The Southern Dwarves did a great job."

"As soon as you're settled in the Xenia, come to the coliseum for training. Your men are in for the exercising of their lives."

Pingius looked up with a fierceness Friar had never seen. "The Dark Warriors will soon learn the price for invading our lands."

"As per your plan, Ritari has been directing the nighttime supply drops into Aon Intinn," Storlax explained. "I have to admit, I don't mind flying supplies and materials in and men out. However, the next phase of your plan has me nervous."

"We did something similar with Liberum when we left for Trepas," Friar said.

Storlax nodded but grimaced, the reference dredging up painful memories.

"They're going great since you gave us the idea of using griffins for drops and dragons for cover. Wyvern don't like battling Vioma or Saatana. The Northern Dwarves are reporting few losses," Lidenskap said. "The walls of Temple Aon Intinn are still surrounded by Dark Warriors. The good news is the fortifications are holding up against the barrage of attacks. The temples on the Proliate Islands are also surviving."

"You need to persevere for another eight weeks for our plan to take shape," Friar stated.

"Better make it six," Lidenskap said. "The Dark Warriors are fanatical. It's almost like they want to die. That said, I'm stunned at the ferocity of the Piscinians and Emperor Fanga."

"Impressive job, that's for sure. The Dark Warriors' new strategy of focusing massive troops to overwhelm a few targets at a time will play into our hands nicely."

Lidenskap grimaced critically. "Is throwing all of our resources into one battle wise?"

Friar smiled. "My brain works best when my troops are outnumbered and in need of desperate victory."

Remembering the horrors of Ovest and Trepas, Lidenskap nodded. "You do scare me."

"Ah, but it is the Dark Warriors who should be afraid."

"Where're you coming back from this time?" Ritari asked. "You were gone a long time."

"This one's a surprise! Wait, that's Veli Pingius?" Friar asked, almost stumbling.

"Yep," Lovag said.

"He's lost…" Friar started.

"Three-fourths of himself," Ritari finished.

Loose skin, reluctant in responding to weight loss, jangled back and forth, alone and desperate to find its long-lost adipose companion. The rest of his body was muscular and his step light. "I feel like gravity has loosened its hold upon me!" Pingius said, his smile back. "What? Don't recognize me without my dirty cloak?" he said, running his hand over glistening armor.

"Yeah, that's it," Friar said, warmly embracing him. "Ritari and Lovag, get to training, I'd like to talk to my favorite Veli."

"Your *only* Veli, and castle-less at that."

Friar looked down, shaking his head. "This is true, but I still hold hope." He looked up at the well-armored and drilled army formerly of Toil Shaor. "That's quite the transformation."

Veli Pingius' face fell.

"I meant it as a compliment. Your Knights look as good as any I've seen."

Pingius looked to his hard-training Knights. "Perhaps it's me, or maybe it's a universal trait, but until threatened, it's hard to appreciate something's full value. Only once my status as a Veli and my Knights were about to be taken away did I recognize the significance of them. After giving up our last castle and barely making it to the Citadel, I vowed to be appreciatory of each Knight, each day, each person I meet."

"That's as good a bit of life advice as one could hope to give or get," Friar said. "During my days of torture, I had a lot of time to think about life and what we're doing. Is there a path to peace for us, or must we understand peace as a choice? Is there a journey that will lead you to happiness, or is it a choice to be happy with your journey?"

With tears sprouting in the corners of his eyes Pingius put his hand on Friar's shoulder. "I took so much for granted. Am I the reason the Knights failed?"

"Blame has no shortage of people and decisions it can alight upon, including me. We need to let the past be and move forward," Friar said.

"There's so much I would go back and change if I could."

"We all carry the burden, and perhaps scars, of our past decisions, actions, inactions, but that does not mean we need to be defined by them, or let them define our future."

Pingius looked down in thought before his eyes met Friar's. "I always tried to be the nice guy, the friend, and it was stressful on my waistline. Now I'm the tough guy. I realize that preparation and discipline are really ways to show you care. I appreciate we're the last, and for the first time in many centuries, the Knights could cease to exist. I can't promise whether we'll win or lose, but I can assure you we'll hit them hard enough they shall remember the Knights."

Scroll 19: What Choice?

"You can lead us to the sinkhole in this sewage-land?" Sankari asked, glaring angrily at Viridi the next morning while marching on a small hill through tall grass and wildflowers.

The Pixie murmured under her breath, "Yes, for the hundredth time." Out loud she added, "Definitely. We're coming up on a village, we should skirt—"

"It looks busy," Lontas interrupted.

Several large boulders sat outside the village, and Bellae felt magnetically drawn to them. Sankari tugged on Lontas' shirt before she and Viridi flew towards Bellae while he jogged.

"What are you thinking?" Viridi whispered.

Before Bellae could reply, a Dark Warrior began shouting to gathered villagers.

"He's saying the perverted beasts ruled by the evil Blue Wizard are preparing an attack," Viridi translated, swatting her hand towards Sankari before she could explode at the inaccuracy. "I'm only translating. Alright, he's announcing the ruthless hordes from across the Great Ocean will soon attack and…must move up the draft age."

"I didn't think I could hate these people more!" Sankari huffed.

Viridi shook her head before continuing, "Volunteering their children guarantees Vartija status, those you call Dark Warriors—but if they're forcibly taken, they're trained as Tumma Vartija or the Horde."

Several kids who had been playing outside the village startled at a Dark Warrior's yelling. Tearfully they ran back to wooden houses and structures that were well built in a "V" formation with one end leading to a large well and the other opening to a series of cooking sheds.

"He's telling the children the time for crying will come soon enough," Viridi translated.

Stop this injustice! the crystals chided. *How many have to die before you listen!* Closing her eyes, Bellae felt her exhaustion steaming into anger. *Why did my ancestors steal the crystals? Why did some work with the White Wizard?* Bellae could feel the rage building and her determination to quiet them exploding. Taking several deep breaths, she rejoiced in a moment of silence. Lontas was gently shaking her when she finally opened her eyes. Enjoying the hushed tranquility, she watched his lips move.

Slowly, sound returned. "…but I think you did," Lontas finished.

"Did what?"

"I think you had a seizure. You were totally out of it."

"I was just enjoying a moment of peace," Bellae said, turning to the village.

A child was sprinting towards the rocks where they were hiding.

"There's nowhere to run without being seen," Sankari said angrily. "Nice job, Bellae!"

A Watcher they had not perceived before suddenly flew forward, carrying the boy's mother, landing in front of the fleeing child. The boy fell to his knees, sobbing hard enough to agitate his entire body. His head lopped forward, tripoding on the earth as his mother, also weeping, knelt to comfort him. The Watcher jabbed one of his claws into the back of her neck, racking down, sketching a line with her blood as cloth and skin parted like a wave.

Without looking at the four-winged creature, she wiped her eyes, suppressed the pain, and began talking soothingly.

"She's telling him he can do this and she's proud of him," Viridi said as the mother spoke in the halting language of Ifrean.

Lontas looked down. "I always just thought of them as monsters, not little kids."

"Yeah, and not forced into it," Bellae added.

"Monsters are made, not born," Viridi added with a shudder before continuing to translate. "The boy's saying he wants to stay home with her."

"Speak in the tongue of the land of the blue devil," the Watcher said, turning towards the rocks where the League quickly ducked down.

"You'll go straight to the Paradise? You and Dad, if I learn to fight well?" the boy asked.

"Of course. We're so proud of you," the mother said. She forced a smile, but it was weighed down by consummate grief and fettered by doubt which pulled at the veracity of the words she tried so hard to make sound convincing, willing the boy to get up.

"You go learn to fight for our Sovereign in White, but you come back to me," she said, tears coating her already drenched eyes. She embraced her son, using her sleeve to wipe away the wet manifestation of her sadness.

The boy slowly rose, and they walked back to the others as groups of children, most younger than seven, were herded into cramped buggies, little more than cages with wheels. The parents gathered around and waved, trying to keep their emotions in check. It was only once the Dark Warriors and Watcher escort disappeared from view the parents collapsed into despair.

"Psychos," Sankari said.

"You think those kids or parents have a choice?" Viridi asked, sympathy coating her words. "You so easily condemn the Dark Warriors, but what's their alternative when they're plucked from their homes as children and beaten repeatedly on the forge of violence while believing if they perform well, their family will be transported to Paradise, a land of plenty, where they never have to work and live in luxury?"

"Uh, people believe that load of rubbish?" Sankari asked.

Viridi looked at the emotionally devastated mothers and fathers. "I'm not sure what percentage believe, but I think the dream of the possible, the longing for hope, lets them get up in the morning and be able to send their children off to savagely fight and brutally die."

Scroll 20: People Trees

"Do you think the cretin children are actively avoiding the sinkhole?" a hidden Nishi growled the next day. "Seriously, they've walked around it like four times!"

"Their incompetence makes me hate them more. Consume that rage. Let it build for when we capture and torture them."

"We should've run into the sinkhole," Lontas said, unaware of the watching specters.

"I agree," Bellae added, trying to avoid a sarcastic comment from the irritable Sankari. "Maybe we backtrack towards that last big rock then change course?"

"I think we're too far south." Lontas sighed. "You shouldn't have run Viridi off."

"It's her fault, entirely, completely, absolutely, undoubtedly!" Sankari snapped. "Wait, I see something." The Fairy fluttered forward, using the terrain, a mix of trees and bushes surrounded by copious wildflowers. Sankari suddenly flew in panicked circles before diving behind a hedge, gesturing wildly.

"I think she wants us to follow," Lontas commented.

As they began walking, her motions became more erratic, so they began jogging. When closer, they could hear shouting and quickly ducked behind the large thicket with Sankari.

"I was telling you *not* to come!" she whispered angrily.

Bellae mouthed "sorry" before asking, "Why are they screaming… at trees?" As she consciously said the words, she knew the reality was too horrible to comprehend.

"Those aren't trees," Sankari added, tears flowing down her cheeks.

Without asking Bellae weaved her way forward, staying behind cover—the other two reluctantly following. Once closer they could clearly see on the other side of a clearing, mixed within a normal-appearing forest, were a large number of unusual structures lined up in a row with several Dark Warriors walking around them yelling.

"You think you're more important than Troldmanden?" a Dark Warrior asked. "You like to slack off? Well, just lie on back and relax. Spin 'em!"

The reality of what they were seeing sharpened, realizing the structures were windmills. A different member of a family was tied to each of the blades or sails. Soldiers were frantically turning cranks, and the windmills began spinning violently.

"Troldmanden told you to build a road from here to Dunmharu *and* get the grain ready for our troops battling to keep us safe from hordes of child-eating fanatics from across the sea."

"Let me off. Please, I'm pregnant and getting sick!" a woman yelled.

"Did you hear that disrespect?" the leader asked. "I'm trying to give a speech ordered by the Sovereign in White, and I get interrupted? Torch it."

Flaming arrows flew to the windmill with the pregnant woman. The whir of the arrows thudded to a stop, quickly followed by gurgled cries. Bellae struggled, her mind ablaze with millions of whispers from the crystals overlapping to create chaos in her brain. *Save them! Don't wait until you have all five sets. Unleash our power upon those wicked men! Take us out of this prison and liberate our influence through you! You can safeguard the world.* Bellae's eyes turned white, and her body began thrashing.

"What's wrong with her?" Sankari asked, fluttering with a mix of concern and fear.

"I don't know. I don't know," Lontas kept repeating while trying to support her head and keep her from injuring herself through the convulsions. Once she stopped, Lontas' voice gradually wormed through. "Come back, Bellae. It's okay. I've got you."

Bellae's eyes slowly returned to normal, but she continued violently struggling. She knew the voices in her mind were correct—she could use them to stop the madness. *But at what price?*

"They've seen us!" Sankari said.

"Behind those bushes, get them!" the leader shouted. "Bring them here to join this party!"

"They're coming!" Sankari yelled.

"We have to run!" Lontas said. Bellae slowly focused, eventually getting up and running. After their confinement on the ship, all three were tiring quickly, and the soldiers were gaining.

"Did you miss me?" Viridi said, appearing in front of them, the vegetation around her body vibrating frantically. "If you want to live, follow me to that crop of trees!"

Once within the copse, Viridi veered north, weaving her way through the large trunks. The vines from her body were flagellating along the leaves and branches of the forest, occasionally briefly embracing them.

The Pixie led them around a hillock. "Somewhere just beyond these trees is the sinkhole you seek."

"Thanks for coming back," Bellae said, hearing the Dark Warriors gaining.

"You would have been here long ago if you had let me help," the Pasture Pixie said.

Before Bellae could reply, a Nishi appeared right in front of her.

"Each footfall forward is one step closer to your DEATH!" the apparition declared, the last word a scream, its mouth opening widely, revealing a twitching tongue and filed teeth.

Bellae moved to the side, but it floated over. "Keep on going! That's it! Get the crystals for *us*. Fetch them like a good, grubby pet before you die! Like animals being led to slaughter, move forward, child!" Before she could say anything else, Lontas rushed forward, slamming his talisman from Trelos into the specter's fanged face. With a profane howl the Nishi disappeared.

"Those things never get old," Sankari huffed. "Seriously, always a joy to see."

"Move! We have to stay ahead of them!" Viridi yelled, flying back.

They continued weaving their way through the forest as quickly as possible as Viridi flew in the rear, scouting for their attackers.

"How much—" Lontas started, but the ground dropped out from underneath them.

Sankari soared back to Viridi, her sword flashing menacingly. "You led us into a trap!"

"I didn't! That's the sinkhole you seek," Viridi pleaded as Lontas and Bellae fell through a large, almond-shaped chasm. "Fly down and join them. I'll lead the Dark Warriors away."

As they fell, Lontas and Bellae bounced off thick brown vines crisscrossing over the concealed opening. With each collision the vines tensed in exasperation before rebounding, sending the children bounding away only to bitterly vibrate at the intrusion. After falling in fragmented sections for several moments, they splashed into pale blue water. Bellae frantically confirmed Grym was okay and that the crystals were safe.

"I guess we found it?" Bellae said, treading water.

"Careful what you wish for," Lontas added.

Looking up through the latticework of vines, they could see beams of sunlight fighting their way through the congested web of vegetation which masked most of the sinkhole's opening. There were numerous trees surrounding the eye-shaped aperture engaging in a slow-motion race for sunlight, fighting to nudge their branches and leaves past their competition for precious territory in an imperceptibly sedate dancing brawl.

Sankari came streaking through one of the small apertures. "Wow, this is definitely *not* a trap! If only I'd warned you about that weed! We're surrounded by a sheer wall of rocky cliffs!"

"Don't panic," Bellae said, as much to calm herself as the others as they gazed up at the precipitous stone barrier rising around them.

"Swim to that ledge," Lontas said. As they moved closer, they realized there was a good-sized stone overhang perching over a ridge for them to hide under. Once on the small rocky shelf, Lontas whispered, "Quiet."

Soldiers were shouting above as they tried to calm their breathing. Several moments later, thankfully, the yelling moved away. Despite the wet rock, Sankari instantly fell asleep, still clutching her peccary sword and occasionally muttering warnings to the absent Viridi.

Lontas' eyes were heavy as he looked at her, managing to conjure a weak smile. Bellae crept over and let her head fall against his shoulder as Grym twisted to find a comfortable place on her chest. Exhaustion had rooted in so deeply it was paradoxical fighting against sleep.

Bellae's hand wriggled over to engulf Lontas' and squeeze. "I miss Arend, Kainen, Scelto, and Gimelli, but it's always been the two of us—it's always been me and you."

"I can't remember anything before us. It's funny how time blunts the sharp edges of life's experiences and smooths the rough borders of pain so that the negative parts of memories don't seem so bad the further we journey away from the events. I was thinking of the River Vita Monster and Squire Battle. Those were terrifying, but when I look back, I miss Liberum, our adventures, the library, Finn. Then my tripping and being bullied were the biggest problems—not creatures of lore, life-and-death situations, and the small issue of the fate of the world."

Bellae squeezed his hand tighter. "We long for those past times because we can never go back, never experience them again."

"Maybe that's why transitions are so hard. I guess we can only see through the 'us' of the now. If we went back, we would see things differently, and appreciate those things better."

Bellae sighed deeply. "I need to tell you something."

"Okay."

"There are voices almost constantly haunting me from the crystals," Bellae said before proceeding to explain their persistent haranguing. After a moment of silence, she twisted her neck to see if Lontas had fallen asleep only to find him staring ahead in concentration. She slumped back down and let him process the information.

"I could tell something was going on. That's what happens when your eyes turn white?" Lontas asked. "You're conversing and somehow siphoning their power?"

"Even when they're not white. They're constantly begging me to use their power."

Lontas shook his head. "The fact that they are incessantly calling to you seems like a warning. They hold too much power. I think they're trying to wear you down."

"What if I *could* use them to help people? Maybe that's an option."

Lontas sat up and looked at her. "We, and remember it's we, need to be careful. I think the Ainmhi Caint knew that the Macht Crystals hold inordinate, otherworldly power. Way too potent for anyone to control. It would eventually begin to take over and dominate you."

"You think I couldn't handle it?" Bellae asked, feeling hurt as the crystals prodded her anger internally.

"I trust you, but not the crystals. They have too much power, and I don't want to lose you. Don't let these crystals change us or you. My story is your story. Your story is mine. Together our tale is woven in the time of our hours, days, weeks, months, years of experiences. If the crystals and their power are driving a wedge between us, that's another red flag."

"Sometimes I just want to say yes to the crystals and have this end."

Lontas nodded. "I get that. Desire's a funny thing. If it's for riches, passion, or drink, it easily slides into hedonism. If it's for learning, success, to improve the world, it is hard work and aspiration."

"The target matters."

"Exactly. The goal matters. Whether it's earned or given makes a difference. If it's a quick and easy pleasure or a hard-fought, uphill endeavor matters. I think it's a balancing act, and easy to be pushed off into the quicksand of indulgence and intemperance, where you lose self-restraint, and in so doing, lose yourself. There's a reason that for millennia the Knights have had temperance as part of their code."

"I'm so glad you're with me. I couldn't do this without you. Your brain, your heart."

"You and me."

"You and me."

"After all we've had to endure…it's just the beginning," Lontas said. "I can't see any ending that isn't serious trouble. These Macht Crystals are unlimited power, and anytime such things exist there will be vast numbers seeking to control them and dominate the world."

The reality she was forced to bear and the stress of the ordeals they endured began to boil within her. Tears that desperately desired to be set free were held back, kept down under the gravity of fatigue and anxiety. "I'm most worried about the 'big two.'"

"Veneficus and the White Wizard," Lontas answered, rubbing his temples as a headache blared. "With the elaborate quest your ancestors laid out, I can only hope they have a solution at the end—a way out of this mess."

Scroll 21: Down There

Angry shrieks woke Lontas up. He had slept so soundly the entire left side of his body felt cold and numb. He flopped onto his back where he battled to shake out the pins and needles.

"The Dark Warriors are back," Bellae whispered.

"The voices are getting closer," Lontas said. "The bottom part said: Dive down…head north, through the stalagmite crown. Rise up and breathe, for your test."

"We need to hurry," Sankari warned. "I can now make out what they're saying."

"This is the north side of the cenote," Lontas said confidently. "There must be a hidden tunnel that we need to dive down and find."

"Are those brats down there?" a voice above asked.

"I don't think so. We were right behind them and didn't hear a splash as we passed," another replied. "We chased a green Pixie for quite a while but never caught it."

Holding his finger up for them stay quiet, Lontas gently lowered himself into the water. After taking a large breath, he dove down. After going down and up several times, he said, "There are many small crevices and openings, but they don't lead anywhere."

"I hear something down there!" a voice yelled. "Sir, come back."

Lontas' eyes shot open in fear of the Dark Warriors and disgust at how loudly he had spoken. With newfound motivation he dove again. He came up, shaking his head.

"Lower the lines!" the leader shouted. "Bring them up alive!"

Lontas plunged under. He shot up just as a dozen ropes snaked through the net of vines into the water. "I think I found it."

"This isn't something you just *think*," Sankari said. "If you're wrong, we die!"

"If we stay here, we absolutely die," Bellae said, sliding into the water.

"Call up when you reach the bottom," the leader shouted as sounds of warriors climbing down the ropes grew louder.

Bellae gently cradled Grym and her bag as Sankari reluctantly joined them in the water. "I'm not some dimwitted spriggan. My wings aren't meant for water."

"Take a good breath. It looks like a long way."

"You didn't swim through?" Sankari questioned.

"No," Lontas replied truthfully. "But I did see a faint light at the end…I think."

"Oh, you think? You think?" Sankari said too loudly.

"That's them! Move, move!"

As the League took deep breaths, the boots of Dark Warriors slunk down, now visible, pushing away the meshwork of vegetation above. As they went deeper, the water greedily swallowed light, voraciously transforming into green gloom as several spears veered off course around them—eventually stalling into a soft freefall as frantic air bubbles angrily rumbled towards the surface. Sankari tucked her wings back but was struggling. Lontas, thinking of *the stalagmite crown*, pointed to an oval aperture with columns pointing up like a diadem.

Sankari shook her head, bubbles of lifegiving air screaming out of her mouth as terror enlarged her eyes. Lontas grabbed and boosted her through the opening. The enveloping darkness blurred into the cave walls, and they blindly swam forward.

Finally, a whisper of hope emerged—the hint of light at the end of the tunnel that stretched cruelly long. The oxygen bubbles, escaping in decreasing numbers, floated to the top of the tunnel, bouncing in agitation before settling into black crevice tombs. Aching pain in their muscles at paddling was surpassed by the burning hunger spreading wildly through their starving lungs. As the last of their air departed, both body and mind screamed for oxygen. The swiping motion of their arms began to slow as the faint gleam ahead leisurely grew in tune with the flourishing lightheadedness in their brains.

Use our power! the crystals called out within Bellae's mind. *Otherwise, you die!*

Sankari's head dipped lower as her arms twitched more than pulled her body forward, her wings ineptly thrashing. Lontas grabbed and pushed her forward, then took turns with Bellae to keep her momentum flowing. As desperation flared, the opening materialized. Lontas thrust Sankari's limp body forward before he and Bellae squeezed through a circular opening. Pushing off with their feet, they struggled to rise, ravenous for air. They fought through the dense water before suddenly popping through a thin, cloudy layer which, in turn, led to crystal clear water. The translucent water instantly felt different. They ascended through the clearer fresh water before finally escaping into air, immediately gasping violently. As soon as he was able, Lontas held up Sankari's limp body, slapping her back.

She's going to die unless you unleash our power! the crystals sang to Bellae, who was fiercely sucking in air. Eventually, the Fairy sputtered, spitting out water, coughing, gagging, and inhaling rabidly when her body's spasms permitted. When their lungs started to relax, they took stock of their surroundings. It was a large cavern with strands of leafless vines hanging in strewn disarray from the ceiling. Several small circles of light shone down on the middle of the pool, each ray ringed with trickles of water. A small ledge and cave were visible. Several anemic plants grew on the shelf, awkwardly lurching towards the light falling from holes above. The three slowly worked their way to dry ground. When the searing burn within their lungs faded to a dull irritation, the three League members lay back and rested in daydreaming pseudo-sleep.

Chapter Four

Battle of Châlons

Scroll 1: Whispered Machinations

Jumeaux waved from one of the cave entrances, relieved to have Veneficus flying off on a griffin. As the magically created rock wall used to seal the gateway rematerialized, he turned into the stuffy, torchlit cavern, nearly running into Fino.

"Sorry," Jumeaux said, gazing cautiously at the troubled-looking Magician. The bags beneath his drawn face seemed deeper.

"Veneficus off again?" Fino asked, seeming to suck in his already gaunt cheeks.

"Yeah, just."

"Do you wonder where he flies off to and what his ultimate goal is?"

"He wants what all Magicians want, to get the Macht Crystals and save Verngaurd."

Fino scoffed. "I've always held you in high regard. I hope my faith's not misplaced. Veneficus looks out for one person only and always—himself. His only goal is to keep power. I, like others, feel he has ruled long enough. Don't you agree?"

Jumeaux hesitated, taken aback by the question—the idea of standing up to Veneficus unthinkably absurd. *Is this a trap?* he wondered.

Fino put one hand on Jumeaux's shoulder while raising the former squire's chin with the other. "You're smart, having the foresight to abandon your family, leaving the doomed Knights. So, you recognize when switching allegiances keeps you on top of the rabble. That survival instinct will serve you well. Victory often goes to those who know when to switch sides."

"I'm not betraying him," Jumeaux said, still wondering if this was a test despite the resolve in Fino's eyes.

"Betrayal's a cheap word used by feeble minds on the losing side to describe those who end up winning."

I didn't betray my family, the Knights? Jumeaux wondered, the words gliding across his thoughts as a query, not a declaration.

"Many are sick of the tyranny that is Veneficus' rule. The rumbles began with the creation of the Academy of Magic, which was supposed to help smoke out the Chosen One but only served to dilute our power and waste the increasingly scarce mindre crystals, which led, foreseeably, to its closure and our vulnerable position. Look how few Magicians were allowed to travel with him, and how many were simply thrown out. Now we're scattered to the wind and humiliatingly weak, and it's time for change. The attainment of the Macht Crystals, which you've been instrumental in acquiring, is a chance for a new beginning. Remember at the Tournament when the Knights' weapons were checked for enchantments?"

Jumeaux nodded, cobwebs falling off his memories.

"Veneficus requested I be in the back of the chamber when the weapons from Liberum were checked. Then later I get blamed for sabotaging the Knights, and my good friend Veneficus ends up interrogating *me* with truth spells! Tells me to be there then blames me!"

"Did Veneficus sabotage the weapons?"

"Unlikley. He seemed very upset. In fact, he later told me I was there to help watch out for the White Wizard or the traitorous Tacet-Vand, as he suspected they would attempt something. He said he had to interrogate me to make it look 'official' to the Knights since Finn died. Bottom line, Veneficus looks out for Veneficus."

Several Magicians walked into the corridor. Seeing Fino and Jumeaux, they stopped, glaring at them. Jumeaux could feel the sweat jolting onto his forehead as his robes suddenly felt heavy and restricting. He looked down. *I can never betray him—he's too powerful.*

"I must go," Fino said. "I know we can depend on you when the time comes."

Do they think I betrayed them? Jumeaux wondered, thinking of his sisters, fellow squires, and Knights. He leaned against the side of the cavern, his throat feeling constricted. It felt hard to breathe. *I have no friends, thanks to treachery—both given and received.*

Scroll 2: Adolescent Odor Congealing

"Are you sure?" Kainen whispered.

Arend sighed in frustration, being cooped up in a cave for six months was not helping their camaraderie.

"Okay, so I'm thinking that the huffing and eye rolling mean you're sure the Dark Warriors retreated," Kainen uttered, looking to Gimelli, but she shrugged her shoulders.

Scelto was busy doing pushups, feeling increasingly claustrophobic in their cave.

"Actually," Gimelli finally said, "the smell of three boys is ripening aggressively. We should get of here."

"Come to the ridge and see," Arend encouraged.

Silently, all four made their way up the beach to a small knoll overlooking Haavi.

"That's a lot of fires," Gimelli said dejectedly.

"Yeah, when I scouted, the Dark Warriors were torching any areas of the city they controlled before pulling out. The majority of their troops, including Nishi and Watchers, moved north, likely to attack Pescare or even Taiheart," Arend said before tensing. "Get down!"

"What?" Kainen asked as Scelto put his hand on his sword.

Before Arend could answer, shouting and shrieks echoed towards them.

"Dark Warriors," Scelto seethed, drawing his sword. "Don't care what you're going to say. Not worried about being discovered. Not bothered by the fact you'll be mad at me. I'm sick of being trapped except for scavenging and guard duty. I'm going to kill them all."

As Scelto sprinted towards a group of twenty Dark Warriors, Arend nodded in appreciation of his words before hungrily taking to the sky.

Gimelli unslung her bow while shaking her head. "I guess we're done hiding."

Kainen was up, deftly moving with an arrow already nocked. "Let's flank them while those two oafs charge straight ahead."

"We don't retreat!" a Dark Warrior yelled. "What will the White Wizard think?"

"Not retreating, heading to our next objective in the north."

"This isn't north!" a third answered. "We turn and fight!"

At that moment, Arend let out a loud squawk from above.

"How did they get in front of us?" the first Dark Warrior asked as they came to a stop.

Arend continued screeching to distract them as Scelto stormed into their disorganized line. His first sword strike cut down diagonally, nearly severing the head and cutting deeply into the soldier's chest. As that warrior fell and the others were turning, he withdrew and slashed to his right, decapitating a second. With his left hand Scelto took out his dagger and slammed it into the face of a third, letting it fall, imbedded in the dead fighter, while grasping his sword with two hands. Arrows began flooding into the Dark Warriors from the side as Kainen and Gimelli took up position. At the same time, Arend dropped down. Using his sharp talons, he ripped two soldiers upwards, his claws piercing deeply into their carotid arteries before he tossed them into other warriors, knocking them off balance and immersing them in the rapidly evacuating blood.

As the Dark Warriors were starting to regroup, dozens of Elven warriors descended from the north. After firing arrows, downing most of the remaining enemy, they switched to kama weapons and with several swings found themselves face to face with Scelto and Arend.

"Reckless!" Ailante shouted, pushing through his warriors.

Kainen and Gimelli joined the tattered League members staring at a wall of angry Elves.

"We had a scouting report," Scelto said, nodding to Arend. "Everything was under control." Seeing the Elf leader bristle, he added, "However, we appreciate your assistance."

"Follow us," Ailante said before spinning towards Haavi.

They walked in awkward silence until the smoke and heat from the burning parts of the city were palpable, eventually arriving at a camp on the southern edge of the city ablaze. With a quick motion Ailante directed his warriors to take up guard duty next to several Piscinians. Reluctantly, the League members followed Ailante into the noisy, heavily protected tent. Emperor Fanga was pounding a table as if it had offended his mother while shouting at the largest Eaglian they had ever seen. The ruler stopped abusing the furniture once he noticed Ailante and the children enter, but the anger remained firmly bonded to his face.

"Ah, I see the other members of Verngaurd have finally sent a formidable army to our assistance!" Fanga growled. "Four children? If only they'd arrived earlier, maybe over half of Piscium would not be razed to the ground!"

"We're all battling our own struggles, Emperor," Ailante said calmly. "These are the League members I was sent, along with Ollmhór," he pointed to the massive Eaglian, "to find. As I mentioned earlier, Eaglian scouts caught sight of Arend, and we wanted to see if the children needed help. The prophecy is at hand, and once we recover the crystals, we shall have the power to rebuild all of Verngaurd, including Piscium!"

Fanga scoffed. "Those rumors? My father's father spoke of such things, and I imagine I shall glean as much worth from them as he did—exactly nothing! The people of Piscium need immediate assistance of arms, food, and supplies, not fantasies, wishes, and prayers!"

Ailante took a deep breath, his demeanor and voice remaining calm. "It's easy to doubt, it is hard to believe, but soon we shall have the power of the Macht Crystals, control all magic, the ability to repair, replace, and heal while assuring final victory over the Ifreanean attackers."

"What's this *we* stuff?" Arend said. "The prophecy clearly states the League of Truth, you know, the guardians of the prophecy bestowed by the Ainmhi Caint, has final say."

"The insolence!" Fanga thundered.

"Forgive the boy," Eaglian Ollmhór said calmly. "He's been battling for our benefit his whole life. He's tired and hungry. I apologize, great Emperor Fanga."

"Sorry for the outburst," Arend said under the pressure from Ollmhór's prompting stare. Turning to Ailante, despite Ollmhór's warning looks, Arend continued, "You haven't exactly been a great proponent of the League…no offence."

"None taken," Ailante replied—his scrunched-up face speaking otherwise. "I have had doubts in the past but always supported Patuljak, Kempe, and the others of the League. I might add, I recently discovered I'm, in fact, a descendent of one of the initial League members!"

"Convenient," Arend wheezed.

"What?"

"Nothing," Arend said, moving next to Ollmhór as Kainen moved to Ailante. "All I'm saying is we swore allegiance to the League and to see the successful conclusion of the prophecy as *it* outlines. Not to be swayed by those outside the League. My loyalty's to Bellae."

"Would you let my people starve, homeless, rather than help?" Fanga thundered, again beating the table covered in maps.

"Of course, he doesn't mean that, and certainly we'll use their power for good, to rebuild Verngaurd," Ailante said.

"Sorry to interrupt, but isn't the last scroll going to tell us what to do with the crystals?" Gimelli asked, resisting the urge to grab Scelto's hand. "I think that's all Arend's saying."

"On this quest we've learned, undoubtedly," Scelto added, "that it's been well thought out with meticulous planning. They must have something in mind at the end."

"Of course," Ailante said. "However, we have dire needs, and the crystals will provide us with the power to fix many ills. We, the leaders, and longtime guardians of the prophecy, should have some say in the conclusion."

"Are we not League members?" Scelto huffed, his agitation growing.

"You are, of course, League companions," Ailante said slickly with an escort smile. "You must realize that generations upon generations of Elves, Fairies, and Eaglians have lorded over this. You, younglings, are newcomers."

"It doesn't mean they're less a part of this," Arend said. "They've bled, fought, and suffered as much as any League member, past or present."

"No one doubts that," Kainen replied. "However, what we're saying is, if there's a chance to fix major problems, and help people, we're obligated to do so."

Ailante nodded. "We are the League. This is why our ancestors sacrificed. This is our due. Honor us, the living, not some old scroll or long-dead creators and race of animal talkers."

"Bellae is a member of that race, an animal talker, and the whole point of the League was to respect the Ainmhi Caint and their wishes. They came to us because of our honor, morals, integrity, and ability to see the greater good over self-greed," Ollmhór said.

Kainen shook his head. "We're saying the same thing. This *is* our opportunity to save the world. Don't you trust Elven leadership? Don't you trust your own leaders?"

"My allegiance is to the cause, and I *will* honor the original agreement, not some revisionist writing of it," Arend added.

"We're getting ahead of ourselves," Gimelli said. "Kainen's right. We might be saying the same thing. We've been repeatedly told to take one step at a time."

"The girl's correct," Ailante said calmly. "Let's not get ahead of ourselves."

"The girl," Scelto said angrily, "is Gimelli. We need to get back. Emperor Fanga, I'm truly sorry for all your country has endured. Your fighters are brave and fierce."

"We'll check on you in a few months, my fellow League members," Ailante said.

With that the four left the tent. They could overhear Ailante talking about Friar and a plan for an upcoming battle, but Emperor Fanga went off on a rampage about his country needing assistance. The tension was palpable as they walked back to the increasingly oppressive cave. Gimelli pulled Scelto between Kainen and Arend—both sanctimoniously angry with the other.

"At least the Dark Warriors are moving away from Piscium," Gimelli said, flashing a smile that no one else saw. Drawing closer to the cave, she tried again. "We're in this together. We'll figure out what to do when we finish getting all five pairs."

"Getting food," Arend said, bursting up into the air as Kainen huffed off.

"We're in this together, right?" Gimelli said, to silence. "Verngaurd is fractured. I'm not so sure we'll find peace and unity at the end of this trail."

Scroll 3: Don't Look Up

"Over here," Lontas called out, standing near the entrance to the cave on the ledge.

"How long did I sleep?" Bellae asked groggily, her arms and legs still protesting.

"A few hours. I found writing at the opening and a symbol on the floor just inside."

Sankari groaned. "Everything hurts. All of Ifrean is horrible. Why do I taste salt?"

"Cenotes are sinkholes, and the bottom has salt seeping from an underground pathway to the ocean. Groundwater and rain come together in sections also. Because the salinity of ocean water is denser than fresh water, it stays on the bottom. That thin smoggy area between the fresh and salt water is a halocline. The barrier between the two densities creates a cloudy—"

"The only cloud bothering me right now is the hot air coming out of your mouth!" Sankari said. "I'm tired, hungry, and soooooo not in the mood for a lecture."

"I'm pretty tired too," Bellae said, joining him. There was a large, partially fractured slab of stone complete with fading letters carved within.

"There is no mystery or trial.
Just a decision to revile.
If you want set four,
Make a decision you will abhor.

Proceed into the cave.
Pick your best friend and tell them to be brave.
A symbol is on the floor.
Your **FRIEND** must stand on it to learn more."

"That's it?" Sankari asked. "One of us, and by one of us I mean one of you because I don't think they had Fairies in mind, just has to stand on a symbol?"

"It seems way too simple. Let's—" Bellae started.

She did not finish as a loud *click* reverberated off the cave walls. Bellae and Sankari quickly looked at each other before frantically moving into the cave where Lontas was standing on a large circular rock with a symbol carved on it. He was smiling and gave an awkward wave.

"After I stepped on it, writing became visible on the wall over there," he said calmly.

"Lontas, what did you do?" Bellae pleaded—fear at the repercussions flooding her brain.

"What needed to be done. We remember what it said. Someone dies, you or another. The words at the entrance clearly say the other is a friend. So, I'm ready for whatever comes."

"Lontas?" Bellae said weakly, her heart drenched in fear of losing another she cared for. "Remember, it's me and you," she whispered as Sankari fluttered to the far wall of the cave.

Lontas looked down. "Sometimes, as you know, there's no choice."

"The words are hard to make out," Sankari said. "Bring some light."

Bellae felt like she was dreaming. *No way can I lose Lontas,* she thought, moving next to Sankari while holding out the magical compass given by Jumeaux.

"Tell your friend not to move.
Or failure it will prove.
Your friend stands on the Sacrifice symbol.
Follow the words, keeping **YOUR** mind nimble.
Another emblem is on the wall.
Push it, and the stone shall fall."

Bellae instantly stopped reading and moved back to Lontas. Looking up into the high ceiling, she could see a cylindrical rock with another sacrifice symbol carved upon it, seemingly floating within a chiseled-out tube directly above.

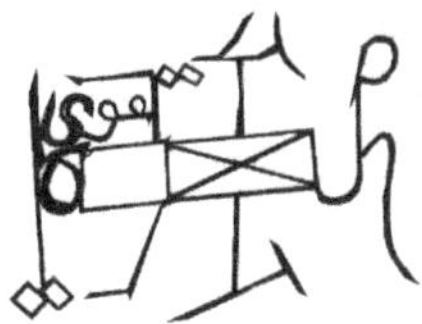

"No, no," she cried, enduring images of Crann's emaciated and beaten body being slowly digested, Borb drowning, Finn spitting bloody sputum—his body shredded.

"Just read the rest," Lontas encouraged, standing incredibly still, resisting looking up.

Bellae gazed at Lontas with pleading eyes but eventually returned to read,

"This test demands the Sacrifice of Love.
Freely giving oneself to the rock above.
Do this, and the next scroll you untie.
Resist, avoiding the Sacrifice stone, and you all die.

Push the button now.
Your friend's death you avow.
Reward for Sacrifice is great,
When a Sacrifice of Love triumphs over Hate."

Sankari hovered nervously as Bellae and Lontas stared at each other. Finally, Lontas smiled. "Look, it's simple. If I get…" he swallowed, "crushed by the boulder, then you get the crystals and save the world. If I move, we all die and the quest ends. It's an easy choice."

"Lontas, this is *not* happening," Bellae said, gazing at Sankari for support. "Aren't you going to say anything?"

"Fine, I will. Lontas is right—full stop. The prophecy is clear. In fact, this is the first time the riddle's easy. We lose Lontas or we lose the world to evil," she said, fluttering around the cave. "Fairies were founding members of the League of Truth along with Eaglians and Elves for a reason. The Ainmhi Caint chose us because we're rational and understand sacrifice for the greater good without being blinded by human greed and selfishness. With a name like 'Sacrifice Crystals,' it's not surprising this pair demands just that."

"Press the button, Sankari," Lontas pleaded. "I'm okay with this, Bellae."

"Wait!" Bellae yelled, the words reverberating off the cold stone walls.

"It's not going to get easier. Push it now!" Lontas demanded.

"I just want a chance to say goodbye!"

Lontas nodded, and Sankari landed on the cave floor to rest her wings.

Slowly, Bellae walked towards her old friend. "Thanks for everything," she said, her eyes filling with tears.

"Thank you for *always* being a friend when everyone else in the world was making fun of me," Lontas replied. "It's always been us versus the world…or at least it felt that way. I thought it would always be that way. Don't forget me when I'm gone. I'll be with you in spirit, until the end. You and me, right?"

Bellae took a ratty series of sucking deep breaths, attempting to control her sobbing.

He continued, "You lifted me up every time I fell. You encouraged me to keep going when I wanted to quit. You held my hand when I needed it most. So, yeah, thanks. Not the way I wanted this to end, but it really is okay. It's okay."

"Don't forget how great a friend you were to me—always going along with my schemes," Bellae said, a giggle escaping through her veil of tears as flashing memories streamed by. "I love the person you've become—strong and confident. Thanks for walking this far with me. I couldn't have done any of it without you."

"Don't worry about me. This is a small price that only I can pay. If the prophecy is true, you can rid the world of evil. If this puts a stop to the White Wizard? It just has to be. Plus, I'll gladly do this for you, any day, any time. You loved the clumsy, nerdy, always-late, always-reading-in-weird-places, and sitting-on-flesh-eating-logs me!" he said, smiling through the fear.

"Lontas, you're my best friend. The best I'll ever have." Bellae turned. "Sankari, go ahead and push the button. I'll stand here for a moment to hold your hand and then run," she said, smiling through weeping shudders, thinking she should say something else, but the right words seemed clouded in the fog of deep emotions swirling in her mind.

Wordlessly, Sankari flew up and pushed the button. Bellae lovingly squeezed Lontas' hand like she had so many times before. With her other hand, she took out and nuzzled Grym. Above they could hear the grinding and cranking of ancient gears and chains. The boulder lurched, and they all gasped. It held for a moment before falling.

Scroll 4: Blindside

"These are the latest battle formations out on the Vahse Plains," Lidenskap said, pointing to the map.

Storlax stared. "How many enemy surround Temple Aon Intinn?"

"One hundred fifty thousand Dark Warriors. After their defeat at Abhainn and struggles in Piscium, they're concentrating their forces at individual targets."

Storlax shook his head. "The size of their army is like nothing ever seen. When you combine their numbers around Verngaurd, including attacks on our Isles, they must be over a quarter of a million. Thankfully, the Elves defeated some seventy-five thousand."

"Imagine if we can defeat those attacking Aon Intinn?" Lidenskap said. "Friar suggests the Catalaunian Fields, north of the town of Châlons."

"Even with his misguided attempts to rally all of Verngaurd, with our ridiculously high losses, I'm not sure we have much chance. Battles are relatively brief, if not radically violent, glimpses of human strife, but their weight on our future is staggeringly out of proportion."

Lidenskap nodded approvingly. "The formerly rusty Knights from Toil Shaor are getting into shape. They've constantly been on the practice field."

"How are they taking it?" Storlax asked.

"The Knights are responding well to the discipline. The former embarrassment that was Veli Pingius has been transformed. I just—" Lidenskap was cut off by the sudden explosion of red flames in the center of the chambers.

"Guards!" Storlax yelled.

They could hear the soldiers struggling to get in, but the door was magically sealed. Red flames abruptly shot towards the two Proliate leaders, coiling around them like a snake. Lidenskap smiled, feeling a deep sense of peace. "It doesn't burn!"

The flame continued to hungrily swirl before shooting back to the other side of the desk, twirling like a small tornado before forming a flaming phoenix.

"Tallcon!" Lidenskap shouted, quickly kneeling. "I've awaited your return. Thank you for coming in our time of need."

Storlax stood open-mouthed, stunned into silence.

"I've something important to tell you," the flame hissed in a hollow, eerie voice that Lidenskap recognized from his encounter on the mountain.

"Please!" Lidenskap bellowed, tears of joy flowing down his face.

"Ha, ha!" the empty voice bellowed.

Lidenskap looked at Storlax, confused, unsure if he really heard the phoenix mockingly laugh. Instantaneously, the flaming figure turned into a bearded man wearing a white hooded robe and leather tunic leaning in the same direction as his pointed white hat tilted across his face.

Lidenskap rose slowly in disbelief. "The White Wizard?"

He waved them off as if batting away praise while the guards outside desperately pounded on the door. Abruptly, the White Wizard's eyes snapped out in a wide, crazed look. "Anyway, I just wanted to drop by and say hi."

Totally dumbfounded, the two Proliate leaders stared at him.

"Actually, I cleaned house for you. As you've been such good lackeys, I thought you deserved a bit of my time."

"What do you mean, 'clean house'?" Storlax asked.

"Oh…nothing big. Just a cleansing. I went through your holy sites and killed most of your Master Clericus Magicians," the Wizard stated.

"What?" Lidenskap demanded. "This sacrilege will not go unpunished. First impersonating him, now this? Tallcon shall bring swift retribution upon you!"

The White Wizard scrunched up his face sarcastically and hunched over as if he were fearful of retaliation. He stood up and pretended to wipe the sweat off his brow. "That was close. I was really worried there for a second."

"I may not know the time and place, but I can guarantee that you shall pay for your insolence!" Lidenskap bellowed.

Without flinching the White Wizard pointed his staff at Lidenskap and blew his body back against the wall. The general slammed into it with a loud thud. He grunted, the pressure of the magic making it hard to breathe. He lingered, prostrate for several moments before the White Wizard made a flicking motion with his staff, dropping the general to the floor.

"I hate interruptions. Let's avoid them in the future."

"I don't understand what's happening or what you're talking about," Storlax exclaimed as Lidenskap slowly picked himself up.

The Wizard huffed in annoyance and sat down on air, floating upwards. "Faith without contemplation is blind devotion, and no one, I mean no one, fulfilled the role better than you two stooges and your flock of faithfully devout flits."

When they looked at him in a daze, his form morphed back into the flaming red phoenix. The shimmering figure continued, "Wow, you're dense! I'm Tallcon. I made him up. I'm not impersonating the phoenix. I '*created*' Tallcon!" The two stared open-mouthed in continued disbelief. "Which is to say, there is no Tallcon. It was all me."

"You lie!" Lidenskap howled.

"Not possible," Storlax said.

Smirking, the White Wizard magically transported Lidenskap back to the mountain where he had first made himself appear as Tallcon. Although he relived the entire series of events when the White Wizard had impersonated Tallcon, it took only a few seconds.

"You're trying to deceive with your black tongue," Storlax spat.

"No, fools, I've been deceiving you—this is the truth. General, wasn't the flame you just saw like the one you encountered hunting the tilkeri on the mountain when I turned your sword red? All it takes is one or two appearances, and your puny minds take the idea and run with it. I didn't have much work at all with your religion for this round of Na Cearcaill. Your ancestors were kind enough to make up all the rituals and writings. I particularly loved the Sanctus Kirja Flamma. Not as long or pretentious as ones in previous Na Cearcaill. Tallcon will go down as one of my favorite fake deities."

"What in the name of Tallcon are you talking about?" Lidenskap demanded, his head spinning with a mix of uncertainty and dread.

The Wizard just rolled his eyes and looked at Storlax pleadingly. "Surely you, Mr. High Commander, grasp what's going on."

"If we believed you, which we don't, why this elaborate ploy?"

"I used the phoenix religion to manipulate and mold you. Just like I've been pitting the countries of Verngaurd against one another, I needed you to self-destruct at my bidding," the Wizard answered happily.

"Why tell us now?" Storlax asked in a subdued voice.

"To crush your spirit so I can cleanse your kind from this planet. Just like I helped groom you to prominence to rid the world of the Knights." He suddenly started laughing. "A magical phoenix who offers rebirth and healing flames? Fools!"

Lidenskap drew his sword and rushed the Wizard. "Blasphemy!" His blood-red sword sliced forward but pierced nothing but air as the White Wizard disappeared.

The general stared at his sword, still trying to figure out how it missed. Slowly, the red color began to drain from the sword. The general dropped it. As it clattered to the floor, they could hear the Wizard's fiendish laugh. The door to their office suddenly burst open, and dozens of Proliate rushed in, their eyes wide with terror.

"Sirs, someone has killed nearly everyone in the temples. You have to see what they did to the Clerics!" one of the guards said.

In stunned silence the two followed them to the Great Temple. Even from a distance they could see that most of the Master Clerics in the city had been pinned to the outside columns with large swords. Several of the Proliate guards with them began to vomit. Shrieks of horror and torment shattered the normally calm courtyard. There was blood splatter everywhere. Even the beautiful trees were showered in crimson.

"Did the fiend put masks on them?" Lidenskap asked.

"No," another guard stated solemnly, refusing to say anything else.

As they moved closer, they saw that the Clerics had their eyes plucked out. Dried black blood stood encircled in fresher, gurgling red within a skinless face.

After arriving, Friar, seeing the general's dazed look, took command. "Proliate and Knights to my left, get these men down now! Those of you to my right are in charge of cleaning up the courtyard. I want this place shining in the suns!"

"Ritari!" Friar yelled as he saw his captain enter the courtyard in front of the temple. "Take command of the detail responsible for getting these clerics down and buried per Proliate customs. I'll head up the courtyard crew."

Ritari began to slowly walk towards the temple in horrified silence. Friar grabbed his captain's shoulders. "Watch your response. The Proliate are traumatized. We need to lead by example and get this done as quickly and efficiently as possible."

Ritari nodded. "You heard Friar! Everyone move with a purpose."

"General," Friar said. "We still have the battle for Verngaurd to fight. Your men need you. I need you."

"What for?" Lidenskap mumbled hopelessly. "My world has been ripped apart. The White Wizard was Tallcon? All this time, we've been played the fools by some twisted Wizard?" He hung his head, crying softly. Several Proliate stopped to gaze upon him in shock.

Friar looked to Storlax, who relayed the story.

"General Lidenskap, you're a strong and worthy leader. Don't let the White Wizard win without a fight," Friar said.

"Why?" the general whispered.

"For your men. For Verngaurd. For me and all your friends."

Lidenskap just shook his head.

"I can't explain what just happened or why. I don't think any sane person could grasp the psychopathic White Wizard's actions. But, I can tell you this, for the first time in a long while the men and women of Verngaurd have hope. All of Verngaurd is coming together to fight his evil. We have a chance to knock the Wizard on his arse and send the Dark Warriors whimpering back to Ifrean." Friar let the general sob, turning him away from his troops.

"We all want that higher power, but we, the collective us, are that higher power. We just need to do our part in the eternal chain. Ideas, when loved too greatly, can bind truth, and fanaticism is born."

Lidenskap took several deep breaths. "In my heart I know what he says is true, but that doesn't make it less painful."

"The truth never has, and never will, make promises to be pain-free."

"But my faith has defined me. It felt so real," Lidenskap said.

"Perhaps the faith part is genuine. It's just the target, Tallcon, that was false."

Lidenskap nodded but looked unconvinced. "I always fought for Tallcon and the greater good, now...what do I fight for?"

Friar spread his hands around. "These are still your brothers. Verngaurd is still your home. You can't choose whether war exists or wish it away with congenial thoughts, but you can choose how you define a warrior and the code with which they model their character. Thus is born our Knight's Code. Trying to make an insanely complex issue and turn it into something simple is massive miscalculation. The very fact this statement is an oxymoron does not make it less true: we fight for peace, both metaphysical and existent."

The tears had ceased, but Lidenskap still looked doubtful.

"If nothing else, general, revenge on that vile enchanter and his underlings might go a long way to help heal these wounds."

Lidenskap nodded his head. "Revenge? That I can wrap my head around."

"It's all trickery," Storlax said gruffly, abruptly approaching them. "Just like his deceptions about you, the Elves, and Dwarves, his words are false."

Friar raised his eyebrows, unsure of what else to say as Storlax and Lidenskap argued.

"What in the world just happened?" Lovag asked, approaching with Ritari.

"I'm still processing it," Friar said. "The White Wizard appeared at the Great Temple as a flaming phoenix and revealed he had made Tallcon up as some sick and elaborate hoax."

"Phew!" Ritari said, removing his helmet to wipe the sweat from his forehead. "I didn't see that coming."

Several arguments were breaking out amongst the Proliate between those who still believed in Tallcon and those who thought he was a creation of the White Wizard. Lidenskap managed to take control and get the men back to work.

"This conflict within the Proliate is only going to grow," Friar said.

"I'm sick of saying this, but the world just keeps getting weirder," Lovag said.

Scroll 5: In Reality, Is Reality

"Go, Bellae!" Lontas screamed, flinging her hand away while anxiously balancing on the symbol. His face reshaped into disbelief as Bellae's turned fierce. He reflexively grabbed Grym after she gently tossed the squirming mouse. Bellae lowered her shoulder, slamming into Lontas, sending him backwards, falling and skidding off the damp rock. Bellae quickly stepped onto the carved circle, her tear-streaked face looking up calmly as the stone dropped.

"You fool!" Sankari screeched, the boulder continuing to fall. "You doom us all to die!"

"No!" Lontas screamed, struggling to stand and cradle Grym as the boulder sped towards her head.

CHING! Massive chains locked and the boulder stopped several feet above Bellae, who had closed her eyes in anticipation. A fine shower of dirt and dust settled on her face as the stone swayed precariously above. A *click* came from behind Sankari, followed by a stone door moaning open. A loud groan, followed by rattling chains, came from above.

"Get out of there. A door opened!" Sankari screamed. "You did the right thing! You weren't supposed to let your best friend sacrifice himself!"

Another loud wail from above prompted Bellae to jump and roll out of the way as the stone above crashed to the floor. Dust and debris shot up as the two symbols smashed together and quickly consumed the room. The only sounds were loud coughing and the tender crunch of debris falling. Bellae put her cloak over her mouth, closed her eyes, and waited. A murky light, diluted by the rubble, fought to stream into the cave. Eventually, the dust settled enough for the three to gather their things and find each other.

"Bellae, I'm not sure if I should hug or kill you!" Lontas declared.

"I vote hug."

"I'd better give him back. He's less than happy."

"I'm sorry I tossed—"

Grym ranted, *"You mean heartlessly hurled, pitilessly propelled, cruelly catapulted!"*

"I was trying to save Lontas."

"Oh, sacrifice the mouse for the klutz!"

"I hate to interrupt the little tiff," Sankari said. "But the 'door' that 'opened' stupidly revealed another *closed* door. This quest is super endearing. Anyway, there's writing on the new stone door, but the reason we need to hurry is that the one that had originally opened is inching closed. So, you know, seems we have a delightful time limit to solve this riddle."

Bellae used the lighted compass to read:

"Willing to Sacrifice self, you gained victory.
Love and Hate are contradictory.
Consequences be damned,
Your friend's defense you manned.
Refusing to Sacrifice another for your gain,
You both avoided death and pain.

True Love is Self-Sacrifice.
Hate is Sacrificing Love and affection for selfish device.
Your friend's death you temporarily avow.
To that ultimate fate we all eventually bow.

You need **THE** Strength to win.
$F_n = F_{n-1} + F_{n-2}$, find the tenth within.
But the reward for a willingness to self-Sacrifice is great,
A Sacrifice of Love triumphs over Hate."

"There's more down there," Sankari said, fluttering below.

Lontas knelt where a series of numerals were carved into the stone. Each figure had two chiseled-out slots above them. "Look, there are seven numbers: VIII, XIII, XXI, XXXIV, LV, LXXXIX, CXLIV. Above each number are two spaces where the crystals we have could fit." Lontas jumped as the stone door that had opened earlier jerked towards shutting. "Sankari's correct. The door is slowly closing."

"Did you think I was lying? Hmmm? Would that make any sense?" Sankari asked before wobbling her head and impersonating Lontas. "Sankari's evidentiary hypothesis is indeed correct. Her thesis does meet corroborating scientific criteria." She soared to the stone blocking their way, pounding it with her fists. "I didn't sign up for this load of shite! What does the tenth whatever, whatever thingy even mean? There aren't even ten blasted numbers!"

Lontas and Bellae looked at each other, unsure whether to join her tantrum, break down and cry, or solve the riddle.

Grimacing at the pain and deep weariness written on Bellae's face, Lontas went up and hugged her. He whispered, "You and me." Turning to the Fairy he added, "I figured it out. We've got this. It's okay."

"Nothing, absolutely nothing, about this is okay! Join the League, Sankari. Don't worry, Sankari. Our family's been members of the League for eons, and nothing ever happens. It's just a prestigious title for you and the family! What a load of peccary excrement!"

"Bellae, it says we need 'THE Strength' crystals. Place them in the slots above the 'LV.' That's the tenth number in the Fibonacci sequence—fifty-five, assuming we start with 1, which Leonardo did. The Fibonacci sequence is a series of numbers where each number is the sum of the two preceding numbers: 1, 1, 2, 3, 5, 8, 13, 21, 34, 55, 89, 144, 233, etcetera. What's absolutely beautiful about these numbers is that you can visualize this poetic sequence in a graph form and create a Fibonacci spiral by connecting the corners of the boxes. See those winding and curling figures on either side of the door? Those are Fibonacci spirals. The squares fit so well together because the ratios between the Fibonacci sequence approximate to the golden ratio of 1.618034." Lontas picked up a rock and drew the numbers within one of the spirals.

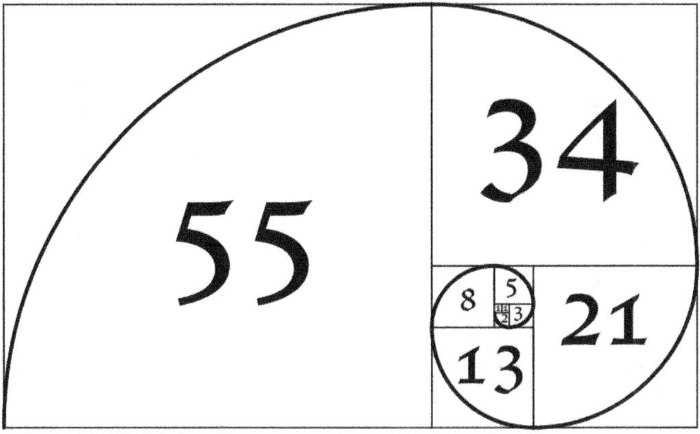

"Bellae and I ran into the golden ratio with Fiacla—"

Lontas abruptly stopped as Sankari, who had been deadpan staring, rushed to get in his face. "Out of curiosity, what percentage of your brain is telling you this is absolutely, no question, the 'perfect' time for a bloody lecture on stuff that no one but you cares about? Hmm? Is it fifty percent? Seventy-five? Huh? Hmmm?"

"You don't have to care about it for it to be important," Lontas said, more than a little hurt. "The golden section and Fibonacci sequence show up all the time in nature. In fact, plants produce alternate leaves at Fibonacci fractions. What's really interesting—"

Bellae gently guided Sankari away. "I've got the crystals. Fifty-five, the LV?"

Lontas nodded as the door that had previously opened began closing in quicker twitches.

"The time limit is speeding up, lovely!" Sankari huffed. "This, Lontas, would be the perfect time to start lecturing on the Fibing-rhino-malarky sequence!"

As Bellae pushed the two Strength crystals into the slots above the L and V, both the original barrier and the stone door with carved numerals immediately jerked and started to open. Bellae quickly removed the two crystals. Once both doors were completely open, they gazed into a dark tunnel stretching out before them. Distant torches magically lit down the entire passage.

Bellae put the crystals back in the bag, and the three cautiously entered the tunnel but Sankari dropped to the floor, weeping.

"Lontas give us a minute," Bellae said. As he walked away the Fairy buried her head into Bellae's shoulder as the two embraced. "I've got you," Bellae said as Sankari continued crying.

After the tears stopped the Fairy asked, "Promise me everything will be perfect when we get through this. Give me your word all of this will be worth it."

Bellae closed her eyes and sighed, thinking of what she knew but could not tell. "I can't."

Sankari huffed, wiping her wet eyes. "What can you promise?"

"To do my best and keep moving forward, together with you, my dear friend."

Sankari wrinkled her nose in displeasure.

Opening her eyes Bellae looked at the Fairy. "I know the sacrifices you've made for me, for seeing this journey through, for your family and your people. I understand and appreciate it."

Sankari looked into the distance before facing Bellae. "Corny…but acceptable."

"Keep flying with me, all the way to the end, whatever that may be?"

Sankari nodded. "Yes. I've got your back. I'm with you until the end."

"Until the end," Bellae echoed as they let a deep hug linger.

Joining Lontas Bellae grabbed his hand, forcing a smile. "Thanks again. We couldn't do it without you."

"Oh yeah," Sankari said, her wing speed increasing, "thanks for sharing about the Fibbin-notcha-cocky-numbers! Super interesting." The Fairy stopped, pretending to think while tapping her lip. "I've changed my mind. I meant *stupor-inducing*, not super interesting. Silly mistake!"

Bellae suppressed a laugh as the Fairy shot her a jarring glance. *She's acting like that to hide her pain,* Bellae thought. Her face fell as she held the glowing compass to see that the tunnel abruptly ended with a carved head staring back at them. The brown stone held the face of creature with massive eyes, spiked eyebrows, a large bull-like nose, and fearsome fangs. The flickering light twirled the shadows across its gruesome features and made it appear to be alive, reminding him of the Tunnel Glanha back at the Tournament of Flags.

"Only the chosen may enter," a voice called out from behind the statue in Ainmhi Caint.

Bellae translated as the voice began repeating the others had to leave.

"Okay, I get it!" Bellae replied as the others reluctantly moved back down the cavern.

"Lontas, while we wait, can you explain again about that super cool number sequence?" Sankari said, quickly drawing her peccary sword. "That was sarcasm, no speaky-speak!"

When they were gone the entire wall, including the demonic head, began to flicker, growing dimmer with progressively more of the stone becoming translucent until it disappeared. *"Enter, child,"* a deep voice boomed in Ainmhi Caint.

Bellae moved into a massive circular room with graded steps down to a central platform as if it might hold performances. There were various carvings around the top, lit up by rustic-looking lanterns indifferently handing out listless light. As Bellae stared at one of the sculptures, it wavered before changing from a dragon to a horned bull. Confirming no one else was in the room, she approached the recently changed carving, tentatively reaching out. As her fingers brushed across the cold, rough rock, it suddenly shuddered between overlapping images of a bull and a Tilkeri. She stepped back as it fluttered before solidifying into a saber-toothed cat.

She caught a shadow moving in the corner of her eye and turned to see long blur of black slicing around the back of the room before disappearing. *Is that a massive snake?* she wondered, backing up before abruptly stopping, not trusting leaning against the morphing wall. Shimmers of elongated black mist appeared and disappeared randomly around the circular room.

Bellae felt like screaming in terror and crying in exhausted depression. *I'm tired of being afraid,* she thought as flashes of the lioness Hamata, the decaying mirror guardian, and the fearsome Fiacla clamored in her mind, begging the question, *What's in here?*

A voice spoke, but she could see nothing. "Your ancestors set up this test betting the chosen would sacrifice self instead of a friend." As if on a delay from the words, a ribbon of inky fog returned. "I, however, would have set it up so that your friend had to die in sacrifice."

"That's super horrible!" Bellae replied angrily. "I've 'sacrificed' plenty along the way, and we both know a lot more will be lost before the end of this catastrophe of a quest."

"Your anger surprises me. Remember, these are the Sacrifice Crystals, and part of love is renunciation of self. You, being a child, should not even be here," the inky form said.

"I don't remember being given a choice."

The form solidified into a black snake-like dragon, startling Bellae, who recognized the face resembling the carving outside the room. She backed up as it glided forward. Its snout was long but ended in a bulbous nose, which sat over massive fangs, two much larger than the rest. Its charcoal eyes were surrounded by armored scales and topped with a row of red feathers. Fluttering on either side of thick scales that protected the head were vermillion feathers. Between its raven eyes sprouted spikes that glittered in the pale light. Pairs of red wings sprouted along the entire length of its long ebony body, which slithered around the large room. Despite the wings, the creature seemed to float more than fly. As it moved uncomfortably close to Bellae, she held her ground, trying to control her trembling. A red bifurcated tongue flickered out, each branch of the ending 'Y' arching around to latch onto her face. She closed her eyes as the two slimy tongue tentacles caressed her forehead and cheeks. She tried to slow her breathing, inhaling and exhaling only through her nose, as disgustingly moist saliva dripped down her skin.

"I'm Kāla, master of time and death, and hence reality and life."

When he stopped caressing her face, she opened her eyes. "How great for you."

"Insolence!"

"Tiredness," she replied, using her sleeve to remove the slobber.

The winged black dragon whirled around behind her, pushing her away from the wall. One of his feathered wings brushed harshly against her back as he circled around, enclosing her within its long body. Once surrounding her, Kāla's face slithered around to face hers.

"I wasn't going anywhere…kind of need those pesky crystals," Bellae said of the vice-like prison of his body.

"Why do you resist seeing the truth? Just now I felt you back in time at the coliseum being told the truth from a blinded creature, but you suppressed it."

"That was a long time ago, and it was a little stressful. Finn was badly hurt."

"Time is a concept born from our experiences, and how we live within a world that materializes in your intellect. You finite mortals love to slice up sections of time: a minute, an hour, a day, a week, a month, a year, a decade, a life, a century, a millennium. However, those are illusory partitions of what is, in reality, one long continuous stream of existence that is all intertwined and interconnected but always unbroken. In reality, is reality."

In reality, is reality? Bellae repeated.

Scroll 6: Battle of Châlons-Acid Rain

"We left our homelands exposed, for you," Ailante, the Head Archerian of the Elves of Creber, said.

"This battle is *not* for me, but all of Verngaurd. This is the perfect opportunity to try and tip the scales of battle in our favor," Friar replied.

"We're still outnumbered three to one," Duende, the new head of the Western Elves after Ailante had killed Bondi at the Battle of Trepas, said. "Plus, my troops are either teenagers, barely finished with basic training, or those well past their primes. Herra Isanta and our experienced troops were killed." He stared hard at Friar and Ritari as he finished.

Ritari scoffed, remembering when Herra Isanta almost killed him—saved only by Sorea. The thought of his old friend dying horrifically on the last verndari of Liberum sent a shiver of remorse through him.

"The time for this sort of talk is over!" King Abernan bellowed. "Every one of us has lost a great deal. If you want to go home and rebuild, then let's stop bleating and start beating the Dark Warriors! Time to stand and fight!"

Friar nodded. "We have plenty of surprises in store for them. For victory, for Verngaurd, we avenge all of our losses!"

All the other leaders of the Alliance went to stand with their armies except for General Lidenskap, who lingered. "If I don't make it, I want to thank you for this battle plan. I wouldn't want to be the Dark Warriors."

"I'm honored to fight with you and regret ever standing against you. For honor, for family, for friends, let us bring triumph home today," Friar replied.

The two embraced briefly. Friar could still see Lidenskap's puffy red eyes through his intimidating winged helmet. As the general picked up his shield, Friar saw that the emblem of Tallcon had been scorched off, leaving a burnt black smear.

"I'm...deeply sorry for your news," Friar said.

"Obviously many don't believe we were deceived, but I know."

"You should feel proud of your ability to move on. A long-held belief, when proven false, creates discomfort to acknowledge. Loyalty can bleed into stubbornness," Friar said. "Deeply wishing for something can ooze ignorance to fictitious reality."

"I believe the White Wizard thought the revelation of himself as Tallcon would break us." He paused, looking out on the horizon. "It has had the opposite effect. I feel a rage that I shall pour into his soldiers with such ferocity they shall regret being born."

Friar nodded, a shiver of hope rising within.

"As for those who still believe, they are more resolute in their conviction than ever. Any soldier standing across from us shall suffer greatly."

"Will the enchantment on the hippogriffs last?" Friar asked.

"The Magicians said as long as they stay with the griffins, they should be useful. They couldn't guarantee when the enchantments would wear off for the harder-to-control hippogriffs. They did warn that when it does, they might attack the griffins or us."

"Not comforting." Friar commented.

The general shrugged his shoulders, turning towards just under half the Proliate, the ones sharing the belief the White Wizard had deceived them. Storlax led the majority, who still held fealty to Tallcon, believing it was another of the Wizard's deceptions. "If..." Lidenskap hesitated, his faith shattered by the White Wizard's vile act stopped him from saying, *If it is the will of Tallcon.* "I'll see you if it is to be. I must say, we look like quite the shoddy and tattered bunch of misfits. Not very intimidating."

"Let them underestimate us," Friar replied. "That means they misjudge what we have on the line. With everything in our world imperiled, threatened with annihilation, we have everything to fight for. We shall unleash all the ferociousness we have left at our disposal. We shall attack like wild animals, but our strategy and purpose shall be as wily as the fox."

Lidenskap nodded.

"Make them pay," Friar added as the general trotted off to the far-right flank of the Allied army to join the Disbelieving of the Proliate, a mix of silver- and red-clad Proliate.

Lidenskap marched in front of his troops, looking over them and offering encouragement. A select few seemed demoralized, but most were outraged. He walked up to a hulking young man who had vambraces but no sleeves or chainmail, showing his massive arms. He had added several spikes and extra plates at various places on his armor, and like many of the Disbelievers the image of Tallcon was burnt off of his armor. "What's your name, soldier?"

"Chy...sir." He emphasized the sir enough to convey disdain.

"Ready to fight?"

Chy smiled. "I happen to have an inordinate amount of hate-fueled rage needing to be unleashed."

"Good, son. Untether your fury. It was disheartening to have our faith shattered, but use that as motivation."

Chy barely held off a scoff. "I didn't need the White Wizard to change anything. I was raised on hate and cynicism."

The Allied army was just behind the last small ridge of the Vahse Plains before the flatland known as the Catalaunian Fields. The besieged Temple of Aon Intinn sat beyond the prairie. The army was arrayed left to right as follows: Proliate Believers, Elves of Creber, Northern Dwarves Saatana Division, Knights, Northern Dwarves Vioma Division, Southern Dwarves, Ager, Western Elves, and Proliate Disbelievers. Behind the lines were the remaining war birds and a scattering of Magicians and Southern Dwarves proficient in prestidigitation.

Friar stepped up to the top of the ridge in front of the entire Allied army with an enchanted Huuto. There was a patchwork of hardened, but exhausted, veterans mixing with green recruits from all over Verngaurd. "Finally, the cloud of evil has revealed itself after nearly tearing us apart. But I see here an army determined to fight for their

Figure 8: Battle of Catalaunian Plains

friends, families, and countries. We fight as one, united against the tyranny of the Dark Warriors. Make no mistake about the reality. There's nowhere to run, nowhere you can be spared from the devastating evil of Ifrean and the Dark Warriors. They do not accept surrender. So, there you have it. Today we fight until victory or death. For Verngaurd—to victory!"

A loud cheer roared through the Allies. As one, they moved over the hill. There, across the open field, was Temple Aon Intinn surrounded by one hundred and fifty thousand Dark Warriors. Many of the interior buildings were on fire, and the Dark Warrior siege engines were pounding the cracking walls. Their infantry was formed up in a "U" shape around the Temple—the fourth side protected by the Hino Mountains.

TABLE 1 Battle of Catalaunian Plains

~~Dead/destroyed~~ *Reduced number*

Allies		**Dark Warriors**	
Knights of Toil Shaor:	5,000	**Infantry:**	150,000
Proliate (Believers):	15,000	**Wyvern:**	375
Proliate (Disbelievers):	10,000		
Elves of Creber:	7,000		
Western Elves:	2,000		
Southern Dwarves:	1,000		
Ager:	3,500		
Northern Dwarves:			
Vioma Division: (Green)	8,000		
Saatana Division: (Red)	7,000		
Griffins:	700		
Hippogriffs:	500		
Magicians:	16		
Surprise troops:	/////////		/////////
Total:	**>59,716**		**>150,375**

While the other flying beasts stayed to the rear of the Allied infantry, a solitary griffin flew to Friar. After climbing on, Friar was flown above the Allied army.

Using the enchanted Huuto, Friar shouted, "Victory for…"

"Verngaurd!" the entire army shouted.

Startled by the surprise appearance of the enemy army, the commanders of the Dark Warriors instantly began issuing orders. Half the Dark Warrior force outside Aon Intinn peeled off from the siege and headed to face the approaching Allied army. The other seventy-five thousand spread around to once again encircle the Temple. With surprising efficiency the Dark Warriors lined up opposite the Allies. In typical disdain, two commanders sauntered out front wearing surcoats with a patchwork of colors, including pink, purple, yellow, and blue, and began to juggle small swords back and forth to each other despite the fact the Allies were advancing.

"Ow!" one of them yelled after missing. One of the swords lanced into his abdomen. With blood oozing out over his surcoat he began laughing hysterically while his soldiers pointed and jeered as if they were a thousand miles from a battlefield.

"Infantry, hold!" Friar yelled. "Archers, fire!"

Archers within the Knights, Elves of Creber, and Western Elves began firing. Repeatedly, the arrows found their marks on the lightly armored Dark Warriors.

"Kill the commanders!" Lidenskap yelled, knowing that would get them to charge. His Proliate were beyond rage and impatient to spill Dark Warrior blood. Friar had given express orders to avoid the commanders in hopes of letting the arrows do as much damage as possible.

"Steady now!" Friar yelled, still circling on his griffin, through the enchanted Huuto. He could see into Aon Intinn and knew Lovag was awaiting his signal. "Stay in position! Keep your order." The Proliate on either end of the Allied line were pushing forward, willing the fight to start. When they didn't respond, Friar flew down to the right flank.

"General, we're outnumbered and at risk of being outflanked. If you pull too far forward, you're going to get cut off. The Dark Warriors still don't know the size of the force within Temple Aon Intinn and could divert even more troops here any moment," Friar pleaded.

Lidenskap nodded, reluctantly giving the order to get back into lines. Friar decided to stay on the ground, moving over to the Knights. Finding Ritari, he stood next to his captain. A lean and fit Veli Pingius looked over and nodded.

"I'll have no regrets on how I fight today," Pingius said. "My mind is already burdened with enough of those."

"Time to put aside the contrition we all bear, and fight," Friar responded.

"You have to give them credit. They have no fear of death," Ritari said, watching those killed by arrows coldly passed back as the next in line stepped forward to die.

The commanders of the Dark Warriors began angrily pointing to the Allies and yelling.

"Bring them down!" Friar yelled. No sooner had the order been given than a host of arrows showered down on the two leaders. They were hit with so many that their bodies were nearly covered as the Dark Warrior infantry rushed towards the Allies.

Since the ground dipped down in between the two armies, Friar ordered the Allies to hold and let the Dark Warriors tire by running down, then part way up the small hill. Once the forces were about thirty yards apart, Wyvern hurtled over the Dark Warriors towards the Allies.

"Shields! Shields, now!" Friar yelled. The front lines of the Allies knelt and hurriedly formed a shield wall with the second line. The black wyverns had thicker scales than their dragon cousins but were vulnerable in scattered patches of grey-black fur. Without front arms they flew streamlined and fast. Their two back legs were straight out behind them, and their axe-like tails were helping to steer their bodies like a rudder.

"Signal the air force!" Friar yelled as the command quickly moved back in relay.

The wyverns loosed a high-pitched screech, then retched their thick green acid at the Allied lines. It splattered on shield and armor, quickly eliciting screams of pain and disgust.

"Griffins! Hippogriffs!" Friar howled with desperate urgency. His attention turned to his soiled shield. He quickly threw it down as the corrosive sputum ate through metal, leather, and wicker. Ritari's shield was holding up better but still sizzled. The stench was so putrid, several soldiers vomited as the smell spread around the front lines.

Air was the one place the Allies had a numerical advantage and with piercing shrieks, the Allied war birds slammed into the wyverns. Although larger, the wyverns' size discrepancy was not as noticeable compared to dragons.

"Their acid is killing us," Ritari said.

"Good news, wyvern have a limited supply," Friar responded.

Initially the wyverns' acid proved an enormous advantage, causing griffins and hippogriffs to fall in great numbers, their bodies leaving a trail of green acid and smoke. The giant birds screamed in utter agony as their flesh melted away, leaving bones and scraps of flesh to free fall next to their mutilated bodies. Several of the injured beasts were slashed by the wyverns' back claws, bitten by their massive teeth, or sliced in half by their axe-like tails.

Things quickly turned after the wyverns' acid ceased. The numerical advantage of the griffins and hippogriffs took over. With no front legs to defend themselves, the wyverns were susceptible to attacks to the chest and upper abdomen—a fact the griffins quickly learned. With the wyverns embroiled in battle above, the Allied infantry prepared for the Dark Warrior charge.

"Forward!" Friar yelled when the Dark Warriors were almost up the hill. The Allied line jerked ahead, and the two sides slammed into one another. The difference in experience and training of certain members of the Allied army quickly became apparent. Some areas of the line buckled, while others easily pushed the Dark Warriors back.

The inexperienced and hastily trained Western Elves were thrown backwards, as was the small force of Southern Dwarves. Both Proliate armies fought with fanatical zeal and jolted the Dark Warrior lines into reverse. The mountainous men of Ager pushed forward as well.

Scroll 7: Tattered Shred

"The illusion of past and future is a product of your perception. In truth the only moment with any worth, or weight, is the present. It is time for you to awaken and see what is right in front of you," Kāla said, sneaking his spiked tail around. Bellae did not have time to duck as it zoomed towards her face. Nearing her, it dematerialized, becoming an inky fog that she soon found herself immersed within. At first, she could see nothing except pitch blackness. Slowly the roar of a crowd, the smell of surrendered blood, desperate, forged sweat, and a misty image of battered red began to rise. Steadily her senses sharpened until she was staring at the mass of pain that was dragon Hullus from the Tournament. His right eye was a blackened, coagulated mound of ruin while his left—littered and disfigured with blades and resultant blood from Finn's hailstorm weapon—stared lifelessly into her soul.

Suddenly Hullus' words flooded into her brain, and she understood who repeatedly tortured him, who was behind the death of Finn, the massive civil war, and Na Cearcaill itself. She saw flashes of the eons of deadly cycles echoing through time to destroy, level, and remake the world in the twisted image of the culpable one. "No, no, no!" Bellae screamed. Kāla's vice grip loosening, Bellae dropped to her knees in desperate sadness, falling out of the dark haze. "How could I not remember this? I should have warned them! I must tell Lontas, all of Verngaurd!"

"Now is the time you must *SACRIFICE*," Kāla's voice hissed as his body again twisted around, lifting her up and tightening. "Keep this information to yourself, for now. It is out of *LOVE* that you want to inform the world, and you *HATE* the truth you cannot tell. Be assured, others will find out soon enough. Whether Na Cearcaill continues will be up to you."

"How could anyone want it to happen once, much less repeatedly?"

"Power is an addictive affliction to most who suckle from it, corrupting the soul from the inside out. The honey-sweet stickiness of lust adheres the object of your desire into your brain, then covetous strands pierce into your thoughts, pulsing the promise of happiness and satisfaction. Eventually, only a shell of justification remains around a decayed, rotten husk. Excuses and rationalization become the language of their putrefied-by-greed heart."

"This cycle, Na Cearcaill, just keeps repeating?" Bellae asked, overwhelmed at the recurrent, and unfathomable, death toll.

"As the name implies," Kāla said impatiently.

"How does no one know…or remember but the League of Truth? Aren't extinction, or near-extinction, events something people would remember?"

"Given the expansive length of time between the cycles, it is quite understandable, and frankly predictable, that they would not. Truth becomes legend, legend becomes fairy tale, fairy tale becomes dismissed and forgotten as time erodes the original meaning. Our lives are just small, tattered shreds of fabric woven together into the unfathomable, enigmatic sheet of eternity. Connected, yet separated by innumerable lifetimes of material time and abundance of other lives. We are the shred, but the thread is in the cloth of our life, and as it stitches into completion through our actions and interactions with the world, we, the individual, become the whole, and the harmonious whole becomes the individual tatter—interwoven, inseparable, within existence. Our stitches—actions—shape the fabric of the world to be inherited by the next generation. We would do well to be humble at the reality of our small scrap of existence and understand the intimate attachment to all other living beings—to realize we are all inextricably linked within the fabric of the whole, the fabric of *the* consciousness."

Bellae stared at his sable eyes as the red feathers around his head fluttered. Time seemed to slug forward as the creature floated in silence. She tried to calm her breathing and stop her tears, realizing the beast could easily crush her. "So, what else do you need?"

Kāla's head slowly tilted to one side as if studying her. "To earn the crystals, besides keeping the secrets you have learned, you must answer questions to my satisfaction about the subject of these crystals. What is love?"

Bellae closed her eyes, her face scrunching into annoyance. Her mind drifted to her dead: Borb, Crann, Finn—and living: Gimelli, Lontas—and everything making those relationships special. Images of Honey and the painful betrayal mixed with others she had grown up with at Liberum. *What made them enemies, acquaintances, and not great friends?* "What is love?" she repeated, her words coming out slowly, as if drained, as her mind relived past interactions.

"Love is just…a simple title of four letters. Anyone can say it. Anyone can throw it around, using it but not meaning it. I think love needs to be proven, demands action. It can be as simple as just being there. But love means your presence not only when the suns shine but in the storms of life. It can be encouraging words. It can be total silence. It can be standing up for them. It can be holding them. It can be letting them go. Love is a simple term but extremely difficult to create and even harder to sustain. I guess it comes down to giving of yourself: time, a hand, a word, silence, helping. Love is true giving."

Small tendrils of mist huffed out of the beast's nostrils before it spoke. "The amazing gift of life is that the more you sacrifice and give, the more, exponentially, you receive and grow. The opposite is true for its diametrical opponent. The more you feed hate, the more it burns through our compassion and eats at our gifts from life, shrinking our souls. Love is accepting. Love is listening. Hate is a rejection of our connectedness in the giant fabric of eternity. I felt your love with Finn. However, your affection was not tested."

"What does that mean?" Bellae asked angrily.

"Love is a time-sensitive affair with disparate pitfalls and different delicacies and requirements as it ages. Your devotion, dying early, did not suffer under the rutted scrutiny of time. Early love is easy love, a honeymoon. Then, the grit of mundane interactions grinds away the initial luster of the emotion, and the scuffed pedestal the object of your love was first placed upon descends under the direction of reality and thwarted frustration. Then you're left with drudging hard work to keep love afloat."

Bellae scrunched her nose. "That seems…negative."

"Doubt of, or disagreement with, reality does not make it less factual," Kāla replied. "As it ages, the gears of love grind into hard work, taking persistent, determined, and monumental effort to refocus selfish motives and covetous desires for self and center your heart on the 'we,' on the 'other.' That is when *true* love is revealed and grows. Hatred is always effortless, fueled by shallow ego. It springs up and burns rapidly like a rabid, scalding geyser scorching you from the inside. How easily hatred can be ignited, sometimes with the slightest injustice against the self. Egotistically cultivated hatred makes a minor injury seem like the greatest tragedy. Love is created from sacrifice of mind, body, spirit for another. Hate is forged from the fire of insensate, inconsiderate self-obsession and sacrifices affection. What damage do you think hate does?"

Bellae's tired brain clunked out an answer. "I think it destroys what's good in us as individuals and hurts others."

Kāla snorted in displeasure. "The prideful, dangerous aspect of hate is that its fire consumes not only reason and logic but burns out the goodness in the hater's heart. If you do not think hate has weight, you have not seen its true burden blurred in the fiery, disjointed mind of the one breeding out the loathing. If you doubt hate distorts rationality, you have never seen the wide-eyed look of awfulness it commands. Hatred is vanity. Propping yourself up to a level of importance that demands retribution and justice for any wrong, any difference, any cause, however delusional. An injustice never forgotten does not eat away at the one who served the cruelty, just the one who holds onto it. It becomes a weed, spreading its destructive roots to bind the heart, and sprouting angst vines throughout the brain.

"Hate can be reactionary—self-hate because of those *we* have injured—or rationalization, self-righteous justification—what we did was acceptable because they *deserve* to be hated. To receive these crystals, you had to be willing to pay the price of your life. Love is sacrificing self for another, and hate is self-harm, sacrificing the best parts of our own spirits on the altar of vengeance. You now receive the Love and Hate crystals," Kāla said, his body consuming her.

The black mist surrounded her mind, and she saw flashes of battles. She saw death, including Lontas dying brutally thanks to a swipe of the spiked arm of a Cyrn-du. The horse then drove its horn into Lontas' chest. His eyes grew wide with pain before life drained away.

"Wait!" Bellae screamed. "The mirror guardian showed me Lontas goes on to have many descendants. I saw them!"

"The future will happen as it always does, but is, crucially, yet to be determined. The future, before it materializes, is hope, is despair. It is all that could be. However, it is entangled with an almost infinite number of possibilities stretching out like innumerable paths before us, only collapsing into one present reality once it becomes the now—crushing all other possibilities that could have been. You saw one realizable future, but what is to come can only be delivered into the present by actions and sheer will.

"The mirror guardian distorts space and time, but the basic rule is unhindered—constantly forward. There is a price for acts that sin against the natural order. I saw him in your mind's eye, and he's not healthy. You mistake life and death as separate entities when they are, in fact, one force briefly breathing permission into your existence before ruthlessly pulling you back to the insensate. A false sense of mine versus a true sense of time," Kāla said, disappearing.

As the black mist receded, the soft glow of two new crystals and a scroll appeared on the floor. Bellae moved down the large stairs. As soon as she touched them, her consciousness was transported to the eternal silence of the infinite. Just as her heart began to race in the panic of the terrifying quietude, a muscular warrior, his eyes ablaze with loathing, materialized in front of her. Abruptly, flames shot out of his eyes, creating flaming bars which spread to confine him.

Hatred divides and separates us as individuals and society, isolating the hater in a prison of abomination—a fiery dungeon of our ego's fabrication. Hatred divides compassion and breaks apart empathetic connection with others, locking us away in a cage of our own making!

Bellae felt herself spinning around, faster and faster until her brain hurt. When she stopped, her head felt like it was still rotating. Slowly, the image came into focus—a circle divided in two by an S-shaped line with a larger bulging section tapering to a thin triangle. One half held the image of hate. The other, two winged hearts under a crown.

To let love reign you must sacrifice for others. Love only takes flight when those involved all beat for the purpose of keeping the other aloft. Sacrificing thoughts of self for others is when the giving becomes growth, when the connection becomes an inseparable bond.

Bellae felt like she was free falling before suddenly collapsing upon the floor, the crystals' words pouncing into her mind. Closing her eyes, she yelled, "Stop torturing me!"

When Bellae opened her eyes, Kāla materialized so fast it startled her into sucking in her breath and scooting backwards. "Temptation, girl, does not arise from something foreign or external. Its life is intimately

Figure 9: Bellae experiences the interconnected emotions of Love and Hate.

birthed from our own seduced and vulnerable hearts. Our souls, like most things, are a dynamic system, paradoxically complementary yet polar. Around they spin with part of ourselves submerged within the opposite. There is friend in our enemy and enemy in our friend. There is some hate in love and some love in hate. The luring desires whispering in your mind have their origins in your own self."

Bellae shook her head. "I did not hear them *until* I got the first crystals!"

Kāla shot forward, his red feathers fluttering angrily as he zoomed within inches of her, forcing her to fall onto her back. "You, with short-lived existences, always make the same mistakes! Conjuring fictitious, gnarled, and horned demons to justify and explain evil and ignoble, as that concept is easier to stomach than seeing it in your own reflection."

"Are you saying the voices from the crystals are my fault?"

"In asking the question, you have answered it. However, no more or less than any other mortal could you be responsible for your sins' desires. It's true the crystals do have a voice to entice you, but they also amplify and magnify what's inside your head. It's a bit of both and unfortunately hard to tell the difference. Gold internally calls, convincing you it should be yours. Power exclaims that the job is rightfully in your hands. Greed, power, wrath, hate are always there, whispering to us, preying on our pride and envy.

"If evil and cravings arise from within, then so too does the good. The character of our being is the end product of balancing carnal impulse and soulful virtue, beaten and shaped from fire and ice upon our mind's forge. Most decisions come down to the interactions of desire and control, emotion and temperament, along with knowledge and obtuse stubbornness. Choose wisely," Kāla hissed before dissipating.

Bellae pushed herself to a sitting position, carefully putting the newest crystals away. Taking several deep breaths, she began walking. She squeezed her eyes shut, willing the crystals, and perhaps her own mind, to stop.

Understand the Ainmhi Caint were magical people, a voice from the crystals whispered. *It is your destiny to become our overlord. This is your ancestors' desire.*

I highly doubt they wanted one person with such power! Plus, I'm getting stronger! Bellae screamed in her mind, feeling the power course through her. *I control the good!* With a sigh of relief at the silence, she opened her eyes before trudging back down the tunnel.

Lontas squeezed Bellae in a powerful embrace as she emerged. Sensing her trembling, he arched back. "I can tell you had more horrible experiences, but guess you can't tell me?"

"I want to. You have no idea how much. But I can't."

"I understand," Lontas said despite resentment slithering up from deep inside to permeate, planting seeds of bitterness within his mind. He took a deep breath, knowing he should not feel this way but also understanding the birth of discontent is not something chosen. "I decide to not let that bother me. It's not your fault," he said, determined not to fertilize bitterness with selfishness. "Thanks for saving me. Despite what I said, I didn't want to be squished."

"I didn't want that either, and you're welcome," she said, trying to sound cheerful and hoping her fathomless exhaustion was not coming through.

"There's no denying how brave you were. Still, you're the only one who can complete the quest and need to be more careful," Lontas said. "How did you know?"

"As important as this mission is, I wasn't going to let you 'sacrifice' yourself for me or anyone. Plus, I had a feeling they wanted me to be willing to sacrifice myself," Bellae admitted. "It said something about 'freely giving *oneself*.' When I heard that, I was sure the prophecy wanted me to be willing to sacrifice myself for you."

"You have to be more careful, but thanks."

"Remember, you were willing to give your life first with no fear."

Lontas started laughing.

"Keep it down!" Sankari gruffed. "We don't know if there are Dark Warriors around."

"What's so funny?" Bellae whispered.

He leaned towards his friend, knowing she was the one person in the world he could tell such a secret. "Actually, when the stone started to fall, I peed my pants a bit."

"What now?" Sankari asked.

"Let's take a look at the next scroll," Lontas said. "Please have us go back to Verngaurd."

"I never even thought about that!" Bellae said.

"Okay, this is in Verngaurd. We can solve it on the way back or once we arrive," Lontas said after pouring over the next riddle.

Before Bellae could reply, a surge of power rushed through her. She could hear Sankari and Lontas yelling but could not make out what they were saying. White light took over Bellae's eyes, blinding Lontas and Sankari, who turned away. For Bellae the light softened to a vision of a massive number of troops in battle, and then she was standing in front of Friar.

"Where did you go?" Lontas asked when, after many minutes, she returned.

"I spoke to Friar," Bellae said exhaustedly, explaining she saw him in a great battle.

"Is he okay?"

"Uh-huh. Must rest." Exhaustion dripped from her words as she closed her eyes.

Scroll 8: Battle of Châlons-Through the Flames

At Temple Aon Intinn the seventy-five thousand Dark Warriors and dozens of siege engines assaulting the fortified city came to a stunned halt as the front gates were thrown open and the portcullis raised.

"Prepare for their charge!" the Dark Warrior commander shouted. "They must be out of supplies!" The besieging Dark Warriors formed up lines and braced for a Proliate attack. As the minutes ticked by, an awkward silence settled on those surrounding the temple.

"Why aren't they emerging?" sergeant Tikkari asked. "Could they be surrendering? Look, sir," he suddenly added, pointing to the walls.

The Proliate force manning the walls disappeared. The cool wind began to howl through the empty battlements. A loud cackling laugh suddenly boomed from behind the castle walls, and the Dark Warriors found themselves in the unique position of feeling a shiver of fear at the surreal scene of an apparently empty Temple with its gates open.

"What's happening, commander?"

"I love the enthusiasm, sergeant. Lead the men through the gates and find out."

"Yes, sir," Tikkari replied as the order for attack was sounded. "Follow me to certain death!" As he reared his head back and howled with unbridled excitement, the rest of the Dark Warriors cheered wildly. When they finished, they yelled as one, "To die!"

With Tikkari leading them, the Dark Warriors began pouring through the temple gates. Their fierce shouts mellowed to a confused buzz as they stormed into the ghostly silent and entirely empty courtyard. The sheer mass of soldiers pushing through the gates compelled those in front to keep moving into the vacant bailey. Unfortunately for them, the ground had been presoaked, turning it into a muddy, slogging mess. In addition, there were wooden and metal obstacles slowing their progress and distracting them.

"They're all gone," a Dark Warrior said, gazing up at the empty battlements and courtyard.

"Spread out and search building by building for the cowards!" the sergeant yelled. "It is our honor to die for the Sovereign in White!"

"Hold," Lovag whispered in the temple tower, just below the red statue of the seemingly debunked Tallcon. He was with the roughly two hundred Proliate Red Guard still in Aon Intinn. The rest had been secretly flown out at night to reinforce other temples as supplies for Lovag to build welcoming gifts were flown in.

The Dark Warriors streamed down empty streets, unable to open any doors, which had been boarded up from the outside. Eventually they ran into solid walls bricked across the streets—blocking all paths the Dark Warriors could take. As more soldiers streamed in, they found themselves completely packed into the front half of the temple with nowhere to go.

"They have at least thirty thousand soldiers inside the gates and reached the barricades," Slaemur-Rass, one of the Proliate defending the temple, said.

"Give the first signal," Lovag replied.

With a few quick thrusts of his red signaling flag, the last few Proliate sprang into action. Immediately, a large portcullis slammed shut, sealing the thirty thousand Dark Warriors in the Allies' trap within the temple. Those still outside the gate continued to push forward, crushing and killing hundreds of their comrades against the reinforced steel of the portcullis.

Next, a series of twenty reka sla were triggered. Each one of the spiked wooden rectangles shot up and out from their shallow underground hiding spots. Traveling with blistering speed, the spiked wooden platforms slammed down onto the Dark Warriors. Tikkari was in front of his troops when one smashed on top of him. One of the spikes caught him right between the eyes. His pain was short lived as the modified catapult snapped his body backwards before flattening him to the ground, along with around twenty of his comrades. Their thin armor quickly relegated to guarding slush as the torsion-based, spiked platforms crashed upon them.

"Release two!" Slaemur-Rass yelled.

At his command the Acus weapons used vainly in the defense of Liberum were unleashed. All along the crowded streets of the temple before the barricades were rows of the spring-loaded, needle-firing weapons. The stinging waves of thin projectiles bit into the Dark Warriors trapped in the roadblocked thoroughfares. As round after round of the weapons fired, the soldiers stuck there fought to push their way back into the courtyard, which was itself completely full. The only breathing room was created when fellow soldiers died, producing a tiling of the slain. Next, several of the Proliate approached four tall polls straddling the crowded streets. The back poles were shorter and had wooden rectangles between them loaded with crossbows. Two ropes led from the box to the larger poles.

Slaemur-Rass shouted, "Three! Mors desuper!"

The Proliate released a wooden cover plate and cut ropes holding boxes loaded with crossbows. As the boxes swung down, trigger mechanisms released, and the four rows of crossbows fired as it fell in a curved path of death dictated by the cables connecting them to the taller poles. Droves of Proliate were downed by the bolts.

Lovag stood and howled, "Let them fly!"

As Slaemur-Rass signaled the next order, Lovag took a few steps back before rushing forward, jumping off the top of Tallcon tower. His arms pinwheeling, he plummeted towards the ground. He was about halfway down when a Vioma dragon came whipping underneath him. He landed with a thud on the neck and a pang of groin pain.

"Nice of you to drop in," Dwarf Abhac said. "If I can be critical, your entrance was a bit dramatic, for my taste. Better hold on, tough guy." The battered Soma did several three-hundred-and-sixty-degree loop de loops, awaiting his dragon brothers.

"Ahhhhhhhhhhhh!" Lovag yelled, holding on for dear life.

"I probably should have let you strap in first," Abhac cried out while smirking.

If his throat had not been full of tangy bile, Lovag would have attempted a tart comeback. After the third time around, the other Vioma dragons had caught up. Struggling to strap in, Lovag weakly called out, "Forward."

"Eteenpain!" Abhac yelled with incredible ferocity. "Kill them all, my Aer Ridire!"

Within the temple Slaemur-Rass ordered the firing of the platform-based hailstorm weapons used by the sapper units of the Knights outside Liberum. They were strung all along the walls of the bailey, tilted down. They fired their one and only cargo of diamond-shaped blades. Hundreds fell in death, and thousands dropped in injured pain.

As the hailstorms finished firing, the entire sky above the Dark Warrior army trapped within the temple was filled with Vioma dragons and their Aer Ridire. Each Vioma had a large circular drum, complete with abrupt-looking curved spikes, strapped below its underbelly.

"Release the drums filled with naphtha!" Lovag yelled, his stomach still spinning.

"Julkaisu!" Abhac yelled in the rough language of the Vioma dragons.

At Abhac's command, the Aer Ridire released the barrels, which still carried the forward momentum of the dragons. The Dark Warriors were so packed into the courtyard they had nowhere to run as the barrels crashed down. The deadly spikes impaled the soldiers before the drums exploded—splattering the sticky and oily naphtha all over any nearby Dark Warriors.

"Light them!" Lovag yelled. The Aer Ridire lit two crossbows on each of the dragons. As they came back around, they released the blazing bolts. The courtyard erupted into a ball of fire as the naphtha exploded in flames.

As the screams of the trapped Dark Warriors erupted, a riot of anger went up from those outside the walls. The dragons retreated to the back of the temple. The Dark Warriors still inside the walls pushed forward, unknowingly towards Lovag's newest machines. They were an improvement of the sidus heulwich, or sun star, which had been used so effectively at the Battle of Trepas. It now had nine rows of preloaded crossbows on a rotating A-frame.

Outside the walls, the enraged Dark Warrior commander ranted, "Push up the siege engines! Now we go over the walls and kill them." The screams of the burning Dark Warriors still echoed as the flames continued to ravenously consume.

"Fire!" Slaemur-Rass yelled. Instantly, the courtyard filled with thousands of bolts, which ripped into the front ranks of the Dark Warriors. Of the thirty thousand who entered, there were now only a few thousand left alive.

"Charge through the flames before they fire the new weapons again!" one of the Dark Warriors screamed. "For the White Wizard and revenge!"

With complete disregard for their own lives, the remaining soldiers lurched through their dying comrades and searing flames towards the couple hundred Proliate.

"Turn the crank! Get the next side ready!" Slaemur-Rass shouted.

Calmly, and with their characteristic efficiency, they turned the large cranks on the A-frame structures of the sidus heulwich. Slowly, empty rows of crossbows moved down and back as the next rows rotated forward, ready to fire. The Dark Warriors were only a dozen yards away now—many on fire and all with the light of flames dancing in their deranged eyes.

"Release!" Slaemur-Rass yelled. Again, the bolts ripped into the Dark Warriors until there were several hundred left. The Proliate turned the cranks to bring up the last crossbows.

"Kill!" the last few Dark Warriors began to chant eerily. They repeated it over and over again as the stoic Proliate set about their business.

"We're ready to fire…sir?" a Proliate pleaded to Slaemur-Rass.

"Hold," he answered.

Time slipped sluggishly along as the remaining Dark Warriors plodded over the piles of dead and burning. Gurgles of pain rained up from the field as the sickening smell of burnt flesh invaded the nostrils of everyone in, and outside, the Temple. The statue of Tallcon, now covered in a hazy shroud of black and angry smoke, stared down impassively at the grisly scene. The Dark Warriors, now only ten yards away, stung the stoic Proliate with a pang of urgency.

Five yards. They actively resisted the urge to release.

"Fire!" Slaemur-Rass finally called out. With inhuman force, the bolts sliced through the Dark Warriors. Many were hit with ten or more bolts and blown back several feet.

"Sir, that was close," a Proliate commented.

"I wanted to see their faces when they died as they saw the faces of all the helpless villagers killed," Slaemur-Rass declared. "Thirty thousand of their soldiers dead to none of ours. We'll take that ratio all day."

"Still, the Dark Warriors are fearless."

"So are we," Slaemur-Rass countered.

Scroll 9: Perfidy Pain

The next morning, Bellae and Lontas woke to shouting. Sankari had her peccary sword out, brandishing it towards Viridi. The Pixie's strands of grass and flora vibrated angrily, creating a soft buzzing sound.

"How, exactly, did you find us?" Sankari growled.

"I was searching for you in case you needed help!" the Pixie replied. "I heard something last night but waited until it was light to search this place."

Bellae guided Sankari away. "Welcome back. Thanks for leading the Dark Warriors away."

"My pleasure," the Pixie answered, sticking her green tongue out at the Fairy. "I think you said you're on a deadline to get back to the Cove of Pain? I want to help."

"I can smell a rat, and you reek!" Sankari huffed.

Bellae looked down, Honey's betrayal still stinging her heart. "She's been good to us. If you're willing, please help us get back in time."

"The Dark Warriors left ropes. I took the liberty of moving one over to this opening so you can climb up without having to swim down and under again. While you two climb, my bestest buddy Sankari and I will fly," Viridi said, mouthing something unpleasant at the Fairy.

"By my calculations we're right on time," Lontas said, days later, as they emerged from a weed-filled path onto the beach.

"We would have been here faster if it weren't for long-way-loser Viridi here," Sankari said, glaring at the Pixie.

"As I said previously, if you didn't want another run in with stone pixies, then we had to walk the extended path. Since Bellae and Lontas can't fly, this seemed reasonable."

"Plus, Bellae was obsessed with avoiding Cyrn-du," Lontas said.

"I had my reasons," she said, reliving the visions of him being impaled by a unicorn.

"Bellae's right to think like that," Viridi said, abruptly shuddering.

"Hey!" Sankari said, fluttering wildly and flashing her sword down the beach. "Isn't that our pirate guy with a bloody Nishi?"

Bellae instinctively felt for her protective talismans as Lontas X'ed his together with a clang in preparation. Suddenly, Viridi began laughing. They swiveled to see the Pixie fluttering with several other Nishi, who were spouting vile, wide-eyed looks.

"I told you, oh fluttery, green one, they're stupid and gullible," a specter said.

"Master knew they would fall for the ruse if I played myself off as an outcast," Viridi replied. "Oh, poor me, shunned by my fellow Pasture Pixies! He knew you'd lap it up…you know, because you're a freaky animal talker and Lontas is a la-la-loser. How did you get this far and not die? Seriously? How? Walking into a field of stone pixies? Brainless! Couldn't find an enormous sinkhole that *was on the map!* Incompetent! Watching Dark Warriors cleansing half-witted villagers? Imbecilic."

Lontas and Bellae looked at each other while Sankari muttered obscenities.

"What? Is that stupid staring at each other supposed to help, or do you have to discuss how you survived being so incompetent before answering? Go, run along with the mariner to get the last pair of crystals, then our master will torture and kill you."

"Troldmanden's going to inflict so much pain on you!" a Nishi hissed.

"The hordes Troldmanden has prepared?" Viridi added. "Let me spoil the ending: everyone you care about, know, have ever seen, or even thought about—they all suffer and die."

"Actually, everyone you have not seen too," a Nishi said. "Like, totally every single one!"

"That's kind of the meaning of *everyone,*" Viridi replied. "Everyone, by definition, includes, you know, everyone!"

The two Nishi glowered as the mariner, hearing the rant, meandered over.

"Hey Mor-Leider," Viridi said. "You simpletons know he works for Troldmanden?"

"Bloody pirate!" Sankari hissed.

"It's mariner!" he replied, drawing his sword.

Bellae clenched her teeth and despite wishing it would not, a tear leapt from her eyelid, winding down the hills of her cheek. *Shouldn't I be used to betrayal?*

"Don't give me that look!" Mor-Leider said. "It's just business."

"It's a little more than that for us," Bellae replied, quickly wiping away her tears.

"Spread your scorn as thick as you'd like. This is a double payday for me. Mariners survive by making as few enemies as possible and never, ever, double crossing a Wizard. I'll keep my word and get you back to Verngaurd true enough. That said, I don't see how you get out of this alive with both the Blue and White Wizard observing your every move and desperate for power and control. Those vices can dominate more than the strongest, most ruinous drink or vilest, most destructive drug."

Lontas shivered, suddenly feeling the eyes of all-powerful Wizards boring into them.

"I need to navigate through the waters of my life sure as anyone else, and these be dark times," Mor-Leider said.

A Nishi slithered towards the mariner, running its grimy fingernails down his cheek. "Be a good servant and you might just survive this Na Cearcaill, boat boy."

Another hissed, "Might, might not!"

Mor-Leider glared at the apparitions, resisting the urge to hack through them with his sword. "As I said, I'll keep my word."

Viridi fluttered next to Bellae and several blades of grass that served as hair elongated, seizing hold of the former squire's face. "Let me spoil the ending. You die. Troldmanden steals the crystals. Verngaurd's purged in the purifying destruction of Na Cearcaill."

"You'd better hope I never see you again!" Sankari said, waving her peccary sword.

"Or what? You'll do nothing but die like the rest, you poop-colored pest!" Viridi said as several Watchers floated down to back them up.

"Time for the pestilent children and excrement-brown Fairy to head to their death in Verngaurd," a Watcher said, his eyes blazing.

"See, I'm not the only one who thinks of you as shite!" Viridi laughed.

With surprising gentleness, the mariner guided the slumped shoulders of Bellae and Lontas towards the small craft as Sankari flew backwards, glaring angrily and gesturing rudely at Viridi and the others. As they approached, the waiting boat arced a rhythmic, circular dance at the behest of the waves. Its rollicking gyrations seemed a lighthearted mocking of their dejection.

"I'll be done with you having that pathetic look," Mor-Leider eventually said.

Bellae, ignoring the mariner, caught Lontas' attention as he rowed their dingy and mouthed, "Always, you and me."

He nodded and sighed, deeply sick of the world's treachery but grateful to have someone to fully trust. Sankari hovered in the back, scowling at the White Wizard's minions on the shore.

"I've seen less puckered faces on an old crone sucking a lemon!" Mor-Leider said.

"If we didn't need you to get home, I'd cut you!" Sankari said, rotating around now that the shore had bleached into an unfocused blear.

After another awkward silence, the mariner spoke, "Ah, five of the moons be in full phase. That means good sailing."

Lontas shook his head. "The moons actually don't go through 'phases.' Our *perception* of them goes through regular, and quite predictable, phases. Now one can easily argue the size of tides are affected by their orbits, especially Stor-Manen, as it's the largest. It's quite preposterous to think the moons themselves are changing! I mean, what are they doing? Putting on various-sized dark cloaks? 'Oh,' says a moon, 'let me put on this black cloak to cover my figure'—"

Lontas abruptly stopped speaking and rowing as the points of both of the mariner's heavy swords pressed into his nose. "You, parrot, trying to tell an experienced sailor with generations of mariner blood that I don't know how the moons' phases affect my sails?"

"Uhhhhh, sure."

"Sure, parrot?"

"I-I-I mean you're correct, sir," Lontas said. "I'm sure each moon has a lovely assortment of cloaks that cover part of their figure, and it has absolutely nothing to do with reflected light from the three suns. I stand corrected." He would have nodded to add emphasis but was prevented by the two swords dimpling his skin. After an uncomfortably long silence, Lontas added, "I totally defer to your sailing skills. I'm sorry."

"Run," the mariner said.

Bellae squinted, unsure of what he could possibly mean while on a boat.

"If you want my advice, and I'm sure you don't, run fast and hard. If you complete this mission, both Blue and White Wizard shall be waiting, whispering some combination of sweet pledges and tantalizing assurances versus cavernous threats and dire warnings.

"When you hear promises and pledges, especially from the powerful, deception and pain are sure to follow. Deceit and corruptness are born within the greedy burning within the hearts of us mere mortals. It is our own weakness, but we hide behind made-up personifications of evil. Any time someone with power promises with eloquent fluency, usually flashing a charismatic smile, you're sure to be greeted with hardship and tragedy. Nothing's free, and anything that sounds too perfect is a fabrication, sure enough."

"What promises are you talking about?" Sankari asked angrily.

"Don't think for one second that the most powerful beings on both sides of the Dark Sea aren't watching and assisting you, not out of kindheartedness, to complete this quest. They both hired me to get you to Ifrean and back. Why? If they don't outright kill you, they'll offer you some reward for giving up the crystals. Spoiler alert, they'll not be honoring those pledges.

"Just because someone looks you in the eye doesn't mean they're trustworthy. A deadly cobra will look at you before it strikes and kills.

Just because someone reaches out to support you doesn't mean they have good intentions. A python will give you a hug and squeeze…until you die. Just because you love and trust someone doesn't mean they return the affection or their trust is deserved. The deceivers of the world don't always use magic but still swindle, defraud, and cheat. The rich and powerful never just hold what they have but constantly grab for more."

"The League *will* have an answer in the end," Sankari countered.

"However you think this is going to end, you're wrong," Mor-Leider replied. "I spend most of my life on the waves because the sea and storms are honest about trying to kill you."

Lontas stopped rowing and let the dingy glide forward under the weight of his stare focused on the mariner. "We're not running. We're going to finish this."

"You'll die," Mor-Leider said. "When you fight two colossus powers, the ending is already writ, boy. Don't think they aren't guiding you to a conclusion of their choosing."

"For countless generations the League has been preparing for this," Sankari said, pride leeching into her words as she imagined the string of her descendants in a long line behind her.

"Evil's been planning for even longer," the mariner said. "Plus, hope is fool's currency."

"If there's even a small chance we can stop this depraved cycle, we have to try," Lontas said. "Caring takes more effort, but not more energy. Kindness and positivity require you to make that choice, recurrently—day by day, and sometimes moment to moment."

The mariner paused, rubbing his forehead for a moment. "If you try to catch the air, you fail. If you try to race the wind, you lose. If you accept the gale and enjoy the breeze, you'll be happy. If you raise a sail and humbly implore the wind, it can be your brother, helping you fly across the waves. You can't beat it, but you can, sometimes, manage it."

"If by 'manage' you mean let this power fall to evil, that's not happening," Lontas said.

"Son, you never stop evil, not truly. All you can hope to do is change its moniker because always, always, the next wicked player is there, lurking in the shadows. Sometimes it will be better for the world, and sometimes worse. Oh, it will have a different name and a different face, but it is the same evil driven by some combination of the same things: vainglory, greed, wrath, lust, envy, shiftlessness, and gluttony."

Lontas glanced to Bellae, but she was looking out on the waves, small tears falling gently despite her expression of resolve.

Scroll 10: Battle of Châlons—At Our Back, in Black

"The siege towers are nearing the wall, sir."

"I want the mongrel Proliate barbecued when we take this temple. Survivors should not be killed so we can slow cook them," the Dark Warrior commander said.

"Reports are all thirty thousand who entered the temple are dead."

"Praise Troldmanden, blessings to their families entering Paradise," the commander said.

The two hundred Proliate left to defend Aon Intinn went up to the ramparts to man the walls. They divided into groups of twenty opposite each of the ten siege engines approaching. Each group had archers with flaming arrows.

"Isn't that cute, sir. The Proliate defenders have little flaming arrows."

"It will be adorable when we jam them through their heads. Still, why have so few defenders on the wall? Any word on the wyverns?" the Dark Warrior commander asked.

"They're not doing well. I doubt they'll be able to help us in the siege of the temple," a soldier informed.

The siege towers were only a few yards away from dropping their planks and storming over the temple walls. Still the Proliate archers held their fire.

Cries of "Hyokkays!" cracked the skies behind the Dark Warriors as the Dwarves of the Aer Ridire encouraged their dragons to attack.

The commander saw a swarm of Vioma dragons bearing down on them from behind. The Aer Ridire riding them released the cord to nets filled with dozens of clay pots full of naphtha and metal shards. The sky filled with thousands of the deadly projectiles. A musical whirring sound filled the air as the missiles dropped. Many of the pots bore painted images of Tallcon, skull and crossbones, or the words 'mors desuper.'

Before the commander could issue an order, the ground exploded as the released projectiles crashed around them. Squeals of pain blistered the air as the metal shards sliced and ripped into the Dark Warrior infantry. The oily naphtha burned in the fresh wounds pocking their bodies. It was then that the Proliate on the walls released their flaming arrows.

The Dark Warriors gazed in horror as the arrows found their marks. The area in front of the temple erupted into a moat of burning misery. The dragons and their Aer Ridire riders headed to the rear of the temple and disappeared.

"Puhh orard!" the battered commander yelled, his jaw and lower face deformed by shrapnel. With unthinkable courage, the Dark Warriors still alive struggled to push the flaming siege engines forward.

"Duck down!" Slaemur-Rass yelled.

All two hundred Proliate squatted down and pressed against the ramparts as the Vioma dragons shot overhead, returning from picking up fresh projectiles to hurl at the siege engines. The defenders could feel the rush of air and sense the adrenaline coursing through the dragons as they zoomed overhead. As the naphtha filled pots slammed into the wooden towers, the sticky and viscous liquid splattered on their sides.

"Light them!" Slaemur-Rass ordered. Within a few seconds, all ten siege engines were ablaze—the naphtha overcoming the watered-down animal hides coating them.

"Follow the ramparts to the back of the temple," Slaemur-Rass ordered.

The Vioma dragons, for the first time using their own fire, circled around the back of the Dark Warrior siege towers, bathing them with flames. With the invaders' air support battling to the south there was nothing they could do, save cry and die. The screams of the Dark Warriors cooking inside joined those on the ground. The Vioma dragons broke formation and began looping around to indiscriminately shower flames on any standing Dark Warrior. To add to the terror, they occasionally flew close enough to claw or chomp them.

With all commanders killed, a young sergeant took stock of the situation. All of their siege machines were destroyed. Around seventy-five percent of the troops left to capture the Temple were dead or burning. Turning to the remaining troops, he yelled, "Everyone south! If we cannot take the temple, we must destroy their infantry."

The twenty thousand Dark Warriors fit to fight abandoned the disastrous siege of Aon Intinn and headed south towards the battle raging on the open Catalaunian Plains. As they marched away from the inferno of death, the cries for help from the burning and dying were ignored. Charred black forms dotted the burning landscape, their former human forms rendered into unrecognizable seared clumps.

"Look," a Dark Warrior said to the field commander of the seventy thousand Dark Warriors still battling on the Vahse Plains.

Rotating, Drepa lit up at the sight of twenty thousand troops coming down from Aon Intinn, wrongly assuming that things had gone well and the flames were the city burning.

"Signal them to our left flank. The enemy's right is weak," Drepa ordered. "Move. The wyverns are about to give out, and then we will have their beasts buzzing from above."

Veli Pingius, having detached to talk with Friar, said, "Our left flank and center lines are doing well. The Proliate Believers, Elves of Creber, Saatana Dwarves, and Knights are holding their own or making headway against the larger force of Dark Warriors."

"Ah yes," Friar agreed. "Recent converts and those with their faith cast into doubt are the most fanatical. I would not want to stand across from the Believers this day."

"Our right flank is struggling," Pingius observed. It was hard for Friar to believe the transformation in his last Veli, armor highlighting his new muscular form. "The warriors of Ager and the Proliate Disbelievers are fighting so savagely they're pushing deep into the Dark Warriors' line. Unfortunately, the Western Elves are getting flung back, and the Southern Dwarves are almost completely wiped out."

Friar nodded. "That's putting both Ager and the Disbelievers at risk of falling victim to their own success and being engulfed in a pincer." He signaled Lidenskap.

"Send two thousand troops to replace the slovenly Southern Dwarves, now!" General Lidenskap bellowed. "Thin out our lines, or we're going to get flanked. When the body is tired and drained, it is time for the spirit to rise!"

The reserve Red Guard arrived just in time to carry out both orders. The Southern Dwarves had turned to try and flee but were quickly cut down by the advancing Dark Warriors. Luckily for the Allies, the Dark Warriors were taking their time killing the retreating Dwarves instead of exploiting the gap in the line. This gave the Proliate time to fill the breach before the men of Ager were surrounded. The unseasoned Western Elves refused to retreat but were about to be overrun when the Proliate thinned their lines to support them.

Lidenskap's troops had stabilized the line. However, things began to deteriorate quickly as the twenty thousand Dark Warriors who had survived Aon Intinn rushed into the battle, slamming into the Dark Warriors' left flank, opposite the recently thinned Red Guard Line.

The influx of fresh Dark Warrior troops forced Lidenskap to thin his lines even more to deal with the massive surge in enemy troops. The sheer weight of the extra warriors was enough to drive the Proliate Nonbelievers backwards.

"Friar, twenty thousand Dark Warriors are trashing our right flank," Gleoi Dei said.

Nodding, he yelled, "Release the sabers!"

Just as the Proliate Disbelievers were about to be overwhelmed and outflanked, several hundred griffins who had been hidden with prestidigitation shot up from behind Allied lines. Each one carried a large crate. After flying over the enemy, they circled around. Diving towards the rear of the Dark Warriors, they released the crates, which flopped down and crashed open. Immediately the growl of the untamed tilkeri could be heard. Two large saber-toothed cats stormed out of each crate, savagely attacking the rear of the unsuspecting Dark Warriors. Their dagger-like teeth instantly impaled and killed any they fell upon. Several were ripped so savagely their spines snapped as they were wrenched backwards. Others used their sharp claws to shred through flimsy armor.

In the skies the last of the wyverns fell, having proven tougher than anticipated. The griffins immediately began attacking the rear of the Dark Warriors' line, their claws and beaks easily crushing and puncturing their lightweight armor. The hippogriffs flew in confused circles above the battle for a few moments before flying off.

"The hippogriffs are leaving," Ritari informed Friar after detaching from the front.

"Better than attacking us or the griffins. We should save our few Magicians with crystal power. None have enough to renew the control enchantment for any length of time," Friar replied. "Where are the Proliate with our next surprise?"

Ritari just shook his head as the two gazed at the still-precarious right flank.

"A true warrior is at his best when the adrenaline fails!" Friar yelled after walking to his Knights. "This is where we call upon the strength of our training, the energy of our ancestors, the honor of being righteous warriors!"

The brutality of the tilkeri saber-tooth cats and the surprise of the griffin aerial assault temporarily halted the Dark Warrior advance, sparing the Allied right flank from being overrun, as they had to split their lines and turn to protect themselves on two fronts. A loud cheer went up from the Allies as over one hundred spraks appeared on the eastern horizon—being ridden by Proliate Believers using massive chains. Their awkward twisting gait was exaggerated as they scurried at their top speed.

"I'm happy they're fighting with us," Ritari said, "but it dredges up some bad memories."

"All fighting this day have plenty of horrific baggage in their hearts," Friar said.

The sight of the lizards bearing down was enough to make even the fanatical Dark Warriors pause. When the spraks were ten yards away, they opened their red sails. The black and yellow center resembled large eyes staring through the enemy. The Proliate riding them all had heavy merja spears. With the twenty-foot-long spraks bearing them, the force of the spears was incredible as they slammed into the newly arrived Dark

Warriors. Many of the spears kabobbed through. Leaving the embedded spears, the riders drew their swords, but there was little work for them to do as the hungry spraks ripped and shredded. Body parts, blood, and ribbons of tattered armor and flesh filled the air around the advancing beasts. Besides intimidating the Dark Warriors, the charge of the spraks forced their lines to scrunch together. The closely packed soldiers had their movements restricted and their fighting efficiency reduced.

The Proliate Disbelievers were fighting with fervor. Chy used his shield to block an axe strike before nearly severing the attacker's neck with a stabbing blow from his sword. Leaving the sword embedded, he grabbed the attacker's axe before it fell and slammed it into another Dark Warrior's head. As blood gushed out, the Dark Warrior's eyes opened wide before he dropped. Chy bent down, grabbed that warrior's mace, and brought it up swiftly under another's chin. The jaw obliterated, and he fell. Chy spun a three-sixty, slamming his shield into several Dark Warriors. He used the newly created space to step back, slurping out his embedded sword.

"Stay in line, youngling!" a grizzled veteran shouted.

"Keep up or shut up," Chy grunted.

The griffins added to the devastation, diving up and down for surprise attacks at various places along the rear of the Dark Warrior lines. Several spraks broke off from the dark warriors and turned on the tilkeri cats, their natural enemies on the Proliate islands. The soldiers struggled to regain control of the increasing number of spraks interested in the saber-toothed cats. As the tilkeri suffered under a combination of spraks and the back lines of Dark Warriors, a loud war cry went up. The male warriors of Jaa appeared from the north in black pants and shirts. Their women warriors were sprinkling bits of dirt taken from Jaa in front of the advancing male army.

"Their law states the men, other than royal guards and dignitaries, must fight only on Jaa soil, but the custom does not say how deep the soil must be."

Ritari nodded, appreciating Friar's workaround.

"Jaa! Jaa!" they shouted. Twisting and barbed tattoos curled around their well-muscled, bronze bodies. With each cry of their homeland, they raised their intimidating guanduo weapons—long poles with large and deeply curved blades at the ends.

Drepa, the field commander of the Dark Warriors, was embroiled in combat with a Northern Dwarf when one of his sergeants pulled him back.

"Commander, the male warriors of Jaa are at our back, in black."

"What? They never leave their lands!"

"Apparently, they do," the sergeant replied.

"Move! Let me take a look."

The three thousand five hundred warriors of Jaa formed four lines, one behind the other, about thirty yards apart. Each line had around nine hundred warriors as they steadily advanced towards the back of the Dark Warriors.

TABLE 2 Battle of Catalaunian Plains

~~Dead/destroyed~~ *Reduced number*

Allies		**Dark Warriors**	
Knights of Toil Shaor:	*4,000*	**Infantry:**	*79,500*
Proliate (Believers):	*12,700*	~~**Wyvern:**~~	0
Proliate (Disbelievers):	*8,000*		
Elves of Creber:	*6,000*		
~~**Western Elves:**~~	0		
~~**Southern Dwarves:**~~	0		
Ager:	*3,000*		
Northern Dwarves:			
Vioma Division: (Green)	*6,250*		
Saatana Division: (Red)	*6,000*		
Jaa (male warriors)	3,500		
Griffins:	*650*		
~~**Hippogriffs:**~~	*0 (fled)*		
tilkeri (saber-tooth cats)	10		
Magicians:	16		
Surprise troops:	/////////		/////////
Total:	**50,126+ (13,200 casualties)**		**(70,875 casualties) 79,500+**

Drepa made it to the rear of the Dark Warrior lines to see the fearsome male warriors of Jaa. "Back two lines, turn and attack!" he shouted. "Encircle and shred them!"

The rear lines of Dark Warriors rotated and advanced towards the men of Jaa. When they were about five yards away, the first line of Jaa Warriors sprinted forward and brought their long-reaching guanduo down in sweeping overhead arcs. Their incredible strength combined with the large, heavy blades of the savage weapons created instant devastation. Several of the Dark Warriors' heads and upper torsos split in two—each half flopping to opposite sides.

After their quick and savage attack, the front line of Jaa warriors, now splattered red, abruptly turned and sprinted backwards, retreating behind the rear lines of their fellow soldiers. This formation and tactic accomplished several things. The most important was to prevent their small force from being enveloped while keeping them on Jaa soil and helping pull part of the Dark Warrior army away from the front line.

This relay pattern continued—the forward line of Jaa savagely attacking before briskly displacing backwards, replaced by fresh troops in the next group. The Dark Warriors' lines were becoming increasingly pulled away from the main force as they tried to knock out the intense soldiers from Jaa—taking more pressure off the Allied line.

Laughter suddenly broke out from the western edge of the Dark Warriors. They were looking at a small dust storm moving quickly towards the battle from north of the Storm Fields. On closer inspection you could start to make out the diminutive forms of Fairies. Some were flying while others rode tusked peccaries. Around the Fairies were the colorful, six-inch-tall Sprites riding their matching spriggans, appearing like a swarm of colorful insects. When they were about three hundred feet away, the Sprites suddenly dropped back, seemingly retreating.

"The bugs are retiring already!" a Dark Warrior cried out.

Undaunted, the Fairies continued advancing. Drepa was still wondering what to make of the miniature army when the skies filled with large throwing darts from the atlatls of the Fairies. Using a throwing stick with finger slots to improve their grip, the Fairies were throwing three-foot-long darts great distances.

The Dark Warriors had their grins replaced with looks of pain as the sharpened stone tips of the atlatls rained down on them with surprising force. They fell by the hundreds. The tips of the darts had been dipped in curare poison: a sludgy liquid made by boiling down bark from young trees found outside Cappadocia. The paralyzing toxin began to work almost immediately. The soldiers who were hit hissed in terror as the poison made movement impossible. Spasms turned to looks of terror, until finally suffocation.

"You!" Drepa yelled to a lieutenant. "Take a battalion over to destroy those flying insects. If you can capture a few, we can eat them at our victory feast tonight."

"Yes, sir," the lieutenant replied. Around a thousand Dark Warrior troops headed west to destroy the several hundred Fairies and Sprites.

King Kuningas was riding in a small chariot pulled by three peccaries wearing leather armor. Wide-eyed, he was yelling orders, causing his chubby cheeks to flush with excitement.

"It's been thousands of years since Fairies fought in battle. We will make a grand impression. Fire at will, my brave warriors!" Kuningas shouted.

"Fairies and sprites?" Ritari asked.

Friar shrugged. "Kuningas was insistent. Do they not have as much right to fight for their freedom as anyone else?"

Working in teams to reload, the Fairies were able to unleash a blistering barrage of poisoned atlatl darts on the approaching Dark Warriors.

"They won't hold up well," Ritari said as the Dark Warriors plowed into the Fairies.

As the mismatched armies collided, the Sprites suddenly returned. Flying on their spriggans, the Sprites hovered in a swarm above the Dark Warriors. Using blow guns, they unleashed a hailstorm of poison-tipped darts, aiming the needle-like projectiles at the face and neck. Screams of surprise and pain rippled through the Dark Warriors as they fell to the ground, writhing from the paralyzing poison. The frustrated soldiers from Ifrean waved and slashed their weapons at the hovering Sprites, who were careful to stay just out of reach.

"Given the size discrepancy, the Fairies have little chance at close-quarter fighting. Their small peccary tusk swords are no match for the much longer and heavier weapons of the Dark Warriors. If we fire arrows, we could hit as many of our allies as enemies, and if we detach our troops, the Dark Warriors, who still outnumber us, could split or roll up our entire line. We must save our surprise reserves," Friar replied as King Kuningas screamed, "Retreat!"

Scroll II: Don't, Not, No. You Know?

"If you're not thinking it, no, if you're not unthinking it, no, as well, because I'm not saying I'm not, not starting to kind of partially not not like you parrots. Under no circumstance am I denying you start to grow on a person, but then again, so do warts and fungi. Once more, I stress, not in an endearing way, more like barnacles on a boat. That spoken, I feel my health would have been better served if you hadn't made it back."

The three League members looked at each other with confused expressions after Mor-Leider's bewildering abuse of double negatives.

"What exactly are you saying?" Lontas asked.

"Get on the Amathia, you insolent and dim-witted parrot! I was saying I didn't expect you to make it back, or even get this far, thereby having a proper excuse to leave you to die without any regret in my head, guilt within my heart, or officially breaking my promise. But now that you're here, I have a tinge of feeling that could rightfully be considered not ungrateful."

"Is there a school for emotional poverty?" Sankari said, gesturing rudely at the mariner. "If so, especially if they teach grammar, sign up posthaste."

Still utterly confused, Lontas and Bellae stepped onto the rickety rope ladder, climbing out of the small boat.

"Thanks," Bellae said, still wondering whether he truly betrayed them or had no choice.

His response was a grunt.

Sankari fluttered in front of his face as the others ascended. "Don't think your honey-coated words, especially with the blatant abuse and frankly, criminal exploitation of language, will sway my opinion—you're a traitor."

"I navigate through life on the waters presented, riding the boat available. My goal is simple—stay alive while sailing on the game board, as a small piece, mind you, I did not create."

Sankari's face scrunched into revulsion. "It's only a fair game if we know the rules."

"That's the thing about life," Mor-Leider replied sympathetically. "None of us really get told the rules, and by the time you figure out some of them, most of your time has left with the tide. All we can do is muddle through with our best sails unfurled."

Sankari shook her head angrily before flying to join the others in their cargo hold that increasingly felt like a prison.

"It seems like we never left," Lontas groaned as they settled into their crates.

"At least we never didn't not unleave," Bellae said.

Lontas shook his head.

"Too soon?" Bellae said, trying to sound cheerful. "At least there's a lot more food."

"Are we going to read the new scroll?" Sankari asked.

"Let's wait," Bellae advised. "I do not not need a break."

Sankari pulled her sword, ominously shaking her head. "That needs to end, right now!"

"We can get everyone's input when we get back," Lontas quickly added.

"I bet they've been having a better time than us," Sankari said sourly. Suddenly, she somersaulted in the air as the ship lurched out of port.

"Shhh!" Sankari said sharply. "Just because you guys aren't sick doesn't mean you can get us caught. Superstitious sailors could still kill us."

"Riding the western currents has made this a smoother ride," Lontas said, his seasickness of the initial trip replaced by boredom. Suddenly, he looked up, his face wrinkled with concern as the ship began to pitch and yaw in tune with the battering patter of portly rain.

The rats scattered as the sound of the ship battling weather and waves intensified.

Sankari, Lontas, and Bellae hunkered down in their crates. The twisting in their stomachs intensified as they felt and heard the storm escalating. Loud footsteps crashed down the stairs, occasionally mis-stepping due to the monumental reeling of the ship and wet boots slipping.

The mariner suddenly appeared. "You have not been as careful this trip back," he admonished, moving in a tipsy but rhythmic way between support beams for balance. "Bottom line is everyone knows that you're on board but will pretend they don't. All it took was me alerting, any mentioning these travelers shall be answering to the White Wizard himself."

Lontas was turning green, holding on for dear life. "Seems we've run into quite a storm."

"No!" Sankari said, fluttering against the rocking of the ship. "You don't say?"

The mariner shook his head. "The Fairy stays, but you two? Time to feel the naked power of nature that only experience can appreciate."

"You want us to go up…there?" Lontas questioned.

"Your sickness shall subside if you go topside."

"I'll say this as I fly, go up and you'll fall overboard and die," Sankari said, wagging her head. "You're not the only one who can rhyme, mariner. Anyway, Lontas will definitely not feel sick from the sea once murdered by it."

"It's a sight worth seeing, my parrots."

"They're not *your* parrots!" Sankari huffed as the three stumbled their way up the stairs.

The roar of the storm pounded angrily, and the violence of the waves thundered louder as they approached the door. The mariner used all his weight to keep the door from being torn away as the squall growled into them, instantly soaking them in a blanket of moisture.

"Keep up enough speed to allow my Amathia to ride the waves but watch the strain on the masts!" Mor-Leider yelled to the struggling crew before guiding them towards the side.

"This can't be safe!" Lontas yelled as they hydro-skated towards the taffrail, which seemed decidedly flimsy and disgustingly inadequate next to the raging tempest surrounding them. Water deluged down from the skies while the ocean angrily hurled surges from below.

Bellae tried to slow her breathing as dark waves rolled to obscene heights in front of them. Not to be outdone, the sky trundled violently—shades of grey and black storm clouds wrestled each other while rumbling across the horizon. Massive spikes of skeletal lightning punched across the heavens with raging fervor, quickly followed by concussive roars of thunder.

While Bellae and Lontas clasped desperately to the railing, Mor-Leider looked incredibly calm, his legs bending in swaying tune with the storm's orders. Torrents of rain recklessly sprinted around the curves of his face before being lost in his already soaked beard. "I find my peace within the storm. I find perspective in the unfathomable power of the wind and rain reverberating above and manic ocean waves showing their zeal but also diving below to mystifyingly cryptic depths. I clearly see myself for what I am, a small blip of weakness against the vastness of nature. I had to get lost at sea to find who I truly am."

Although they knew they probably should, pure spiked terror dimmed their ability to appreciate his words.

Scroll 12: Battle of Châlons-In Front, In White

The exhausted Fairies made a dash towards the Storm Fields. After the heavy losses they suffered, the infuriated Dark Warriors were not keen to let them escape.

"We have to do something," Ritari said.

"High Commander!" Friar yelled. "Get the griffins to help the Fairies escape!"

Storlax nodded and began shouting orders. Several squadrons of griffins flew west. They looped around and slammed into the surprised Dark Warriors, allowing the worn-out Fairies and Sprites to retreat from the battlefield. King Kuningas' chariot had been destroyed and the peccaries pulling it killed. His injuries necessitated being carried by several struggling Fairies. Noting that the residents of Cappadocia had safely retreated, Friar smiled. The miniature warriors had managed to kill hundreds of Dark Warriors and stretch out their troops. Suddenly, his grin disappeared as a strange new sound permeated the battlefield. A series of loud shrieks startled everyone, including the griffins. They turned to see five hundred Eaglians flying towards the battle from the north.

"The Eaglians are here!" several cried as a cheer went through the Allied army.

"Keep the griffins away from them!" Friar yelled, afraid their mutual hatred would spill into conflict. When they were still far out of reach from the battle lines, half a dozen portals opened in the sky on either side of the Eaglians' flight path.

"The last of my birds, attack!" a voice boomed.

"Was that the White Wizard's voice?" Ritari asked, a shiver of fear running through him.

"Unfortunately," Friar replied.

A loud buzzing sound was followed by hordes of Stymphalian birds zooming through the portals. Eight eyes, four large, four small, arched terrifyingly over honed beaks lined with sharpened teeth. A crown-like appurtenance circled their heads. Their four-foot-long bodies had two massive wings and ended in a pair of fins for stability. Four of their legs ended in sharp points capable of impaling their victims while two ended in claws. As one they opened their mouths and let out an unearthly screech as clawed tubes projected out between their sharp teeth.

The Eaglians immediately turned to face the birds from the Ifreanean swamps. Their throwing darts flew with deadly accuracy, piercing their relatively fragile eyes and skulls. With bestial shrieks the Stymphalian birds fell in droves. When all darts were thrown, they switched to swords. The strength advantage of the Eaglians was clear. However, the Stymphalian birds' agility, due to their dual-stabilizing rudder system, put the Eaglians at risk.

The large eyes of the Eaglians made irresistible targets for the avian attackers. Their large, clawed tubes shot from their mouths into the massive globes of the Eaglians, exploding into the orbs with a moist clap followed by an eruption of ocular fluid. Their larger optic nerves made the path to Eaglians' brains more susceptible, and the grotesque muscles of the tubes began their wavelike contractions to feed, slurping large sections of brain with each guzzle.

Eaglians began falling en masse, the Stymphalian birds hanging on to suck as much cerebral matter as possible before shooting off the corpse just before impact. The Eaglians went wing to wing in groups of five—the pentagon shape an attempt to create some overlap defense. In close-quarter fighting, the Eaglians, seeing their comrades' fate, used their hulking beaks to shred the entire front part of the birds' heads.

With a cheer from the Allies, griffins emerged behind the two sets of Stymphalian birds. Their appearance compressed the Ifreanean creatures between themselves and the Eaglians, minimizing their one advantage—greater mobility. A few Stymphalian birds began to retreat back through the portals as their numbers exponentially dropped. The portals abruptly closed, replaced by a blindingly vivid white light shining brightly behind the Eaglians.

"What's that, Friar?" Ritari asked.

"No idea."

The fighting slackened to scattered swordplay as the majority of combatants stared towards the increasingly dazzling light. The griffins withdrew behind the Allied lines, leaving the enraged Eaglians to battle the remaining Stymphalian birds. A humming sound was getting louder as the light expanded. Shrill screeches filled the air as the light shot forward and overtook the Eaglians. Their majestic forms exploded, and the few remaining Stymphalian birds were also incinerated. The radiance abruptly disappeared, and the sky filled with thousands of wyverns. The black beasts crashed through the shattered Eaglians, spitting acid on the fragments of their ranks or taking bites from their broken bodies with their wolf-like heads.

The wyvern immediately set into the griffins, who had returned, but this time the beasts from Ifrean enjoyed an almost two-to-one numerical advantage. Simultaneously, the white light that destroyed the Eaglians floated towards the battle.

"Honor to Troldmanden!" some Dark Warriors shouted.

Friar and Ritari looked in disbelief as the White Wizard appeared within the light in his white robe and hat, carrying a gnarled wooden staff and wearing a leather surcoat.

"Cheer, fools. Cheer for your own demise," the White Wizard whispered while moving towards the warriors from Jaa.

Friar turned to the dozen Magicians cowering behind them. "Time to earn your keep!"

A tall, thin Magician, Pitkä, scoffed, "That's suicide."

"If you don't try, we all die," Friar said.

"We're not sure how much magic we have left," Venlig, the Magician who had helped Friar in the dungeons, said.

"I understand that," Friar replied. "However, you can take what you have left to the grave or you can fight, and maybe go home with empty crystals."

"Our magic is not powerful enough to kill him," Pitkä said.

Friar paused. "I have seen on several occasions the Wizard Tacet-Vand push back evil creatures with a band of light. Could that work here?"

"The lux veritatis spell could work," Venlig said.

"Perhaps if we all work together," Pitkä replied.

"The Sameina spell, in conjunction?" Venlig suggested as arguments about the practicality of combining those two spells broke out amongst the others.

By this time, the White Wizard was floating about thirty feet above the Jaainians. He swept his staff around in a wavelike motion before raising both arms above his head. A dark cloud suddenly formed above the Wizard. It swirled and rotated wildly. When he lowered his arms, a massive number of lightning bolts roared out of the cloud. Loud thunderclaps followed as the air between the ground and cloud filled with streaks of hot light. The fried bodies of the Jaa warriors merged with the ground, turning a scorched black as they were repeatedly struck. All remaining Dark Warriors who had been battling to the north were also sacrificed.

Achieving sufficient mortality, the strikes stopped, and the Wizard pointed his staff towards the spraks digging their way through the flesh of the Dark Warriors' line. Streaks of red magic in the shape of arrows blasted out. As the scarlet flames hit the beasts, they exploded, enveloping and then disintegrating them in an inferno.

Motivated by the appearance of their leader, the Dark Warriors ferociously struck out at the shocked Allies. Dead griffins were splatting down, overwhelmed by the massive number of fresh wyverns. With the men of Jaa destroyed, the Fairies and Sprites in full retreat, the spraks dwindling, and the griffins entangled with the wyverns, the Dark Warriors were able to advance and spread out without fear of rear or side attacks.

"Call out the dragons from the Temple," Ritari said in desperation.

"Friar!" a Proliate Disbeliever shouted before he could answer. "We need help on the right flank, or it *will* fold!"

"Signal Lovag to stay put," Friar said. "He's not to bring the dragons out."

"Sir, if we don't call the dragons, we're going to die."

"Ritari, the dragons will instantly be targeted and obliterated by the White Wizard. We have to give the Magicians a chance." Turning to the Proliate, he said, "We'll send five hundred Knights and a thousand of your Believers."

"I doubt that will do anything other than delay the fall," he replied.

"Understood. I'll see if I can get some Elves of Creber as well," Friar said.

As he ran back to General Lidenskap and the hard-pressed Disbelievers, Friar sent five hundred of his Knights to the right flank and messengers to Storlax and Ailante, asking for help from the Believers and Elves of Creber.

"Friar, we can't win this," Ritari whispered.

To his surprise, Friar smiled. "Oh, I wouldn't be so sure. Why don't you head to the right flank and cause some trouble. You're worrying too much, hanging out with me."

"Yes, sir!" Ritari said with faithless enthusiasm before running off.

"The Magicians are going to get slaughtered before they have a chance to cast whatever spell they're thinking of," Ailante said, having disengaged from his line to assess their right flank and oversee a few hundred of his warriors shifting over.

"I can help with that," Friar said, giving an urgent signal.

Moving out of a veil of prestidigitation previously hiding them were thirty Knights on horseback. Gleoi Dei led them, surging towards the Magicians, who were just moving around the burnt corpses of the spraks, hunted by fifty Dark Warriors.

Gleoi Dei gave orders, directing the cavalry to intercept the attacking soldiers. Most had bows drawn and loosed before switching to swords. The arrows had evened the numbers, but the speed and power of the horses gave the Knights a violent advantage. Slashing down with the added momentum of their steeds, the cavalry quickly demolished the foot soldiers. A loud shout rang out from the back of the Dark Warrior lines as several hundred detached from the rear of their lines, charging towards the cavalry.

"Form up a defensive line around the Magicians," Gleoi Dei said as more and more Dark Warriors began to withdraw from the battle towards them.

"Do what you need to!" Gleoi Dei yelled.

"Let's hope this works, Venlig," Magician Pitkä said, thrusting his crosier as high as he could. The others pointed their crystals at his while, as one, they chanted loudly. Glaring light burst out of their crosiers, converging upon the tallest Magician's crystal. Pitkä screamed in pain, his crosier lowering briefly before he struggled to raise it again and chanted, "Lux veritatis!"

Irradiant light detonated upwards with the power of all gathered Magicians. The beam slammed into the White Wizard, catapulting him backwards. In disbelief he found himself immersed in pain and forcibly flying in reverse. Only when his figure was obscured by the rumbling clouds far in the distance did the Magicians' light cease.

Noticing that many of the Magicians' crosiers had stopped working, the Dark Warriors converged on them, howling with fury at what they did to their leader.

"Ride off, quickly!" Pitkä said to Gleoi Dei before linking arms with the other Magicians and casting a spell which whisked them behind Allied lines.

"Congratulations and thank you," Friar said.

Pitkä glared off into the distance. "We just wounded him, and likely very little damage done at that. It's a protection spell, not a killing one."

Many stared mournfully at their hapless crystals, some walking south, off the battlefield.

"Those of you brave enough to stay," Friar said, "watch the skies for his return."

"We won't be able to do anything about it," Pitkä said.

"Whatever you can do, it's more than us," Friar replied.

Just then the White Wizard landed, slamming into the snow- and ice-covered landscape of Jaa, skidding backwards and leaving a crater burning into the frozen ground. Particles of ice, snow, and dirt flung outwards in a wave until he finally came to a stop.

I didn't see that coming, the Wizard thought. "Imbeciles! They don't know the end game! Go on, kill each other. It makes what comes next all the easier." Shaking his head, he banished a wriggle of doubt whirling in his mind. *No, it shall be like every other bloodletting in my never-ending cycle of cleansing. They all die. I live forever.*

Back at the battle Friar yelled, "Archers! Take down the wyvern before they turn on the ground troops!"

Arrows lit up the sky but not enough to stop them all. Friar startled as humungous green figures abruptly plowed into the wyverns just as Lovag landed next to him on Soma.

"Looks like you need some help," Abhac yelled from his perch on the shabby dragon.

"Most certainly," Friar said, grateful to see the impressive beasts.

"With the White Wizard gone I took the liberty of unleashing the dragons," Lovag said, unable to stop smiling, while looking down from the wooden carriage.

"Wise decision," Friar said. There were only a handful of griffins left, but they retreated as the dragons slammed into their smaller, flameless cousins. Many of the wyvern had spent their poison and were no match for the heftier and enraged dragons.

"Back to the battle, all but Lovag!" Friar ordered. "Hit them hard. We don't know if, or when, the White Wizard will return! Time, as ever, is not working for us."

Before Lovag could dismount, Friar's eyes turned white and his body hardened, his arms stiff at his side, his sword clanging to the ground. He was unable to move. At first, all he could see was blackness. Slowly, a misty haze began to swirl around him. Panic bounded in his brain.

Scroll 13: Month Four: Past Sins

As a courtesy Mor-Leider rang the bell, alerting them of his approach, sending the portly rats in a lazy ramble to the shadows.

"Brought you limes and the studious parrot another book."

Lontas shot up, trading him for the one he had finished. "Thank you! I wish I'd known you had a library in your quarters on the way there."

"I wouldn't be letting a fledgling, retching seafarer such as you touch these prized possessions." Mor-Leider used an old barrel for a seat before continuing, "So, what did you parrots make of the Dark Warriors?"

Sankari perked up. "Horrible, rotten, smelly creatures."

"As I feared, you learned nothing," Mor-Leider said.

"Well," Bellae said, an anxious glance to Sankari. "I feel sorry for them. After seeing all they deal with, how they are made, it's hard not to."

Mor-Leider removed his tricorn and wiped his forehead, mostly succeeding in just smearing the grease inhabiting his brow. "Tis a true lesson learned. It's harder to hate your enemy once they're known. Beware anyone or thing that makes the idea of killing routine. All leaders, on both sides of any conflict, being duplicitous, will try and sway you by using their authority to dehumanize the so called 'others.'"

"I can muster the strength to still hate them, and continue despising your betrayal," Sankari said angrily, her wing speed increasing.

"I understand, but you should know that others' words and wishes do not change reality for the world, or those whom they spite. It is we, internally, who thrust our own penances upon our souls. Hanging chains of guilt to deform them, punish them. Noxious gases of culpability, remorse, and regret leach up to our brains."

Lontas smiled, stunned he had misjudged the mariner when first seeing him in the grimy pub. "I misread you and the Dark Warriors."

"He's fooling you," Sankari said. "Too much alone time at sea warped the old brain."

The mariner twitched towards his two swords but stopped, making Lontas and Bellae wonder how much of his blustering was show, hiding his true form beneath. Sighing, he said, "Only being tossed about in dark waters in the middle of the night can my mind shake loose the honey-coated, fraudulent shackles of ignorance. Only when sunlight fades, along with its false whispers of contentment, and treacherous promise of boundless time, can we truly see. The price of such knowledge is the freefalling, sour feeling of knowing we shall drift back into the blackness of eternity. Past sins haunt me sure enough, but you don't cross the ocean dark without being tossed about. No ship sails for long without bearing damage, and no being walks the earth without accruing regrets. You'll only have to bear my presence a bit longer…parrots."

"Nice job," Lontas said, glaring at Sankari as he ascended the stairs.

"What? Just because you two suckers fall for evil pretending to be nice, don't blame me. I'm going to say it like it is, and you're welcome. My job is to protect Bellae, even when you're being stupid. You realize he stole the whole 'honey-coated' line from me?"

Scroll 14: Battle of Châlons-Fanatical Fanatics

Am I dead? Friar wondered as a misty form took shape in front of him. Although recognition was instantaneous, true understanding did not immediately occur.

"Hello, Friar."

"Bellae?"

"Yes, not exactly sure how or why I'm here with you, but I think I'm supposed to give you a message about the battle."

"Are you *actually* here?" Friar wondered, amazed at how much she had changed.

"No, I'm far away in Ifrean and from what is my past, but I can feel the conflict."

"Really?"

"Yes. We found out some Dark Warriors get extra brutal training, the Tumma Vartija or horde. If you have not seen them yet, they're coming." The hazy outline of her face looked down. "Be gentle with the Dark Warriors."

Friar's mind twisted in confusion. He loved his former squire, but the last sixty years had dampened his sympathy for the invaders from Ifrean.

"Their situation is…complex," she said simply.

"What does that mean?"

"Their actions are not for the reasons you think. They don't have a choice—"

Friar cut her off again. "There's always a choice."

"Sometimes...there isn't." Bellae's form seemed to solidify as she looked up again. "Sometimes the choices are between terrible and horrible. Ifrean has been twisted and perverted by the White Wizard."

"I understand, but even if I sympathize, even if I don't fully blame them and the situations which led them here, we still have to fight. I don't want their twisted world infecting Verngaurd. I shall kill them all."

Bellae nodded, using the power of the crystals, she forced into Friar's mind all she had learned and seen in Ifrean. "I must go now. Watch out for other creatures as well." Blackness swirled as her face disappeared.

Slowly blinking Lovag into view, Friar could see the clouds swirling above him. "Am I...on the ground?"

"Yes, lay here a bit," Lovag commanded. "Your eyes shone and body stiffened."

"How long was I out?"

"Several minutes."

Slowly, Friar sat up, and the scene came into focus.

"Another vision?" Lovag asked.

"Sort of. It was Bellae warning of fanatically trained Dark Warriors called the horde. They should be joining the fray soon. She also cryptically mentioned other creatures."

"Maybe Watchers or minotaurs?" Lovag wondered. "I—"

He did not finish as Lidenskap pushed his way through the crowd around Friar.

"What happened?" Lidenskap asked but did not wait for a reply. "Our right flank's in peril. It's time to bring up the reserves."

Friar struggled to stand, his knees cracking their age. "They'll stay put. If you think we've seen the last of his surprises, you're most mistaken."

Before the general could protest, shouts from the Magicians made them look to the southeast. Dozens of Watchers appeared in the sky. Their grotesque desiccated skin flaked off as they pointed ominously.

Their eyes and the deep ruts carving through their skin glowed blue as they began chanting, which opened twelve ground portals.

"Portals?" Lidenskap asked questioningly.

"Portals," Friar confirmed without saying 'I told you so,' before shouting, "Alert Pumilus and the Southern Dwarves to release hidden stage two!"

Two massive ballista, pointing upward, shot a flag tethered between their bolts. As the banner rose, it showed the Isle of Hirmulisko with a creature in silhouette.

Lidenskap looked confused, not knowing all of the reserves Friar arranged. He did not have long to contemplate the flag's meaning as a thundering sound came from the portals. At first, only a dust storm was visible, but soon large black forms could be seen charging forward. The earliest things visible as they burst onto the plain were their monstrous, single, black horns soaring out from their foreheads. Their massive spiked and barbed arms were out to their sides as their four hooved feet beat against the ground angrily.

"Are those…unicorns?" Lovag asked.

"Should we turn some the rear lines on the right side to face them?" Lidenskap asked.

"There's no need," Friar replied, just as Pumilus abruptly appeared in front of them, having hidden himself with prestidigitation until the last moment.

"Although they smell horrific, I would bet on our friends from Hirmulisko," Pumilus said, ruffling his red hair. "They should come out of our screening magic any…second…now!"

As his words faded, a herd of centaurs appeared to the south of the unicorns. They growled in rage, startling the enchanted beasts from Ifrean. The unicorns slowed, caught between the desire to attack the Allied infantry and innate hatred for centaurs.

"They're violating our ancient agreement!" Lidenskap said. "Centaurs can't be here!"

"They're here at my request," Friar responded. "Unless you have another solution to the unicorns? Or, perhaps, you'd like to tell them to leave yourself?"

"Are the centaurs wearing armor?" Lidenskap asked, ignoring Friar's questions.

"Yes, a condition of their agreement to assist. Most carry immense swords, but some have axes or maces. Nearly all have chest plates with a few scattering vambraces."

"Arming savages?" Storlax seethed. "What could go wrong? They strike me as more dangerous than the Dark Warriors."

"They are dangerous…to our enemy."

Storlax scoffed, disgusted at the sight of beasts from Hirmulisko. "Should you go guide your little undomesticated projects?"

"They're highly intelligent and need no direction," Friar said as a quarter of the several hundred strong centaurs took off due east. As they did, the portals closed, leaving two hundred unicorns on Verngaurd's soil.

"Your mind and preparation for battle is…terrifying," Lidenskap said.

"Once you've choked on the bitter sludge of defeat, you do everything in your power to never suffocate on that bile taste again."

As the two equestrian combatants were about to come together, it became apparent that even with the imposing swords, the centaurs did not have a reach advantage given the unicorns' impressive, spiked arms. As the two sides clashed, there was instant death. The unicorns used their barbed arms to decapitate several centaurs. While the centaurs speed helped, their clumsy use of the weapons made them less effective.

"Looks like they could use some training," Storlax gloated.

"Ah, well," Friar replied, "perhaps I should ask our friends from Ifrean if we can have a respite while we train them? What do you think? Is a week enough?"

Storlax huffed back to his lines just as Cruba managed a colossal overhead strike, which flowed down a hulking horn before cleaving a third of the unicorn's face off. The creature dropped immediately, but Cruba stomped it several times out of caution. As the fighting became close range, the unicorns took to uppercut motions with their powerful, sharp upper arms. The razor-edged spikes easily tore into the centaurs' flesh, impaling under their chest plates and ribs, instantly decimating their hearts. They also used their sharpened teeth to gore any exposed flesh. Despite a numerical advantage, the centaurs were being thrown back by the power and ferocity of the unicorns, complicated by their lack of practice with weapons.

As Friar contemplated sending the Gleoi Dei led contingent of Knight cavalry into the fray, the section of the centaur army which had initially broken off reappeared. They had swung east and north and now returned at speed to the rear of the battleline. Sabots, the massive centaur Friar had met in Hirmulisko, was leading this flanking movement. They spread out in a C formation and slammed into the unsuspecting unicorns. Sabots wielded an imposing axe, which he used to sever a unicorn's spine, almost bisecting it through its flank.

"Friar!" Magician Venlig called out, "Watchers to the south!"

The same twelve Watchers reappeared due south. As a fresh round of ground portals opened, they could hear chanting in the language of Ifrean. Soon legions of hardened soldiers came streaming through. To a man they had deep scars and inured skin.

"The horde," Friar seethed, nodding to Pumilus.

The former Rebelde Plains Dwarf stepped forward with his two loitsia sticks, moving them rhythmically. Soon, a prestidigitation-summoned banner rose with the number 3, Tallcon, and massive crossed spears. As portals closed, the teeming horde of brutally trained Dark Warriors lined up. The sarissa-spear-wielding Proliate abruptly appeared behind them with long spears tightly packed in a phalanx. They lurched towards the fanatical Dark Warriors.

"How did you know they would be needed back there?" Lidenskap asked.

Friar shrugged. "I perseverate on every possible negative situation and then come up with at least one solution."

Wearing deranged expressions from months of sleep deprivation and near-constant training, the Tumma Vartija did not hesitate charging the massive spear wall. A fleshy squelching sound sploshed across the field of battle as they slammed into the sharpened tips. Many jumped to impale themselves, their lifeless bodies serving as an anchor to weigh down the spears and disrupt the phalanx. Exploiting the cracks within the spear wall, the Dark Warriors rushed towards the front-line Proliate. Because they all had two-handed spears, they could only scream as the enemies' weapons rained down.

"They're going to flank them," Lidenskap said. "The hordes' back lines are flooding around the ends of the less mobile phalanx. Once around to the sides, they'll do massive damage.

"Release four!" Friar shouted, even though Pumilus was right next to him.

"Would you repeat that? I could barely hear you," the Dwarf replied before using his loitsia sticks to summon a magical banner with the flag of Jaa with a silhouette of a creature.

"What's that calling?" Lovag wondered.

Before Friar could answer, heavy creaking sounds echoed across the battlefield to the east of the horde. Formerly hidden female Jaa warriors cranked large wheels, which pulled taut chains attached to hooks on twelve wooden doors, which began to rise up out of the earth. As the hatches opened, massive howls reverberated out. Princess Hamaza could be heard yelling orders. Massive Valkea Osolobos shot out of the trap doors.

The enormous wolf-bear of the north had white fur covering its tall frame. It mostly walked on its large back legs but occasionally descended to lope with all four clawed paws as it sprinted towards the horde. One stopped to howl loudly while the other eleven bounded towards the dark guard wreaking havoc on the sarissa spear lines. Vaulting upwards, the Valkea Osolobos came down with claws slashing and powerful jaws severing. One of them broke a Dark Warrior's neck while the claws slashed skin and muscle of the face off. Another crushed a skull with a powerful bite. A third easily ripped one of the warrior's heads off.

"Our right flank is going to fold," Lovag said. "Permission to join the fight?"

Friar nodded, and Lovag sprinted off with Lidenskap to help shore of their right side. Turning to Pumilus, he asked the Dwarf for the final messaging flag. First an entire company of female Eaglian warriors descended from the west. Over a hundred flew into the back of the main Dark Warrior fighting force. From a distance they used their throwing

Figure 10: Friar, expecting deception and ruses, unleashes his answers with violent fervor.

darts, killing the enemy in droves. Those left standing were soon set upon by swords and talons.

The dragons finally returned from finishing off the wyvern and set upon the other end of the main Dark Warrior line. The warriors from Ager and the Disbeliever Proliate were at risk of having their line turned just as the dragons slammed into the enemy. The Dwarven Aer Ridire used their bolts to mop up any the dragons did not annihilate.

Friar signaled several Vioma to go and help the sarissa-spear-wielding Proliate as the horde were living up to their name and starting to overwhelm them. With the help of the all-female Eaglian company the Allied left flank began to roll up the Dark Warriors' right. Soon the Eaglians, Proliate Believers, and Elves of Creber routed the entire western end of the enemies' line until meeting up with the dragons.

The female Jaa warriors were struggling to regain control of the Valkea Osolobos but eventually got them into large, barred crates for transport back north. After wiping out the unicorns, the centaurs came over to Friar—the healthiest of their ranks carrying their dead. Sabots towered over Friar. "Do not forget your word. We shall return to our homeland."

Friar nodded. "I won't forget. You may keep the armor or return it at the Eluvies Delta where you picked them up. I do not know how it will affect your long swim."

Sabots scoffed. "Do not forget your promise." Without waiting for response, he led the entire centaur contingent away.

"Good luck," Cruba, the first centaur Friar met, said before heading south.

Looking up, Friar saw many blue falcons circling above on overwatch of the centaurs. With the Allied left line obliterating the Dark Warriors, and the dragons turning the tide on the right, the regular troops from Ifrean were soon encircled and eradicated. The Tumma Vartija were the last of the Dark Warriors alive. They had squared up and were now surrounded by the Allied army. They chanted in the language of Ifrean and continued to fight fanatically. With the dragons and female Eaglian warriors joining the fight, the last one was killed within moments.

"What now?" Lidenskap asked Friar.

"Now we go clean out every last pocket of Dark Warrior infection upon our lands."

"Agreed. I'm surprised the White Wizard did not return."

"I am eternally grateful," Friar said. Looking up at the bloody field, he resigned himself for the gruesome cleanup. "Freedom, like wisdom and behaving ethically, is not a destination. Instead, it must be fought for repeatedly and frequently. The price is visible in the smears of blood and life forces scrawled into the mud of this place."

Chapter Five
It's Almost Over

Scroll 1: Vision of Evil?

Kainen woke up with Gimelli over him. She was talking, but he could not hear, having just woken from a dream of Bellae after obtaining the last crystals. The power overwhelmed her, turning her evil, and she was destroying the world.

"You okay?" Gimelli repeated.

Kainen sat up, took a drink, and realized he was still shaking. "Bad dream."

"What was it?" Arend asked, the tension between the two friends still palpable.

"Even though the prophecy mentions a child, we interpreted it to mean they would be a child when their gifts were discovered, *not* that they would fulfill it *as* a child. Surely you can see the dangers of someone so young with such power?" Kainen said. "I just had another vision of her destroying the world, succumbing to all that power."

"Bellae? Are you serious?" Gimelli said. "You said it yourself, it's just a dream."

"It felt like a lot more," the Elf replied, still taking deep breaths.

"You're just looking for an excuse to be Ailante's flunky, turning your back on the League," Arend said.

Scelto burst into the cave. "Someone's approaching. I think one's an Eaglian."

"You *think*?" Arend said sharply.

"I don't have your eyesight."

Arend huffed and went outside. "It's the Eaglian we met several months ago, Ollmhór, carrying Ailante," he said a short time later as Gimelli and Kainen joined them.

"Ah, children," Ailante said after landing. "As promised, we came back to check in, bringing fresh supplies, including fruits and vegetables."

Ollmhór thrust a large sack towards them.

"Thank you," Gimelli said, smiling.

Later, a Fia Asteikko roasted as Ailante told of the Allied victory.

"Thanks again," Gimelli said, trying to break the silence after he finished.

"So no word?" Ailante asked.

"No, sir," Kainen answered. "It'll still be a couple months."

"Ah, they left in winter and shall return to it, I think," Ailante said. "I know you're trapped in this cave, but the rest of Verngaurd is suffering greatly under the Dark Warriors and White Wizard."

"It's not like we have a choice," Arend said.

"Of course. Just like those homeless and starving Verngaurdians have no choice," Ailante replied tersely. "We'll be grateful to see the end of the prophecy and the benefits of it. The good we can do with the power of the crystals is unlimited. I was thinking—"

"We should honor the prophecy?" Arend interrupted, his head spinning at the treacherous prose. "Isn't that what the League is supposed to be about? Isn't that why countless generations of our families sacrificed what they wanted in order to serve the prophecy?"

Ailante's face scrunched in anger. "We are the League. We owe allegiance to the League here and now. This fact has been hidden from you, but some believe it was actually the Ainmhi Caint who were responsible for Na Cearcaill, not some nebulous evil. In fact, there's concern about Bellae's ability to handle the power of the crystals at her tender age. We can—"

Scelto interrupted. "Bellae's done everything and anything to see the success of this quest. She's never wavered, even when others of us did. She can handle whatever 'it' is."

"Trust me. Trust us. Trust those who fight and sacrifice in the now. You owe no allegiance to those so old even their dust is gone," Ailante said. "We are the Elves and Eaglians spilling our blood, the Eaglians and Elves fighting for our existence, as the very present White Wizard and Dark Warriors attack our forest and patrol the skies."

Ollmhór put up a hand to the children's protest. "I understand your frustration, and let's wait and see what the Ainmhi Caint have to say in the final scroll."

"Forget about a long-dead race," Ailante said, taking over again as Kainen nodded. "A race that may have caused all of this chaos and pain. Think about the ones here and now."

"They're not all gone. Bellae's an Ainmhi Caint," Arend replied.

"All the more reason *not* to trust her," Ailante replied.

"I'm a descendent of them as well," Gimelli huffed, struggling to maintain her cool. "I don't appreciate you maligning my ancestors or my sister."

"No offense was meant," Ailante said, forcing a smile. "All I'm saying is, caution and the greater good are the best attributes, and they align with using the crystals' powers to heal."

Scroll 2: Month Six: *Sea Serpent* Fashion

"The village your parrot eyes glimpse far to the south is North Visser," the mariner said, seeming uncomfortable on dry land after Lontas rowed them ashore. "Proceeding north, the peninsula narrows. After it expands again, you're fairly close to the cave where your friends rest. Now be off," Mor-Leider added gruffly, quickly pivoting and walking away.

"Mor-Leider," Bellae called as Lontas restrained Sankari.

"She'd better not thank the traitor!" the Fairy seethed.

"Shhh!" the mariner said, holding his finger to his mouth. "Do you want to be found and dispatched? There could be Dark Warriors about."

"I want to thank you for getting us there and back," Bellae explained. "We appreciate it and enjoyed our talks."

The pirate stopped, caught off guard by the thankfulness. "Dimwitted parrot! Why'd you have to declare such a thing as that?"

"I forgive and appreciate you, that's why."

"I don't know whether it's better to wish for your parrots' success or failure."

Before he could protest, Bellae embraced him in a hug. He stiffened at the gesture. "I know you didn't have a choice in any of this. I can relate. I don't really have a choice either."

Mor-Leider kept his head down, the tip of his tricorn hiding his rapidly blinking eyes. He turned quickly, forcing Bellae back. Walking towards the dingy, he muttered, "Foolish parrot."

"I can't believe you fell for that backstabbing goon's act!" Sankari said. "Reminds me of that stupid, green Pixie menace who what? Yeah, that's right, also tricked you. Thank goodness you had the sense to bring me along to look out for you."

Bellae, ignoring the Fairy, tugged on Lontas' sleeve, and the three headed down the beach under the cover of darkness. Although Bellae and Lontas felt off balance on the shifting sand, Sankari was fluttering in large circles, happily stretching her wings.

"There's a fire, and I think that's the cave we stayed in before," Bellae said near midnight of their second night. "But they're being too loud. They wouldn't be that careless?"

"It was a year ago. I can't remember if that's the cave," Sankari said.

After creeping closer, they could make out forms sitting around the fire, talking loudly.

"Sankari, can you see what's going on?" Bellae asked as the Fairy wordlessly fluttered forward.

"I lost sight of her," Lontas complained.

"She won't allow herself to be caught. I—" Bellae did not finish, as a handful of torches suddenly started sprinting towards them.

"You head south. I'll run west to distract them," Lontas said as they heard shouting.

Bellae shook her head. "It's Gimelli!"

Once the others arrived, the two sisters embraced for a long time as Kainen, Scelto, and Arend patted their returning friends on the back.

"You guys are brazen. We'd better put out the fire in case the Dark Warriors come," Lontas said, shivering at the memory of human windmills.

"No need. They left this whole area," Scelto said.

The members of the League of Truth—Kainen, Arend, Bellae, Grym, Gimelli, Scelto, Sankari, and Lontas—headed towards the substantial fire. Once settled, Lontas and Bellae told of Mor-Leider, their rough trip to Ifrean, the Lion's Mane Rock, the stone pixies, the initially helpful then betraying Pasture Pixie, the cenote, the Sacrifice Crystals trial, Kāla, and what they found out about the Dark Warriors.

"The Dark Warriors aren't really evil?" Scelto questioned.

"I don't think anyone starts out evil or good. I think they do evil things because they're trained or forced to," Lontas said.

"If you choose to be evil, you earn the title of evil," Arend asserted. "They're the ones wielding the weapons killing innocent people, often by horrible methods. They're responsible for torturing and burning villages."

"Exactly! Thank you, Arend," Sankari said.

"It's hard to call it a choice when they have their families as prisoners," Gimelli said.

"Would *you* commit those horrible crimes and then justify it?" Kainen wondered. "I doubt it. Everyone has to take responsibility for their own actions."

"Living in terror and committing atrocities in the name of fear is just an excuse for being a coward," Arend replied.

"What about the next set of Macht Crystals? What did the scroll say?" Scelto asked.

Bellae carefully handed the scroll to Kainen, who read:

"By offering to **Sacrifice** yourself for a friend,
The boulder did not descend.
The Chosen One will be called to sacrifice more in **Love**,
When **Hate** you are free of."

"**Wisdom** crystals are *the* end.
Prepare yourself to offend.
Knowledge, easy to utter, hard to achieve.
You must break the evil one's **Ignorance** weave.

The conclusion is finally in sight.
Two more trials to set things right.
Go first to the only island in Verngaurd's South.
Only the Chosen One's tongue and mouth,
Can convince the creatures you need.
In the **large** bay find half to swim, half charging steed.

Once they are on your side,
Head north where **GIANT** crystals hide.
Seek the place sailors steer clear.
Where jagged cliffs rise sheer.

With new friends journey down,
To a land, for them, renown.
A world of light where it should be dark.
There, you disembark."

"What does 'two more trials' mean? I thought this was the last pair?" Gimelli asked.

Bellae looked down. *The last trial is for me alone.*

"It means the prophecy, the one, you know, the League is sworn to protect and see to a successful conclusion, will tell us what to do with the crystals," Arend said, glaring at Kainen.

"I get what you're saying," Kainen said, trying to ease the tension. "However, there's zero doubt the world's in enormous trouble, and when the five pairs come together, we have a chance to use their power to fix it."

Arend stood up, his wings snapping in anger. "Our duty is to the prophecy, the League, and Bellae. That's what we swore to protect, not what Ailante or any other ruler spews."

"Wait, what's going on?" Lontas asked, uncomfortable with the strain.

"We've been visited several times by different leaders, including Ailante," Gimelli said cautiously. "They seem to think they should get a chance to use the power—"

"Wait what?" Sankari thundered. "Ailante always belittles the League!"

"Now that we're almost done, he suddenly declared himself a descendent of the League and—" Arend was interrupted.

"That's unfair!" Kainen said. "He just wants to do what's right for Verngaurd."

"That's the problem," Arend said. "Every ruler's going to have a different need, a contrasting vision for their use!"

Bellae's head was spinning. The crystals increased their chatter. *They're confirming what we've been telling you! Everyone will try and take us from you and abuse our power. We need you to help save the world. We only want to help, not be misused.*

When she came back to the conversation, Scelto was talking, "... we won't know how this ends until we get the last scroll. Do you think the riddle means the South Proliate Island, with Temple Barsk on it?"

"No," Kainen said. "It's the Isle of Hirmulisko—the island of creatures and its bay."

"Correct, and the creatures they are talking about are hippocampi," Lontas said. "A hippocamp has a head that's roughly the shape of a horse, the 'half charging steed,' but with horns, and instead of hair, their mane is sea serpents. Their tail is like that of a dolphin, and their front legs end in webbed feet with claws. That part would be the 'half to swim.'"

"Sounds lovely," Scelto said. "Who doesn't enjoy a creature with sea serpent hair?" As he finished, he flicked Gimelli's hair up. "Snakes instead of hair, huh?" She smiled and playfully bumped her shoulder into his chest. He took the opportunity to put his arm around her.

"Ew, stop! I'm going to be sick!" Sankari said. "Not in front of children and Fairies."

"Can we get back to the prophecy scroll?" Kainen advocated as Scelto blushed. "This 'jagged cliffs rise sheer' has to be the Cliffs of Karst."

"Great, it looks like we head to Hirmulisko, find our sea-serpent-haired friends, then go to Karst," Scelto added. "Either that was easy, or we're getting good at this."

Arend agreed to do watch even though the Dark Warriors had left. The others retreated to the cave, leaving Arend, Bellae, and Lontas.

"We sure did miss you," Lontas said.

"Likewise. It wasn't the same with you off at sea," Arend replied.

"Did you stay on target?" Lontas asked, standing to grasp forearms with Arend.

The Eaglian let out a half squawk, half chuckle. "Always. However this ends, I've got your backs."

Lontas took his seat and looked down. "Even before the little argument, I've been wondering, who exactly should we trust?"

"We should be able to trust each other," Arend said, glaring into the cave. "We'll finish this like our ancestors intended. Don't expect the struggle to be over once we get the crystals. One thing's for sure, it's only the beginning of our troubles."

Scroll 3: Half-and-Half

"This is amazing," Kainen said outside Temple Ensjel near the Eluvies Delta. "All of Verngaurd's united, and one set of crystals away from finishing! Ailante said once we find the last two, we go to the Citadel for a great council so they can decide what to do with them."

Arend shook his head. "Not this again. We will honor the prophecy."

Kainen shot Bellae a quick glance. She had her eyes closed and was frantically petting poor Grym despite his squeaky protests. The crystal's promises of unparalleled power and prestige were interrupted only by murmured compliments and flattering remarks.

"Even though this prophecy was written eons ago, it had a clear purpose," Arend continued. "The Chosen will read their final wishes after the last set of crystals are secured."

"We should wait and see," Bellae said, her voice coming out frailly.

"You haven't eaten anything," Gimelli said, worry clouding her eyes.

Forcing a smile, Bellae took a bite and chewed slowly. It tasted horrific—nausea was now a constant companion. Somehow the power of the Macht Crystals had destroyed her hunger yet managed to leave her feeling hollow. *I can be your food,* a voice whispered in her head. *Accept the power of the crystals and never hunger again.* When she finally forced herself to swallow, Bellae had to resist the urge to vomit.

"Isn't this lamb good?" Scelto asked, hungrily going for thirds.

"Yes," Bellae managed, the truth shrouding the words until they were barely convincing.

"It would taste better with a big glass of torahammas milk," Lontas said, smiling.

"Funny," Scelto retorted, his stomach flipping at the catastrophically profuse memories.

Bellae closed her eyes. The others laughing pierced her brain, making the voices from the crystals distort. *I control the good! I control the good!* she shouted, her restraint lessening.

"So we get the last two crystals and then go to the council at the Citadel. Right, Bellae?" Kainen asked, his gaze piercing.

"Yes," Bellae said, trying desperately to sound convincing. *They will try to persuade me to "use" the crystals for good, not caring about the price,* she thought.

Now you've got it! a slithering voice called out in Bellae's mind. *Only you can bring peace to the world and quell their ambitions. You don't need those fools. You have more potential than the Blue Magician to keep the world safe and full of magic.*

"Excuse me," a Proliate Red Guard said. "We have the boats requested."

"Thank you," Kainen said. "We'll rest for the night and head out first thing tomorrow."

"Is there anything else?" the guard asked, barely hearing "no" before marching off.

"We're getting close to the Isle of Hirmulisko," the Proliate guard said the next day. "Are you certain you want us to just drop you off? There'll be no ships coming for you."

"We'll be fine," Bellae spoke, despite the fact he had been addressing Kainen.

Kainen nodded in affirmation, even though he lacked Bellae's confidence about heading to the mysterious island with no foreseeable way off.

Bellae let her fingers gently skim the deep blue surface. As they moved closer to the white sandy shore, the water amended itself to lighter blue before turning see-through by the time the small skiff rubbed its belly against the sand. As the Proliate guard helped the others out, Bellae took off her boots, watching her feet sink into, then lift out of, the wet sand. Wriggling her toes, she let the sand crawl around her skin as her feet sank.

"Good luck," a Red Guard said before wading back onto the skiff that brought them ashore.

"Tell me again why we can't just go to the Cliffs of Karst?" Sankari questioned.

"No way can a boat survive near them. The current's strong, it's too jagged, and we'd die," Kainen said. "Plus, it sounds like the hippocampi will know exactly where the crystals are. The Cliffs of Karst are actually quite large."

A brisk wind coming in from the bay made Sankari shiver, prompting her to move inland.

"Where do you think you're going?" Kainen asked.

"To get out of the wind!" Sankari huffed. "I'm going to the trees."

After putting her boots back on, Bellae moved forward with Gimelli. After a few steps, the sand became dry and less forgiving.

"You know they call this the Isle of Creatures?" Kainen asked. After looking anxiously at the trees, Sankari flew back to the League. The Mardin sun was past the midpoint of the sky, and Luminos was well past the horizon. Yet the League sat quivering on the cold beach.

"Do you think we should swim out to find them?" Scelto finally asked.

"Great! The water's freezing, but, by all means, jump on in, big guy," Sankari huffed.

"Relax, Sankari. However, it's too cold to stay out in the water for any length of time," Arend said, looking nervously towards the woods. "Something's watching us."

"I can sense them," Bellae said.

"Hmmm," Sankari piqued. "The reason you didn't mention this before?"

"I sense no ill will."

"Oh, you sense no ill will…" Sankari paused, putting a finger to her chin. "That makes it okay then. Especially after almost dying by rock pixies and horrifying unicorns!"

Silently, Bellae moved towards the woods. "We can't just sit here." Knowing her sister and Lontas would protest, she looked to each of them. "You can come with me, but I think it'd be better if I go alone." When she was close to the edge of the forest, she spoke in Ainmhi Caint, *"We've come to talk with the Hippocampi. Once we do, we'll leave."* After a brief pause with no response, she continued, *"Please. We don't want anything from you and will not stay."*

"You'll need that language with the hippocampi, but, while I understand you, it is not necessary with me," a rugged voice called out.

"I'm Bellae. Will you come out, *or do you want me to come in?"* She asked the last part in Ainmhi Caint to avoid her sister worrying.

Something rustled in the top part of the tree nearest the edge. Emerging from the forest was a magnificent creature with the head, arms, and torso of a human man attached to the body and legs of a horse. Thick brown hair swung down his back, turning into a mane before joining his horse body. He carried a massive sword, courtesy of the Northern Dwarves.

"My name's Cruba, son of Chiron," he said, a series of horns jutting out from the top of his human head and cheeks.

Bellae smiled and nodded. "May I come closer?"

"Yes," Cruba answered. "After decades with no visitors, now we have many."

Bellae moved to gently rub the horse's back. "I've never seen a centaur before."

"We were forced here, but may be moving home," Cruba said. "Humans and Dwarves used to hunt us, fearing anyone more powerful."

Scroll 4: I'll Try to Make Sure They Don't Kill You

A short while later, most members of the League joined Cruba in the shallow water of the bay with large conch shells provided, along with instructions, by the centaur. The rounded shells were about ten inches long and smooth, save for the open edge, which was flayed out. Kainen, Arend, Bellae, Gimelli, Scelto, and Lontas were blowing into them with the other end under water. Sankari protested and refused to help when, in reality, the shells were too large for her.

"I don't think you guys are trying your hardest," Sankari yelled from the shore, fluttering in a zigzag pattern out of frustration and the wind.

"Is she always like this?" Cruba asked.

"Unfortunately, yes," Scelto answered. "They can really hear this?"

"Do you doubt my word?" Cruba asked, standing up to his full height and splashing his front hooves in the water.

"No," Scelto replied. "I was just wondering how well sound travels under the water."

"The hippocampi are very curious creatures with excellent hearing," Cruba said. "They shall come. However, you might regret that they did."

"What does that mean?" Gimelli questioned.

"They don't like mainlanders—especially humans. Once—"

Cruba was cut off by Bellae screaming. Lontas dropped his shell and ran towards his friend. A large bird, mostly brown but with blue feathers, was fluttering around her head. It had long pointed wings, each one with a thin blue stripe running down the middle.

"Cruba, can you help?" Gimelli screamed in a panic.

"Why?" he asked calmly, as they realized Bellae was laughing.

"That's my friend Gorm, a blue falcon. He doesn't usually take to new creatures but seems to like humans," Cruba announced, thinking of Gorm's response to Friar.

"I'm not exactly sure what you mean by 'take to new creatures,' but it sure looks like he's attacking her," Gimelli said, cautiously approaching her sister.

Tired from laughing, Bellae moved back to sit in the sand. *"Can you please stop for a second?"* she begged, feeling Grym spinning nervously in her pocket.

"I thought you were too dimwitted to speak to majestic birds?" the falcon chirped.

"I wouldn't say people are dimwitted. But you're right. Most can't speak this way." Bellae pulled the edge of her cloak up over her neck where the falcon had been tickling her.

The falcon settled on her shoulder, and Bellae introduced herself and the members of the League. He bobbed his head in greeting to each of them before abruptly swiveling towards multiple white streaks of agitated surf frothing furiously towards them.

"Here come my friends," Gorm said. *"I'll try to make sure they don't kill you with their horns or poisonous snake manes."*

The League watched dark forms cresting above the angrily foaming water, each surge forward casting sprays as they bobbed up and down with incredible speed. The creature out front of the others had writhing forms wriggling angrily off its head.

One in the back arched high out of the water, shouting, *"Ceffyl-Mor! Stop right now!"*

Its head was similar to a horse's, but its nostrils were set on top to allow it to breathe easier when surfacing. Instead of hair, hissing sea-serpents lined its neck, slithering around stripped ram horns in a terrifying mane. Its belly and front legs were that of a horse, except the lowest part, which ended in webbed feet instead of hooves. Pale blue-green scales lined its back and shoulders, transitioning to the smooth grey skin of a dolphin complete with a powerful tail.

"The hippocamp out front is young and curious, much to the angst of her overprotective parents," the falcon explained.

Figure 11: A roughly horse-shaped head is adorned with sea serpents for a mane along with curved horns. Front legs end in webbed feet, and they are powered by dolphin tails.

"Bellae, back up!" Lontas begged as Gimelli nodded.

She waved them off as she and Cruba moved forward.

"Hey horseman!" the girl hippocamp called out, bursting through the water to stare at Bellae. *"Where'd you find that funny thing?"*

Bellae froze, staring at the mostly green and blue sea serpents with bands of color that whipped around and on top of the hippocamp's head, hissing at her.

"Only two legs? No fur except the top of its head? How odd. What is it?"

"I'm a human from the mainland, and my name's Bellae."

The young hippocamp abruptly glared, her sea serpent mane flaying out. Each serpent gazed angrily at Bellae while their bifurcated tongues flicked ominously.

"Wait, you understand me?"

"Yes. In fact, I came to find you," Bellae answered.

"My name's Ceffyl-Mor."

"I heard someone calling after you."

"My dad! He's always stopping me from having fun. He does the whole 'I have larger horns and am older, so you should listen to me' thing," Ceffyl-Mor said. *"Did you notice my purple scales?"* she asked. Using her powerful tail, she pushed herself out of the water and, turning side to side, revealed two rows of purple scales surrounding the blue and green ones. *"Only I have them. Mom says that makes me uni-kay."*

"It's beautiful and unique!" Bellae replied.

Several male hippocampi, their sea-serpent manes thrusting forward and hissing, rushed towards Bellae, baring their sharp, pointed teeth.

"The middle, angry-looking one is my dad," Ceffyl-Mor whispered to Bellae. *"Relax. This is my friend, Bellae, and she can speak to us!"*

An adult female hippocamp swam up to them, looking from Cruba to Bellae.

"Hello! My name's Bellae. It's nice to meet you."

Something softened in her eyes. *"My name's Capall-Mara, and this is my willful daughter. You must pardon our unpleasant greeting, but humans are not welcome here."*

"I thought they were supposed to be bad?" Ceffyl-Mor said.

Capall-Mara tipped her head side to side. *"Most have been cruel to us. This Isle is supposed to be protected, and we have learned to fear the two-feet takers."*

"We're only here for a short time," Bellae stated before leaning forward. *"Gorm, would you stop pecking at my neck!"*

"It seems the falcon likes you," Capall-Mara commented, seeming to relax more. *"So why do you encroach?"*

"There's a great war going on, and there's something we need to find. If we can get these last two things, it could stop the fighting," Bellae stated.

"It seems to me that's your business and none of ours," an elder hippocamp stated.

"Sooo much death, so much destruction," Bellae said, closing her eyelids, but not before tears streaked out, dropping into the ocean. *"I have to try and stop it. Please help."*

Capall-Mara stared at the young girl questioningly. *"Perhaps. What do you seek?"*

"Kainen, please bring the scroll to me so I can read it," Bellae requested.

It was Gimelli who brought it, wanting to be close to her sister. "Bellae, why are they baring their teeth, and their snakes hissing aggressively?"

"They don't like humans," Bellae said, translating the scroll into Ainmhi Caint.

"What do you want there?" the mother hippocamp asked concernedly.

"We need two crystals—" Bellae started, immediately interrupted by the hippocampi's angry shouts and threatening gestures. Loud hissing wriggled through the air as the sea serpent creatures on their necks seethed loudly.

Ceffyl-Mor raised herself out of the water in front of Bellae, *"Let my new friend finish."*

"Your 'friend' wants to steal our sacred crystals!" one shouted.

"They are two-feet takers!" another added as a screaming match started between the hippocampi while their sea serpent passengers furiously hissed.

"Bellae, what did you say?" Sankari shouted.

Lontas shot the Fairy an annoyed look before walking forward. "What's going on?"

"I'm not sure," Bellae admitted. "I just read the prophecy, and they seemed to know the place, but when I told them I needed to find two crystals, they went crazy."

"Bellae, you won't really take our sacred crystals will you. I mean, you didn't come here to steal them?" Ceffyl-Mor asked in a hurt tone.

"I don't want to steal anything," Bellae replied.

"What did you mean by taking two crystals?"

"I've been questing to find special crystals and already have eight but need two more."

Ceffyl-Mor shot her new friend a questioning glance. *"Where are these crystals?"*

"In my bag. Right here," Bellae answered, patting her sack.

"They fit in there?" Ceffyl-Mor asked.

"Of course," Bellae answered, carefully pulling one out.

"Those are the crystals you're looking for?" Ceffyl-Mor asked as it pulsed blue.

Bellae nodded. *"I need two more like this."*

"She doesn't want to take our giant crystals. She's looking for two small crystals," the young hippocamp explained.

Slowly, the adults stopped bickering. The largest of the adult males swam closer.

"This is Csarff-Mâ," Ceffyl-Mor said, wriggling protectively towards Bellae.

"We do not have those types of crystals. You're wasting your time. Now go!" he cried. *"Two-feet takers are never welcome!"*

"I promise we'll leave as soon as we have them. They'll be hidden," Bellae explained.

"Girl, no one but our kind has been in the hallowed area for over a thousand years. It's venerated ground and not to be soiled by foul two-feet takers. We have our marriages and initiation ceremonies there," Csarff-Mâ declared.

"Believe it or not, they would have been hidden way over a thousand years ago by people who could speak with you, like I can," Bellae assured. *"Please, we're so close. Will you let us look? If we find them, we leave. If not, we leave."*

The adult hippocampi whispered amongst themselves. Even as their heads looked inward, the squirming serpents writhed angrily towards the league.

"There's nothing there, but we'll take you to the Cave of Crystals. One person per hippocamp. Do not touch our manes!" the fearsome Csarff-Mâ said.

Bellae translated for the League.

"Thank you for your help, Cruba," Bellae said, hugging the centaur.

"You're welcome. Good luck, child. I hope you'll come back someday."

Bellae smiled though tears. *I won't be coming back.* "You'd better take Gorm," she said.

"He goes where he chooses. We're friends, and he'll come back when he's ready," the centaur replied, collecting the shells.

Bellae thought the falcon might fly away, but he did not. Just to let her know he wasn't leaving, he tickled her neck.

"Have you been looking for those crystals for a long time?" Ceffyl-Mor asked, swimming back and forth and spritzing Bellae and Gorm.

Bellae nodded but could not help the tears from flowing faster.

"What's wrong?" Ceffyl-Mor asked.

"It's just been a long journey is all," Bellae said, wiping away some of her tears. *"Do you think you can carry me, or am I too big?"*

"I can manage!" Ceffyl-Mor answered excitedly.

Once the members of the League, except Arend, who carried Sankari, had a hippocamp to ride, they set off. Arend was circling high overhead, and Bellae could tell he was enjoying soaring on the high sea winds. She turned, waving to Cruba. He returned the gesture.

Ceffyl-Mor swam by raising her head while bringing her tail down and then reversing the motion—using the back-and-forth rocking to swim. *"Is my mane bothering you?"*

"Not at all." The sea-serpents lining Ceffyl-Mor's neck were calm, facing forward, skimming in and out of the water.

"Do you control them?" Bellae asked.

"Not really," Ceffyl-Mor answered. *"My mood affects their attitude. If I get angry, they're angry. If I'm happy, they are."*

"Are they poisonous?"

"Only when I want them to be!" Ceffyl-Mor answered.

Not reassuring, Bellae thought. *"You're very impressive, all of you."*

Several of the sea serpents turned towards her, curious but silent.

"Do they have names?" Bellae wondered.

Ceffyl-Mor slowed, and Bellae could feel hurt radiating from her. The young hippocamp started swimming faster at the chiding of one of the adults. *"Of course, they have names!"*

"Sorry, I should have known that." Bellae felt herself relaxing with the rhythmic movements and calming cadence of the hippocamp's swimming. *Just one more pair,* she thought with a mix of relief and horror.

Scroll 5: Are You With Me?

"She wouldn't tell me much," Jumeaux informed Veneficus and Fino within a small alcove of the elaborate cave a group of Magicians had taken refuge in. "She refused to tell me where they were. However, I could see they were in the ocean outside the Cliffs of Karst."

Veneficus nodded. "Very good. They near the completion of the quest, going to get the fifth pair of crystals?"

"She didn't confirm this directly, but yes, I know they are."

Turning to Fino, Veneficus said, "Get the griffins ready. We travel to the Cliffs and must be ready to pounce before other beings with magic show up."

Fino nodded and left as Jumeaux relived the betrayal of those he thought of as friends. *I know Veneficus put them up to it,* he thought. *But no way will I confront him.*

Veneficus looked at Jumeaux, sizing him up. "You have the unfortunate task of living in dark and uncertain times. A peaceful future is holding on by its fingertips in this rapidly changing world. Chaos blankets us like a damp morning fog. You can help clear the vision of the future and secure hope and prosperity that will last thousands of years. To achieve this, I must get the Macht Crystals. Only I can let the suns shine through all the death and misery.

"When I was young, a very long time ago, I heard a wise man say, 'Anyone can fail, but only a few get up.' What do you think of this?" Veneficus asked—the weight of his stare laced solidly with great expectations.

What does he want? Jumeaux wondered. Nothing notable came to mind, so he answered, "That sounds right. I mean it does take a lot to rise and try again."

"Reasonable," Veneficus answered, but his eyes were knotted with disappointment. "However, the more I thought about it, the more I felt it's only part of the truth. The point is, it takes courage to stand and risk failure. We don't ever really know the future—we only glimpse snippets, not knowing the reality of it until it is upon us. Too often, disappointingly, the actual future depends too much on other people and their actions or inactions."

Jumeaux nodded.

"Magic creates stability and peace, keeping the inhabitants of Verngaurd in touch with nature. That's why I must succeed. Greater security leads to loftier goals, which breeds a superior way of life, but only up to a point. Eons ago, Verngaurd lost touch with nature and almost discarded me and magic for faithless technology. They began to worship it over anything else. It consumed their very lives! I saved the world from utter destruction then and have done so other times. Of course, I had the Macht Crystals at my side for those battles.

"Every creature alive bends down to something, and of those, technology is the worst of these false gods. This is why my experience and knowledge is so important for the world. That is why it is vital to every inhabitant of the planet that I get those crystals. Can I count on you to help me finish this?"

"Of course," Jumeaux answered, nodding vigorously.

"I'm putting my faith in you. There are few whom I have trusted in my many lives. The bloody Ainmhi Caint were the last. Those vile, backstabbing animal talkers are the cause of this mess. Concocting a story of some 'great evil' as an excuse to steal *my* power." Veneficus' voice rose, and his face flushed with anger. "I know your family and friends treated you shabbily, and you rightfully hold a grudge, so I don't need to mention this, but if Bellae and that League of Lackeys do not willingly give me the crystals…let's just say life becomes extremely unpleasant for them…and *anyone* assisting them."

A twinge of regret rose within Jumeaux, mingling with his fear of Veneficus. *You're the one who told Chy and Kaveri to befriend me. Everything with you is false. You don't really care.* Visions of how kind Bellae and Gimelli had been to him flowed by. He may not have felt at home as a squire, but he had never feared for his life like with the temperamental Veneficus. A small seed of second-guessing sprouted in his mind. *Is this life the fake one and I discarded the real one with the squires and Knights? Is everything with Veneficus a lie or coercion?*

"Jumeaux?" Veneficus prompted, his expression a hybrid of resentment and anger.

"I'm with you, sir. Until the end," Jumeaux finally said, despite his doubts. He could not stand against the Magician's fierce gaze.

Scroll 6: Two Tasks Left

Arend and Sankari perched precariously on the jagged Cliffs of Karst while the water aggressively churned, swirling and frothing around the rockface. Wrathful white waves threw themselves at the dark stone with reckless abandon, slamming off the serrated edges before being launched back to the ocean, broken into drops.

"If we get too close, the current will smash us into the rocks," Ceffyl-Mor said as the others glared anxiously at the never-ending number of jagged outcroppings lancing into the sky.

Ceffyl-Mor's mother, Capall-Mara, swam to Bellae. *"The winged creatures, especially the large ugly one, cannot follow. The journey's too dangerous."*

Bellae interpreted, leaving out the ugly comment.

"We'll take you two-foot takers to the entrance, but you must never tell another soul," Csarff-Mâ, the large hippocamp, warned.

Keeping their distance from the swirling waves, the wingless members of the League were taken around to the far side of the cliffs.

"We swim very fast towards the rocks, take one last deep breath while jumping out of the water, then head below," Ceffyl-Mor warned. *"Make sure everything's secured."*

Bellae explained to the rest of the League, but Gimelli was talking telepathically with Jumeaux. "What did he want?" Bellae asked uneasily.

"He said to help," Gimelli said, "but this time, I got the worst feeling. I can tell there's something deeper going on. It seems like he's truly worried and deeply sad."

Bellae nodded before saying, *"We're ready."*

"Hang on tightly!" Capall-Mara warned as the hippocampi sprinted towards the cliffs.

The League gazed anxiously at the rapidly approaching sharp crags. Just before they were about to hit the rocks, the hippocampi bucked up, flinging their bodies, and reluctant League riders, above the swirling water. Gazing down, they could see the harsh waves and abusive current gyrating around the rugged rocks. The League breathed deeply before being immersed into the wetness, startled at the violence of the turbulent water. They eventually swam through an underwater passageway morphing the dark green water into complete darkness. The only benefit was the tempestuous water relaxed, and they could only feel the water pushing them back as their mounts rushed forward.

Lontas' air hunger exploded, generating tormenting visions of the terrible journey in the cenote. Thankfully, light above grew brighter, joined by tantalizing hints of ripples dancing overhead. The hippocampi gave a few more tail and arm thrusts before erupting out of the water.

"Wow!" Bellae said, noticing the light within wasn't coming from the suns shining through holes in the cavern but from an enormous crystalline forest. Crystals as big as trees shot up at odd angles. Their brilliant glow lit up the huge underground chamber and reflected off the other crystals to create a dazzling brightness. A maze of uneven pathways seemed to haunt the crisscrossing crystals. "This is so beautiful," Bellae said.

Lontas squeezed his friend's hand, glad to see her face brighten.

"Alright, we brought you here," Csarff-Mâ said resentfully. *"Now hurry up, but do not touch our sacred crystals."*

"We tried to warn you there's nothing here," Capall-Mara added.

"It's superhot," Scelto commented before Bellae could answer.

"It must be a hundred and twenty degrees," Gimelli added, wiping the sweat mingling with saltwater on her forehead.

"It's also crazy humid. That must be why the crystals grow so big," Lontas said.

"Okay, now what?" Gimelli asked.

"A world of light where it should be dark. There, you should disembark," Lontas quoted. "What? I memorized it," he replied to their stares.

"While that's great, it doesn't really help us," Scelto said.

"It means we don't have anything specific to look for. So there must be a symbol or writing," Kainen said.

"Are there any symbols or markings that could help us find our crystals?" Bellae asked.

"We stay in the water, obviously, but we've never seen any," Capall-Mara answered. *"We've been coming here for thousands of years. I think we'd have noticed something like that."*

"Can we please take a look around?" Bellae asked.

"Go ahead," the intimidating Csarff-Mâ answered. *"Do **not** injure our crystals."*

Their mounts swam to the edge, and the League members carefully disembarked. As they stood on the black rock ledge, the enormous crystalline structures seemed even more imposing, crisscrossing from floor to ceiling at odd angles. As Bellae took out Grym, she suppressed a smile at his contemptuous look.

"There's nothing you can say that will convince me you're not trying to drown me."

Bellae squinted her damp eyes. *"I wish Borb was here and that everything was different. I yearn to be eating Cookie's food and hearing Finn laugh. I wish to ride Crann and to never have met Honey, but none of those things can come true."*

Cautiously, Scelto, Gimelli, Kainen, Lontas, and Bellae entered the crevices of the glowing structures, wondering just how safe it was to walk underneath them.

"Another dead end," Scelto said, his large shoulders almost stuck. "Maybe Bellae could get a little farther, but I don't think so."

"Even with crawling, all paths lead to an impasse," Gimelli added, brushing the glowing dust from her knees. "I saw several large broken shards, so at some point, they must break apart and fall. They could kill us if the fragment was big enough."

"No choice. Keep looking," Kainen said, his thick skin insulating against the soupy heat.

Grym finally came scurrying back to Bellae. *"I made my way around most of the edges. Nothing but solid rock. Nothing hidden I can see. It's soo hot in here. I need a break."*

Bellae nodded, putting him on her shoulder. After weaving their way through a labyrinth of dead ends for hours, the League was sweating profusely and jumped in the water to cool off.

Csarff-Mâ snorted loudly. *"I told you this was a waste of time. Your very presence is a desecration of our sacred temple."*

"Is there any way you could check underneath the water?" Bellae asked. *"It could be small. Look for something a person carved."*

While the adults dove down to look, Ceffyl-Mor nudged Bellae playfully. Exhausted, Bellae could only manage a weak smile as she drained the last drop of water.

"Do you want me to get you more water?"

"Could you?" Bellae asked.

Ceffyl-Mor nodded her head vigorously, and her sea-serpent mane perked up, hissing excitedly at the chance to leave.

"Thanks to all of you, as well!" Bellae said to the sea serpents as the League carefully loaded their drained waterskins into a sack fitted around the young hippocamp's neck.

"Cruba will do it for me. He complains I'm too curious, but so is he. He'll stand at the edge of the forest until we come back with an update," Ceffyl-Mor stated.

"We have to consider that one of these giant crystals has grown over writing, or perhaps even destroyed it," Lontas suggested as the young hippocamp submerged.

"Could these things do that?" Scelto asked. "When I stepped on the small shards on the floor, they crunched like glass."

"Keep in mind we're talking about thousands of years. Over that time, it's possible these things grew and broke so many times they wore the rock thin like the old grave markers that…used to be at Liberum," Lontas explained.

"Did anyone see anything, however small?" Kainen asked.

Everyone shook their heads as the adult hippocampi finally came up. *"Definitely nothing below but plain rock,"* Capall-Mara announced before asking, *"Where's Ceffyl-Mor?"*

"She went to see Cruba and get us water. I'm sorry if she wasn't supposed to go. She offered, but I should have asked you first."

"I'll get her," Capall-Mara huffed, diving out of sight.

The League went back onto dry land. Sweat poured off, but with the sticky, humid air of the cave adamantly refusing to absorb any of their perspiration, it saturated their clothes and sat triumphantly on exposed skin until they were encased in its salty cocoon. The League felt they were about to collapse when Ceffyl-Mor and her mother returned.

"It was my fault," Bellae admitted, helping get the satchel off. She passed around the water, her hand stopping when she saw the surprises.

"It's okay. She's okay," Capall-Mara replied.

"Cruba says hi," Ceffyl-Mor reported. *"He added fruit."*

They were feeling recharged after draining the water skins and eating.

"What about over there?" Lontas suggested, pointing to an isolated, small ledge across from the vast one they were on.

"How did we miss that?" Kainen asked. "Over there the crystals are thinner, smaller."

They swam to the compact rocky shelf, and Bellae stated, "It's still hot, but cooler."

"I bet there's a crack allowing fresh air in. That's why they're not as big here," Lontas said.

"If we don't find something soon, we'll have to try again later," Gimelli said.

Bellae looked cautiously at the hippocampi glaring intently and thought, *I'm not sure they'd let us return.*

"What are we missing?" Lontas asked after they scoured the ledge without luck. "We can't find any writing or symbols. Then maybe we aren't looking for the right thing."

"What do you mean?" Scelto asked.

"That!" Lontas answered. "There are ten small, but distinct, depressions in the rock. They're near the wall where the hint of a breeze is coming through."

"So?"

"Eight of the indentations line up vertically. The other two are lined up horizontally on either side of the vertical line. We have eight crystals that could fit in those vertical spots. We need to put the crystals in those depressions," Lontas replied.

Bellae was already grabbing the damp bag of crystals. Taking a deep breath, she opened them. Slowly and methodically, she began placing them in the indentations. Each time she did, they changed color—the first two red, third orange, fourth yellow, fifth and sixth green, seventh blue, eighth indigo. As the last one went in, a secret door opened where a faint breeze had been.

"Hey, the crystals won't come out!" Bellae complained, trying to dislodge them.

"Maybe they release when we find the other two," Lontas suggested, climbing up and over a few smaller crystals to get to the opening. "There's writing.

Only two go through.
More, too many. Less, too few."

"Are there any symbols, or is there any other writing?" Scelto questioned.

"Not that I can see."

"Obviously, Bellae goes," Kainen said. "She should decide who goes with her."

Bellae looked from person to person anxiously, knowing that whatever decision she made someone would feel bad. "Lontas," she said, mouthing, *You and me, always.*

Lontas smiled brightly then paused. "Do you think Grym will count?"

Bellae scrunched her nose. "I really don't. Plus, if they're that picky...I'm not worried."

Lontas entered, followed by Bellae. Once she was through, she removed the lighted compass. "We'll be out as soon as possible."

"There's a symbol on the floor," Lontas said, pointing to an intricate design. "Written underneath it is, 'Wisdom.'"

"I guess this is the symbol for wisdom," Bellae speculated. "I don't see any other markings or words…so maybe we should step on it."

Bellae grabbed Lontas' arm as he started to move forward. "It's almost over, isn't it?"

"We're getting close. Then everything can get back to normal," he said, seeing fear and sadness overlying her silent smile. "What is it?"

"I'm just worried, that's all," she replied unconvincingly, wiping away tears.

"We can stand here, or you can start telling me what's going on," Lontas demanded.

"I promise I'll tell, but first, let's get these last crystals."

As they cautiously stepped on the emblem, there was a loud *click* quickly followed by a circular area around the symbol sinking several inches. The sound of stone grating against stone filled the room. The small door behind them shut while one in front opened. A gust of stale air blasted into them but was quickly followed by a cooler, less humid breeze.

"I guess we aren't leaving that way," Lontas said.

"It may open when we solve the next step," Bellae replied. "We have to be able to get the eight crystals we left stuck in stone."

They stepped into a large cavern, roughly oval, marked by jagged, black rock walls, except for one section, which was completely flat and smooth. Small holes above them let in a few rays of light, which were directed towards the flat wall. Occasionally, water from a particularly harsh wave splattered through the holes and into the room. As they moved closer, they saw the flat wall was covered in a large number of identical squares, each with writing.

Bellae counted. "There are twenty-five squares."

"There's writing in the squares *and* on the floor," Lontas said. "It looks pretty worn down." He looked up above just in time to see a spray of water splatter down on him and the writing. "The top part says, "Warning...read this...something. The rest is clearer.

"Four sets of Crystals found.
Two more tasks bring the finish around.
Wisdom comes at the end.
A life of **Knowledge** to comprehend.
Ignorance and its haunts to suspend.

Even if you succeed in this,
The world is not free from the abyss.
The Evil One grows frantic.
The last task, gigantic.

Symbols before you, twenty-five.
A solution for each you must arrive.
Find the **two** of which you **search**.
Pick the wrong one and you are in a lurch.

Once you find the two,
Push them and you are through.
Then you finally learn what to do.
Generations of many, saved by the few."

"So each of the twenty-five squares on the wall has a riddle?" Bellae wondered.

"Yeah, and after we figure them out, we have to push two," Lontas added.

"How will we know which two to press?"

"Not sure." Lontas looked closely at Bellae's tired and frail appearance. "What's this about two more tasks? Gimelli mentioned it, but you blew it off."

"Most people are not going to be happy with the final instructions, and many will try and steal the crystals. We have to follow this to the end, you and me. Even our friends may try and take them or tell us what to do with them. We have to make them think we're considering their ideas while following the plan laid out in the prophecy scrolls."

Lontas nodded, feeling there was more to the story, but also knowing she had told him all she was going to for now.

Scroll 7: Sick of the Water Motif

"I'm finished," Lontas said, after, away from the water sprays, drawing a large rectangle on the floor using a thin rock. Within it he drew twenty-five squares. "So we solve the riddles and write the answers in the corresponding boxes I drew. Once we figure out which two are correct, we push those."

"Sounds good," Bellae said as Grym ran in circles, avoiding being splashed by the incoming water. "I'll read the first square,

This can be for good or bad but either way,
Is done to accomplish something.
Only those alive can perform this.
What is it that can speak volumes in total silence,
But makes the performer strain or even sweat?"

"We have to do twenty-five of these? This could take all night," Lontas said.

"I'm just glad you're here," Bellae replied. Looking back to the top square, she added, "It could be a thought? Only someone alive can think, and it is done in silence."

"Good idea, but you don't strain or sweat when thinking. Let's see, could it be a goal? A behavior maybe?" Lontas suggested.

"Uhm, what about...action?" Bellae asked.

Lontas reread it with action inserted. "That's the answer! One down." He scratched 'action' in the matching square.

"I'll read the next one," Lontas said.

"We are born into this,
And as we age, we slide back to succumb to it when elderly.
At any age this can manifest as a physical or mental defect.
Both could potentially be changed,
But only through training and consistency.
The body is easier to alter.
For creatures it shows as a lack of strength and energy.

For the suns it would be less heat and light if they became this."

"Let's see," Bellae said. "Okay, the 'born into it' part is weird. Could it be helpless? We are born helpless, and when we get really old, we fall back to that—like in the infirmary."

"That's a good thought, but then this part that says it could be changed though training and consistency? That almost sounds like... getting stronger, so maybe weakness?" Lontas said.

"That fits!" Bellae declared. After rereading it to confirm, Lontas marked the answer in the second box.

Even though it was cooler in this section of cave, both were incredibly thirsty by the time they were onto the eleventh square.

"All right," Bellae said, trying to stay cheerful.

"It can grow from working at it or experience.
It can shrink, especially if you ignore it.
Even as it grows exponentially, it never takes up more space.
It can be more powerful than a mountain but weighs nothing.
Despite having a power beyond all others,
It can be extinguished in a second."

"Hmmm. This one's interesting. We might have a winner here."

"What do you mean?" Bellae asked, wiping the sweat from her forehead.

"Let's try to go about this a different way," Lontas said. "We should try working backwards by taking the words we think we are looking for, and plugging them in, so we would take wisdom, knowledge, and ignorance and see if they fit."

"I think wisdom and knowledge would fit," Bellae said.

"I agree. However, I'm leaning towards knowledge. It just fits better," Lontas said.

"All right. Mark it down as knowledge but put a little "W" in the corner, just in case."

"High tide," Lontas said an hour later, pointing to the back corner of the cave where water was now pouring in.

Bellae looked up to realize the light was withering. "We don't have much time on two fronts. Let's solve the last five splitting up. You start at that end, and I'll start here. Look to see if one works for wisdom or ignorance." Pulling out Jumeaux's compass, she started reading.

"I think I have it!" Bellae exclaimed on her second square. "Listen to this: A void that takes up space to no end. Despite its complete lack of substance, the ghostly form can do great harm to those cloaked in it and those who come in contact with it. Over time, it can be transformed with hard work and determination into an agent for good. But then, it is no more. In one sense we are all born with it. The collective society is accountable for allowing it to fester and rot, or changing it to a flower to bloom, its fragrance changing to that of benefit."

Lontas nodded. "Ignorance. I certainly don't have anything over here. That means we've found 'knowledge' and 'ignorance.' I wonder if we need to find the 'wisdom' one?"

"I don't think so. It mentioned two. This last pair of crystals, ignorance and knowledge, are the 'wisdom' crystals, right? So let's press those squares that we've already found."

"Right. I'll take twenty-two, you do eleven," Lontas said. The two looked at the rising water that had advanced to right behind them, seemingly alive as it lurched forward, coming in faster and starting to swirl where it was gushing in. "Okay. One, two, three!" Lontas cried out.

They pushed the two squares. Lontas' moved easily. Bellae was having trouble getting enough leverage, so she quickly spun her body around and pushed. Nothing. The ceiling started to shake, at first a slight tremor, but then it moved more violently with bits of rock falling around them, some plopping into the progressing water.

"You can do it, Bellae!" Lontas screamed.

She lurched forward with all her weight, and the square went in. The shaking slowly stopped, but there were large cracks in the roof and a haze of dust hanging in the humid air. After a loud *click*, a small stone panel slid open next to the twenty-five squares.

After an anxious glance at the water flowing in, they moved to the newly opened panel.

"What's this?" Lontas asked, completely annoyed at wooden pieces sitting behind the panel. "No crystals? You've got to be kidding me! We have to solve a puzzle box?"

Bellae peered in to see a half-formed wooden cube. Each piece was carved into odd shapes that looked like bones. The missing sections were lying randomly at the base of the cube. She reached in and took the cube. Lontas then picked up the small pieces.

"Hey, there's writing carved here. Give me your glowing compass.

"Fix what needs mending,
The water level is not suspending.
Once the repair is complete,
Insert it where wall and ceiling meet.
Make sure from the **start** you are **right**.
Or you will never make it to the light."

Lontas reread it, knowing the water would soon cover the words.

"So we have to repair this puzzle box thing and then find a spot for it?" Bellae asked.

"I guess," Lontas replied, suddenly feeling tired. Taking the incomplete box from her, he moved to a spot where the rock formed a small ledge and set the cube and pieces down. "Why don't you look for where this thing is supposed to go while I work on this?"

Bellae noticed at the top of the flat wall a cube-shaped shadow that looked to be the same size as the puzzle box. She knelt down in the water to reread the writing for herself. She uselessly tried to splash the water away, but it kept lapping back, covering the riddle.

"There must be a piece broken or missing!" Lontas howled in frustration.

Bellae shook her head, remembering all the complex armillary spheres she had mauled but that he built in class at Liberum. "I think we need to take it all apart first."

His tired brain did not want to accept such a thought.

"'Make sure from the **start** you are **right**' means starting from scratch."

"That's ridiculous," he complained.

Bellae shook her head. "Everything about this has been ridiculous. It's another test to trip us up. We…well, you, can do this."

After a frustrated sigh, he quickly took the wooden box apart as she joined him near the ledge with water leaping higher.

"It's obvious now that the inside two pieces were put together incorrectly," Lontas said, trying not to panic as the water crept higher. "After all the work I did getting it apart, and seeing which pieces were under tension, putting it together won't take long."

"How do we get the cube up to that hole?" Bellae asked when he finished. After several failed attempts to climb the wall, the two sat on the ledge. "It's too high."

"We have to wait for the water to rise, floating up," Lontas said sheepishly.

"I have to admit, I'm getting sick of the whole water theme my ancestors keep throwing at us." Bellae looked at her mouse friend. He was thin and dejected without Borb—looking like she felt, tired and lonely. *"You better get up on my shoulder, Grym."*

"You know, Lontas, part of me thinks you'll look back on this and think it wasn't so bad. It's been quite the adventure," Bellae said softly.

Lontas looked at her with hard, questioning eyes. "You mean *we'll* look back on this?"

"We," she said simply, resting her head on his shoulder. Weighted with what Kāla said and memories of what was lost, she sighed at what had yet to be given.

"I think I can put the cube in," Lontas said hours later, paddling to stay afloat. At the top of the flat wall, he reached up and stuffed the puzzle box into the slot. "It fits!"

The seconds bled into minutes as they continued treading water.

"Is something supposed to happen?" Bellae asked nervously.

Lontas pushed the cube deeper into the gap. A loud splash came from the middle of the cave. A small rectangle of the ceiling had fallen. Brilliant sparkling light danced down on the surface of the advancing water. "This can't be good."

Scroll 8: I Must Apologize

"Can we get up there?" Bellae wondered.

"I think so," Lontas replied as the two stared up into the opening in the ceiling, fearing what could be beyond the light.

"Are we just going to splash around here or actually do something?" Grym questioned.

Treading water, Bellae nuzzled him as best she could. Looking to Lontas, she summoned a feeble smile. "You and me…again."

He nodded, motioning her forward. Once she was under the dazzling light, he grabbed under her shoulders, kicking hard, he pushed up, being dunked under for his effort.

"You okay?" he asked upon reemerging, but she had disappeared. His mind panicked. *What if she's gone and I'm stuck here?* His heart began to race and breath quicken.

"Bellae!" he cried out, reaching up while kicking but could not grasp the opening.

Suddenly, a hand burst through the light.

"Come on," a voice whispered that sounded muffled and far away.

"No choice," he said, kicking his legs as hard as he could and reaching.

Their hands clasped, and he slowly rose. Frantically, he reached into the light, his hand scraping against rough stone that wobbled. Slowly, with the help of Bellae, he rose. Once up, he could make out a thin rim of wildly teetering rock. Slowly it's waggle quieted.

"There's, nothing…nothing," Bellae said as the two locked hands and backed together on the small oval rock precariously floating in pitch-blackness so massive it seemed to have no end in all directions. "The light was from the opening itself, I guess?"

Finally, Bellae whispered uneasily, "Black dragon of eternity."

Lontas looked over to see her hyperventilating. "Like we talked about in the desert."

She nodded, huddling closer. "But you're here. That's infinitely better."

As time wore on, their ears ringing in the absolute silence, Bellae said, "I feel like death's staring at me with easy confidence, certain of victory. Those of us afflicted to see the darkness are forced to bathe in it—submerged within its unfeeling cocoon, knowing its undressed cost. I see the darkness every time I close my eyes and sometimes when they're open."

Lontas was stunned at her maturity and amazed at how much she had changed on this journey. "I'm not sure what to say, but just know I'm here with you."

Grym's squeaking made them look up. Slowly, a thick webbing of glowing ropes began materializing around them in a crisscross pattern. Bellae petted the top of her mouse friend's head as he squirmed into her pocket. They watched the large cables intersecting all around them.

Lontas said, "Look where they meet. At each node of the net is a polished jewel."

Strung across the endless darkness was a three-dimensional net stretching out in all directions. Occasionally, small quivers of radiance would shoot down one of the meshwork of threads, sending small vibrations of light across all the gems like waves in a disturbed pond.

"Can I get down?" Grym asked, peeking out again.

"Okay, but be careful."

"It's not like I can go far," the mouse replied.

"You can hear a musical chiming as the light ripples around," Lontas said. "I wonder where the illumination is coming from?"

Bellae shook her head. "What do you think we need to do?"

"No idea."

Lontas got on his hands and knees, carefully scooting to the edge of the precarious rock floating in the blackness broken only by the net. Bellae grabbed onto the back of his shirt for support just before the top of the rock started to tilt.

"Oh, no!" Lontas said, sliding closer to the edge. "Move to the other side!"

Bellae cautiously backed towards his feet, still holding on. Lontas guardedly scooched forward so his head was peeking over the precipice. After gazing around, he cautiously slithered backwards as Bellae scooched forward. Once in the middle, they stood up.

"Well?" Bellae asked.

"As far as you can see an infinite net with jewels in the nodes in all directions. The doorway to the water is definitely gone."

"How thick is this rock we're on?"

"It's just a small shard of floating, tipsy rock. The endless-in-all-directions vastness of this space kind of makes me want to vomit. Not sure how this is possible. We know we climbed up here from the cave."

Bellae sighed, feeling trapped on the swaying rock. "Thanks for being so smart and helping me through…whatever this is."

"It's nice to be needed and useful," he said as the meshwork continued vibrating, sending glowing light around. "There has to be something. The prophecy wouldn't leave us stranded."

"How can you want something over but dread that it will end at the same time?"

Lontas nodded. "One more pair. Seems like yesterday—and, at the same time, a hundred years ago—when we left Liberum for the Tournament."

Bellae could feel the dread of riding away from her home seeing the Knights and flags decorating the now-destroyed walls of Liberum. "Sooo much has changed. If someone had told me half of the things we'd endure, I'm not sure you could have made me go."

"A lot's changed. However, some things haven't. You and me."

"You and me," she echoed.

"What do you think this net stuff is made of? I mean, seriously, this stuff is super tough and almost…sticky," Lontas marveled, stretching up to touch it. "It's definitely not rope."

"There's something carved on this floating rock of death," Grym interrupted.

"Great job," Bellae said. "Okay, it says, 'Indra's Net' in large letters. Below that:

Each jewel is reflected in and, in turn, reflects all others.
Touching one touches another and another—like sisters and brothers.
In fact, one is bound to, and is one with, all:
Emotions, thoughts, positive, negative, whispers, loud call,
Each one resonates through my coiled net.
Whether seen or recognized, an intertwined existence is met.
And so it goes,
Interconnectedness imposed.
Reality is sometimes below the veneer,
If you peel it back like a seer.
Appearance is but a reflection of reality.
Consciousness is the light, in actuality."

"All righty, then," Lontas said, hunching next to her on the precariously levitating rock.

"I've seen Grym be skittish, but never like this," Bellae said as Grym went berserk.

"He literally just flipped backwards," Lontas added.

"I must apologize. I think I'm making him nervous," a strange voice called out.

Lontas and Bellae looked at each other, almost afraid to look up. When they eventually did, they gasped at the sight of the intimidating creature.

Scroll 9: Weave-Entwined

"I'm Arachne." The creature had a female human head and upper torso that merged into a spider's body with eight hairy appendages. She had two separate pairs of humanoid eyes with nests of spider eyes surrounding them, while a solitary human eye sat in the middle of her forehead. Her nose looked skeletal, and she had four hairy appendages, pedipalps, from the sides of her pointed ears, and two chelicerae above her tongue. From the human torso a pair of human arms ended in webbed human hands. Projecting from her spider body were four sets of hairy spider appendages, the last one ended in a large, webbed, palmate foot for swimming.

"I'm Bellae. This is Lontas," she replied, glancing at her friend, his mouth agape.

As they stared, they noticed in places the pale outer flesh began dissolving, melting into dripping strands of tissue, which revealed blood vessels, meaty red muscle, fibrous white tendons, and amber sheens of fat. Web-like strands of dermis shot across the gaps of exposed muscles frantically trying to mend the degrading skin as a roving battle meandered around her human face and torso of alternating decay and nets of restorative flesh skirmishing for dominance. Viscous fluid oozed out of the deteriorating sections while saliva rummaged over her lips and occasionally through dissolving skin, which, when reforming, reabsorbed it.

"Are you the guardian?" Bellae asked, the silence growing uncomfortable.

"Yes," the graceful Arachne answered, spinning around the net as if gravity held no dominion here. Closing her many eyes, she seemed to be feeling or sensing something.

"Uhm, your net's amazing," Bellae eventually said.

Figure 12: Within a void of an infinite web of jeweled nodes, they meet Arachne, the last guardian.

Arachne opened her eyes, torquing her head to the side. “The net I travel on is Indra’s.”

Lontas, continuing to stare, mumbled something about the net quivering while Grym violently scratched at her feet. Bellae quickly put the mouse in her pocket.

“We all travel through our own time and place, but despite those bonds, we are interconnected through space and time,” Arachne said, waving her hand out to the seemingly infinite net with gems at each node. “Each and every one of us has the ability to leave a legacy vacillating for the future. Strive to vibrate with greatness.”

"Okay," Lontas wheezed, still staring at her decomposing and reforming skin.

Arachne used her human hand to brush back the blackest hair they had ever seen. Even the skin on her hand was decaying, only to be rebuilt after giving an unsolicited view of the flesh beneath. "I felt you working together and can tell you're good friends. Listening to the vibrations of the world through this net can grow tedious. Via the web's quivering I can feel when inhabitants of your realm are heading into trouble but can do nothing about it. Greed, pride, and narcissism are top offenders."

"How far...how long...is this place?" Lontas asked.

"Infinite in all directions."

Lontas cocked his head to the side. "How does that work?"

Arachne smiled while shuffling forward with blurring speed. "I can feel everyone and everything of your world, but I am not *in* your world. This net lies over the existence you know and expands in all directions, unbound."

"You can feel...everything?" Bellae asked.

"For some reason most don't like the idea that everything's interconnected. But, in reality, we are all just a few simple acts removed from all others—fettered as one. None are better or worse, just different. We cling to the myths of us versus them and good versus evil. However, this is an illusion created by circumstance and experience. There are simply actions and intentions. Each person and their deeds are reflected in, while simultaneously reflecting all others," the spider-woman said, pointing to the gems placed at each node in the net.

"Lontas and I were in Ifrean and learned about Dark Warriors. After those experiences, we thought of them differently," Bellae said.

Arachne nodded. "We see in a new light once we understand someone's path. It's comforting to think we would act differently if forced into another's situation, yet think of yourself as one of these jewels. We are all but reflections of all others. We see the light filtering through our own jewel in others, and theirs in ours. You could think of the light as consciousness. It flows through each of us, and while you can't touch it, you can feel it, and the vibrations of our actions resonate across the net.

"If one jewel is touched, all the others in the net sense the change. As the Chosen One, you have a choice and a chance. You have the power to strum the strings of the world into harmony and redistribute the magic of the world, or…unleash the alternative you have been seeing and feeling. There are critical times in your life when the choice you make reveals, or removes, your character," Arachne challenged. All of her eyes bored into Bellae, who, for the first time, noticed the large eyes seemed to have webs flexing across them.

"When someone does an action with selfish, negative intentions, it is a reflection in, and of, all of us. When someone does something good, it resonates a spark of good energy through the universe. Bellae, you can even out the brilliance of the world. Break the cycle of false control that has been strangling its progress. Loosen the grip of the One who's been controlling us." As Arachne finished, the last two crystals appeared, moving down towards Bellae, wrapped in the thick silk of Arachne's web.

"I have a scroll, but only for the Chosen. Please read the message but keep the words to yourself. Once finished, place the note upon the last two crystals."

Bellae took it. Despite the words she was reading on the last instruction scroll, she forced herself to smile through the terror. After finishing, she placed the note on the crystals, and it immediately burst into flames. Arachne closed all save the top middle eye, which seemed to glass over in a faraway look. Her various spider legs moved backwards along the various net fibers, sensing their barely perceptible vibrations. After perceiving multiple strands for several minutes, all her eyes snapped open. "Now, child, shall you feel the full pressure swirling around you, which is coalescing its force. All with any inkling of magic shall descend upon the scent of power radiating from all five crystal pairs while those without magic lust for their potency, even the League, and various leaders on both sides of the Dark Sea."

She paused as if gathering her thoughts. "We all live on the webs we forge from our desires, our priorities. Some spin their world out of greed. Others desire for power. Some, hedonistic inclinations. Others, out of the impassive. When the right temptation or prey triggers their web, they pounce. Gold doesn't in itself corrupt. Giving your heart over to greed is the perversion. We all kneel to something, just a matter of what we choose. You are not headed for glory, but that is good. Glory holds the weight and noise of empty air."

Arachne scuttled closer. "When the Ainmhi Caint were being hunted into extinction, they left a pathway and created the League of Truth, knowing the gift would return within a child. Later generations of the League, including the current, thought it should be an adult. The pathway became a prophecy, and the emergence of one who could speak to animals became the Chosen One. But do not despair. Your kind were gentle, giving, and wise. You can overcome your last trial."

Bellae blew out a long breath. "I can feel it, the pressure. I can hear in my head all the voices and their perspectives on what to do with the crystals. It's overwhelming."

"Is it?" Arachne asked. "Do you not already, deep inside, know what you are to do?"

"Why didn't the Ainmhi Caint just get rid of the crystals when they were being hunted?" Bellae asked, her frustration rising.

"There were many arguments I could feel on my web at that time. Some thought it wise to get rid of them, but others wanted to save them, convinced that in the future the collective consciousness would mature, and they could be used wisely, and therefore, pushed the decision down through the ages. Others of your kind turned to Ifrean and dark magic."

"The Watchers," Bellae breathed. "So my ancestors thought it would make more sense for a child, some unknown time in the future, to handle the crushing obligation of dealing with the immensely powerful crystals?"

Arachne brushed her human hand against Bellae's cheek, wiping away a tear. Bellae could feel the skin dissolving and reforming as it swept across her. At one point she felt something moist and assumed, with a shiver, that it was exposed sinew and muscle.

"Remember they were being hunted and try to understand the pressure and violence arrayed against them. We are all just a series of nows, of the presents, of each fleeting moment. At our base, we are simply a series of fluttering instances that, when we look back, are woven together to make the fabric of our forever within the infinite. From birth we are doomed to continually, and only, look through eyes of the present, but most have the vision of the now colored by the looking glass of past events and the fog lost amongst future hopes. Living in your own time is a web. It can ensnare your body and mind. The more invested you are egocentrically, the more chains of ignorance dig into your flesh, embroiling you further into your own pathetic, minuscule perspective."

"Are we not all a product of our time? Is it not a requirement?" Lontas asked.

"Not a requirement, but ninety-nine percent are stuck in that mental quagmire."

Bellae shook her head. "I was just thinking about how absurd this is. Some random mutation allowed me to speak to animals. Stralande told me there's nothing special about me other than I happen to have the reappearance of animal talking. That, unasked for, led me here, through everything else. It's amazing, wonderful, and at the same time, ridiculous and absurd."

Arachne seemed to settle. "Your ancestors set this up so that only a descendant would be able to claim them. Nothing more, nothing less. It was the League, over generations, that made this into some fantastical prophecy, distorting the words and thoughts of the original makers into some kind of chosen."

"They changed it?"

"Slowly, the way mountains rise—a little at a time. But a little off course, over the eons, becomes drastically different. Small changes became complete revisions as people interjected parts of themselves and their beliefs. The League twisted this multiple times."

"You don't seem to like the League, the ones who helped us so much."

Arachne twisted her head. "I can feel the webs of temptation pulling into them, the eggs of greed germinating to pull apart their best-laid objectives. Good intentions do not outstrip the consequences of a negative action. You will have more than Watchers and Proliate to deal with. Those you value as friends will try and take what's yours. Be careful whom you trust."

Arachne turned to Lontas. "Could you stand back?"

He cautiously shuffled in reverse, his eyes fixating on the nearing edge. Before he could look up, Arachne spun around, flashing two large spinnerets from the back of her abdomen, which shot out silk at amazing speed. Moving with lightning quickness, she was quickly upon him, rapidly encasing his chest in the sleek white web. Before Bellae could react, Lontas found himself hanging high above, bobbing wildly. Stunned, he opened his lips to protest. Before any sound seeped out, he felt himself being spun around as the spinnerets covered both his mouth and ears in ivory lace.

"Privacy," Arachne said, scurrying with dizzying velocity back and pointing to the tiny rock, "is required and hard to come by."

Looking up at Lontas, still spinning and thrashing, Bellae felt guilty at having to resist laughing at his predicament. His eyes, wide with terror, quickly drained any humor.

"I'll retrieve him shortly, and all shall be whole," Arachne said, her den of eyes nestled across her face staring deeply. "I could feel the vibrations of your movements and never expected you to live long enough to make it here."

"Thaaanks?" Bellae replied.

"You're welcome," she responded, looking out on the vastness of the crystals and darkness surrounding them. "I realize this is, has been, an unfair hardship. The crystals you've collected are a burden, with more to be added. I can feel the weight growing within your mind and soul. You've been encumbered by the awakening. You see it. The darkness?"

"See and *feel* the emptiness," Bellae said.

"The presence of darkness is *not* the absence of light. Warmth is not the truancy of cold. It is, in fact, light and heat that are intruders into the universe, and their trespassing can never outlast the cosmos' baseline, darkness...biting cold. Life and light are the rarified exceptions in a world ruled by lifeless blackness. The reign of light is necessarily weak, as, like us, it is but a temporary visitor. Darkness and death both have infinite patience, being predestined to win.

"Do not despise the light for its frailty, or your life for its impermanence. Do not be angry that our individual being is but a wisp of perishable existence—you might as well be angry the ocean got you wet, such is the way. We are not the creators of, nor did we even consciously choose to participate within, this contest. Do not fix your mind on the impossible. The rules of the game are beyond our power to change."

Bellae stared back, a fierceness entering her eyes, her mind tempted. *Maybe I can keep them. I can stop the darkness.* Out loud she said, "I don't want to let darkness win."

"Darkness is the predestined victor. Ordained to win on the very day light entered the universe. Light and life are the great deceptions of the cosmos, intended to rage against shadows for as long as possible. The most life and light can hope for is to hold back the darkness."

Scurrying along the web, she held her hands out, gesturing to the various crystals. "Each crystal represents a soul living in your world. Our lives, while we live, are all interconnected. Our life, in the past tense, becomes part of the extensive web of all existence. It is in the darkness that we find our reality, our truth. Once you understand that, once you embrace the eternal darkness on either end of life—your non-existent existence—you truly appreciate living as a miracle, the miracle. Despite its great shortcoming—its brevity—it is a marvel."

Bellae scowled. "Non-existent existence? Embrace eternal darkness? Does that mean everything I've done is useless?"

"Quite the opposite. Being the whole of what we have, our individual, meager existence literally means everything. However, you can only see the truth of it to the extent you see the interconnectedness," Arachne said, waving her arms to the various fettered crystals. "All of us alive together are interconnected. All who came before, and all who will come after are linked in the web of creation. It is only seeing that, only in understanding the togetherness, that we can make sense of our being. Examining the world thinking only of yourself is like examining a drop of water and thinking it is the ocean. Understanding the drop, truly, only within its greater context, means you understand the ocean and vice versa.

"Only in comprehending the minute can we comprehend the infinite. To truly see the microscale, we must be open to grasping the limitless." Arachne closed her eyes. "I can feel the vibrations of all the actors performing their lives on the shared stage. Humanity starts from a platform of potential, then moves forward, each decision and action collapsing into a certain reality. Most never see, but I acutely feel, that when we hate another, we are actually hating ourselves. When we harm others, we afflict the reverberations of suffering upon ourselves.

"If we expend the time and effort of our valuable souls on any deep connection, whether it be love, hate, combat, or war, long enough, you will find, eventually, you are staring at part of yourself in the reflection of what you love, hate, or are fighting with. When we love each other, casting aside petty hostility, that allows growth. Greed, gluttony, ego, self-obsession, all of these are poisonous emotions. The wielders of such frailty do not feel, do not understand, that those passions eat away at their core identity, nor do they comprehend it is like poisoning the well from which we all must drink. Desire deceives the will. Unbridled pleasure exploits the body. Greed stains the soul. Self-inflicted laziness decays the body. Lust rusts our hearts and rots our ability to love. Cheating cheapens victory. Hatred putrefies in the same measure forgiveness emboldens. Gluttony abuses body and soul as the line of enough is crossed. Fear devours optimism and conviction. Such evils, I think you are coming to understand, are subtle, traveling under the guise of corrupt whispers born of the internal rustle of greed and malcontent."

Arachne paused. Several moist bits of her constantly reshaping skin fell. During their drop, the fragments of flesh seemed magnetically pulled towards her, slurping in to rejoin her body. Moving to Bellae, she used one of her human hands to grab Bellae's, pushing it against the net. "Do you see it? Can you feel that?"

Closing her eyes, Bellae could sense a temperate quiver. Soon the vibration began to resonate up her arm until her whole body fluttered. Voices, jumbled at first, flooded her mind. Images flashed within a wave of noise inundated her thoughts. Squeezing her eyes tightly and concentrating, she began to make sense of the individual vocalizations. Thoughts, emotions, hopes, and dreams, good and the bad mingling together. Her body shuddered under the exertion. She could feel the actions and their reverberating effects across the net.

Arachne ripped her hand away. Bellae fell back on the angrily jostling rock. Slowly, the internal turmoil from touching the net and vibrations of the external rock slowed. She opened her eyes, wiping away sweat beading on her forehead. "That was intense. Can I try again?"

"Tasting the connections is enough. Notice no jewel has a more prominent position. None sit in the center. None are relegated to the fringes. Each and every jewel is not just *its* center, it is *the* center in that it reflects all the other jewels. The Macht Crystals will try to manipulate you, twisting your worldview to focus on your own importance."

"It's been…tiring," Bellae sighed.

"Silence highlights a scream's power. Both are necessary for effect and understanding of the other. It is cold darkness that reveals light's warmth. It is in being lost that one appreciates a beacon home. Cold defines heat. Hunger highlights sustenance. Loneliness shows love's value. Struggles, like what you're enduring, allow true joy and contentment to blossom during peace."

Bellae let her chin fall. Despite the wisdom she was experiencing from the guardians, she could not help feeling exhaustion at "inspirational" talks.

Arachne smiled. "There's no hiding from me. What you call a burden, others would call an opportunity. The world's problems have answers, but realizing the inhabitants lack the will for change is heartbreaking. I ache for the possible. I weep for the good that could be."

"I…" Bellae hesitated, trying to entice her thoughts into a coherent idea. "What you describe makes sense. Ever since I collected the first crystals, I started to see more than I wanted, understood things I would rather not, but sensing the suffering of the world? Is the worst."

Arachne flashed a sorrowful smile. "Try not to let the sheer enormity of the world's misery, or the brevity with which good can shine, discourage you from walking a path of light. Sometimes I catch my breath as the wretchedness of the world echoes within my consciousness. All of us can only do our part to spread love and happiness with the time we are given. You can grasp opportunity, but not control the time you are allotted to achieve the goal. None of us can fix the world's problems alone, but that doesn't mean we shouldn't try. Seeing the truth is hard. It's difficult to mobilize people to act, and nearly impossible to achieve it."

Bellae could feel the voices of the crystals rumbling in her mind with a physical pressure. Mentally she struggled to keep the door of resistance closed against their advances. "I know what I have to do, but…I do not want to," she finally said, tears eagerly arising from her sorrow.

Arachne smiled. Gently, she grabbed Bellae by the shoulders before using one of her clawed hands to raise her chin. "Time is *the* gift. Using it wisely is *our* gift in return. Even when long forgotten, your actions will echo along the eternal fabric of time and be felt. The decision as to what to do with the crystals is your burden."

"Why don't you take them? Hide them here," Bellae said, a glimmer of hope desperately trying to rise out of the vice grip of reality.

"No guardian can bear the crystals without suffering a terrible curse, courtesy of your descendants."

"Just keep them…whatever this place is!" Bellae added, wiping away her tears.

Arachne shook her head. "The sands are already falling within the hourglass of time for you to decide. The crystals are already calling out to any and all creatures with a hint of magic." All of her eyes turned to focus on the bag with the crystals.

Bellae recoiled slightly at the desire misting behind them. "I trust you to keep them safe."

A tremor wound its way through Arachne, and the yearning for the crystals seemed to waver. "You know that's not true. The combined crystals shall not accept sitting idly by, and when that much power is at play, hordes shall come looking. It shall never end until the end. They will never stop searching for a soul to corrupt, to master."

Scroll 10: The Gift

"Each changing of the guard, as generations rise and fall, is born of ignorance balanced by precious, and oft neglected and misunderstood, opportunity," Arachne said. "At birth, with our infantile perspective, we are lulled by the deceptive, black-hearted lullaby of permanence. Most only see but a pinhole of light weakly shining down on their fragile present, your desperately brittle life, and think you are quite clever and ever so indispensable to the world. However, child, I see the immortal darkness surrounding you, encircling me, besieging life. Many have smashed through the world, looking for a way to stay or at least be remembered. Whether you give into the crystals deceptive melody will depend on whether you remember we are born from darkness and are destined to return to it.

"Most fail to examine, much less seek to understand their, our, impermanence. If more could break the fleshy chains fettering us in the underground cave of ignorance and rise up and turn away from the shadows cast on the cave wall, we would understand the preciousness of every moment in the now of our existence. Too often our minds are distracted by past failings or seduced with hope for an unpromised future."

Bellae sighed. "One of the worst things about this whole journey? Cryptic 'life lessons.'"

Arachne nodded. "We must be mindful not to become too devout to reductionism. Such perspective loses the beauty in the whole. You're missing the gift of the opportunity born *from* the hardships of the path here. If you take a butterfly and microscopically examine its body, the thorax, abdomen, you would walk away unimpressed and perhaps convinced it is quite ugly. If one were to but widen their perspective, ah, then you see the beauty of the wings and grace of its fragile flight. Too often we miss the greater splendor, concentrating on the minutia."

"I complained about the journey, but now that it's ending...I'm terrified."

"To truly live a full life is to know eternal life. Your fondness for existence, or lack of it, does not change the truth. I know you're scared. I would challenge you to not think of 'living well' as ease or opulence but striving and fighting for, and achieving, your potential. Measuring your life based on someone else's standards or goals is living for something outside your own."

"Will the ending hurt?" Bellae asked.

Arachne brushed aside Bellae's hair. "I shall answer with two stories. There once was a man sentenced to beheading for multiple murders. Before the hooding, he complained to the executioner about the unsanitary nature of the axe. Looking down at the wooden platform, he complained the boards were weak and unsafe, asking if they wanted him to fall through and kill himself or perhaps die of infection? Should the condemned be burdened by such worries? The second involves a queen going to a feast. She's despondent, understanding that it will end and she will have to leave. Should that taint the joy of good friends and fine food? Should the queen whine during each course about eventually having to leave?"

Bellae shook her head. "Those are...ridiculous."

"Aren't they, though? Does it make sense for those of us invited to life, like the queen to the banquet, to complain about the bumps in our journey? In both, we know that we have to leave. That does not mean we should not enjoy the time. What is the value of a condemned man complaining of the hygiene of the implementation? Make no mistake, pain will be a part of either path you take. I can tell you from past experience, darkness and temptation shall follow you like a shadow in the desert if you choose to succumb to the crystals."

Bellae nodded. "It's all about perspective and seeing what's important."

Arachne smiled. "We are but lonely travelers borrowing life for a moment, but if we see the interconnectedness, we understand the greater fabric of reality. We should strive to serve as a light during our tattered shred—not worry about what will be in a millennia and beyond. That is not our remnant of time to inhabit. If one is to pursue wisdom, they must first lay down conceit and arrogance. If they are to find peace, they must first throw away greed and vice. If you wish to discover truth, you must shed prejudice and unquestioned belief." Quickly turning, Arachne scurried to Lontas. Using her claws, she shredded the binding silk. Lontas coughed and sputtered, pulling web fibers from his ears, mouth, and nose as he unceremoniously tumbled upon the precarious rock. The motivation to complain melted at the sorrow radiating from Bellae. *Didn't we do it? Don't we have the crystals?*

Arachne leaned in close and whispered to Lontas. "Just be there. That shall be enough." She stood erect and stared until he was forced to turn away. "Life beats up empaths, tearing holes in the fragile fabric of their caring souls. What others would thoughtlessly walk away from weighs heavily upon you—forcing you to build a patchwork of repairs as you forever wear the event thin as it replays within your mind. Humility is a gift bestowed only to those who endure suffering trials. Humbleness is born from strength of will by those who keep rising after being knocked down. Do not regret your past. It has formed your present and guides your future."

Lontas blushed at the thought she felt all the times he stumbled or was bullied. "A part of me will always be the scared kid whose only home is solitude in the library."

"Your trials shall make you a kinder and better person for the rest of your days," Arachne said as Bellae lifted Lontas up.

"Maybe regret and wisdom are two sides of the same coin. Maybe remorse is the mountainous path we must climb on the way to finding ourselves, and maybe truth itself," Lontas said.

Arachne smiled. "Most things important for life and growth as conscious beings are tied to the toll of time and suffering endured through adversity. Sagacity, common sense, rationality all demand a hefty price as we trade bits of our lives for wisdom. Our years and experience are payment for the growth, allowing us to live better. But, by the time we are prepared to live, our bodies are ready to give up, returning to dust. A gift and a curse.

"To continue the mortal journey, the body demands sustenance. Any living creature knows this. However, to grow the mind and soul, the truly wise toil to feed them through learning and growth. The answers are not as important as asking the questions and searching for truth. Those hording obscene wealth suffer corruption of soul and perspective. Those who covet truth value words and knowledge. I presume you're ready to go back to your friends?"

"Yes!" Lontas replied, a little too excitedly.

As Bellae touched the crystals, her eyes turned white, her perception immersed in blackness. Eventually she saw letters, then words, then sentences, and finally an entire codex. Letters swirled off the pages, twisting faster and faster until coalescing into an arm holding a torch rising out of the book. In her mind she heard, *Wisdom guides the questions to ask on the path of Knowledge while the accumulation of Knowledge births a life of Wisdom. The light and life of Knowledge demands profound toil but reaps its reward in lighting up a life full of meaning and Wisdom.* Stuck under the shadow of the codex was a man, his eyes bound, chains around his neck and waist holding him in place, his hands over his ears. *Willful Ignorance binds the senses into impotence for all swaddling themselves within its numbing and terrible embrace.*

"You okay?" Lontas asked, his face crunched with worry.

Throwing out a fake smile, she nodded before brushing off the crystals and placing them in her bag. Arachne grabbed the two of them with surprising strength before taking off through the net, moving with unbelievable efficiency.

"Aren't we going back down?" Bellae asked, dodging the glimmering jewels and net.

"You don't want to be thrown back in that water. I agreed to help your ancestors, having lived through the horrific vibrations of many Na Cearcaill. Everything you perceive as a burden, the tests, the different guardians is, in fact, a gift, one given in hopes of preparing you with knowledge and wisdom to make the right decision."

Bellae's head wobbled. "I think I understand."

As Lontas was turning green, Arachne stopped and began chanting. They could abruptly see a long stone staircase appear within the blackness, net, and jewels.

"So your net overlays the entire world?" Lontas asked.

Figure 13: Bellae sees the manifestation of Knowledge versus Ignorance.

"I'm part of many worlds," Arachne said before grabbing Bellae's arm as Lontas descended the stairs. Bellae swiveled, trying to avoid the impulse to pull away from the worm-like movement of the spider-woman's skin. "I shall see and feel your decision—one I do not envy. Heed what the last scroll says about the storm fields. They should block the signal.

"Few in this world, and none with endless wealth, ever see the easy truth standing in front of us, staring at us. Giving of ourselves builds us and the world up. Helping others assists us, helps all. Taking and hording destroys the self, demolishes the all."

Bellae looked after Lontas ruefully.

"I know you cherish him. Genuinely being satisfied with what is allows the path to true contentment. Those who truly live and strive for understanding have a long life no matter how short the actual time. Those who can know themselves and conquer base desires will find strength regardless of the size of their muscles. Make the virtuous decision."

Before Bellae could reply, Arachne and Indra's net disappeared and darkness enveloped them. She carefully took out Jumeaux's gift, the glowing compass. Holding it out for light, she found herself staring at a stone ceiling. On the last step was carved, *Memento Mori.*

"Remember, you have to die," Lontas said, climbing back up. "That's what it says," he clarified at her hurt expression. Walking up to the ceiling, he pushed before throwing his shoulder against the rock. "It's not budging."

Bellae sat down, and he joined her, rubbing his sore shoulder.

"How long do you think we can just sit here?"

"As long as you need," Lontas replied, seeing the weight upon his friend.

The burden and hideous options fleshing out before her made Bellae's head fall and eyelids close. "Stralande and Kāla told me some rough, horrible things of the reality before me, but only after Arachne and the last scroll do I see the true implications."

"You don't have to store those secrets. You can share them," Lontas said.

"Just because I want to doesn't mean I can."

Lontas sighed. "Just remember, you and me. Right?"

Bellae nodded. "As I looked up to see you gagged, hanging from a magical net, something occurred to me. Sometimes I feel sorry for myself. I didn't ask to talk to animals. I didn't want to go on this quest of horrors. But you didn't either. Despite that, you always stood with me. So, I'm sorry I got you into this."

Tears decamped from his eyes, breaking across his cheeks. "What are you talking about? That you would think of me, with everything you've been through, is the reason I'm here."

"I'm sick of enduring the guardians saying, 'Just enjoy the journey.' Basically, with what we endured and have to do, just smile and keep faith."

Lontas nodded as she sidled her head onto his shoulder. "Smiles and hope can be expensive accessories." Bellae lifted her head and smiled. Lontas wiped away his tears. "But they're worth the cost."

"Somewhere along this journey, I stopped thinking about my past life. By choice and circumstance we've been pushed further and further away from our previous life, and I will never get back to it."

"Don't talk like that," Lontas said with real fear. "All things change. I fear when things stop changing more than change itself."

Bellae looked at him questioningly.

"Once things stop changing…meaning, death."

"When we left Liberum, the world felt enormous, and life full of endless, boundless possibilities. Now that we've been out here battling for so long it feels like the world is closing in and has gotten quite small," Bellae said before whispering, "At least for me."

Scroll 11: One-More-4-the-Road

After finally moving down the stairs, Lontas and Bellae arrived at a dead end. Holding up the compass for light, Bellae sighed. "They couldn't just let us leave?"

"Of course not. Another riddle." Lontas shook his head before reading:

"A building constructed upon a foundation of the heavens.

Order from reason—reason from the order writ.

A structure with innumerable doors to open and unroll.

The more you unfurl, the more you know, eventually realizing the goal is unattainable.

Once through, only aspiring and persevering gains true entry—acquires true sight.

Seeing versus the ability to truly see. Intent, passion, imagination: they matter.

Let our tongue be heard one last time. Though long swaddled in eternal slumber, we, perhaps, shall stir."

Lontas looked to Bellae, seeing the invisible, but crushing, weight she bore. "The true riddle is really the printed—the italics are commentary."

Bellae sighed, exhaustion pulling her down. "If you know, just tell me."

Lontas tried to hide his disappointment at her lack of enthusiasm. "This is based upon an ancient riddle, and the answer is school. The lessons, the foundation of learning, are based on precise mathematical truths—as if given from the heavens themselves for us to discover. You must have the right motivation and persevere. If you enter the school with the correct intent, and work hard, you'll leave with sight, truly seeing. It's a journey, not a destination."

"Sooo…school?"

"Yep, so school."

Bellae gave him a hug. "Thanks for being here." In Ainmhi Caint she yelled, *"School!"*

A loud rattling ensued followed by a clunking sound as the stone with the writing began to slide to their right. A woosh of dust and debris showered out, and they covered their mouths. As Bellae held out the compass for light, she could see several of the massive crystals, now broken, that had grown into the door.

Wordlessly they started through the maze of crystals, eventually hearing the voices of the other League members. They again found themselves sweating from the heat.

"Bellae!" Gimelli shouted, embracing her sister as they emerged.

After explaining what happened, Bellae placed the new crystals into the two remaining depressions. The rock hungrily drew them in. The different colored lights sputtered before turning their standard blue. With a high-pitched clang, the ten crystals released. Before Bellae could pick them up, a wave of energy pulsed out, blowing Bellae and the rest of the League backwards. Several of the closest large crystals shattered outwards, sending a shower of broken shards throughout the cavern. Bellae's crystals came together, trembling violently until a rainbow of light shot up in an explosion that obliterated a hole in the rock ceiling. Perched outside, Arend, Sankari, and the falcon Gorm startled into the air as a rainbow of energy burst through the top of the rock. Inside, debris and chunks of rock were raining down everywhere.

"Can you stop it, Bellae?" Lontas questioned.

Shrugging, Bellae reached out towards the group of crystals. *They are calling out.* Despite the shuddering and light, they felt cool. She tugged, but they did not separate. After several tense moments, the crystals finally came apart and the energy stopped.

"Put the crystals away," Scelto implored nervously. None of the League members had been seriously injured, but all were coated in dust and grime from the exploding ceiling.

As the League dodged debris, the hippocampi were screaming as the knock-on effect of the blast was damaging their sacred crystals in a cascade.

Bellae bent down to pick one up, and visions slammed into her mind. White light shot from her eyes. *You will be all-powerful and can prevent suffering. Take our power now!* Bellae began to see flashes of burning and destroyed villages. *See what happens if you reject the gift of the crystals?* Dead bodies—some tortured, some burned, some dismembered—took turns violating her mind. *Don't listen to the scrolls! Use the power of the crystals and become the most powerful being ever! Bring peace to the world through magic!* Bellae fought to clear the images and voices from her head. *I control the good!* she repeated within her mind until the voices stopped. Gradually the rumbling cave came into focus.

"We have to get out of here now!" Scelto yelled, almost tumbling to the side as the entire cavern seemed to shift, dispatching fragments of ceiling to rain down.

Bellae swiftly placed the crystals in her bag while the hippocampi cursed them. As the League ran towards the pool, the cave began to shake more violently. Larger pieces started to rattle down. The last of the massive crystals shattered as the League jumped into the water.

"Our Cave of Crystals!" Capall-Mara cried out in anguish. *"I knew you were trouble! How dare you deface our temple!"*

"I had no idea this would happen, I swear!" Bellae replied.

Dust clogged the air as the cave continued to fall apart. Shards of broken crystals were flying around the room like thrown daggers as the giant crystals shattered beneath falling rocks.

In all the chaos Bellae found Ceffyl-Mor. *"We have no right to ask, but please, can you get us out of here?"* The sea serpent mane thrashed angrily towards her as the young hippocamp wore a look of betrayal.

"How could—" Ceffyl-Mor was cut off as massive chunks of the ceiling began plopping down. She turned, pleading with the furious hippocampi. Whatever she said caused the others to move towards the League, weaving to avoid the cascade of stones plopping into the water all around them.

"Take a deep breath!" Ceffyl-Mor uttered as the hippocampi dove down.

Bellae turned to glance behind. Large chunks of the ceiling were piercing into the water. Each one followed by a trail of turbulent white bubbles.

Scroll 12: Message on a Bird

Despite her air hunger, the instant Bellae popped her head out of the water, she knew something was wrong. Arend let out a shriek to confirm her suspicions.

"Gorm!" Bellae yelled. The falcon instantly dove to her. *"My friend, I have an important mission,"* she said, strapping something around his neck and whispering instructions including, because of Kāla, where they were to be taken. As she finished, Arend began yelling, describing what he was seeing as the others emerged above the surface. Gorm took to the air, flying northeast as Bellae had instructed him to fly around those approaching from due north.

"Jumeaux just told me he's the one Arend's seeing. Veneficus is with him," Gimelli informed. "Do you think they want to help? I'm not sure what we should do."

Bellae shrugged, not mentioning she already knew he was coming.

"You saw what Bellae did. Ailante and the others are right. She's dangerous," Kainen said to Arend, who had flown lower. "Without trying, she destroyed the hippocampi's cave."

"We know, and should trust, her," Arend replied.

As the two argued, Gimelli asked, "Did the last scroll say what we do with the crystals?"

"We have to take them to the council at the Citadel," Kainen said, moving away from Arend, who was floating with Sankari on the stiff breeze above.

"Bellae needs to do what the prophecy told her to do," Lontas said defensively. "She's the one whose been putting her neck on the line, time and time again."

"Like all of us haven't been risking our lives?" Kainen shot back. "We've all paid a price on this quest, and we should all have a say in where they end up. The council will know what to do. We've already seen how powerful they are. Used correctly they assure victory over the White Wizard and Dark Warriors. In the wrong hands, they could kill everyone."

"Why are you looking at Bellae?" Gimelli asked protectively.

"The power of crystals should be given to the collective wisdom of the ones who have been protecting them, and their secrets, for eons, the League of Truth," Kainen said. "It's nothing against Bellae. She just shouldn't have that responsibility."

"What did you find out, Bellae?" Scelto asked.

"Right now, we should get away from Veneficus," Bellae said, trying to block out the crystals and the hippocampi. "Maybe head to back to Cruba?"

"Arend, how long do we have?" Scelto asked.

"Minutes."

"Let's move," Gimelli added over Kainen's protests.

"Please take us back to Hirmulisko," Bellae asked of the hippocampi, who were still crying at the loss of their sacred Cave of Crystals. *"I'm really sorry you lost your special place."*

"I don't understand what happened," Capall-Mara said, glaring angrily at the League.

"I'm honestly not sure, but could you please help? There are people we need to avoid coming to get us from the north."

After arguing amongst themselves, the hippocampi took off. Their shock and anger translated into a much choppier ride complete with hissing sea-serpents.

"Did you get your crystals?" Ceffyl-Mor huffed angrily.

"I did. I'm profoundly sorry," Bellae replied, anxiously clutching her bag.

"I thought we were friends, but you betrayed me," the young hippocamp said.

"They're closing on us!" Arend yelled. "They must be using magic to speed their flight. There's no way to outrun them." Soon a series of griffin shrieks rang out from above.

"Stop!" the thin Magician, Fino, called out, riding a large griffin. Jumeaux and Veneficus also circled above.

"Did you find what you were looking for?" Veneficus asked, pointing his crosier ominously towards Bellae.

"We found them. We'll meet you at the Citadel tomorrow. There will be a council to decide what to do with the crystals," Kainen said.

"There's no need. I'm the one who must have the crystals. You don't want them falling into the White Wizard's hands. Think of all the times Magicians have helped. Remember, they were mine for ages before the backstabbing Ainmhi Caint stole them. Even with good intentions to 'protect' Verngaurd, they were misguided. Look at the death and destruction resulting from their theft. Come with me to a safe place, and we'll talk about their future."

Suddenly, a dozen griffins dropped from the sky. Several of the fast-flying warbirds rammed into the young Eaglian, who tumbled backwards. A lion paw raked across his wings, and he cried out in pain.

"Stop this now!" Bellae thundered, reaching for the bag.

Veneficus snarled, pointing his crosier at the bag, mumbling an enchantment. A beam of light shot towards the crystals. As it neared, it suddenly split apart, arching away in a half-sphere, as if it were hitting a shield. Bellae could feel him pushing harder with his magic, trying to take the crystals. She was not creating the barrier—the crystals did it independently. Veneficus huffed, the beam of light stopping. He uttered another quick enchantment, and a red beam shot from his crosier. It formed into a giant rope and coiled around Arend, squeezing him tightly.

"You'll never get them!" Bellae shouted. "I—" Bellae's remaining words went muffled as a second red rope blasted from his crosier and wrapped around her body and mouth just as Arend let out a painful cry, the enchanted rope squeezing his injured wings. Sankari flew to Gimelli knowing the magical lashings could kill her.

The scared hippocampi bolted south, towards the Isle of Hirmulisko. Many of the League members were forced to hold on for dear life as the creatures sped forward. Ceffyl-Mor took off even though Bellae was still being squeezed by Veneficus' magic. The connection between Veneficus' crosier and Bellae disappeared, but the squeezing rope remained. Veneficus threw Arend into the sea, and the red rope that had been compressing him disappeared. Arend struggled to stay above water as his crushed wings fluttered, becoming soggy and heavy.

Veneficus began chanting. The water around the hippocampi turned black and began to swirl, spiraling faster and faster until they were whirling around helplessly.

"I can't swim out of this!" Ceffyl-Mor cried.

"Watchers and specters, master!" Fino shouted.

Barely looking, Veneficus summoned a silver light from his crosier and obliterated a dozen Watchers and Nishi. "Don't need them, but I know who *should* join our party."

"Jumeaux. Help us!" Gimelli cried out.

After looking fearfully at Veneficus, Jumeaux looked down.

"He knows his place and understands what's at stake. You have no perspective of the world, nor any understanding of what's truly going on."

"What are those things?" Lontas asked, his head dizzy from spinning, as horrifying red shapes zoomed up from the depths below.

"Bellae, something's coming!" Ceffyl-Mor cried out. The young hippocamp pulled her head out of the water, looking at Belle with pure horror. *"Viper Squid and—"* Ceffyl-Mor cried out, unable to finish, pain ripping through her mind. She began thrashing violently, flinging Bellae into the swirling sea. The other League members met similar fates as their mounts bucked violently, floundering in brutal agony. Griffins swooped down, ripping the League members from the water, careful to stay above the twisting whirlpool.

"Fino, bind the wretched League and get them on griffins," Veneficus ordered. "This is the last night we sleep on cold hard stone!"

Scroll 13: Mind Splinters

Falcon Gorm made it to the Citadel. His keen eyes easily spotted his target. Friar pushed down the bows of those next to him on the ramparts. "Everyone, hold! I recognize that bird."

The exhausted falcon landed heavily on his chain mail. Gorm rocked his neck forward, causing the necklace Bellae had secured to pendulum forward. Friar instantly recognized it and screamed, "Get me a Vioma, now!"

Unpuzzling the Inion Medallion off Gorm, Friar asked, "Will you lead me to Bellae?"

Within minutes, Northern Dwarf Abhac landed precariously on the battlements. "You rang?"

Friar quickly scaled the tottering rope ladder, pausing to pat Soma on the shoulder underneath a few new scars before ascending into the carriage with the Aer Ridire. After strapping in, he gently tossed the falcon up into the air. Gorm flew back down, landing on one of the wooden beams, repeatedly pointing with his beak towards the southwest.

"I guess he wants to ride. Smart bird. It's not wise for a snack to fly in front of hungry jaws," Abhac said before shouting commands.

The red creatures grew steadily larger, rising closer to the surface.

"Help, Bellae!" Ceffyl-Mor cried out. *"Make the screaming stop!"*

Tethered by magical ropes, Bellae could not move or speak. She could only shed tears at the desperate plight of the hippocampi as their panic thumped her insides. *Take control of the crystals. Spread mercy,* a voice whispered. *Promise your life to us forever, and it shall be done.*

Several of the male hippocampi began slamming their fearsome horns into the water as the rising creatures slowly materialized. Clawed tentacles broke the surface, quickly coiling around the wriggling hippocampi until digging deeply into the sides of their victims, generating gushes of blood and howls of pain and fear to torment the air.

"Take the prisoners to the caves. Jumeaux and I shall join you shortly," Veneficus said. "This is the good part."

The long, arrow-shaped bodies of the viper squid came into view as their eight arms and four tentacles slithered around the tails of their writhing targets. They slowed, enjoying the panic, feeding off the fear and suffering of their prey. Even traveling away, Bellae closed her eyes against the surge of pain radiating from the hippocampi. *I got them killed,* she thought as the crystals chimed in, *Release our power, and more deaths need not happen.*

The viper squid raised themselves out of the water enough to show their enormous black eyes and jaws with massive, spiked teeth.

"That's the viper part—sharp fangs instead of beaks," Veneficus added before chanting. As he finished, the swirling waters began to calm.

In easy motions, the squid spread their spiked teeth apart and chomped into the heads of the hippocampi. Their serpent manes shot in vain towards the squids' bodies, their own fangs barely scratching the tough skin of their attackers. With a sucking noise, the squids submerged their victims. Loud splashes and bloody bubbles filled the voids of the dying hippocampi.

"Show's over," Veneficus said, beckoning Jumeaux north.

Jumeaux let his gaze linger on the water, still marking the butchery with red and black hues which joined fleshy chunks, and he imagined the horrific scene playing out below. The spiraling water slowed, allowing scarlet and sinewy bits to spread apathetically along the surface. Fighting nausea, Jumeaux swiveled, catching up with the Supreme Master.

"Why did the hippocampi go nuts before they were touched?" Jumeaux asked.

"They were being subjected to high-pitched sounds from the reclusive mer-sirens. They have long, spiked tails, webbed hands, and human upper torsos and heads, complete with gills near their ears. They are freakish beasts whose singing drives most creatures insane—all except the viper squid, so they hunt together, the mer-sirens not having to get their claws dirty to eat."

Seeing his concern, Veneficus added, "Never forget our actions are for the good of all. Everyone helping the Chosen One is doing so to spite me and thwart our plans. You realize the League of Truth is a direct descendant of the traitorous Ainmhi Caint? Those villains started this mess—deluded fools thinking they are protecting Verngaurd from some made-up evil."

"Isn't the White Wizard evil?" Jumeaux ventured. "Wouldn't it be devastating if he ended up with the crystals?"

"Do you doubt my power?" Veneficus thundered. Before Jumeaux could answer, he uttered the prodigiosis volo enchantment, sending both griffins lurching forward.

When they arrived at the cave entrance, their griffin mounts were taken to the stables while they journeyed to the large meeting chamber in the next room. Fino was vainly trying to calm a Magician writhing on the floor, his body arching in pain. The flesh of his hands was mostly gone, the edges blackened and burned.

"Did the fool honestly touch the crystals?" Veneficus asked.

Fino nodded. "He took a pair out of the girl's bag, thinking he could use their power if he attached them to his crosier. The prisoners are against the far wall. They've been thoroughly searched and their weapons removed to the side."

"Fino, guard the League of Inequity," Veneficus ordered. "Jumeaux, untie our League of Deception guests. Are you proud of yourselves for getting all my Macht Crystals? You shouldn't be. You wouldn't have survived without me. I saved you multiple times and got you to Ifrean!"

A Magician approached Veneficus. "Hordes of Watchers and Nishi are advancing."

Snarling brusquely, Veneficus ran back to the cave entrance to dispatch them as Jumeaux chanted. Slowly, the magical binding encasing Gimelli dissolved.

"Jumeaux, how can you do this?" Gimelli whispered.

"I have no choice," he answered telepathically, a glance to Fino.

"There's always a choice. Stand with us."

"He'll kill me," Jumeaux replied, looking down. However, Fino's words stirred some hope of taking down Veneficus.

"He's definitely killing us, but how long until he turns on you? Remember, I love you."

Jumeaux cringed, remembering his traitorous friends, also betrayed by Veneficus. *"You don't even like me,"* he said, raising his eyes to meet hers.

"You don't have to always like someone to love them. That's the deal with family."

Jumeaux paused. *"I know I was always a little different and a lot angry. Sometimes when I was trying to be funny, it came across as mean, and sometimes when I was being mean, I disguised it as humor."*

"Every one of us, every single day, makes mistakes. We still love you," Gimelli said.

Jumeaux fought the acrid emotion refluxing into his mind. *"I try to move beyond my past mistakes, but they weigh down my heart and soul, never leaving my mind. Each one, by itself, not heavy...but together? They are hard to bear."*

Gimelli let tears flinch out from the sentiments in her complex love for her twin. "Nothing that's been done cannot be forgiven. Nothing said cannot be left behind. Help us."

"I can't remember why I was so angry. None of you deserved it. I knew Veneficus was priming you for this moment. I helped him, betraying you. There's no coming back from that."

"I can see you felt we betrayed you as squires and I understand why you ran to Veneficus. Right now, help us, then we all move forward together."

I don't know who to trust, Jumeaux thought. Speaking telepathically, he said, *"You can try and reach back in your mind and poke around painful memories, but the reality is, regrets stab out in our remembrances like monstrous spears with pennants marking our failures in time along the path of our past. Banners we can't change and never forget."*

"You're right. We cannot change or reshape the past, but we can learn from it. We can change and move forward."

Jumeaux shook his head. *"Each regret is like a splinter in my mind, making me uncomfortable and grief-stricken. I can never reach in and scratch the itch from those shards of remorse. I don't know who I really am. I was sleepwalking through much of life in Liberum."*

"Well, you're awake now, and we can dig out those splinters of remorse together with good actions, grand deeds, and helping others. Slowly, day by day, we'll excavate each one, replacing them with pleasant thoughts and memories, together. Twins for life. Family forever. Knights undyingly."

"You live in the sunshine, Gimelli, and it's hard for you to see those of us forced to subsist chained within the shadows."

"Keep moving, Jumeaux! Did you shite your pants or something?" Veneficus yelled upon returning. "Unbind the rest! Fino, don't stand there like a post. Keep the boy moving!"

Jumeaux moved to Scelto—he could see the hatred boiling behind his former nemesis' eyes. *Nothing's changed. Nothing will change,* he thought.

As soon as Scelto was free, he pushed Jumeaux. Fino immediately slammed the wooden end of his crosier into Scelto's abdomen, dropping him in pain. He groaned in agony as Gimelli tried to comfort him.

Fino smiled as if he had done him a favor. Jumeaux managed a grin, weighted by fear as uncertainty fizzed within his stomach.

Scroll 14: Mouse's Measure

After Jumeaux unbound her, Bellae whispered, gently squeezing his hand, "I know it's scary, but you need to know I love you. There's still time to do the right thing."

Arend, who was in and out of consciousness, moaned.

"Veneficus, please. We're all working for the same goal—to rid Verngaurd of the White Wizard," Kainen stated. "Let's go to the Citadel and meet with the council."

"You don't know as much as you think, stripling. There are larger contrivances at work. The League of Incompetence is merely an extension of those responsible…the cursed Ainmhi—"

He was cut off as blinding light flashed before quickly dimming into the forms of Tacet-Vand and IleZuri. The Wizard shuffled forward, his eyes glued longingly to the Macht Crystals.

"What are they doing here?" Scelto whispered to Gimelli.

She shrugged her shoulders, but a tinge of fear raced in her mind. *Was he the one who blocked the weapons against Hullus at the tournament? Is he the evil one biding his time?*

"I knew the scent of power would entice all sorts of magic-addicted rats hoping for a bite of their energy," Veneficus said as Tacet-Vand pointed to his throat.

Veneficus blurred towards the Wizard before abruptly stopping and harshly thrusting his crosier forward. The crystal flared angrily before transferring a stream of magic light to Tacet-Vand's throat. The Wizard's head was thrown back, eyes closed, his face crumpled in pain. The shifting light stopped, and Tacet-Vand fell to the floor, vomiting a thick, black material. He retched two more times before IleZuri, brandishing his bladed bow, moved to help his friend up.

"We've made it to another Na Cearcaill!" Veneficus said. "How many have there been?"

"How old are they?" Lontas breathed. Bellae shook her head.

After taking several drinks of water, Tacet-Vand swallowed repeatedly before breathing deeply. He tried to speak but only managed a gagging cough.

"You're always so dramatic, brother," Veneficus said.

"Wait, what? Brother-brother, or like friend-brother?" Jumeaux asked.

"He is, unfortunately, my brother of the same mother," Tacet-Vand said, finally able to speak, but rubbing his throat.

"I hope this little punishment left no hard feelings?" Veneficus asked.

"Little punishment?" IleZuri raged. "Millennia without a voice? Age upon age he has been forced to wander until Na Cearcaill returns."

"Watch yourself, Defender of the Wizard," Veneficus said ominously. "His was a just penalty for denouncing and then betraying me with the cursed animal talkers!"

"I've been forced into a desolate life of wandering for much longer than the last Na Cearcaill," Tacet-Vand said, tears streaming out. "I only lost my voice with the Ainmhi Caint."

"How old are you two?" IleZuri questioned.

"Proper social demeanor dictates never asking someone's age," Veneficus said, turning to Tacet-Vand. "See, brother, all has unfolded according to my will. I can only hope your desolate wandering has given you a change of heart to see reason and rejoin my team. Without you, my partner, splitting time as virtuous and iniquitous has been *exhausting*."

"Splitting time?" Lontas mouthed to Bellae, who partly closed her eyes and shook her head as doubt and exhaustion heaved to surround her mind.

"I'm done being a lackey to your deranged plans," Tacet-Vand said.

"Mere mortal creatures are trapped in their own brief window and cannot see as we do."

Tacet-Vand shook his head. "We, being trapped in the present, can only and forever live in our collective prison of today. We can never change the past, nor is it prudent for any living being, including you, to manipulate what lay ahead."

Veneficus scoffed. "That's pathetic and ironic coming from you, one bearing as much guilt as me. You know the truth. My actions protect Verngaurd and its creatures."

"You speaking of 'truth' makes me physically ill. Maybe you saved us from some dark times, but you staved off amazing ones as well," Tacet-Vand replied.

Fino stepped forward, glancing at the League he was guarding. "Uhm, we need to be caught up. I can safely say no one has a clue what you're talking about."

Turning slowly, Veneficus moved towards the groaning Magician foolish enough to touch the Macht Crystals, whose cries were growing louder.

"Thank you, Supreme Master!" the writhing Magician said. "I'm sorry. I shouldn't have touched them. Spells didn't work, so I grabbed them. Thank you for taking away the pain!"

"Don't mention it," Veneficus said calmly as Tacet-Vand used the distraction to drink several elixirs hanging along his belt.

IleZuri grabbed the Wizard's arm, whispering, "Should you drink that much at once?"

"There's nothing to hold out for…not anymore."

Veneficus pointed his crosier at the man, yelling, "Eldur hnottur!" A fire ball shot out of his crosier, blasting the man's head off. The flame was so hot it seared the neck, a black eschar commanding no blood come out. Veneficus then blasted three other Magicians who happened to be in the room before turning to Bellae. He smiled as the last fire ball shot out of his crosier.

"No!" Lontas screamed, diving towards her.

Tacet-Vand's body shook ferociously. When the movement stopped, the quivering revealed a shrunken and shriveled form, half the stature of the previous version. His skin was like that of a Watcher, desiccated and run through with deep crusting pits. His back was hunched and his muscles wiry. Despite his sorrowful appearance, his form blurred with indescribable speed to Bellae. Once touching her arm, he chanted. As the fire ball flew just over Lontas' outstretched arm, everything and everyone froze, save two.

Tacet-Vand let go. "I can't hold time for long. Veneficus will kill me, of that I'm certain. I want to tell you we all have a brief time to walk in consciousness. During that time, we accrue baggage from mistakes and now must carry them. What's important is to use those defeats as lessons. You must fight to keep Na Cearcaill from continuing." His face grimaced as a shudder went through his decrepit form. "I'll try to block the blast but am weakened from creating this moment. I see you looking, and yes, this is my true form, a punishment for ingesting magic, for *everything* carries a price. Avarice for power and greed to covetously hold onto life have twisted my form. What will you do with the crystals?"

Bellae recoiled, thinking, *How can I trust him?*

"I understand your hesitation. This has been a trying time." Pain flashed across his face. "Can't hold. Follow the prophecy your ancestors laid out. If you won't trust me, trust—"

He was cut off as time lurched ahead. Instead of blocking, Tacet-Vand managed to slow and diminish Veneficus' blast before it slammed into Bellae's chest, shooting her backwards, her frail body crashing against the hard rock. Tacet-Vand was also dashed to the floor.

"Did you think you could keep my powers at bay?" Veneficus thundered as Tacet-Vand's form slowly returned to the shape of a kind elderly man. "I made a mistake trusting those Ainmhi Caint and I clearly see, you, brother! Did you know I gave the animal talkers the chance to know the truth of this world, to see behind the curtain of Na Cearcaill? The fools threw away the opportunity to know the secrets of the universe and live forever!"

Gimelli rushed to her collapsed sister and cradled Bellae's head in her arms, sobbing. The exploded fireball had left a black charred mark in the shape of a starburst on her cloak.

"How did it not blow a hole through her?" Scelto whispered, joining Gimelli. "Not that I wanted it to," he added quickly. "Tacet-Vand must have slowed it."

Jumeaux stared in stunned silence at the blackened mark on his sister's cloak. He could hear the other members of the League shouting and gathering around Bellae. Looking up, Jumeaux caught Fino's gaze, his eyes widening in an 'I told you so' manner. *He's right. All Veneficus wants is power. He won't keep me around.*

"No need for hysterics," Veneficus announced. "I can use Bellae's dead hands to move the crystals into place, so no need to worry your unattractive, misshapen heads."

"You're a monster!" Gimelli yelled.

Sankari muttered obscenities and rushed towards Veneficus. Fino sent out a stun spell, but given her petite size, it fiercely blasted her backwards. Her head crashed first against the wall with a crack before bouncing off the floor. Blood streamed from her nose and ears.

Scelto jumped up and ran to her. "She's not breathing," he said, trying to revive her.

With his own eyes blurry with tears, Lontas brushed Bellae's unruly hair out of hers before touching the charred section on her cloak. "It's warm," he said, watching sluggish plumes of steam rising. The blackened section moved, and his hand jerked in surprise. "Hey, what the?"

Gimelli put her cheek to Bellae's mouth and stopped sobbing. "She breathes!"

Curious, Lontas touched it again. The second push made the majority of the burnt residue slide off her chest. Flipping it over revealed a singed tail. "That dark spot…is Grym. I think Tacet-Vand protected her and Grym jumped to absorb the rest of the power."

Gimelli's sobs alternated with gasps of relief. "Grym saved her."

Tacet-Vand, drained from stopping time, rose to one knee.

"Looks like you took a harder hit than initially perceived," Veneficus said, unaware of the time discontinuance.

The Wizard spoke telepathically to Jumeaux, *"Everyone loves to talk of our lives as a journey, but they seem to hold their perceptions of us in static wretchedness, focusing in on our past sins—not what we have done since, how we have changed. What we did in the past forever defines us in their minds. Those judging move forward themselves while holding us bound backwards in time to the person we used to be, the actions we had committed, and therefore, are never truly able to forget or forgive past transgressions. Just because others hold us to the fire of our past mistakes does not mean we need to imprison our thoughts in a never-ending cycle of tormented reliving."*

"Why are you saying this?" Jumeaux replied, looking at Veneficus, confirming he could not hear their conversation.

"Veneficus looks out for himself. I've known him for incalculable lifetimes. Whatever he promised you will only be honored while it's convenient."

"But he's the protector of the world!"

Tacet-Vand shook his head. *"Evil deeds, no matter the underlying motivation, disgrace you alone, stain your soul, not those harmed by the action. The world will always produce unsatiable souls that are never fulfilled, even when suckling at the orgy of greed."*

Jumeaux scoffed, *"You must be confusing me with Bellae, the golden child."*

"It's true she retrieved the crystals, but whether she completes her task will be decided here and now, and you and I have a vital role to play. Let the past go. Move forward. Although Bellae's important, how you act, what you resolve to do, will decide everyone's fate."

Chapter Six
Deceptions Divulge

Scroll 1: Tangled Woven Web, Unwoven

Tacet-Vand's concentration broke with Jumeaux as he was lifted harshly by several Magicians who entered the chamber, having stepped over the four Veneficus had killed.

"Hold yourself together, brother," Veneficus said as Tacet-Vand's form oozed and sagged, morphing sporadically into the shriveled form several times before solidifying into the shape they were used to seeing.

"What just happened?" IleZuri asked. "What's going on?"

"I see my brother, who likes to point fingers of wrongdoing at others, failed to mention all that sleeps within his troubled soul."

"Do not lump me in with your actions or those you bend to your subjugation," Tacet-Vand said, taking a swig from one of his vials.

Veneficus smiled. "It takes literally no effort for people to hate. All one needs to do is manipulate them, quite easily, into seeing and thinking it is 'us' vs 'them.' A quick rumor here, an innuendo there. People fall into the 'I belong to this category' so easily it's pathetic. The only thing people descend into easier than hate is pathetic love."

"Anyone who loves power, glory, money, can never appreciate, nor truly love, intelligent beings." Tacet-Vand turned to Jumeaux. "Let no one think that a creature like my brother, who loves no one but himself, can ever truly love them."

"Jumeaux is loyal," Veneficus said, "knowing his place, unlike you. I always give more than I take, even if your miniscule brain cannot fathom it."

Bellae groaned loudly.

"What's this?" Veneficus demanded. "Jumeaux, check your sister."

"I'm glad she's okay," Jumeaux whispered, stepping over Arend—who was unconscious. Scelto, joined by Kainen, cradled Sankari behind them. The tears flowing down surprised him as the others, having focused on Bellae, did not comprehend the Fairy's death.

"Brother, we have one life, but we live out our lives as more than a single person. We aren't the same, journeying through the stages of being, not really. It's time to turn the page on the past and come home."

Jumeaux scrunched his nose. *That sounds like Tacet-Vand. Are they teaming up to make a mockery of me? Plus, I'm never the hero.*

"Experiences test and teach, and through it all we grow, evolve into different versions of ourselves. Each dawn is a chance to use those lessons and become better. The version of my brother I see today...makes me proud."

Jumeaux shook his head in a mix of skepticism and remembrance. The bullying, both administered and experienced, the failures, the jokes that fell flat, the times he was unnecessarily cruel, the sarcasm that hid his true feelings. All of those experiences felt like a massive weight, tethering down any chance for growth. "It feels like all the mistakes and disappointments happened to lead me right here and now. I'm always the villain."

"That you could articulate such thoughts proves you've matured way beyond that overwhelmed squire. All things are possible, but only if you start forgiving yourself. The past can never be undone. Who we *were* cannot be changed. However, who we can become is always open. We can move forward together."

"You do seem different," Lontas added.

"Hey, man, no matter what, you'll always be a klutz," Jumeaux replied, his eyes moistening, his face dispatching a sad smile, his insides felt like they were being torn in two.

"Well, you'll always be a jerk…but my jerk," Lontas said, locking Jumeaux in an embrace.

"Jumeaux!" Veneficus screamed. "This isn't a squire reunion! How's Bellae?"

As Lontas released him, Jumeaux mouthed, "Lo-lo-loser."

"Numnuts," Lontas replied.

Annoyed, Veneficus briskly moved over, pushing past Fino, poking Bellae. Her body began to writhe. *The smallest detail,* he thought. *Maybe I can use her before she dies.*

"Don't do that again!" Scelto said, gently setting down Sankari. With blurring speed several Magicians surrounded him and Kainen, forcing them back as Gimelli finally grasped Sankari's demise.

"You killed her!" Gimelli said, glaring at Fino. Visions of the sometimes derisive but always truthful and passionate Fairy flashed across her mind as tears streamed out.

"You're hardier than I thought," Veneficus said, kicking Bellae, prompting Gimelli to move protectively back to her sister.

Bellae struggled to sit up. Her chest felt sore, and each breath hurt.

"Thanks, big brother," Bellae said in a hoarse voice when Jumeaux conjured water.

"Surely, you know he's not your brother?" Veneficus challenged. "By the way, Jumeaux, assist her again without permission, and I'll strip off your skin."

"Oh, he *is* my brother," Bellae interjected, despite the pain of her sternum.

"So sweet, makes me want to puke!" Veneficus claimed. "Well, Miss Know-It-All, do you know *who* killed Mommy and Daddy? I recently found out from captured Eaglians."

Bellae and Gimelli locked glances.

"It figures the League of Deception would leave out that small, but ever so vital, detail. Jumeaux, throw water on Bird-Brain."

Once Arend was up, he felt light-headed, struggling to focus. The last thing he remembered was falling into the ocean after being squeezed by a magical rope. He tried to flutter his wings and grimaced.

Pain, lots of pain, which sharpened his mind as Veneficus continued, "It was Aquila, Arend's father, that murdered your parents."

"Liar!" Gimelli burst out. "Her mother died in childbirth just like mine! Then Bellae came to live with us, and we became a new family."

"Did your fathers die in childbirth as well?" he jeered. "Tell me how that works. I've heard of sympathy pain, but that's stretching reality even for the League of Idiocy!"

"Hamata mentioned our parents," Bellae said, determined not to let Veneficus get to her.

"She can barely walk and swing her tail at the same time. Once I've recharged my crystals, I'll give every freak the Ainmhi Caint recruited to help in their delusion the retribution they deserve. Knowing Na Cearcaill was about to be unleashed, the League went on a killing spree—Aquila killing both sets of parents."

Gimelli shrieked in horror as Jumeaux squinted his eyes, trying to comprehend the words.

"That makes no sense," Kainen said defensively, looking at Arend. To his dismay, he saw quiet resolve in his friend's face instead of rage.

"Actually, my naïve younglings, it's another example that the true 'evil' in this world is the League of Truthlessness. They wrote a false prophecy to misguide me, stating the Chosen One was the *brother* of the girl who could speak with animals. Therefore, for the false prophecy to be true, Bellae needed a brother. That's how Jumeaux came to be with me—I thought he was the Chosen because I had the false prophecy spawned by the great deceivers," Veneficus said.

Doubt bubbled within Jumeaux's head as it spun with uncertainty. He felt reality falling, claustrophobically penning him in. *He never cared about me. He's just using me.*

"Jumeaux proved powerful with magic, and then there's the telepathy with Gimelli that's been so useful," Veneficus continued. "I've been tracking you this whole time with no effort."

They shot Jumeaux a look of disappointment. *Played the fool, again,* he thought.

"After his killing spree, Aquila sent you to be watched over by Friar," Veneficus said.

Bellae couldn't help crying. Emotional fatigue and physical exhaustion swirled with guilt over those she loved dying for her. *Our parents were killed because of me?*

Kainen stared at Arend. "Why aren't you protesting these lies?"

"My dad did nothing wrong."

Kainen shook his head, stunned. Before he could say more, Veneficus began, "Well, now that we know how your family tree was pruned, let me give you one chance, girl. I'm not opposed to having another underling."

"A dragon of the North approaches, carrying Friar," a Magician interrupted.

Veneficus looked suspiciously at Bellae. "Full of surprises, I see. Let him land." After a pause, Friar entered. "How unexpected and unpleasant it is to see you."

A loud roar of a Vioma dragon shook through the cave.

"A dragon? Subtle. Now join the others," Veneficus advised. "Throw your sword in the pile with the League weapons. It will do you no good here."

Friar hugged the former squires, handing the Inion medal to Bellae.

"Thank you," she said, slipping the last part of Finn she had over her neck.

"Enough with the reunion," Veneficus howled. "Time for the unbridled truth. If left unchecked, you insatiable creatures eventually embroil the world in war. War breeds advancement, and eventually you embrace the evils of technology. Both war and technology speed you to a point when you destroy yourselves and the planet. I've seen this future, having lived to almost see it happen long ago."

The League exchanged questioning glances. "What's he talking about?" Scelto asked.

"No clue," Gimelli answered.

"I'm really a savior, a rescuer," Veneficus said.

"What are you saying?" Kainen asked in frustration.

"How do you think the backwater Proliate became a military powerhouse? I manipulated King Udistus with visions until he got it through his thick skull how to make them into a force. Who do you think got the Southern Dwarves to turn on the Knights at the Battle of Petturi? Who gave Friar his visions? Weaken the Knights and raise up the Proliate to destroy each other."

Friar rubbed his head. "Is this…a sick joke?"

Veneficus huffed. "You remember Hullus, the dragon that killed Finn?"

Bellae's eyes widened at the reminder as unbidden and unwelcome images of Finn's gurgling death and what Kāla helped her remember but directed her to stay silent about came to the surface.

"I drove him mad through constant torture," Veneficus said. "I wanted more to die, but one Knight was enough to stir up hate by my machinations."

As he went on to tell them about the village massacres he orchestrated, Bellae found herself back in the coliseum, standing before the dragon's devastated body—his mouth silently moving. "The dragon told me, but I had blocked it out until recently."

Veneficus gestured with a flourish, happy someone understood. "I manipulated the battle even more by enchanting your weapons, making them ineffective for the first part of the fight."

"What?" Friar cried out. "I saw you cast a spell to break the enchantment, allowing my Knights' weapons to work."

"Brilliant, wasn't it? I looked the hero by undoing my own evil enchantment. Friar, you served as a competent accomplice. The insect Bellae started to throw off my plans when she confronted the tortured dragon. I turned the situation to my advantage, playing the hero who slew the evil dragon before he could hurt the runty squire. Of course, I was preventing her from talking to the dragon and finding out about the torture, and luckily my memory-blocking spell seemed to have worked against the wretch. I also compelled Fino be my patsy and loiter around while I was enchanting your weapons so I could blame him later."

Fino's face morphed from one of hurt, reliving all the accusations against him, to one of anger. His eyes traveled to Jumeaux as he nodded slightly.

Jumeaux turned away, feeling manipulated himself, remembering the look in Veneficus' eyes the day he had stormed into his room at the Academy and found out about his telepathic ability. *He was going to kill me. Telepathy saved my life.*

Veneficus continued, "I threw in the idea my brother, Tacet-Vand, could be to blame. I knew your Pantteri would have killed that monstrous dragon instantly and I wanted to make you heroes and martyrs before I tore you down. Everyone loves to see the top dog fall. Everyone."

Scroll 2: It Could be Worse

"I don't understand," Friar said, his brain aching with confusion. "Are you honestly saying you're responsible for Finn's death, manipulating us into a civil war, *and* Na Cearcaill?"

IleZuri looked to Tacet-Vand in mixture of disbelief and anger.

"Friar, do not travel down this road looking for reason or compassion," Tacet-Vand said. "His heart is hardened."

"What of your heart, brother?"

"I deluded myself for eons, but my heart is alive despite my shriveled form."

"Does the truth disappoint you, Friar?" Veneficus asked. "The 'truth' is almost always bitingly disheartening, at least when truly comprehended. Welcome to the world. Greet reality. Because I love all creatures, I protect the future by keeping you in the past."

"So 'love' causes you to punish us for some perceived sin of future generations?"

Tacet-Vand nodded and raised his eyebrows. "Ah, precisely the point I made."

"Nothing, not even magic, stands alone. Crystals and magic have some dependency on belief. It can be, if you do not let me succeed, replaced by the corrupt glow of man's fake magic," Veneficus warned.

"So you just have the right to change and create things as you like?" IleZuri asked.

"I'm a humble chef," Veneficus replied. "I toss in ingredients, and sometimes masterpieces are created, sometimes dreadful horrors. I create good *and* evil, but you have the free will to act within the confines of my play."

"Wait. You're the 'One' they speak of?" Kainen asked dumbfounded. "They stole the crystals from you because they found out about Na Cearcaill and how *you* manipulate the world, not some other evil?" He rubbed his head, having trouble wrapping his mind around this idea.

"They didn't find out," Veneficus answered. "I told them, offering a chance to assist me. The first and only entire race I offered to survive Na Cearcaill."

"So you just pretend to be different people? Playing with our lives?" Friar asked.

"We all play roles. We all act through innumerable parts within the play of our lives," Veneficus countered. "You act differently with me than, say, a squire. I do the same thing on a bigger scale, with a higher purpose."

Tacet-Vand stepped forward. "Please, brother, stop the madness. Get off this wheel of destruction that does as much to hurt you as those you destroy. The famine in your heart for power and control is tearing you down. It's time the world flows where it will."

"I tread with infinitely more care than your rulers. I'm less corrupt than the Knights when ruled by kings. Was I more cruel than Emperor Fanga, who taxed his Piscinians into poverty to fund his decadent lifestyle? If I didn't unleash Na Cearcaill, it would get worse. The weapons get greater but are always outstripped by the depraved greed of the tyrants in charge."

"There's a massive difference in what you do and what rulers do," Friar advocated. "Plus, those dying prematurely would strongly disagree as to the value of your actions."

"The entire span of the longest life amongst you is still nothing to eternity. What does death today, or in twenty years, mean to you puny mortals? To the universe, these small differences are negligible. Left to your own devices, too many problems arise, and, of course, most of your troubles come from internal greed. Soon enough the world will forget all things, and all things shall be forgotten by the world. I alone stand outside time, seeing the truth."

"You most definitely are not eternal, and I know your true form is as contorted and twisted as your greed," Tacet-Vand said. "We started off with good intentions, but look what we've become." At that, his form morphed into a shriveled, desiccated shape, hunching under the weight of time—his scrawny muscles suffering under gravity.

"I comprehend why the perishable short-lived don't understand, but you know they eventually destroy themselves—I just control the demolition and make it less than total." Veneficus turned to the group. "Hatred is your baseline response to any ill will or negative word despite the fact only love can quench hatred's fire. Eventually, man will always find reason to kill magic and justification to destroy magical creatures. They will rationalize it with gods, the God, love, hatred, security, protection, but, in reality, those are thinly veiled covers for a swirling mix of fear and anxiety towards that which is different blending with jealousy. If I keep you humble, we avoid this greater sin. My actions prevent evil."

End this! Stop this. Stop him. Make our power your power. Visions of countless possible futures seared Bellae's mind. With the crystals she was able to see and understand them all. Most ended with the entire earth destroyed under the strain of ignorance, bleeding and burning. Tears screamed out of her at the destruction, the extinctions, the scorching of the planet. *If you stop Na Cearcaill but do not use our power, you see how the world ends.* Her visions shifted to the past, strolling through innumerable spoliations of the world. The tears slowed at the bidding of rising anger. Suddenly, she came back to the cavern where everyone was staring at her. "How often we miss the natural wonders and grandeur of beauty nature has laid out before us in each and every corner of creation, choosing instead to greedily mine for money and demand to 'own' that which should belong to us all." Driven by rage, she started to move towards Veneficus.

"Ah, ah, ah!" Veneficus admonished. "Stop right there. How about I let your pathetic band of friends and Friar live if you place the Macht Crystals in the Regenerator?"

Her face tightened, still twisted in anger. However, as Veneficus' crosier glowed ominously, she stopped, and it softened.

"Good. Jumeaux, oversee your pseudo-sister manually loading the Macht Crystals in the pedestal as I showed, for they cannot be manipulated by mindre crystal magic. Once placed in the Regenerator, incubate as many spare crosiers as possible."

Jumeaux remained frozen, having seen the past Na Cearcaill destructions as Bellae had.

"Well, well," a Valo said as they entered. "That look of stupidity on his face says it all."

"I saw those images too," Gimelli said telepathically. *"Even though Bellae's not our sister, we're still Ainmhi Caint. The crystals must have boosted her power to us."*

"He plays the 'I'm an idiot statue' better than anyone I've ever seen!" another Valo said.

"Jumeaux!" Veneficus said, startling him. "Did you fall and hit your head?"

"No."

"Then we can assume you do not have brain damage. Therefore, summon the Regenerator and have Bellae put the crystals in. Make sure they're in the correct order."

"Yeah, get moving, lackey boy!" a Valo said.

Jumeaux and Bellae moved. She pretended to be afraid, cautiously giving Veneficus a wide berth and creating the opportunity to pass next to Friar, whispering, "Keep him distracted."

Friar kissed the top of her head. "I'll try."

Both of them then moved past the decapitated Magician to the other side of the cave.

"If you met yourself, Jumeaux, I don't think even you could stand to be around the incompetence!" a Valo said.

"Leave my brother alone, you…" Gimelli started, unsure of what exactly they were.

"Oh, with the layers of eloquence within your graceful words I should have known you're related," a Valo suggested while haphazardly throwing out amputated light.

"Don't be so harsh to the girl," another Valo said. "Think how lonely and isolated any thought the girl has feels, being companionless in her cavernously empty head."

"Yeah," a third added. "I imagine her going very far one day. We can just hope it is extremely far away and she never comes back!"

Jumeaux pointed to the bag with crystals next to the dead Magician and nodded.

"Help me, Jumeaux," Bellae said softly while replacing the removed pair.

"Step back a bit," Jumeaux said before chanting loudly.

A section of the cave wall disappeared, and a large, adorned column moved gratingly along the rugged floor. Once the pentagon-shaped pillar came to a stop, Jumeaux guided Bellae to the large and ornate ivory pedestal resting on an onyx plinth. Elaborately carved decorations adorned every inch of the pearly white sides of the Regenerator. There were landscape scenes on the flat spaces, between evenly spaced pillars. Each column was covered with the heads of animals—some common, a few exotic, and others that no longer walked the earth.

"Jumeaux, he's evil. Don't follow him down a path you can't come back from," Bellae whispered. "We're family no matter what he says."

"No talking, you two. I can kill Bellae and use her dead, stumpy hands to move those crystals. How the wretched Ainmhi Caint are able to hold them when I cannot, I will never understand. Place the crystals while I watch. Slide open the ten panels, two per side, then place the Macht Crystals in order before sliding them closed," Veneficus commanded, keeping an unblinking gaze on Bellae as she placed the ten crystals into the large pedestal.

"They're home and shall stay forever. Jumeaux, slide crosiers into the holes on the top in the middle of the Regenerator—mindre crystals down—and let them recharge. Bellae, over there!" Veneficus said, pointing to the far side of the cave. "I'll not give you the chance to take them out. I know they've been whispering to you, and I can feel your temptation."

"I'm not you," Bellae whispered, disappointed at being forced to move away from them.

"No. No, you're not."

Perhaps Jumeaux can do something, Friar thought. "Veneficus, I know you. It's impossible to fathom that you are the one responsible for all this death and war."

Veneficus scoffed. "You know me? I've lived tens of thousands of your lifetimes. For the longest time I frantically ran through the maze of life, trying to find meaning and uncover 'secrets.' The conclusion? The maze never ends. There's no pinnacle, no finish line, no end-all wisdom. There's just a dark journey through a twisting maze, which ends in insensate and numbed unconsciousness. So my brother and I experimented with minuscule dilutions of pure magic to ingest. Initially, we hoped for more power, but it became apparent we would not die. I'm not just a user of the crystals—their power is within, and part of me is inside them."

"I assume the parts you left with the crystals are your reason and sanity?" Friar said.

"Cute." Veneficus shook his head.

"Such power warps the soul and twists the mind, not just the body," Tacet-Vand said. "I'm embarrassed it took so many Na Cearcaill cycles to come to this wisdom."

"I think your unnaturally extensive lives and experiences deformed and minimized, rather than expanded, your perspective," Friar said.

"Your lives are but infinitesimally insignificant points on a cosmically eternal canvas of the infinite. You speak of perspective, but you have none," Veneficus responded.

"Instead of using your gift of time to learn and appreciate a comprehensive outlook, you've lost focus and allowed power and greed to blur your true self and genuine vision. It's not too late. Fulfill your promise and help us rebuild," Friar said.

"That's as quaint as it is unreflective and thoughtless," Veneficus replied.

"When we've talked in the past, you showed sincere emotion for us. I know you care."

Veneficus' face hardened. "The longer I let you scurry forward in development, the more I see the schizophrenic regression of giant empires under tyrannical madmen crash against the isolationist contraction fighting to establish tiny, carved-up states in an effort to huddle together within the 'sameness' of you so you can feel like you belong. You cling fanatically to any group, wedging yourself to 'fit in' with prideful groups. I save you from yourselves and your hunger for belonging in sacrifice of common sense."

"It's impossible to imagine what you're talking about," IleZuri said, angry at his betrayal by Tacet-Vand.

"Of course, you don't understand. Your puny consciousness could never grasp it. I can tell you that left unchecked a new, false magic arises. Technology is cold, heartless, and its soulless core has no memory of the human condition. Logic to the extreme, when devoid of human heart and destitute of unfathomable benefit of beauty, will consume the world, turning it into a barren wasteland that will eventually lead to a complete extinction of biological life."

"Whatever your deluded justification," Friar said, "you've no right to treat us like puppets."

Veneficus sneered. "The choreographers of your actions are born from your own baseness, which weaves individualized prisons out of unscrupulous sordidness. A string here for your vulgarity. A line for desires. A cord there for your loves. A chain for your hate. A strand for your addictions. A yarn for your jealousy. They rule you, making you dance and contort yourselves as you yearn for the false gods you kneel to in order to feed your carnal cravings. You form your own kind of marionette prison born from the lust and yearning you pathetic beings spew. I steer you from weakness, cutting the cords of your sordid hungers. A man's life is but a series of lecherous yearnings and is no more valuable than those decadences and desires."

"Forget the past. Help your sisters," Gimelli said telepathically to Jumeaux.

Jumeaux's emotions swelled at visions of his actions at Liberum, the Tournament, the Academy of Magic. Tears quivered beneath his eyelids as he fought to keep them restrained. *"I know I've been difficult, really unlovable, but I know a way out of this."*

"You, Tacet-Vand, and Bellae should be powerful enough to beat him," Gimelli said.

"What I have to do may not be enough to make up for my past, but my life is all I have to offer as penance. I never fit in, never belonged."

"You'll fit in. This is your chance. Help us, and we go home."

"I've never had a home, not really. I know it's my fault. I had lots of chances but never used them."

"Don't do anything stupid. We—" Gimelli was abruptly cut off as magic cloth appeared across her face. She was thrown on her stomach, her hands magically tied. Scelto made a move towards Veneficus and quickly found himself encased in the same magical cloth.

"I can tell you're talking telepathically," Veneficus said. "Jumeaux knows his place and understands he must be careful to survive Na Cearcaill."

I understand your tone has changed since the crystals are in your possession, Jumeaux thought.

"You glaring at the boss, nitwit?" a Valo said, hovering uncomfortably close to his face.

"Enough," Veneficus chided. "Jumeaux, get to work. You should have already put the crosiers in. Don't let your sisters fool you. They never needed or wanted you."

Bellae made a circular motion with her finger towards Friar to keep going.

"So you have the right to destroy us?" Friar asked.

"You mortals with restless minds are afraid to stare at the infinity barricading you in, so you busy yourself with the aforementioned desires, punctuated with killing sprees of anyone different, not realizing you fight over nothing. I merely guide the combat you crave. Without me, you progress to weapons of ultimate devastation, killing yourselves and the planet. How can the birds sing when forests are cut down? How can Eaglians and dragons fly when the extraordinary are viewed as monsters? What of the blackened sky, choked with black smoke of progress? The answer is, of course, they cannot, and the solution is my cycle of remodeling. Your simple minds cannot deliberate on the food of millennia and drink from the bitter cup of futures failed. My eternal contemplation eclipses your feeble, stringy hold on existence."

"Those deaths, those cultures, and opportunities lost? That evil is upon both of you," IleZuri said.

Veneficus sneered. "You create enough war on your own! People growing up in peace think it's the rule, when it's a delusional exception. If you get rid of me, all you do is plunge the world onto a path of increasingly cruel and sadistic wars. War comes whether I direct it or not."

"What you say about war is likely true, but we would have free will," IleZuri said.

"Would you? Do you? Perhaps you recall our previous discussion of puppetry? Plus, does a peasant born in dirt and destined to toil all his life in abject poverty have a 'choice'?"

"I see your point, they may not have opportunities, but why not use your magic and power to give them chances instead of taking them away?" Friar asked. "What you're doing is controlling, throwing us in cages of your making."

Veneficus smiled. "You've hit upon the key to my success. If you make the cage big enough, no one knows they're in prison. If you make the time scales long enough, no one realizes the disruption. Your perspectives are fettered by the blinders of your pitiful mortality."

"I may not understand as much as I wish," Friar admitted. "However, you still have no right to destroy entire cultures for potential future outcomes."

"You mean as opposed to kings who start wars for riches, or emperors who battle for land? Or perhaps the tyrant who unsuccessfully tries to feed his insatiable lust for more: more money, land, fame as the greed chews from within?" Veneficus questioned. "Do you expect the bad man to be good? You are chess pieces with static capabilities, and I need merely to put you in the right places. Without my intervention an age where man devours everything, repeatedly turning upon themselves until distracted into a depraved egotism."

Seeing Jumeaux grimacing in pain, Friar continued, "What do you hope to gain?"

"I forget how ignorant you are," Veneficus replied. "I'm molding the world by destroying this one and starting over, generating one of my choosing. Your fragile minds need me to inject humility. Reducing you to animals sleeping with pigs is a great way to bolster modesty and stop you advancing to a point you forget about magic. I scrub the world free of past diseases and memories, molding it into my next rebirth. You should be grateful I allowed your brief time here. All people and races of strength grow tired, old, and corrupt. If allowed to run unchecked, they decay and die, but not without infecting the very earth itself."

Friar stole a glance at Jumeaux's eyes, which pleaded for more time, before asking, "Were you behind the first Dark War?"

"I played your father for the fool he was. He swallowed my pacifist advice like a dehydrated man gulps water. The mighty Knights fall. The Proliate rise. Then? You! We had to live up Daddy's failures, didn't we?" Veneficus said mockingly. "You were marvelous as I led the Proliate warriors into your traps at Trepas. If you'd rolled over, I wouldn't have been able to thin both of your herds so nicely. Now, after the Dark Warriors devour Verngaurd, I'll finish them off, and presto, the world starts over."

"So, suddenly, you can defeat the White Wizard, your arch enemy?" Friar goaded before thinking, *Is this why the White Wizard attacks us so ferociously? Are we on the wrong side?*

Veneficus scoffed, then grew fearfully silent, straining to hear. Eventually, he said, "Evil approaches."

Scroll 3: My Life's Eternity

Suddenly, a howl of pain came from the dragon outside the cave, overpowering a whine from Jumeaux. Bellae doubled over at Soma's intense suffering.

"It's the White Wizard!" Abhac yelled.

"Speak his name? Friar, what have you done?" Veneficus asked.

Bellae could hear Gorm screeching.

"Get to safety!" Bellae yelled at the top of her lungs.

Another loud howl came from the dragon. Abhac's bloodied and battered body came flying into the cave. The lifeless figure slammed against the wall before slumping ungallantly. The bloody trail from where he hit followed, flowing across the rock towards his collapsed form. Bellae screamed at the sight while still radiating pain from the dying dragon.

"Veneficus, deal with the White Wizard," Friar pleaded.

IleZuri began swinging his bladed bow, instinctively moving in front of Tacet-Vand despite the Wizard's calm demeanor. A hushed silence settled on the cave as the White Wizard sauntered in, seemingly unconcerned.

"You can defeat him!" Fino encouraged as the few remaining Magicians nodded.

"Everyone stand down," Veneficus thundered, moving towards the powerful Wizard.

"Supreme Master?" Fino asked, crosier at the ready.

The two serenely walked until a few yards apart. Veneficus held out his crosier, and the White Wizard his staff. Veneficus' crystal began to glow, and the top of White Wizard's staff began to dematerialize, flaking into a dusty essence before being drawn into Veneficus' glowing crystal. After a few seconds, large chunks of the Wizard's staff flew off, also absorbed, until it was assimilated into Veneficus'. The onlookers stared, dumbfounded as the White Wizard stood passively by. After sauntering forward, they turned, their shoulders touching. Their bodies began frenetically shaking, oscillating so violently they started blurring together as they vibrated closer, until completely overlapping. Friar looked to Fino, but his mouth stood agape.

"What's this madness?" IleZuri queried, looking to Tacet-Vand, who turned away under everyone's gaze, as if ashamed. The two chimeric forms seemed to completely merge, and the vibration slowed, finally revealing the static image of Veneficus.

"It's good to be whole again," he said, shivering slightly.

"You defeated the White Wizard?" Fino asked, confounded.

"He was pretending to be the White Wizard," Friar hissed.

Fino blurted out, "How could you be both the White Wizard and yourself?"

"Why would you assume the 'real' me is Veneficus? Why couldn't 'I' be the White Wizard pretending to be Veneficus? I appear to you in this form because it's comforting and recognizable. Being both personas allowed me to manipulate things on both sides of the Dark Sea—a task necessary once my double-crossing brother Tacet-Vand suddenly decided he wanted to be traitorous. We used to take turns being the 'bad' and 'good' guys throughout Na Cearcaill's many cycles. Fear and hate are the easiest emotions to conjure and sustain. Playing off of each side made it effortless to manipulate you sheep."

"You knew all along?" IleZuri asked.

"Of course, he knew, dimwit!" a Valo said, having floated behind Veneficus when the White Wizard entered.

Tacet-Vand looked down. "You have no reason to pardon my past. Some sins cannot be forgiven, but, perhaps, my change of heart and assistance will move towards atonement."

Bellae shot a glance at Jumeaux, noticing tears flowing down his face, and wondered about his expression. *More agony than sadness.*

"The White Wizard knows all, is everywhere. How could you be him?" Fino asked.

Veneficus smiled. "Fear and rumors burn faster than wildfire. Humans don't care about the source or validity of information. It only matters *that* they heard it."

Pain is a suggestion, Jumeaux thought, trying to convince himself of what Luchar used to yell when he was a tired little kid. The agony made him want to scream, but he suppressed it. The torment made him want to cry. He resisted.

Friar, discerning Veneficus turning towards Jumeaux, quickly added, "You manipulated us from both sides the whole time?"

"You prop yourself up on the flimsy legs of peace and plenty, but if you peel back the exquisitely delicate layer of prosperity that is the lean skin holding your societies together, a gaping wound of barbarism ready to ooze hate and bleed abominations is revealed," Veneficus said. "With the mask of comfort removed, greed and brutality spring to life with such ease it's devastatingly insulting when your life comforts and securities are torn down. Strip away peace and prosperity, and you undress civility and courtesy. Peel back civility and common courtesy, and you flay away your delicate humanity. Raw and exposed, you are beasts at your core. 'Civilization' consists of frail onion skin layers disguising your true selves. I simply control the process and timing of your destruction at regular intervals."

"Your egocentric logic is flawed. I refuse to condemn this generation and our children's children for something they may never do," Friar said. "They deserve the *opportunity* for a future of their making. There will always be those with the courage to stand against evil. Sooner or later, the immoral, deluded, and those intoxicated with power, like you, fall."

"Calling me deluded and immoral?" Veneficus said, his gaze fierce. "You know nothing of your place on this tiny planet or the wider universe. The rock we're spinning on cares nothing of you. In the end, you return to nothingness after crashing into an unfeeling and uninterested world. Periodically shaking up your world order is doing your pitiful minds a favor, preventing your consciousness from sinking into despair."

"By destroying lives and cultures? With help like that, who needs enemies?" Friar asked, scanning towards Jumeaux, who was working on something in agony.

Several lights floated to Friar. "This guy has a thick skull, master," one said.

"Ah, I should have known your infantile intellect cannot comprehend the absurdity of your affliction. You're cursed with consciousness, which, given enough time, leads you to realize the utter futility of any and all of your actions. You briefly flash upon the earth to taste the fruit of life before burning out into the abyss of nothingness. When you're gone, what can you claim to have accomplished? What can you hope to have achieved that will last more than a blink of an eye? Nothing." Veneficus said.

"Sooner or later, your time will come crashing to an end, and you'll join us in the abyss," Friar countered. "While your infamy may live for generations, it too shall fade. Then what will you have accomplished other than evil? You chide us for rationalizing when that is the origin and justification for your heinous existence. What gives you the right to play God?"

Veneficus looked around mockingly. "Because there was an opening. Do I not fulfill the definition? Is a god not eternal, building and molding the world—guiding and changing the fortunes of mortals? Am I not responsible for creating the moral fabric of the worlds I design?"

"You're delusional, but mortal," Friar said. "All that has a beginning has an end."

Veneficus smiled. "With the crystals your pathetic squire acquired, my longevity is assured. Never again will I trust any fools like the Ainmhi Caint. They, like you, jabbered pretentiously, condemning *me* for my cleansing, refreshing cycle of rebirth!"

"So you hunted and killed them?" Friar asked, glancing at the sweat sprouting on Jumeaux's forehead, his face locked in a grimace.

"You all die soon enough anyway, even if I do nothing."

"You're right. We all die. But what you fail to realize is what matters is how we lived," Friar said. "Living with love, compassion, and honor—these things matter. The Knights' code matters: temperance, justice, wisdom, and courage. Striving to improve, endeavoring for improvement and a better life for the next generation, is important."

"Spoken from the frail perspective of the speck of dust you are," Veneficus replied.

"What about *my* eternity?"

Veneficus scoffed mockingly. "*Your* eternity?"

"It may not be as extensive as yours, but it's *all* the time in the world I have. My brief time here *is* everything to me. It's all any of us have." Friar paused. "I'm not the first or last to be chilled when thinking about endless time and infinite darkness waiting to absorb me. The idea of forever becomes hazy, losing true meaning when our brief time is measured against it. However, I do understand the idea of everything. You can call it my everything, my eternity, or whatever you choose. You can make fun of its brevity, but you *cannot* discount its importance, for it is the entirety of my conscious experience, the sum of all the chances I have."

"I'm the preserver of true life. Without me it degenerates into chaos. When a world I created grows too dilapidated, I replace—"

"You value yourself too much," Friar interrupted. "Do not judge yourself impartially."

Jumeaux let out a groan, but fortunately a Valo, having concentrated around Friar, chimed in. "Don't interrupt the preeminent, unparalleled, transcendent big guy!"

"Can't you see that if past worlds had not been destroyed, the Knights would never have existed?" Veneficus stated. "I'm protector and creator of life."

"Who gives you the authority to decide such things?" IleZuri demanded.

"I am the architect, the builder of reality. I am the spring. Without me, entire worlds would never have existed."

"Without you entire worlds would not have been destroyed," Friar responded, trying to keep his wandering eyes from straying to Jumeaux's painful flinches.

"I tire of this conversation," Veneficus said, raising his crosier.

Friar struggled with ways to give Jumeaux more time. "You abused our trust, misused power, and betrayed countless generations."

"Aw, poor leader of ruble castles is a wittle sad?" a Valo said as the others chuckled.

Veneficus smiled at Friar's pain. "You wish reality to be something else? You desire the world to be black and white with simple good and bad?"

"But I do see good and bad. Spoiler, you're the bad guy."

"Your discomfort with the truth is not my, or reality's, concern," Veneficus replied. "I cannot help the fact that you want evil to be some dark and nefarious being, someone easy to loathe, a villain to provide greasily simple answers. Mortals can only lose that which is theirs, and life is never really yours. For your life is but a skin coat borrowed for a brief time."

"Look at all these skin-coat-wearing sheep!" a Valo said as Veneficus raised his crosier.

He needs more time, Friar thought. "There's some truth in what you say."

Veneficus lowered his crosier. "You understand? You admit I'm right?"

"I admit to being no more than a speck in an enormous universe," Friar said. "But you're wrong about the importance of my life and your fate. Eventually, death will come. When it does, all your countless years will seem to have passed just as quickly as mine. So, you see, we both have only our eternity to live within. I'd choose my life's eternity over yours."

Veneficus shook his head. "Can you feel yourself slipping into the quicksand of eternal sleep? Each day you become weaker, movement becomes harder as you stiffen and slow, breathing becomes more arduous, and then you arrive at your final destination—sucked into the black hole of eternity. Your consciousness, your dignity removed as you return to dust."

Friar scoffed. "In the end, it is not the length of time we walk upon the earth that matters but the quality and kindness of our steps."

"You're obtuse and delusional. You live in the shadow of death like scared rats staying out of the rising light."

Friar smiled. "A life with death looming forces us to enjoy moments in a way you'll never understand. Death shakes the cobwebs out of the mundane. I feel sorry for you, one who never appreciates a simple sunrise. The true miracle of birth and everything in between to death."

Veneficus' crosier glowed angrily. Friar's unblinking gaze met Veneficus' with no fear. Visions of all his failures flickered across his mind. He wanted to scream to Bellae, telling her to find a way to win while asking the world to pardon his sins. "Forgive me. I'm proud of my—" his words abruptly stopped as blue light burst from Veneficus' crosier.

His supplication ended abruptly as the beam of intense heat slammed through his midface. Veneficus quickly moved the beam up and down—slicing him into two charred halves. Each side fell unceremoniously to the ground, sluggishly throwing up eddies of smoke. Bellae screamed, tears pouring out of her eyes as Gimelli and Scelto struggled against their bonds.

"There's nothing to forgive. You served your purpose wonderfully, falling for my visions, leading to my victory today," Veneficus said. Standing proudly over Friar's cleaved body, a smug smile creased across his face, undaunted by the fact he had completely misinterpreted Friar's last pleading. Turning to the former squires, Veneficus cast a spell releasing them. "You should see, and know, the fate awaiting you."

Scelto flipped over and stood, quickly helping Gimelli to rise. She was horrified at Friar's death but distracted by Jumeaux talking to her telepathically.

"Okay, I'll stall. Thanks for helping. Love you." Gimelli shook her head to let the others know to stay put while racking her brain, eventually blurting, "I've seen enough to recognize that your 'help' is really mass murder."

"What a naive perspective. Frailty eventually takes root, weaving its way through the fabric of every culture left to grow without my pruning, especially those once plagued by any level of affluence. It chokes and clogs out the good of the society like weeds outpacing flowers. Sooner or later, power corrupts and temptation chisels away at the soul. You always end up with the have-nots suffering under the yoke of the persecuting haves. Always!"

Jumeaux fought to hold in the cries of pain fighting to get out, the ill-tempered facade he had so tediously built starting to melt. *Everything Veneficus told me was a lie. How can we defeat such a…god?* He looked to Gimelli. *How have I treated her and the others?*

"Jumeaux!" Veneficus thundered. "What's wrong with you? Are you crying?"

"I g-g-guess I didn't know I was," Jumeaux said, forcing a smile despite the agony and tears streaming down. *Eat the pain,* he repeated while closing the last compartment with his foot.

"All you have to do is stand there monitoring the mindre crystals. Once fully charged, they flash. Take them out and place new drained crosiers in. Is this too difficult for you?"

Jumeaux shook his head, but his chin also dropped to his chest under the weight of physical pain and swirling emotions squeezing his heart. All the rebukes, all the failed attempts at sarcasm, all the times he pushed people away all suddenly rolled up, becoming overwhelming.

"Can't take criticism? Crying because your feelings are hurt?" a Valo said, streaming over. Jumeaux put his arms behind his back, shuddering in agony as they touched his robes. The lights took his expressions for sadness, swarming with glee towards his perceived weakness.

"I never thought of amateurish mediocrity as a life goal, but now that I've met Jumeaux, I can see that for someone like him, it's a good one," a light scoffed.

"Jumeaux was a loner, and Veneficus had to bribe people to befriend him," a Valo said.

Veneficus smiled. "He's realizing his true station and that I used him for information."

"It's okay, brother," Gimelli said telepathically, but as he looked up, she was taken aback by his expression—distorted into a tortuous wince. His eyes widened and he moaned, tears rushing out in a panicked hurry from their house of pain while sweat bubbled on his forehead.

Scroll 4: Lend Me Thine Hands

"What now, you dimwitted fool?" Veneficus thundered to Jumeaux.

"I think the little guy's a wittle overwhelmed by the sit-u-A-tio-oon," a Valo said.

"Kid's definitely a lightweight" another added.

"I was born the odd one out," Jumeaux said shakily. "Immersed under loneliness my entire life. In my mind I've been treading the water of deep rejection as long as I can remember."

"Oh, boo-hoo, poor you," a Valo chided.

"Yeah, enough of the sob story, kid," another light added. "No one cares."

"Do you think these tears are in response to your rebuke or Veneficus' betrayal? These tears are born from pain!" Everyone gasped as he held up the burnt skeletal remains of what were once his hands and forearms. Scars of burnt bone were covered in raw flesh and spindly tendons, which abutted up against singed remnants of his robe. Halfway down his forearm was a mess of blood and tissue, some charred and black, some red and raw.

"The idiot touched the Macht Crystals," a Valo scoffed, not comprehending the repercussions.

Gimelli dropped to her knees. Jumeaux flashed a weak smile. *"With this, think better of me,"* he said telepathically before dropping to the floor, his eyes fluttering under the lash of agony begetting weakness.

"Eldur hnottur!" Veneficus yelled.

Gimelli could feel the heat coming for her from Veneficus' crosier. She attempted to swivel away, but it was too late. The fireball slammed into her right shoulder, deflecting back to the wall behind her. Pain seared in her brain as she was spun around. Gimelli hit the floor, clutching the blackened wound as Scelto dove over to shield her.

"Bloody crystals!" Veneficus yelled as light from his crosier sputtered before fading.

"Uh oh, boss," a Valo said. "Looks like only one fireball came out."

"Yeah, that mindre crystal's effete," another added.

"Uh-feet? We don't have uh-legs, much less a feet!" the first said, chuckling menacingly as Veneficus hit the crosier with his hand. The crystal fizzled, but no more fireballs emerged.

Lontas and Kainen moved towards Veneficus, but Fino stepped in front of them, his crystal glowing.

"Fino! Bring me a new crosier, you fool!" Veneficus bellowed.

The sallow Magician ran to the Regenerator, pausing to gaze in disgust at the bits of flesh clinging to Jumeaux's burnt hands as the boy moaned senselessly before descending into unconsciousness. After pulling out a crosier, Fino ran towards the Supreme Master.

Veneficus chanted several times, but the mindre crystal did not even flicker.

"Supreme Master!" Fino said, pointing to Bellae, who had circled around the room and was now reaching into her blood-and-flesh-coated bag. Her eyes turned white as the power of the Macht Crystals Jumeaux had returned from the Regenerator coursed through her.

"Immobilize her!" Veneficus yelled with a hint of panic.

Fino hesitated, his subservient nature running through the options. *Do I turn on Veneficus without Jumeaux?*

"Fino!" Veneficus screamed.

"Verkko!" Fino yelled. Immediately a thick web shot out of his crosier and slammed into Bellae. She was blown rearwards, her back pounding into the cave wall, knocking the air out of her as the web encased her against the rock. The bag of crystals fell uselessly to the floor. As her breath was returning, Bellae noticed Gorm hopping into the cave.

"Looks like wunderkind here took the Macht Crystals out of the Regenerator, big boss guy," a Valo said, looking down at Bellae's bag. "That means no mindre charging for you!"

Veneficus began kicking Jumeaux. "You're as poor a Magician as you were an impotent squire. I offer you a chance for life, and you betray me?"

The repeated kicking pulled him back into consciousness. Holding out his hands, the very air stinging them into agony, Jumeaux stood. Veneficus kicked him in the chest, and he stumbled across the cavern, ending up next to Gimelli.

"I've been drinking crushed up mindre crystals for thousands of years. Do you know what that means? I literally have magic running through my veins to still kill you."

Jumeaux nodded to Fino, trying to encourage the sickly-looking Magician to help as Veneficus took a swig from a formerly hidden vial glowering white. "Adtonitus!" he shouted as out of his palm flew a single bolt of lightning.

Jumeaux cringed, closing his eyes tightly against the coming pain. After a moment, he opened his eyes to see that the strike had carved a hole through Fino's chest, blasting out his heart and leaving a sinewy, blackened gap. Fino's eyes were caught in a look of horror as he fell to his knees, then lifelessly upon his face.

"Did you think I wouldn't know you were plotting against me?" Veneficus yelled.

"Yeah, we heard you traitors!" a Valo said. "No one betrays the Supremiest, Masteriest, Derangiest Magician in the world!"

"Except the evil animal talkers," another added. "Plus, pretty much everyone in this cave as well." As Veneficus' head whipped towards the light, it floated backwards.

"Pull," Bellae whispered to Gorm, who had worked his way around the cavern, his beak nipping at the web. *"No, the bag."*

He hopped down, struggling to pull the bag, his beak occasionally slipping off the strap.

"Adtonitus!" Veneficus yelled. A bolt of lightning ripped through Jumeaux. The strike, however, was not centered, catching him on his right side, obliterating his ribs and lungs. The intense heat cauterized the wound as he fell over, landing with a cry of pain.

"Not a direct hit there, boss-guy," a Valo said.

Seeing her brother fall, Gimelli pushed past Scelto. "Leave my brother alone!"

"Enough of the lovey-dovey drama-rama!" a Valo said.

"Please tell me you realize that you're all going to die. It's only the order that is to be determined. I'm happy to admit I lied to Bellae about letting you live," Veneficus said.

As Arend found the strength to stand, Gimelli touched Jumeaux's head, panic racing as she felt his life force slipping away. *"You did it, Jumeaux. You saved us and yourself."*

"I die, but you have a chance for a great life," he said, raspiness clinging to his voice as his scorched, deformed arms began to shake, his body freezing despite the profuse sweating.

"But you saved your heart and soul, little brother. You did that," she said, tears streaming down her face.

"It may not be enough, but what I did is all I have to offer. I realized too late I want to be your family. We choose our actions, but there's no independence from the consequences." Blood dribbled of out his mouth until an agonizing hack prompted a surge. His face scrunched in pain as blood and pink foam spurted out. His breathing, labored and laced with wheezing, turned to gasps. *"Does the fact that I replay the grating memories of my actions over and over until mental blood is drawn help my pardon?"*

"Of course, all's forgiven."

His body was racked with shaking as she cradled his head. His breathing devolved into a gasping hiss. *"Love you, sis,"* he managed before his head flopped lifelessly to the side. Gimelli rested her head over the intact portion of her brother's chest and let the tears flow.

Veneficus laughed.

Gimelli gently set Jumeaux's head down before rising to face the Magician.

Arend moved closer to Gimelli while whispering to Lontas, "Stay on target, my friend."

"I wanted you to see your twin brother die," Veneficus said. "Now you. Adtonitus!"

As the lightning bolt shot from his hand, Arend snapped his wings, flying in front of Gimelli. The bolt tore through his chest, slicing into his heart and aorta. He did not have time to squawk before falling to the floor with a loud thud in front of the stunned Gimelli.

"Oh Arend," Gimelli cried, dropping down next to him.

Lontas whimpered, "No, no, no," as Kainen rushed to his friend's side.

A gurgling gasp caught in the back of Arend's throat.

Kainen grabbed his hand and squeezed. "I've got you brother. We are the League. Sacrifice for success." Arend's forced breathing fell silent as tears cascaded for the others.

IleZuri rushed Veneficus. Before he could reach him, Tacet-Vand created a portal. "I'm sorry I lied. You'll know what to do," Tacet-Vand said as the blonde warrior was drawn through the magical doorway, disappearing as the portal did.

"Adtonitus!" Veneficus yelled again. Scelto pushed Gimelli aside, the magical bolt slamming into a rock behind them. He then stood in front of Gimelli. Lontas quickly followed.

"Oh, how gallant. The order I kill you is not important. The boys can die—"

He didn't get to finish as a stream of white light blew though his stomach, sending him lurching forward. "Enough," Tacet-Vand said after drinking another elixir. "This ends."

Veneficus looked at his injury in stunned silence. His body flickered to his true form—slight and shriveled, hunched and frail, with stringy arms and legs covered in desiccated skin. Streaming bluish magical fluid competed with dripping blood to escape the injured sections.

"Your true form shows, brother," the Wizard said spitefully.

Veneficus began chanting, and slowly the injuries on his desiccated form began to heal—strands of tissue and skin crisscrossing across the hole, struggling to mend the wound. As they did, his projected body reappeared.

Bellae could feel the power of the crystals as Gorm struggled to bring them closer. Finally, she grasped the bag. "*Thanks,*" she whispered. As soon as her hand clasped the bag, she could sense the web holding her warming and starting to glow. The closer her hand moved to the crystals, the faster the web vibrated and increased in temperature.

Tacet-Vand quickly drained the last of his vials before moving behind Veneficus. He shuddered as the power coursed through him. Closing his eyes, he fought the urge to join Veneficus in his attempt to live forever as the magic whispered promises. *Enough. I've lived enough,* he thought. Clearing his mind, he focused on the magic flowing through his veins, quickly sending several fireballs cascading at the remaining Magicians loyal to Veneficus. After taking a deep breath, he began chanting, a massive surge of radiance blasted from his staff.

Just before the gleaming ray hit him, Veneficus summoned a shield. A loud hiss traversed the cave as light slammed into the magical screen, radiating off and crashing into the cavern, sending rocky shrapnel showering out. Veneficus was pushed back, his feet skidding across the cave floor for several yards.

"Once I kill Bellae and recharge the mindre crystals, I shall hunt down your Defender, and he shall die…slowly," Veneficus said. The ray ceased, and he turned towards Bellae, a look of concern flashed across his face, as her hand had found the crystals, their magic surging through her body battling the web. The net was trembling violently and glowing red with such heat it was shredding the fibers and leaving scorch marks across Bellae's cloak.

Veneficus chanted another web spell to reinforce Fino's original. Chanting again, the crisscrossing webs began to constrict. Bellae gasped, trying to refocus the power of the crystals to stop the tightening from crushing her.

Tacet-Vand released a stream of fiery, magic arrows from his staff. Each time one released, a shrill whistle echoed across the cavern. Veneficus whipped around to face his brother. The flaming projectiles did not immediately head towards the waiting Magician. Rather, they shot out in all directions. With all the other Magicians dead, Kainen retrieved his kama weapon before slinking in the shadows around the edge of the cavern opposite to where Bellae was stuck.

"That's a neat trick," Veneficus said, his respect at the arrow spell leaking into his words as they began zooming indiscriminately around the cave, forcing the League to dive to the floor as one of the floating lights was struck by a wildly flying projectile. Something like a scream escaped it as the orange flame struck deep into its floating face. With a thwack the orb exploded, sending a shower of magical blue dust flowering to the floor.

The magical projectiles began flying more and more erratically while picking up speed. Veneficus ducked and threw up an orb shield as one whizzed over his head. However, the arrows simply avoided it, continuing their zigzagging path, hovering hungrily outside the barrier, waiting for an opening.

"Magic is imbued within the arrows—they can go all day. How long can your shield hold?" Tacet-Vand asked.

Veneficus looked covetously first at the empty vials at his waist and then the Regenerator stripped of crystals. A thin smile hunched across his face. Letting the defensive barrier drop, he chanted, and the remaining eleven floating orbs were magically siphoned towards him.

"Boss!" one of the Valo shouted. "Whatcha doin'?"

"You wouldn't, would you?" another asked, captured by Veneficus' spell. "We've served you faithfully for eons!"

"Sacrifices must be made, and, obviously, better you than me."

"But I thought we were the light of your world—pun intended," another Valo said before Veneficus slammed it into one of the blazing arrows.

"If this is about our load of sarcastic comments," another Valo said, desperately trying to float away, "it's not our fault. We can't be responsible for all the stupid people coming into your office. You know the saying, 'Someone says something brainless, bash them with sarcasm!'"

"That's definitely not a 'saying,'" Veneficus said while grabbing it with magic and skewering it into an arrow. The light exploded, sparks fluttering down.

"But, master, who'll pump up your way overstated and obscenely exaggerated ego? Why not recreate us with arms and hands so we can clap for you? Pat you on the ol' back even! We could get you that disgusting, chunky gruel you call tea," a remaining Valo said.

"No," Veneficus answered, still dodging while sacrificing his magical lights.

"Listen, Supriemiest, Masteriest big guy," a surviving light said. "If this is about the stuff we said behind your back, let me say, if you do know we called you insane when you were absent, how could we know you weren't aware you're psychotic?"

Scelto pushed Gimelli out of the way as an arrow sliced into his arm. Even with her burnt and bruised shoulder, she helped Lontas make a rough bandage for him as the arrows, though fewer in number, continued to zoom menacingly. Kainen crouched in shadows with his kama.

Veneficus, scowling, hurled the Valo who had insulted him towards an arrow. Just before smashing into it, the Valo cried out, "Your true form could cure the world!"

Veneficus narrowly guided the light to avoid the arrow. "What does that mean?"

"Well, if laughter is good for health, then your ugly, hideous, misshapen face—"

The worlds trailed off as the Valo was obliterated against one of the zooming arrows.

"Who's gonna light up your days with sarcasm and humor?" a Valo pleaded.

"You're not as witty as you believe, and your satire grows old," Veneficus replied while sacrificing the last of his Valo to end the arrow threat. "They were growing dull—pun intended." He chanted, calling Fino's crosier to him.

"You were always quite willing to sacrifice others but never quite prepared to offer anything of yourself," Tacet-Vand said before conjuring and unleashing a flaming spear.

Scroll 5: Not My Goal

Veneficus ducked under the spear. He was just about to stand when the Wizard recoiled the flaming weapon, which, again, flew just over the Magician's head.

"Missed…twice," Veneficus said.

Just then Kainen sprinted forward, his kama weapon blurred, slicing into Veneficus' left arm. With a scream, the Magician brought his crosier over, racking the crystal across Kainen's face. Even with his tough Elven skin, it sizzled, burning his bark-like face. Kainen spun around and embedded the beak weapon into Veneficus' side, immediately doubling him over and causing him to shriek in pain as a mix of blood and glowing magic surged out. Scelto and Gimelli charged forward. Veneficus chanted, and both dropped like boards, unconscious. He intoned healing spells for himself but could feel the magic draining from his blood as he desperately thought, *I need fresh crystals.* He stumbled as magic, bred with blood, gushed out.

Lontas rushed forward after retrieving his sword. He slashed Veneficus' other arm. Kainen used his kama to dig into his leg. Veneficus swung his crosier wildly, slamming into Lontas' head. Lontas stumbled backwards, dazed. Ineptly, Veneficus tried to hold the magic in.

"Win, Bellae," Kainen said before going back on the attack. His blade sped forward. Veneficus blocked it with his crosier. As they fought, the crosier's crystal seared into Kainen. The young Elf's face, mauled by deep red scars streaking in angry crisscross patterns, outlined eyes filled with rage. Several of his strikes managed to draw blood, but none were deep.

Lontas was up but moving slowly. Veneficus jabbed the wood of his crosier into Lontas' abdomen before side kicking him in the head. Lontas bounced backwards off a stone, knocked out. Kainen slammed his kama into Veneficus' back. The Magician's form briefly flashed to the shriveled version before fury overtook him. Reciting a different spell, flames burst out of his crystal, showering the young Elf's already disfigured face. Even after the spell had consumed flesh and muscle,

Veneficus kept the flames burning. Kainen's screams turned into a gurgle. Reluctantly, Veneficus used more magic to heal his own wounds. Reflexively, he reached for his vials. Their hollow tinkling reminded him their contents were spent.

Using the distraction from the others to prepare, Tacet-Vand released a massive lightning strike above Veneficus' head. White-hot light ricocheted from the roof, causing rocks to crash onto Gimelli and Scelto, who were just coming to.

"Aim much? I'd—" Veneficus stopped as large chunks of ceiling came crashing down. He barely had time to squat and form a shield orb. The dust and debris spread out in a choking haze, large slabs falling on the smoldering body of Kainen but missing Lontas.

With fine particles still fiercely clinging to the air, Veneficus blurred towards his brother, doing a leg sweep. Tacet-Vand landed hard on the floor as Veneficus twisted his body, slamming his elbow into the Wizard's nose. Soon, the crystal from Fino's crosier was glowering inches from the Wizard's face, blood gushing from his nares.

Howls of pain lit up the cave as the crystal raked side to side, charring sizzling lines of angry, burnt red across his face. Tacet-Vand's form flickered before reverting from the wizened old man to the shriveled form that was truly him. The bright red gashes crisscrossing his already desiccated face became pocked with blisters as he suffered more slashes.

"You can't defeat me, brother," Veneficus roared. "I've *always* been stronger."

After a halting breath, Tacet-Vand wheezed, "I wasn't…trying…to defeat you."

The look of concern that briefly flashed across Veneficus' face was replaced with rage as he stood, flames burst from his crosier, engulfing Tacet-Vand as the spewed fire traveled back and forth. Veneficus gloated over his brother's charred and seared body, which, already withered, contracted more, the fire tirelessly feeding. As the flames slowed, he spitefully kicked the burnt husk at rage's request.

"It's called a distraction," Bellae said, now freed from the web. Touching the crystals, she called upon their power. White light flooded into, then out of, her eyes, thudding into Veneficus, sending him pounding across the cavern, sliding to a skidding stop, his crosier clattering away.

Bellae shook her head against the chatter and enticements roaring in her mind from the crystals. *I control the good!* she shouted. In a flash, her eyes still glowing, Bellae moved to stand over Veneficus. He was gasping for air, and blood was flowing freely from his gapping chest wound. In his blood, Bellae could see bits of crystal reflecting the soft light of the cave.

"I am magic and cannot be destroyed," Veneficus said, but fear swathed his words as his form shuddered between what they had known and the genuine withered and wilted shape.

"Oh, I'm pretty sure I can manage it," Bellae replied.

Before she could unleash more magic, Veneficus flipped backwards and up, his foot connecting with Bellae's chin, sending her sprawling rearward. His dehydrated form seemed comically small. He howled with rage as the warped magic that had come to make up so much of him fought to repair his shredded chest. Chanting, he reached out with his outstretched arm, summoning the crosier of a dead Magician. "No reject like you kills me!"

"But, she's not alone," Scelto said, having freed himself and Gimelli from the rubble. They helped the sputtering Lontas up. He shook his head, still dazed.

Scelto grabbed the Magician's shriveled wrist, holding it firm while slamming his forearm into Veneficus' elbow. A loud crack was followed by a fresh howl of pain as Scelto twisted the fragmented arm back upon itself several times while kicking out Veneficus' leg, blowing out his knee. The Magician and the crosier clattered to the floor.

Lontas grabbed his sword and rammed it into Veneficus' back, piercing through ribs and liver, splurting out magic-laden blood from his front.

Gimelli retrieved the crosier and slammed the crystal into Veneficus repeatedly, using the searing gemstone as a spear. While his arm and leg ineptly tried to heal, he used his good right hand to grab the wood below the crystal, stopping it from slicing into his body. Lontas withdrew the sword, slashing it with all his might along Veneficus' back, sending a shower of blood and magic splattering across the cave. Scelto joined Gimelli, and they pushed down on the crosier, together overpowering the Magician. The crystal sizzled into his jaw.

Bellae yelled, "Move!" while putting her right hand back in the bag.

Looking up to see her eyes overtaken with glowing magic and a look of fury, Lontas, Scelto, and Gimelli complied. Bellae could feel the power coursing through every cell in her body, carrying with it a burden of wrath for her to bear, but the sickly sweet vigor kept her from caring. "You shall pay for all the countless deaths you handed out, but the one that will allow me to finish you? Finn."

Veneficus sputtered a cough, blood and magic spewing out of his mouth. Panic shone behind his eyes. "You're acting righteous, but the crystals eventually win, taking over as they did me." He looked down, truly seeing his withered form before thousands of images of the worlds he had shaped flooded back. All the races, cultures, religions, and creatures he had helped create and destroy played out in his mind.

"So many," Bellae breathed. Realizing she could see them, he forced them to stop. In their place flashed a future with Bellae warped and controlled by the power of magic. Her ability expanded exponentially until she was more powerful than him. Her intellect perceived the smallest changes in a world she manipulated with complete mastery.

Veneficus chuckled. "Soon you'll be stronger than me. If I die, I do so knowing you're the new keeper of magic. You'll figure out what I did and control the world to keep magic."

"I *will* be more powerful than you, but not the way you think. I'm going to be something greater than you—a magic addicted, sadistic god," Bellae declared before moving close, whispering, "I'm going to be the girl who said no to infinite power."

A stream of white light blasted out of her left hand and into Veneficus' chest. His body thrashed and trembled as he howled. His reverberating form shuddered with increasing pain and terror. She could feel his dwindling magic pushing back with fanatic self-preservation. A blue shield of light sputtered around him as he vainly tried to repair his injuries with the faltering magic coursing within. Conjuring images of Finn, her ancestors, Crann, and the dead League members, she poured in all the magic she could draw from the crystals. His protective blue light fizzled and dissolved. He looked at her with pleading eyes.

As Veneficus vainly fought against her overwhelming magic, his speech was halting, "…only did what…was best…I thought—"

"You thought wrong," she interrupted before thrusting all of herself into the magic. His eyes exploded, showering ocular fluid, before his entire shriveled form burst into flames. A thunderous clap shook the cave, sending Bellae, Lontas, Scelto, and Gimelli flying several feet backwards. They shielded their eyes and faces from the heat just as a burst of white light and dust filled the cave, shooting out the opening.

Bellae's visual field morphed from blindingly bright to a darkness marred only by residual flashes of the now-departed light. An intense ringing in her ears was replaced with the distasteful chatter of the crystals. She began laughing, seeing the future with herself all powerful. Every emotion was heightened, but rage and hate exploded. She could not see, nor hear Lontas. Her feet left the floor as her body levitated. Power and control entwined within her body as her mind traveled down various dark paths, fury filling her up at the injustices.

"I can fix every problem! I can cure the world!" Bellae shouted.

Lontas could feel the heat radiating off her. Reaching up to pull her down, he touched her skin. "She's burning up."

Gimelli and Scelto joined him and continued pleading. Suddenly, her head snapped to Lontas before she dropped down, her left hand clasping his throat, slamming him to the ground. He gasped at the pressure and heat, which was burning into his skin. Gimelli desperately tried to remove her hands from his throat, yelling and screaming alternating with pleading.

"You're jealous!" Bellae shouted, her hands tightening around his throat.

"Scelto!" Gimelli shouted.

He ran full speed, ramming into Bellae, knocking her off and sending both to the ground. Scelto removed Bellae's right hand and grabbed the bag of crystals off her shoulder, flinging it away. Lontas was left gasping, rolling side to side in panic with a red streak seared across his neck. Now separated from the crystals, the magic started to fade, the white light sputtering.

"What happened?" Bellae asked, the light draining completely from her.

"You attacked Lontas," Gimelli said.

Bellae could only remember the powerful visions and the scorching rage blending into the belief only she could fix the world's problems. Aggressively, she turned to the bag of crystals lying across the cavern. Assurances of greatness exploded in her mind. Drained, emotionally and physically, she could see the skirmish of light and dark retreating across the universe while listening to promises of all the good she could do in the world, if only she accepted their power. She whispered, "Sorry," before darkness collapsed around her.

Scroll 6: Celebration?

"Bellae, you okay?"

She did not recognize the voice. Her head ached and whirled. *I need to feel the crystals!* Her deep craving for their power embarrassed and frightened her as both eyelids fluttered open. A female Eaglian kneeled beside her in the cavern. Bellae turned to see the brittle, scorched body of Veneficus, still sizzling in a blackened heap. Aggrieved, angry sparks of ember and magic occasionally shot off the crispy corpse.

"I'm Lanella," the Eaglian said, gently guiding Bellae's gaze away from the charred form. "Arend's mother, Aquila's wife." Despite the fact her dearest were dead, there was pride in their sacrifice secured to her words. "You did it. You found the crystals and defeated Veneficus."

Bellae paused. Nothing that happened in this cave, along the journey, even finding the crystals, and certainly what was to come, seemed worth celebrating. She said the only thing that made any sense, "Sorry about Arend. I couldn't have done this without him."

"I'm so proud. He was a great son," Lanella said, trying to overcome the dagger of sorrow. "Selfless parenting is about getting your child ready for their life, performing a million small acts of assistance and praise that will never be remembered or rewarded."

"What about Gimelli, Jumeaux, Lontas?" Bellae asked, panicking. Despite her pounding headache, she sat upright. There were pools of blood, which had dried into black splatters, and scorch marks speckling the cavern, but no bodies except Veneficus' seared remains.

"Gimelli's fine, and Lontas is right behind you," Lanella said.

Bellae spun around frantically. Despite his appearance, she couldn't help smiling. His eyes were red, punctuated with deep bags under them, and his hair was ruffled. However, the relieved smile he wore warmed Bellae's heart. Her head screamed in agony as she stood and shuffled over to hug him. "I'm glad you're safe," she said, burying her face in his chest. "I'm so sorry. Wait, did I do that to your neck?"

"That wasn't you, not really," he answered. "I thought I'd lost you."

She whispered, "I'm so sorry," while giving him a tighter hug. "Thanks for staying."

"They wanted me to leave with the others, but no way," he said. Leaning in, he whispered, "You and me, always."

"Always," Bellae whispered back, knowing it was not quite true.

"The Eaglians flew the others to the Citadel to see healers. They took the dead to be buried," Lontas said, looking at Lanella sympathetically.

"Now that Bellae's awake, she can retrieve the crystals," Lanella stated before talking about a celebration, but her voice was outstripped with screaming within Bellae's mind. *They'll take the crystals from you! As sure as the suns rise, they shall* ***all*** *try. Swear allegiance to us and our power and let us continue to help you. Look at the good you've done, ridding the world of Veneficus and his inane Na Cearcaill that caused so much pain, sorrow, and death.*

I control the good, Bellae repeated to herself, gathering the crystals that had fallen out of the satchel. Each time she bent over, it felt like her head was about to explode, made worse by the sickly sweet promises booming in her brain.

"Everything alright?" Lontas asked.

She forced a smile and dodged the question. "I'm ready."

As Lanella and the former squires walked towards the entrance of the cave, they could see the Northern Dwarves rigging a harness around the Regenerator.

"Don't worry, miss. The dragons will get this contraption to the Citadel for you," a Dwarf boasted as if that were her wish.

Bellae nodded but felt sick to her stomach. *Don't go with them. Arachne said I'd know what to do, but do I? You can't depart from here except by flight. How else can I leave?*

"Let's go off on our own so I can think about this," she whispered to Lontas.

"Come, children," Lanella prompted. "Everyone's waiting."

"Maybe we should go and at least see everybody," Lontas said.

Bellae nodded, but doubt jumped angrily in the back of her mind. Despite her reservations, Lanella carried Bellae, and another Eaglian carried Lontas out of the cave.

"To the Citadel!" Lanella's windswept voice called out. An escort of Vioma dragons quickly surrounded them for the journey.

Did I agree to go because I want a way out? A way for this to end differently than the last scroll instructed? she wondered. Tears broke loose from her eyes only to be violently whipped away by the rushing air. Occasionally, she caught glimpses of Nishi and Watchers greedily observing them from afar, called to her by the beseeching power of the crystals combined.

Bellae glanced out the door, praying it would not squeak. Her vision was met with a wall of red armor. *No chance of getting to Lontas.* She had finished washing up in what looked like a barracks—completely utilitarian. Several Proliate guards had separated them and now stood directly outside their respective doors.

"Are the new clothes acceptable?" a guard asked brusquely.

"Yes…thanks," Bellae replied, coming fully out of the room.

"Boy! Time to go!" a guard said, pounding on the door across from hers.

After they made sure she had the crystals, they moved out of the building only to be instantly surrounded by a dozen more guards. The two were separated by jostling red armor as they formed a block 8 around them. They were forced to perform a stilted jog, trying at once to keep up with the rigid warriors but not step on or be crushed by them. Finally, after sightlessly weaving their way through the city obscured by scarlet armor, they entered the Citadel's Grand Hall. As the cadre of Proliate split off, every eye in the room turned weighty stares towards them.

Bellae stopped, stilted by the force of the carnal hunger radiating from the leaders and important people of Verngaurd. Scanning them, she could see their vision pulled to the bag of crystals she was clutching, enthralled by the promise of power, as well as the fabricated concept such capability would solve all problems—personal and country wide. Bellae's breath quickened. The air turned heavy, crowded by the longing. Starting to feel lightheaded, she spotted two familiar forms pushing through the gawkers.

"Ritari!" Bellae said, overflowing with unrestrained relief, before embracing him fondly.

"Look at you two. I think you've grown a foot," Lovag declared after deeply hugging his former squire Lontas. "But, I think you mean Friar Ritari."

Bellae, distracted by the false conversations brewing as all eyes magnetically drifted to her, self-consciously glanced around the Grand Hall. Even the restrained Proliate could not obscure the beauty of the room. Elaborate paintings of great battles and discoveries peeked behind their standards.

"Hold on now," Ritari said. "We *all* need to decide what comes next, and I will abide by what the council says about rebuilding the Knights."

"Ah!" Lovag scoffed, the idea too ridiculous to comprehend. "We'll rebuild."

"Bellae, nice to see you," General Lidenskap said, approaching. She nodded, and the two stood awkwardly before he inexplicably bent down giving her a cumbersome hug. "I can't wait to see the crystals at the Great Council. I have many ideas of how I—*we* will use the Macht Crystals. It's exciting to think their power will rebuild Verngaurd and secure our future. We should permanently place them on display in the Great Temple."

Turning his body with a flourish, he shouted, "Reveal!" startling Bellae and Lontas. A group of Proliate thundered to the center of the room, removing a large tarp covering the Regenerator. Gasps went up around the room at the beautiful ivory carvings. Several Magicians could be heard arguing that it should be in the Academy of Magic, and a number of leaders rumbled about the safety of their realms as a holding area.

Bellae squeezed the bag from Stralande tighter. Alarms were firing all over her mind. *This is all wrong. I should never have come.* She looked admonishingly at Lontas, who instantly sensed the same conclusion and looked down contritely while sidling closer to take her hand.

"…be great?" Lidenskap finished, but Bellae had not been listening. "Why don't you put the crystals in their natural home? This will allow people a chance to view them until we decide their fate. Of course, there will be guards at all times."

Warning bells raged along with the crystals' sugared words. "For right now, I'll hold onto them," she said while internally repeating, *I should never have come.*

"We have plenty of time to decide what to do with the crystals," Lovag interjected. "You two look half starved. Get something to eat."

Bellae winked appreciatively at Lovag.

"Of course, eat," Lidenskap said, disappointment suffering across his face.

Lontas guided her to the overflowing tables of food before grabbing two full plates. They stumbled to a table out of the way. Lontas ate greedily while Bellae halfheartedly picked, silently watching the rigid celebration—stifled by yearning for the crystals. After the hardships they had suffered, it was odd to be comfortable, clean, and consuming abundant food. Bands from many countries took turns playing, but no one had let their guard down enough to dance. Currently, the Elves of Creber were performing a slow melody on their wooden instruments.

"Look," Lontas said. "The first to dance."

Bellae followed his greasy finger to Scelto and Gimelli slowly dancing. She resisted the impulse to run and greet her sister. *She must have just arrived, otherwise, she'd be smothering me.* Both had several dressings over wounds but otherwise looked well.

"Are they wearing the same outfit, or are they just really, really close?" he asked.

"If you're going to be critical of others," Bellae smiled, "you might want to wipe the chicken grease off your face and hands."

Lontas shrugged and went back to eating as she somberly surveyed the party where everyone seemed to be acting: counterfeit laughing, forged talking, involuntary eating and drinking. She constantly caught ravenous sidewise glances in her direction. The mental pressure of the crystals soared until even the bag itself felt heavy. She looked back to Scelto and Gimelli enjoying themselves, dancing slowly to the Elven music despite the uncertain future. *That's the key, isn't it? Enjoying the moment while it's happening. The future will come soon enough.*

"Bellae, eat something," Lontas reminded.

She smiled, taking a few small bites to humor her friend, though the act of chewing seemed trivial compared to the pull of the Macht Crystals and weight of covetous eyes and jealous hearts encircling them.

"What do you think about the council tomorrow?" Lontas asked.

She looked back to several Proliate standing behind them. One of them brusquely flipped his hand forward, encouraging her to look ahead. "Ignore us. We're here for your safety."

Yeah, and diezmars are simply "castle redecorating" ideas, Bellae thought. She leaned in to whisper, and the guards tilted forward to listen. Sighing, she sat upright. "Do you remember learning about the Teorainn Hills north of the Storm Fields?"

Lontas was so surprised by her question he stopped eating. "Yeah."

Bellae glanced nervously at the approaching crowd of leaders before turning back to Lontas. "That's what I think of the council tomorrow," she said. "Tell no one. You and me." She gently squeezed her friend's arm before turning to sham smile at several leaders anxiously closing in, their self-restraint waning against the gravitational call of access to power.

Scroll 7: Friends Like These

"My dear, lovely to see you. Congratulations," Ailante said, but his tone was impatient, laced with avarice. "I'm glad Kainen specifically, and the Elves generally, were able to assist you on your quest. As you're aware, Elves were chosen by your ancestors to lead the League of Truth. I trace my lineage back to the original members who helped the Ainmhi Caint eons ago. Our forest is a secure, out-of-the-way place to store the crystals. They would sit near where Finn is buried, the Edelia Arbor Breith. The birth tree of our nation."

Bringing up Finn? A dirty trick, Bellae thought, forcing herself to smile.

"You can visit whenever you wish, or you can live with us. I understand Finn was like a father? Having the Macht Crystals there would be quite the tribute."

"Hello, Ailante, children," a Magician they had never seen said. "I'm Hud. As one of the last Magicians, I humbly request to incubate some mindre crystals in the Regenerator." His eyes kept bowing to Bellae's bag under the irresistible weight of desire. "Even though the White Wizard and Veneficus are gone, we need to have a stash ready, as the Dark Warriors are—"

"Wait, wait," Ailante interrupted. "We make no decisions about the crystals tonight. That will be discussed tomorrow at the council."

Weren't you just doing the same thing? Bellae thought.

"Ailante's right," a massive Eaglian declared. "However, I think everyone can agree the Eaglians are the ones who should watch over the crystals. We have no blind ambition but only want to live in peace and harmony within our Giant Redwoods. If there's any group that would not abuse the power of the crystals, it is us. Imagine how safe they shall be hidden with us."

"No creature of any land can claim to be more in 'harmony' with nature than us!" Ailante scoffed. "By your logic, the crystals should be moved to Creber immediately."

"I don't think our Eaglian friend meant it as a challenge," Ritari said, coming over at the commotion. "He was merely—"

"Where did the Ainmhi Caint hide the last of their kind?" the Eaglian interrupted.

"They chose you because you're on the other side of the world and no one would think to look there," Ailante said. "We want somewhere central for the crystals."

"Hold on. The Proliate have bled more for Verngaurd's defense than anyone else over the last half century and *two* Dark Wars!" General Lidenskap interrupted. "We control the Citadel along with the last of the loyal Magicians. The crystals should obviously stay here!"

"Preposterous!" Princess Hamaza of Jaa shouted, having joined the ever-growing throng around them. "We lost fifty percent of our population to this war! Our mystics have foreseen that the crystals were meant to reside near the spiritual northern lights. *That's* where they'll be in harmony with nature and the cooling psyche of the north." Her eyes bored into Bellae. "You've met our mystics and know their peace. Jaa is where they're meant to be."

Gimelli and Scelto attempted to get to Bellae, finally realizing she was there. Bellae could hear her sister's voice, but a large group of Proliate descended to stop them and surround Bellae and the elite of Verngaurd. "Leaders and the Chosen only!" the guards repeated.

"Ager can barely even claim to have a country after the devastation we endured," a mountainous man said, obviously the new King of shattered Ager, carrying a large scepter and wearing a crown. "We're simple, but more trustworthy than any other nation of Verngaurd!"

"Piscium battled the Dark Warriors in brutal street-to-street fighting, putting up more resistance than any other realm. If anyone needs the crystals to rebuild, it's us. Let us use them to reconstruct our country, and then we'll happily give them back!" Emperor Fanga yelled.

"We should just trust you'll give them back?" an Eaglian asked.

"Of course!" Fanga thundered. "If we hadn't bogged down the Dark Warriors, they would have conquered much more territory. We didn't just roll over like Ager!"

"Oh, I see," the immense King of Ager shouted, grabbing Bellae's right shoulder. His exceptional power crushed her muscles so she could not pull free. "First you insult our entire country and then expect we'd ever allow the most powerful objects in the world to be handed over to a country of vice that consorts with pirates? Ha! That's never happening."

As the leaders jostled and screamed, Bellae could see their ambition, hostility, and greed as if they were palpable beings circling their heads and staining their souls. *They're no better than Veneficus. I know their hearts believe they are. I understand their minds think they're doing what's best. However, they significantly underestimate the corrupting power of the crystals.*

King Abernan of the Northern Dwarves pushed through the Proliate guard, encircling them. "The Northern Dwarves and Kirvella dragons are the logical choice. We have power, defensibility, and intelligence. There's a reason the Kirvella dragons were the keepers of the initial scroll. They're incorruptible, and our home untouchable!" A round of scoffs echoed as he moved to grab onto Bellae's elbow. She winced in pain at both his and the King of Ager's grip.

"Are you saying we're unintelligent?" Hud, the Magician, asked, moving to stand claustrophobically close to Bellae. His hands grasped the strap of Stralande's bag.

"Bellae needs to leave. She's feeling sick!" Lontas yelled.

"She can't leave!" Lidenskap bellowed.

Bellae's glassy eyes seemed distant, staring out over deep bags. "I'm really tired, and my head hurts. I must apologize, but I need to lie down and sleep."

Ritari's large hand went to the king's and forced it off her shoulder. "Excuse me, sire. I don't think you know your own strength. Bellae's been through a lot." Ritari moved to displace Abernan, then Hud, before pushing to make room for her.

"We have much yet to discuss!" Lidenskap complained. "She leaves when this is decided." Several Proliate instantly confronted Ritari.

Bellae could see the leaders and their entourage jostling and pushing. A fluttering of wings caught her attention. *Lanella!* Bellae thought, feeling comforted at the sight of her. Lanella was talking with the gigantic Eaglian Ollmhór, who met the other members of the League when she was in Ifrean. He easily pushed through the Proliate.

"Let the girl rest," Ollmhór said, snapping his wings in a show of strength. "This can wait until the council tomorrow, as was predetermined. This child has been through a lot." He let out a muted squawk but opened his massive beak intimidatingly. The large Eaglian who had been trying to get the crystals to the Redwoods squared off against Ollmhór.

Several female Eaglians, under the direction of Lanella, came over to help Ollmhór, but a different group were trying to hinder their progress and arguing loudly.

Cracks are forming everywhere, Bellae thought. She glanced to Lontas, who was wide-eyed and nervous.

"I know—" Lidenskap started.

"The nice thing about our victory over the tyranny of Veneficus and the White Wizard is we have the luxury of some time," Ritari interrupted, seeing Bellae's exhaustion.

Ailante nodded. "The Elves were the cornerstone of protecting the prophecy, and we should act like it. Let the girl rest. We shall have this discussion in the morning." Putting his arms on Bellae's shoulder, he whispered, "Your Knight was an Elf of Creber. I'm sure that makes you realize how trustworthy and caring we are. Especially since Kainen guided and guarded you, we are the obvious choice for the crystals."

"Oh, you pointy-eared serpent! Trying to manipulate the girl to your side when she just told you she wasn't feeling well?" King Abernan thundered, moving closer. "The quest began with the Kirvella, and with them it should end! She knows how safe our mountains are, and the intelligence of our Kirvella dragons. Bellae, we can fly there immediately."

"You two should be ashamed of yourselves," Lidenskap said. He was about to go into a tirade about the advantages of the Proliate watching the Macht Crystals when Lontas jumped up and grabbed Bellae's hand, raising his eyebrows at Ritari.

"Enough!" Ritari thundered. "Let them rest!"

"Let us through, please," Ollmhór said, assisting them. "She rests until tomorrow."

The enormous hall seemed claustrophobic with leaders and their abundant greed. Bellae clutched the crystals with one arm across her chest while Lontas clung to the other. Ritari and the large Eaglian were trying to protect her but were being jostled by the increasingly agitated crowd. Bellae screamed as her hair was pulled forcibly back while another hand grabbed her bag.

"You're not leaving!" a voice called.

Two female Eaglians sent by Lanella grabbed the Magician, who had pulled her hair and led him away. She could feel desperate hands snatching at her and the bag carrying the crystals. Lontas was pushed and nearly fell. Ritari managed to right him as the space around them continued to compress.

"Keep moving!" Ritari yelled as several female Eaglians joined them to help make a path—one forced to sway within the agitated waves of the angry pushing and shoving.

She felt Ollmhór's firm but gentle grip on her shoulders, guiding and protecting. Suddenly, she could hear Gimelli and Scelto yelling for her. *No,* Bellae thought, knowing this hall was no longer safe and she would not be able to control her emotions with her sister. *Seeing you will clutter my last mission, and I don't have the willpower to resist running off with you.*

The crystals maliciously flashed images of the times Gimelli tried to talk her out of continuing the prophecy. *She wants the power for herself. She never wanted you to succeed.* Bellae shook her head, forcing images of all the times those two supported her to the front, but she felt humbled at how easy self-righteous and jealous thoughts can cloud the mind. The leaders continued yelling as a throng, including some recently arrived Southern Dwarves.

"I'll keep them safe for tonight," Bellae shouted, a spark of defiance flashing in her eyes.

"Bellae's speaking!" Ritari shouted over the din repeatedly until the voices quieted.

She steadied her voice. "Powerful leaders, stay here, continue talking about what to do with the crystals. That way, when I bring them to council in the morning, we can avoid this fighting." As she hoped, that spurred massive verbal sparring amongst the different factions.

"Stay on us," Ritari said as he and several Eaglians forcefully pushed out of the Grand Hall. The Proliate assigned to protect her circled around. Seeing a line of Proliate in front of them as they exited, Ritari said, "Brave Proliate, you know your duty. Escort Bellae to her tent to rest." He leaned down, whispering, "This is the best I can do, child. I do not envy you."

"It's more than enough. Thank you for this and everything," she said sincerely, not sensing avarice within him. Gently, she pecked his cheek before the Proliate took up position all around her, shoving Ritari and the Eaglians aside.

"Take her straight to her tent and guard her all night," Lidenskap ordered, having run out of the hall. "Yes, the staunch Proliate shall guard her till morn!"

A fervor broke out behind them as the desirous fray leeched out, continuing to argue.

After marching with no view other than red armor, they eventually arrived at a pair of tents set off from the others. "Boy there, girl here," a guard said.

"Can I say goodnight to my friend?" Bellae asked, the idea of being away from Lontas seeming absurd after all of their time together.

"Quickly!" a guard said angrily while standing with one hand on each of their shoulders, denying any chance to talk privately.

"I'm going straight to bed, Lontas," Bellae said, self-consciously eyeing the guards hovering over them.

"Are you okay?" he asked.

"Of course. I'm glad the quest is over. As I told you in there, I think the council's a great idea and I can't wait to hear what they decide in the morning. You know, we should go just north of where water is made so that humans can turn into fish."

"You're not going anywhere!" a guard protested.

"Of course, once the council is done," Bellae said sweetly, seeing Lontas nod his understanding out of the corner of her eye.

"One last thing," Bellae said as they were separated. "Lontas, do you remember how well and long we slept when we first met Arend in the cemetery? That's what we need tonight, the same amount of restful sleep as that time. Dream of breathing in water."

"Stop talking nonsense!" a guard admonished.

Bellae nodded. "Guards, could you please escort me to my tent."

"All right, Bellae. See you in the morning," Lontas said.

"We'll be outside your tents, all night. You will *not* leave without an escort," a guard said. "For your safety, of course."

"Of course. Thank you," she said before heading into her tent.

Bellae absently felt for her mice friends, smiling at the memories while tearing at the empty pockets. *I miss you guys,* she thought. *Now, I wait.*

Time crawled as she lay on her bed, actively fighting to stay awake and repress the seductive calls of the crystals. *We told you they'd try and steal our power! See how easily they turn to fighting! Only in your hands will the world be protected and safe. Imagine peace and security for the world. You can rebuild everything.*

I bet you said that to Veneficus before you turned him into a shriveled creature addicted to your poisonous power, Bellae replied in her tired mind. "I can't believe I'm still talking to you," she said to the empty tent.

You're stronger mentally and of character. You can handle our power and use it for good! Veneficus was weak and power-hungry!

You offer nothing but addiction and death.

You could not be more wrong, child. We offer life for you and for all of Vern—

"I control the good," Bellae repeated over and over until the voices dimmed to whispers. She bit her tongue as the guards peeked in on her at regular intervals. Closing her eyes and lying motionless on her bed finally induced less frequent visits. Sometime later she thought, *The sound of party goers has finally died down.* She quickly closed her eyes at the rustling of the tent door.

"Yeah, still out," a guard said.

"Crystals?" the other asked.

"Right next to her on the cot."

"Nice to have some stillness settle on the Citadel."

"No kidding," the first guard said. "I can't wait for Lidenskap to seize the crystals and move them to the Proliate Islands, where they belong."

Bellae resisted crying out in anger and despair. The sack with the crystals slid, and she reached to grab them. As her hand went in the bag, her eyes shot open in panic before turning white, and she suddenly envisioned herself as Supreme Master, ordering Magicians around as voices goaded her. *You are all powerful, the strongest being ever to live. You have total command of the weather, earth, water, and fire,* a main voice echoed, while thousands of others whispered things she could not make out. *You'd be able to control death itself. Don't listen to the prophecy. Your ancestors were jealous of the Supreme Master's kind and generous power.*

Finn, Crann, Arend, Sorea, Luchar, Arquero, Abhac, and thousands of others came running towards her. *"Thank you for saving us from death."*

I control the good! she screamed in her mind repeatedly, drowning out the crystals' words until she stormed back to the present. She fought the urge to scream and abruptly froze, hearing the tent flap rustle again as a guard pushed his head through.

"No, she's sleeping. Must be dreaming," he said before closing the tent.

Bellae fought to slow her breathing. After lying still for twenty more minutes, she quietly slipped out of bed and over to the trunk of clothes Lidenskap had sent for her. *Suck up,* she thought. *Your guards spill your true motives.* Carefully, she picked an outfit to wear, using the other garments to stuff into her old clothes like a scarecrow. After placing the dummy under her blanket, making sure to create a bulge where the bag of crystals should be, she set to removing the stitching where the wall of the tent met the groundsheet.

The Magicians will track you if you leave, fool! the crystals shouted when she had a hole.

Bellae hesitated, wondering how accurately magical creatures could track the crystals. *Can they know my exact position or just generally?*

Exact position, the crystals chided before outlining a spell to temporarily throw them off. *This spell will make the power seem like it is coming from your cot and blind those guards to your escape.*

I don't trust you but have no choice, Bellae thought, thrusting her hand into the bag. Her eyes turned white, and she could feel the potent energy thrusting through her body. She chanted as they directed, and when she removed her arm, she could see and feel a false power radiating from the bulge on her cot as the form on her bed morphed into a more realistic-looking one.

Part of her wanted to shove her hand back into the bag, to feel their intoxicating power. Shaking her head, she carefully counted, trying to get the timing of the soldiers walking past. The minutes bled forward. She glanced back at the tent flap. *I need to go!* she screamed in her head, ignoring the crystals' statements about how easily they could help her escape. *Now,* she thought, slipping out between the Proliate walking around her tent.

There were concentric rings of guards, and she had to dive under a bush to let two pass. Moving through the soldiers took much longer than she hoped, but she eventually made it past. Taking a deep breath, she was up and moving, making her way through the makeshift camp. She could now hear an uneven song being belted, alternating between an inebriated chorus of boasting and deep ensembles of snoring from the maze of tents with equal measure and volume. Closest to her, the walkways were thick with Proliate guards, and she had to constantly zigzag to avoid their patrols. Voices and footsteps made her freeze, squatting low. They moved progressively closer, prompting Bellae to look for a way to escape. She could not go back down the aisle, as there were several Agerians talking. She tried to shrink into the shadows.

No choice, she thought, hoping the snoring was coming from the tent she was crouching next to. *That one has no groundsheet.* She carefully slipped under the fabric. It was dark and smelled like a mix of mead, sweat, and dung. Several Piscinians were sprawled on haphazardly placed cots. The floor was littered with boots, overturned, empty tankards, and the promise of morning headaches. A trumpet of gas erupted out of the man sleeping closest to her, and she fought the urge to retch at the revolting odor.

As soon as you leave, the Magicians, along with every other magical creature, will be alerted and come after you! the crystals screamed in her mind before going into the same tired arguments of why she should take control. Her heart rate hastened and sweat burgeoned from her forehead. *Will I even get out of here?*

Outside footsteps stopped right next to where she was, prompting Bellae to become motionless. She recognized Lanella, Arend's mother, saying, "I guess you're right. I'll wait until morning to see her. Thank you."

She heard footsteps move away. Time oozed forward. The only sounds she heard were nasal wailing and malodorous releases from the backsides of her fellow tent dwellers. After several more minutes, her cloak over her mouth for the smell, Bellae collected her things and pried her way out from under the rancid tent. After quieting her breathing, she moved away. Without warning, a massive figure appeared before her. Bellae resisted squealing but could not avoid running into them.

Scroll 8: Honoring Promises to Kill You

Shaking, she slowly looked up, exhaling in relief at the sight of a beautiful Eaglian.

"Hello Bellae," Lanella said. "I've been looking for you. I saw you moving in the shadows. Hiding under the tent was risky, but it paid off."

Bellae suddenly felt exhausted, collapsing into the Eaglian's arms.

"I have you. It's okay. When Arend was little, I used to say, 'Pain is part of all lives. Strength grows from pushing through. Choosing whether to let yourself suffer and wither, or strengthen and grow, from its effect, is up to you,'" she said with weighty sadness. "Sorry. Holding you reminds me of times that are long lost to time."

"He was powerful and true, and I miss him greatly. However, please, Lanella, I can't give you the crystals or move them to the Redwoods. I—" Bellae started.

"Shhh. I know. I could tell you were about to throw up with all those pigheaded leaders, each one spitting false praise and overblown promises."

"So you know what I have to do with them?"

"No, and I don't want to. I've lost my husband and beautiful son to this prophecy. My family's been involved in protecting the descendants of the Ainmhi Caint from its origin. I know they'd want it fulfilled. Everyone's eager to celebrate the death of Veneficus but foolish enough to go right back to where we were with abuse of power. I've come to hate what my family swore to protect. You don't have to look hard to see the drool of greed slavering on the chins within most of Verngaurd. They foolishly think they can control the crystals.

"I know your heart is pure, but power like this? Sooner or later, it can only corrupt. The path would start small...at first. A little bending the rules for the 'greater good.' Then, before you know it, you mutate *into* the rules. And trust me, the rulers of Verngaurd will *always* have some sort of emergency that requires you to use the crystals. Their situations would invariably be important, demanding their immediate use." Lanella paused, looking up at the many moons and thousands of stars glistening above. "No matter what, find a way to complete this as intended, not the politician's way. I do, however, have a favor to ask."

"Anything," Bellae said, still hugging Lanella—now out of relief rather than exhaustion. "I'm so tired of the pressure and this quest."

Lanella gently brushed down the hair on the back of Bellae's head. "It seems to me no one can bear great power or absurd wealth without, to their bones, feeling they're better than all others. How else can they bathe in lavishness when a fraction of their affluence could feed and heal so many? Perhaps they think, somehow, they were innately blessed and preordained to be 'special' with the birthright to rule the rest. As you could tell by the so called 'adults' and their in-fighting, perhaps only the young could resist the temptation of such power."

Tears coerced their way through Bellae's tightly squeezed eyelids. She could feel the weight of the crystals' power and hear the incessant, tormenting plague of appeals.

"The favor? Read these notes but only once at the finish of your journey. I do not want them to distract you."

"Okay and thank you," Bellae said, releasing her grip and wiping her tears.

"I have a team of Eaglians loyal to the League's original mission, and they will help me create distractions if you're discovered."

"Thank you," Bellae replied.

Lanella nodded with sad eyes. "Now go do what you need to. I can't fly you out. That would garner too much suspicion. Try to attach yourself to a large group leaving the main gates. Even at this hour there's bound to be traffic."

Bellae weaved her way through the city. Panic broke through the chatter of the crystals, and she hid in the shadows as two Magicians approached.

"I can taste their power," a Magician said.

"I know. They're so close," the other replied.

If you only knew, Bellae thought.

"We should have taken them from the brat tonight."

"Tomorrow will come soon enough. Even if they're on the Proliate Islands, we'll finally be able to recharge our mindre."

"What are you two doing?" an angry Proliate guard asked.

This is drawing too much attention, Bellae thought, moving around the corner and down a side street. *I have no idea where I am or how long the spell to mislead them about the crystals' location will last.* Trying to slow her breathing, she continued weaving in between pathways and streets in the general direction of the gate.

Eventually, she began to recognize a few streets and could hear the din of travelers, guards, and draught animals. She slid into the shadows of the large open area she had entered with the Knights before the Tournament. Torches lit the area, but darkness still ruled the night.

That wagon, Bellae thought, raising the hood of her cloak and moving to join a party heading out of the Citadel. *They haven't discovered my ruse yet, but...soon.* The crystals implored her to use their power again. *You don't have much time!*

Shaking her head in a vain attempt to quiet their voices and calm her nerves, Bellae tucked herself behind a dozen children and two adults walking around a severely overloaded wagon. The pace was slow thanks to aged horses pulling against the weight.

"Another wagon?" a guard gruffed, holding out his hand until the caravan came to a begrudging stop. The horses neighed in annoyance, knowing the effort it would take to restart.

"Just want to beat the congestion of the morrow," the driver said. "My family's from Ager. We want to get back and rebuild. Our farm was burnt—"

"Yeah, don't care, everyone has a sob story," the guard said, walking around the caravan. "All of these are your…family?"

"The youngest of my children ride within. My sister has four. Her husband was killed by Dark Warriors, so they travel with us, as do four cousins and children of neighbors who—"

"All right, all right," the guard interrupted waving a torch in front of Bellae's face. He paused, staring at her. "Hey, Dovendyr!" he yelled, causing Bellae to jump.

They've discovered me! she thought, but to her surprise, he turned away.

"Dovendyr, when are you letting people out?"

"The line coming in is five times longer!"

The others, through exhaustion, did not seem to notice Bellae ease herself next to the carriage away from the guard. She could hear a mix of snoring and muffled conversation from the children within.

"They're backing up into the streets over here. Let them through, especially this ragtag group," the first guard said, muttering, "Good riddance from our fair city."

The stream of people coming in stopped, and eventually, the line out ambled forward. They were forced to stop several times as the various groups leaving were examined.

One more group in front of us! Bellae thought, now seeing the gate. *I need the spell to last a bit longer.* She caught a glimpse of Lanella watching over her, which calmed her nerves. They started moving again, and she could hear a guard yell, "Keep going!"

Bellae could not help remembering their trip into the Tournament when Lontas almost fell off this overcrowded passageway. She fought tears brewing from sadness of all that had happened, how much had changed, and how this would end.

"Stay with your group!" a guard yelled at main gate. "Are all of you together?" the final guard by the outer barbican asked, not attempting to hide his irritation.

"Yes," the man driving said before rattling off all of those traveling together.

"Another tale of woe? How refreshing. I enjoy hearing each and every one—the greater the detail, the better! Perhaps you'd write down your story, then drop it in our suggestion box, aka the moat. Did the last guard go through your wagon and search each one of you rabble?"

"Yes, yes, he did," the man lied, and Bellae gratefully sighed.

"Great, he can do some work once in a while. Move this peasant procession through!" the guard yelled. "Don't forget to leave me your story. So excited!"

Several warning bells rang out, and Bellae noticed Lanella dart off in the direction of the commotion.

"What's going on?" a guard asked.

"Probably some plebeians wasted on drink and their abuse of our kindness," another said.

"Should we stop this group?"

"No, they're holding everything up."

It seemed like slow motion, but eventually, the family made it out.

After one other family made it through, they could hear shouting behind them. The Proliate lining the road began passing along an order. "Let the riffraff already out continue, but no more shall be allowed in or out of the Citadel!"

Bellae turned to see a group of Magicians up on the massive walls. "I can feel the crystals have left!" one shouted. "It's like they instantly magically transported out!"

Holding on to the wagon for balance, Bellae watched several Eaglians fly to the Magicians. She could not hear what they said but did hear the Magician's response. "You saw her? Where?" After a pause, "But I feel them out there!"

"However, a minute ago, we felt them both inside the walls and without!" another Magician shouted in a panic. "No way could she have escaped. She must be shielding them from us, and the outside source is a trick!"

"How would she be able to do that?"

"She has the source of all magic!"

"Follow us," Lanella said as they flew off into the Citadel. The Magicians argued before angrily mounting griffins and chasing after the Eaglians.

There were still Proliate guards spaced sporadically along the path several hundred yards from the gate. When the soldiers thinned significantly, she moved outwards, drifting to the rear before crossing behind the wagon, quickly pushing her way through the line of angry people and frustrated animals trying to get into the Citadel. Heading north for hours, the well-manicured and controlled landscaping of the Proliate gave way to the open prairie grasses and random trees of the Vahse Plains. After another hour, she settled in for the night, sick of twisting her ankles on the uneven ground. She watched the moons and stars spin their slow dance across the sky.

"Bellae!" Lontas called out.

"How did you find me?"

"Bellae! Come here!" Lontas said.

The hairs on the back of her neck stood on end. "I said, how did you find me?"

Silence.

Bellae grasped the bag of crystals tightly. *They've found you,* a voice from the crystals purred. *Use our power. Otherwise, they will hunt you mercilessly. Unleash our energy!*

Multiple Nishi approached from all sides.

"No hard feeling about our previous conversations," the one closest hissed. "We were rooting for our favorite putrid wretch the entire time. It was the White Wizard that made us come after you. We cherish rotten children."

"Oh yes, we love brats. Simply adore your whining, uh, winning 'personality.'"

Bellae was surrounded with more showing up. "Those 'conversations' did not change my thinking about you. Did you really believe I'd fall for your trick after all the times you failed?"

"Can't blame us for trying. It's what we Nishi do."

Bellae could feel her skin crawl as they slithered closer, crowding around her. Occasionally, one fluttered close enough to have its hair brush her skin.

"Watchers are coming. Better just give us the crystals and walk away."

"Oh, sure," Bellae said, "I have no doubt you'd use their unlimited influence for good."

One of the floating creatures gently put its uncut fingernail under Bellae's chin. She felt a numbed chill rise up into her entire mouth. With one hand she reached into the bag and grabbed a crystal while with the other she swung her armband talisman into the closest one. A thunderbolt of shock flashed across the Nishi's gaunt face before her eyes widened in terror. Instead of disappearing, the entire glowing form of the specter collapsed to a single small point before a loud cracking sound harrowed through the surrounding air.

Murmurs of awe and dread simmered while Bellae used their hesitation to lurch forward, hitting several other Nishi with her protective brace. Loud popping sounds joined the anguished and fearful screams of the encircling wraiths.

"With the crystals you're killing us!" a Nishi howled. "No fair!"

"My heart is heavy with grief at your loss," Bellae said sarcastically while continuing to end the fleeing forms. She paused, huffing at the effort of chasing and dispatching so many.

"I just want to talk," one of the remaining apparitions said, cautiously approaching.

"Can't really say that interests me," Bellae replied.

"You realize any and everything with a hint of magic can feel the five pairs of crystals? You'll never have peace as long as you possess them. It will take centuries for you to garner enough power to dissuade those so inclined from attacking. Imagine all that time looking over your shoulder in constant fear. Give them to us, and we'll honor our previous promises, which were lies, but this one's not, to kill you semi-quickly."

"Not sure if this is the best time to bring this up, but your negotiation skills seriously suck," Bellae said, sprinting forward, quickly eradicating it.

"More, from all over the world, are coming. We can feel them," the last Nishi taunted.

"Right now, I'm just interested in killing you," Bellae said calmly before chasing the last Nishi away. "Lontas? You and me…always," she whispered to the gusting, but unmoved at her tears, wind while looking around at the shadows dancing in anemic moonlight. *Lontas, I need you,* she thought, struggling to block out the voices of crystals. Abruptly, something passed in front of Stor-Manen, the largest moon, overhead.

Wing beats, she said to herself. *No choice.* Touching the crystals, she called on them to hide their power. The flapping grew louder, and as they neared, she could see dozens of Watchers. Quickly she ran, pressing herself under a drooping tree.

"The signal disappeared!" a Watcher said.

"Did she use a portal?"

"Or can she fly?"

"I don't think the ratty urchin can do either, yet."

"Well, obviously, she can. The crystals' call vanished." They were directly overhead now. Bellae tucked her head down and curled up in the grass around the frail tree.

"Without more magic to drink we all die!"

"Don't you think we know that?" one said before pointing towards the Citadel.

Without looking up, Bellae could hear the griffins' angry squawks and Magicians yelling. The darkness exploded in fire balls and blasts of magic. Suddenly, the battle above dulled into a whisper as her focus went to the magic being drawn from the crystals to hide her. As the power flowed in, she could feel parts of herself flowing out—replaced with black tendrils smokily wriggling around her cells, dehydrating them. Small tears compressed their way through her tightly squeezed eyelids. As the battle moved away, Bellae could feel her arm tingling.

She opened her eyes to see pure magical power flowing into her, causing her heart to race and mind to quiver in pleasure. She quickly released the crystals. "This is going to be fun."

She alternated between having the crystals project their power elsewhere while she dozed and walking while manipulating their power to block their magical beacon. With each use she felt more of herself drifting away. As morning dawned, she had the luck of finding a group of Cavalo horses. After some bargaining, she was able to get a horse called Hratt to take her north.

"The others agree to stay, promising to do the favor you ask. You realize the lighting storms are dangerous?" Hratt neighed.

"I do, but they can hide what I carry."

"Alright, let's go," Hratt said.

The Mardin sun had launched a pink glaze over the horizon when they made it through the Vahse Plains days later, each step bringing them closer to the massive wall of storms. It seemed stuck in place, a series of hovering dark clouds with wrathful tempers throwing out rumbling bolts of lightning.

"How close do you expect to get?" Hratt asked nervously.

"Not much further."

When they were close enough to feel the thunder's vibrations, they stopped. Although lighting strikes and resultant rumbles dotted the entire field in front of them, actual rain was more sporadic. After marveling at the wonders of the storm field, Bellae shivered while watching the newborn sunlight sparkle across the frosted ground. Reluctantly, she released the power of the crystals, stopping the shield. *I hope we're close enough to block their power,* she thought as they chided her that they were not, and she should continue to use them.

"What happens when you touch what's in the bag?" Hratt asked. *"I can feel something…not right."*

Bellae paused, knowing she was growing accustomed to their power. After clinging to the nimble horse bareback, she needed to shake out her sore hands and legs. *"I know it's harmful to use their magic, but I'm trying to hide from worse things and an even more destructive outcome. Hopefully the storms shield their magic."*

"You can't cross the Storm Fields."

"We don't have to," Bellae replied. *"If the scroll's right, being close to the storm fields is enough, so we can skirt around them. Let's head west towards the mountains and then along the spine of the range up to Lake Glasere's southern edge."*

Hratt nodded, and the two traveled towards the Tingij Mountains. Once there, the horse gently moved his neck back, rocking the sleeping Bellae up.

"Sorry, dozed off," she said. *"Everything okay?"*

"No sign of trouble."

Dismounting, Bellae sat against the rough, rocky cliff, fighting to keep awake, constantly scanning the skies for Nishi, Watchers, or whatever else may come. The horse paced back and forth restlessly, as if he could feel danger closing in.

"What hunts you, child?"

"Pretty much anything magical," she replied, her eyes fluttering. The metronomic pattern to his hooved gait added weight to Bellae's fatigued eyelids. Eventually, her eyes flittered one too many times and stayed closed.

Scroll 9: Beauty in Your Palm

"Bellae!" Hratt neighed. *"Someone approaches."*

"Crann?" Bellae asked sleepily, her mouth dry, sticking together via strands of congealed white saliva.

"No, it's Hratt. A dust cloud approaches."

Bellae looked east and squinted. The third sun, Pheobus, was already well above the horizon. *"What time is it?"* Bellae asked.

"Time to hide."

Fortunately, the mountain was full of crevices, jutting rocks, and small caves. They easily found places to conceal themselves, and Bellae went back to shielding the crystals' power. She closed her eyes, enjoying the surge of power pouring through her. Twenty minutes later they heard, but could not see, a group of horses thunder by.

"Did they follow us?" Bellae whispered, wondering if they were Proliate or Magicians.

"No, I purposefully walked back and forth along streams to throw off pursuers."

"Maybe they're magical, and I shouldn't have slept."

The group rode north for a few minutes before stopping. Time moved apathetically forward as listlessly and tired as she felt.

"If they could feel the crystals, they would be here, I stopped shielding them to see."

One painful hour later, the riders had not moved, so Bellae crept along the ragged base of the mountain. Sighing with relief she found riderless Cavalo horses. Inching closer, she heard a snort and froze. Someone was noisily sleeping in a crevice to her left. Bellae remained still until a horse neighed loudly. The person sleeping shot up, slamming his head against the rock. Disoriented, he staggered up, stumbling into Bellae, knocking her down. She gasped. The air shot out of her as the person on top of her began screaming and flailing.

"Lontas?"

"Bellae?"

"You found me!" she said, hugging him tightly. "I asked the Cavalo horses to look for you," Bellae explained.

"Thanks, but when they came thundering towards me, it scared me half to death…which seems to be happening a lot." He massaged his sore head before examining the blood coating his fingers. "With them I moved faster and found streams to drink from and berries to eat."

"You're bleeding badly," Bellae cried.

"Remember who you're talking to. I'd know if it was serious. The scalp bleeds a lot, mine in particular due to scar tissue. Lontas took a spare shirt he had brought from the Citadel, courtesy of Lidenskap, and held pressure. "Ow."

"That 'ow' was way too late," Bellae said, smiling.

"There's absolutely no time limit on saying 'ow.'"

"I disagree. You're coordinated now and have forgotten the Lontas Trip Count rules."

"Those days weren't that long ago," he replied.

"Long enough." The smiles pilfered from their faces at all they survived, endured, lost. "We've been through so much. I feel like I know more but understand less." Bellae turned away, not wanting this heavy conversation. "Did you get a chance to sleep?"

"I'd just fallen asleep when you attacked me."

"I most definitely didn't attack you!"

"It qualifies."

"But you tackled me."

"I was merely defending myself," he replied.

"Are you guys trying to draw attention to us?" Hratt neighed.

"Sorry!" Bellae apologized. *"This is my friend, Lontas."*

"So I gathered," Hratt said, scanning the plains to the east. *"Why don't you two get some sleep? We'll keep look out."*

"The fields block the crystals' power, like predicted," Bellae said. "No attacks as long as we border the storms."

After lying down, a soft snow began, dawdling in twirling pirouettes. Reaching out, Bellae caught a snowflake on her palm, her eyes tracing the intricate branching pattern as it started to melt. The snow continued drifting gently down, each unique flake softly meandering towards her until tenderly touching down in a soft kiss before melting on her warm skin. *Snow is clouds crying in slow motion,* she thought. Hratt moved in front of the opening to block the snow. *"Thanks, Hratt,"* Bellae said.

"Thank me by sleeping."

After she fell asleep, Lontas stared at Bellae. The journey around the world and back had manipulated, irrevocably recast, her form: morphing body, soul, and mind into something different. *I guess it changed both of us beyond recognition,* he thought, nervous about what was going to happen with the crystals and dejected she had not told him. *So many secrets.*

Hratt neighed, admonishing him to sleep.

"Whatever happens, horse, I shall never forget our voyage. They are big memories but stained by pain and clouded by time."

Hratt snorted, oblivious to his words' meanings, as Lontas closed his eyes.

Scroll 10: What May Come

Bellae's eyes fluttered to see a different Cavalo horse standing guard. The snow had stopped but still lightly embraced the ground.

"I feel rested," Lontas said, moving out from the alcove.

"I think we slept all night and should go."

After riding north for hours in the early morning light, they came upon Lake Glasere, continuing northeast along its border, battered by the wind raging off the water. After drinking their fill, they turned due east, the Storm Fields now to their right.

"What are you thinking?" Lontas asked, tired of the silence.

Bellae startled at his voice, the glaze over her eyes replaced with focus. "What may come." She paused. "Is what may come a curse or a gift? I believe...hope, it's a gift for in it lies infinite possibilities. The form those alternatives and choices take is up to us. Do we look at it as a burden or opportunity? Hopefully, the world takes what may come as a gift."

Lontas shook his head. "Are we going to destroy the crystals?" The cold and fear conspired to cause a tremble in his voice. "Are we going to throw them into the storm fields?"

Bellae smiled. "Sort of to the first. No to the second."

"Are you going to throw them into the lake or...the magma of the volcanoes?"

"Nope and nope," Bellae answered. "Those are temporary hiding spots. It might not be for a thousand years, but eventually they would be found, and the cycle would continue. If not Na Cearcaill, then at least the abuse and coveting of the crystals' power."

"Who's going to find them in a pool of magma or the bottom of a lake?"

"Remember, they're magic and want to control someone, like Veneficus. Sooner or later, they'd be found."

"Someone would find them *at the bottom* of a *volcano*?"

She paused, gauging her friend. "What we see now seems permanent. We wake up day after day, and everything seems the same.

However, if you move forward tens of thousands of years, Lake Glasere may be farmland or a desert, and a volcano can become a rocky crater. There are lots of things I can see now. With the first pair of crystals, my perspective morphed. I could see the insane changes that have, and will, occur on our planet."

"Does it matter if they're found far in the future?" Lontas asked, his frustration and apprehension fattening.

"The magic within these crystals was never meant to be so condensed. It needs to be spread out. Plus, if all the crystals are together, they call out. That's why the Ainmhi Caint disseminated them so far away from one another."

Lontas started to protest, but Bellae held up a hand. "I wanted you along because I didn't wish to be alone. Let's talk about other stuff."

Knowing she would shut down if he kept pushing, he nodded.

"So do you think you'll get married?" she asked.

"Where in the world did that come from? I don't know. Not for a long while at least."

"Will you come and visit me when you're older, even if you get married?"

"Of course. But this is crazy. I don't even know *if* I'm going to get married—"

"I know," she interrupted. "But just humor me. Promise to bring your kids and lots of animals to see me."

"Sure, but I can't imagine you won't have a ton of animals already."

"Oh, I'm sure I'll have some around, but never as many as I would want."

He stared in utter confusion.

"Lontas, your descendants, many eons from now, when we, and all of this, including our quest, are long forgotten, will build a new type of magic, and it, like the one we know, will have the power to bewitch or enrich, mold with honor or defile, educate or radicalize, grow the soul or rot the person depending on how it's used." He was about to question her when she suddenly stopped on a large plateau. Further north were the small Teorainn Mountains. To the south were the raging Storm Fields, still singing in thunder's seemingly never-ending chorus. A few rocks dotted the rough grass, which was bowing before the wind rushing over the hills.

"What're we looking for?" Lontas asked nervously.

Bellae shrugged. "Let's head east for a while."

Lontas could not fight the mounting dread as they moved along the small tract of land between the Teorainn Hills and the Storm Fields. Several times they startled at the roar of thunder to their south as the width of safe ground narrowed and enlarged randomly. Hratt and Lontas' horse became adept at watching for blackened earth to avoid. After riding for an hour, Bellae stopped. Dismounting Hratt, she closed her eyes and clasped tightly onto the horse's neck.

"Here?" Lontas questioned. "I guess I expected something more… impressive?"

Dismounting, he walked to explore the nearest hilltop. The forceful wind and rising suns had scattered most of the snow, and that which remained looked like a rash upon the ground. All he could see to the north were more hills, which eventually ran into mountains. Turning around, he could see Hratt snorting and shaking his head wildly. He even bucked slightly before bolting off. Lontas was stunned, having never seen an animal act like that around Bellae.

Walking slowly to the center of the plateau, her head tilted down, she said, "Lontas, time for you to leave."

Scroll II: This Kind of Magic

"I'm not going anywhere without you," he answered passionately. "Whatever's happening, I stay." He pointed for his horse to leave, which it did, his mind unraveling while trying to fathom how this could end.

"Ever since we met Stralande, I've known." She looked down, fighting the tears soliciting to escape. She thought back to Finn in the Arena. *He serenely told me a story, calming my nerves when he was the one about to fight a dragon. It's my turn to be calm, and perchance some distant day he'll realize what I did, what I overcame to stay poised.*

"What have you known, and why didn't you tell me? None of this makes sense!"

"I knew how this ends, and it makes sense. To free these Macht Crystals the Chosen One has to give up her life. They need a soul to sacrifice itself to set them free."

Speechless, Lontas stared as two serpentine emotions coiled into his heart: disappointment she had not told him and bewildered misery at the thought of her sacrifice. Closing his eyes, he sucked in a shuttering breath. "That's ridiculous and absolutely doesn't make sense. I hate this prophecy. I loathe this journey. I detest this moronic quest. After we fought for our lives, facing everything from walking trees and horrifying vampires to crazed rocks and unicorns, how can it end in our death?"

"Not ours. Just mine."

"No, no, nope, and no."

Bellae smiled patiently. "When enough years have passed, you'll look back on the adventure fondly, perhaps as the greatest days of your life. As hard as this has been, now that we're at the end, part of me is sorry to have it over."

"But we have to…"

"What?"

He rolled his eyes, frustrated. "Oh, I don't know, figure out the meaning of life?"

"That's easy. The meaning of life is to live a life full of meaning."

"How long have you been waiting to use that?" Lontas scoffed.

"The greatest gift you can give to me, and most significant insult you can hurl at death, mine, yours, this sacrifice, is to live your life well. Seek grand adventures, but deeply enjoy each ordinary moment. After all we endured, once I die, go live your best life. Enjoy your time. It's a simple insult that doesn't, in any real sense, hurt death, but I imagine it annoys the netherworld out of it."

The burden of Lontas' sadness wrung tears from his eyes. He looked at the windswept plain dotted with trees, some still clothed in white, and knew he would never forget this moment, these feelings. "I don't want to go on without you. What you've done will never be forgotten."

"Eventually all deeds and names born of any time, will be forgotten. But those in the future will feel the suns in freedom. They will unconsciously smile at the choices in their life, not knowing, or even needing to know, whom to thank. That's the best I can do, and it has to be enough. In that way our actions, our sacrifices will echo on, and that's enough."

"Despite the Tilkeri and their bullying, I'd love to go back to Liberum to read, attend class with Professor Lehtori. Even the horrible squire battles and practices."

Bellae struggled to understand until a flash of recognition broke through her far away stare. "Our old astronomy teacher. We planned our trip to the cemetery after one of her classes."

"'We' is an exaggeration. It was more of a 'you' thing." His mind spun in despair for a way out. "How can we destroy the crystals on a hill, by ourselves, with no weapons or tools?"

"I'm a little vague on the how it works part," she said as it started to snow heavily.

"Then why can't I stay? Remember the whole you and me thingy?"

Bellae smiled and nodded. Her heart was racing, unsure of what was going to happen and wanting him with her. "Okay, but stay there."

"Wait! We throw one pair into magma at Mount Honoo, wrap chains around a chest, and throw others into the Dark Sea with Mor-Leider, bury one pair on the Isle of Hirmulisko, one in the marshlands, and the others in Lake Glasere," Lontas pleaded. "No one'll know they're there."

"We'd know, and they'd hunt us mercilessly. Even if nothing happened in our lifetime, sooner or later, someone would find them, and the world would be right back here."

"Who cares? We'll be long dead."

"I suppose the people living then would care a great deal," she answered. "The magic within these crystals needs to be spread out, shared with everyone."

"What are you talking about? Is everyone suddenly going to become a Magician?"

"No, not that kind of magic."

"What kind of magic are you talking about?" he beseeched, growing annoyed.

With an artificial smile, she gently placed her hand on his shoulder before silently walking up to one of the Teorainn Hills. After reaching the top, she stopped and knelt as Lontas followed.

"Here," she said, "this magic."

Lontas knelt, looking at a meager, fragile white flower struggling against the blowing snow—its small green stem shivering in the cold.

"Magic is a half-dead winter flower?" he asked, spite leeching into his words.

She opened her arms wide. "The sky, the suns, the moons, the stars, the trees, the lakes and rivers, and the mountains themselves. You. My sister. Everyone, including all animals. It's all a form of magic. The best kind."

Lontas shook his head as her eyes ravenously studied the snow-covered landscape.

"Think of the trackless snow blanketing the world in atonement. It fuses together many different parts of the world as its touch unites us. It's a lesson that we're all interconnected."

"So no Magicians?" Lontas asked, confusion mixing with disappointment.

Bellae smiled, and suddenly Lontas felt immature next to her, even though he was older. There was something in her eyes which he did not understand except to fear it.

"Once the mindre crystals run out, there'll be no more Magicians, but magic will not be gone. The flowers will still bloom, babies will still be born, the suns will rise every day, crops will grow, animals will run, fish will swim, birds will fly, love will flourish, and life will go on. That's magic enough."

"Let's just smash them into a million pieces and be done with it," Lontas suggested.

"You can never really destroy anything, just change its form. The crystals' current form needs to be spread out, to give this gift to everyone on the planet."

"Please, you're not making sense. That you need to die to accomplish this is ridiculous."

"Love is an eternal spark, but only through work and sacrifice. Like everything in this world, it is at risk of dying. You must constantly add fuel to keep it going—it takes commitment and effort. To truly love someone, you must be willing to sacrifice for them. I would happily sacrifice myself for everyone, but especially you, Gimelli, Scelto, Lovag, Lanella…everyone we know. Even for Hratt and every other animal in the world. They all deserve a future. I would love to see Gimelli and Scelto get married someday," she said, her face twisting into a smile veiled with sadness.

"You *can* see that. You admitted if we hide them, they'll be safe for thousands of years!"

"Lontas, you saw how the leaders fought over them. If I don't destroy the power of the crystals, sooner or later, things will go bad."

"So if you do this, things will be okay?"

"I see a new magic, deep into the future, where enormous shimmering buildings rise inexplicably into the clouds. A world where flight doesn't require feathered wings. People can see and communicate across the globe with a new kind of sorcery."

"So the future's a success?" Lontas asked again.

Bellae smiled sympathetically. "The past is concluded, the present is now, but the string of tomorrows? That's not set. What may come is like an infinite series of roads, each with millions of different paths—decisions that mold the future into the solid present. Each choice alters not just the makers but bridges into affecting everyone else's time ahead, even if in some small way. Remember Arachne? We're all interconnected. Whatever future is created, it will involve amazing triumphs and disastrous calamities. There will be ups, downs, and many repeated mistakes. The depraved and greedy rise to the top, no matter their name. Call them kings, emperors, leaders, the ultra-rich. Call them whatever made-up, 'special' name the next generation comes up with. Many will fall for the snare of gluttony. Peace will be hard to come by in the future. Power, greed will overwhelm the souls of most."

"So is what Veneficus said true? We kill ourselves, all life, and the planet?"

"Of the billions of different paths forward, there are infinitely more chances to misstep into doom, but there are paths to a higher collective consciousness. Not great odds, but there's some hope. What Veneficus did not realize is that even though progress may be painful, everything staying the same is conjuring stagnation. It is the very seed within the knowledge that nothing can stay the same that we see rise and flower the hint, the possibility of improvement."

Bellae started to spin away, but Lontas clasped her shoulders. "Improvement, when things are good, is overrated. The enemy of good is perfection."

"The enemy of improvement is complacent acceptance," Bellae countered. The force of her retort made him pause. "There's infinitely more in the universe that we can't visualize than is visible. There's more inside you than you could possibly imagine. Destroying the Macht Crystals gives those who come after a chance to explore our world, the universe, and to move beyond this time—exactly what Veneficus didn't want. People, for ages past, and in a future we cannot see, in worlds we cannot yet imagine, have, and will, toil deeply and sacrifice silver and gold for that which they love. My sacrifice needs to be written in blood, bone, and marrow."

"You speak as if blood and silver were roughly equal. I would much rather be poor of coin than lost from you. Another way to look at this is that the world needs you to guide it."

"Guide will turn to greed and manipulation," Bellae replied, embarrassed to admit the pleasure of magic running through her, their addictive call constantly beckoning.

"I can't lose you and me. I can't lose us."

"Everything ends, Lontas. We know it but don't want to think about it, much less accept it. Even though it all ends, live joyfully anyway. Too often our minds feed misfortune until it expands, leaching the joy out of the life we have remaining. Go listen to birds sing, watch suns rise, taste good food, and most importantly, even though all that you love comes to an end, go find people to love anyway." The wind whipped Bellae's hair around her face, and he could see how exhausted she was. "Courage is a Knightly virtue for a reason. It cannot exist without having to consciously choose between two alternatives. Without thoughtful intelligence and intelligent thought, there can be no growth of spirit or true bravery, true courage. The thought of you continuing on after I'm gone will help me take the hard route."

"Why not use their power to help discern the truth of the world and help those who need it? Imagine what I can learn with several lifetimes."

"I have kissed the rings of truth and caressed the secrets hidden in nature all around us and learned that each 'truth' we walk through is just a portal to dozens of other questions in a never-ending maze and we, collectively and as individuals, will die before we get to the end."

Lontas looked down. "You're...so different..."

"With the crystals I've seen millions of lifetimes and changed a thousand ways a thousand times, so much I hardly recognize my former self. I see the black dragon of eternity coming and I'm scared. I don't want to not exist—nothingness scares me. This is where courage comes in. Greed and power will eventually take away who I am. It may be a slow descent into nothingness, but the result's the same. Whatever path I choose, I lose me, abruptly or slowly."

"But I would get to be with you. Choose slow!"

"Whenever you're around, the world doesn't seem as dark, infinity doesn't seem so overwhelming. Many years from now, you will wring these memories from your brain, and only joy shall drip out. The hardships, the loss, will have dulled, and you'll look back fondly on our adventure, on you and me."

"You said the Chosen was a hoax and you just happened to show up with the Ainmhi Caint gift. So wait for someone else to be born and do...whatever this is. We've sacrificed enough! We got through the trials, faced the riddles, guardians, and deserve to be finished."

"Stralande called prophecies flexible hope composed on parchment in rhyme, vague so they can be interpreted in different ways when the right circumstances congeal. What's important is that others believe. You know it has to be an Ainmhi Caint." She looked around satirically.

"Veneficus hunted and killed the rest. I owe it to them, many of whom died horrible deaths."

"Flexible hope? That's the most demented thing I've ever heard. We don't want to follow people who think like that!"

She shook her head. "I've had an amazing string of todays, most of them with you, my one true friend. I could never have dreamed of such things before we set out on this adventure. It's been…breathtaking." Closing her eyes, she pictured herself soaring over Lake Glasere with the Eaglians, feeling the wind and breathtaking atmosphere of gliding. Next, she was sitting with Stralande, Cappadocia with Fairies and Sprites, solving riddles with Hamata, watching Crann selflessly march to his death, Kāla, Arachne. She pulled power from the crystals and magically relived all their guidance and advice. "All their words and counsel, all the grueling trials, have been leading me here so I could make the right decision."

"It's so NOT the right decision," Lontas said, still in denial.

"The one thing I learned during this journey is that there is no tomorrow, for any of us. All we ever have is a series of solitary todays. Our string of present moments is our chain of events that makes up the entirety of our time, our eternity. You can enjoy it or waste it, but you shouldn't expect there would be anything else. Maybe we shouldn't think about it in terms of 'my' eternity, maybe it's our collective strands of eternities that build one cohesive lifetime."

"Honey betrayed us, Veneficus was evil, a lot of people tried to kill us. We don't owe anyone anything, much less dead ancestors or some nebulous future!"

"Delaying pushes the problem down the line, and the future has enough obstacles waiting. Here." Bellae handed him the sheathed dagger from Friar before taking off her Inion medallion, watching it spin frenetically, as if anxious about being handed over, before quickly slipping it over his head. "Maybe you'll have daughters one day. You, my friend, will resonate part of me as you move forward."

"I won't forget you. I won't forget this," Lontas said, softly sobbing.

"That you will think of me in the future is comforting. Be careful how you wear your past, our past. Don't let this journey become a weighted penance. Remember to live." Bellae paused, and Lontas hated the faraway, detached look in her eyes.

"Use this power to rebuild Liberum, putting in a comfortable reading spot for us!"

Bellae smiled impatiently. "Oh, Lontas. I love you, but you're the only one leaving here. The last companion, my best friend. We made it...success."

"This isn't success, we're supposed to win."

"Oh, it is victory, and we have won."

"Who's going to pick me up when I fall?" Lontas said.

"That's just it, you're strong enough to get back up on your own now. You're the one who broke *into* the library and used that knowledge to save us. That's the guy I see. But what I see isn't important. You need to see the greatness inside you. There's plenty of journey left for you, but it will be without me. You moving forward, having a life, remembering me, the world having a chance to crawl from the shadow of Na Cearcaill, those are the parts to celebrate."

Lontas looked down. "I'd do it again, even the horrible parts, just to get more time with you. What am I supposed to do?"

"Live an amazing life, full of love. We step on the everyday activities as if they're a burden. We race across them as quickly as possible. Our eyes are not on the present but looking ahead to some imaginary goal. Forgetting to enjoy the journey is a crime. Tread softly on your precious mundane days and enjoy each drop of life's water as if it were a king's ransom, because each moment, in reality, is much more valuable."

Lontas began to bawl from a mix of awe of how much Bellae had changed and fear at not having her around. "No pressure though."

"Go live your life and understand the lives that will branch forward from you. We're all traveling together in our collective ship towards our cumulative future. Despite what those in charge say, we can forge it into whatever we want. After the crystals are destroyed, there is freedom to move onward. I'm sorry I can't go any further." Bellae closed her eyes, surprising Lontas by seeming at peace despite his own mind frothing angrily for a way out.

"The guardian of the Strength Crystals said an ending is a new beginning!" Lontas said.

Bellae opened her eyes. "This is a new beginning, but for you, for others. Sometimes, the end is just the end. After this, you'll keep going, one step at a time. Don't worry about the tough times, they can't be worse than what we fought through. Don't worry about the heartaches, they won't be heavier than this. Learn, live, and love. Please know the only home I ever had was being with you, my best friend."

"Are the crystals talking to you?"

Bellae nodded. "Constantly."

Tears, unwelcome and bewildering, streamed down, and he fell to his knees.

Taking him gently by the shoulders, she helped him up. "It's time, Lontas."

She embraced him in a lingering hug, one anchored within past adventures and friendship, a signal of fear and reluctance for the future. It was the deep embrace of two friends heading in opposite directions on disparate journeys. They clasped fiercely for a long time, yet when Bellae pushed back, it hardly seemed enough.

Lontas wiped his tears. "Forever, as long as I have days to walk, my life shall be clouded by the thick cover of our friendship and memories. I need to…do something to show you how much I appreciate all you have done for me."

She took his hands. "Showy celebrations and big deeds don't mean anything compared to the million little things you've done. Walking with me, standing next to me when I needed it, steadying me when I faltered. Always being there has meant…everything. The dark times you picked me up and supported me, the ones no one else will ever know about, the acts that were small but genuine, they add up to the greatest gift of all. The only thing we can really leave behind is love and kindness. You did it. You've already done it, Lontas."

Bellae's eyes suddenly flashed white. When the light faded, she said, "They're coming."

Scroll 12: They Stab, We Block

Sprinting towards them were Cavalo horses. *"Many are nearing,"* Hratt said. *"We'll try to hold them off."*

"I moved too far from the storm fields to block the crystals!" Bellae lamented as the horses formed a ring around the hill. They snorted and pawed at the snow-laden ground, their upright manes fluttering proudly as several spun and exploded out their whip-like tails in anticipation of battle.

"Who's coming?" Lontas said.

Before she could answer, a portal opened and IleZuri stumbled through, taking a few halting steps before the opening shut behind him. He looked around in utter confusion. "I was just in the cavern with Tacet-Vand. How am I here?"

"He must have portaled you here, but that was long ago," Lontas answered.

The steady flapping of wings drew their attention to the air. Streams of Watchers were flowing towards them.

IleZuri looked around. "Me and horses versus that many Watchers? This won't go well. Obviously, Tacet-Vand..." He stopped, a tear coursing over his cheek. "I dedicated my life to someone I didn't know. What do you do after something like that? Defending you, as he must have wanted, is as good as any."

Lontas pointed as a shimmering portal opened. Several minotaurs bellowed as they stormed through. IleZuri spun his bladed bow and moved off in their direction. "I'll do what I can, but whatever you're going to do, do it quickly."

As the Watchers grew near, a series of loud shrieks stung the air. "Eaglians!" Bellae said, initially joyfully, then cautiously, "I hope they're on our side." They soon realized there were two streams squawking at each other. The first group arrived and landed on the hill next to Bellae and she prepared to grab the crystals. She regretted that part of her wanted to use them as their honeyed promises continued to coat her mind.

"We're determined to fight for you, upholding our sworn promise to your ancestors," a small Eaglian said, cracking her neck. "We were tracking the Watchers and some of our less-inclined brothers and sisters must have been following us."

Several Magicians abruptly materialized in front of them. The Eaglians bared their fearsome beaks and drew their swords.

"We fight for you," the closest one said. "We lived through Veneficus' abuses and can see the promise of the crystals' power warping the few of us left. We witnessed the leaders and their infighting. Now those," he pointed to a group of Magicians riding griffins, "they're here to kill you and take the Macht Crystals. Proliate troops are coming as well."

Loud clangs of metal versus horn rang out, and several Eaglians immediately took to the air. Some to help IleZuri battling minotaurs, some to shield against Watchers. Still others faced off against their fellow Eaglians, both sides unwaveringly convinced of their righteousness.

Several Cavalo horses joined the fight. One used its whip-like tail to tangle a minotaur's feet before another smashed its hooves into the same minotaur's shoulder, a third collided with its horned face. IleZuri's bladed bow twirled with deft proficiency, occasionally loosing an arrow when distance allowed. Another portal opened behind him. IleZuri sprinted towards a minotaur about to emerge, jumping he kicked off its chest, pushing himself backwards and drawing an arrow before quickly putting it into the creature's left eye. A second arrow pierced through the mouth of the beast, which was wide with bellowing pain. The portal began to sputter as the Watcher summoning it began to lose control. At first, small, flittering, sand-like disintegrations began to shower away, but as he continued trying to magically hold open the portal, large sections of his flesh splintered, shattering away. With a muted gurgle he completely degenerated, and the portal instantly collapsed, slicing an emerging minotaur in half. More Eaglians arrived and with the horses began to push the remaining minotaurs away.

A Magician who had joined them looked anxiously at his crosier. "We'll help keep the Watchers away…for a bit, but with Magicians on griffins arriving soon, you don't have long."

Scroll 13: Promise Realized

Bellae turned to leave. Lontas grabbed her arm. "Everything's going to change now."

She shook her head as if disappointed. "Everything changes every second. We constantly morph ourselves as we reform simply through living, learning, failing, succeeding. Sometimes the big changes require us to lose old attachments."

"Doesn't mean I have to like it," Lontas said, feeling his words sounded immature.

"Like and reality rarely line up, and certainly have no obligation to do so. I don't particularly care for the facts right now, but they did not ask me."

An Eaglian crash landed a few feet from them, bleeding profusely from innumerable lacerations. "Not the best time for whatever this is," she said before jumping back into the air.

"Thanks for everything, Lontas, but it's time."

He ineptly wiped away the tears that were instantly replaced with new ones as Bellae ran to the center of the hill and set the sack of crystals down. "Stay there."

Lontas felt like the air had been stolen, pilfering his ability to say anything.

She quickly unfolded the notes from Lanella. There were two, written in different handwriting from different ages. *I promised to read these at the end of my journey, and this is the end,* she thought, stealing a hurried look at those fighting to give her time.

"Dear Bellae,

I want you to know killing your parents was the hardest thing my husband Aquila ever did. He would have rather been tortured in a dark dungeon of Ifrean than do it again."

Bellae's eyes turned white, the ache of those words hurting at a chasmic level. Crystal-fueled visions of Aquila and his strange behavior around her flashed, including his tearful and tormented walk from the

Redwoods to Liberum with her as a newborn. As her eyes returned to normal, she forced herself to keep reading through tear-muddied vision.

"Your parents were our friends and loved you very much. Their death sentenced Aquila to life in a prison of profound grief made of unbreakable bars of regret. He advocated for hiding them in our Redwood Forest, but they, and League elders, thought it was too great a risk.

Your ancestors tested everyone in the forest to see if the mindre crystals would burn. Your mother, Thysia, only had minor redness, everyone else was severely burned. That was our first clue. Once she became pregnant, she could speak with animals and touch the mindre crystals without getting burned. It was the final sign of your identity, the Chosen One.

As a first born without an older brother the League had a problem, as it had made a false prophecy to deceive those hunting you. In that fake version the animal talker would have a brother who would be the Chosen. No one knew how much good such a false prophecy could do, but the elders felt that any delay of the discovery of your true identity could make the difference between success and failure. When you're staring at what seems like an impossibly long and difficult journey, you don't know what will make or break the endeavor.

Veneficus never figured out females were infinitely more powerful than men. So they knew the Chosen would be a girl. Only Jumeaux and Gimelli's parents were pregnant at that time. Because so many were looking for you, if your parents were found and tortured, or magically coerced, they could give up your true identity and knowledge of the false prophecy. The League replaced the twins' newborn with you while eliminating the parents. The ruse worked, that's why Veneficus took such an interest in Jumeaux. Your mother was happy to give her life to make sure your identity as Chosen, and the false prophecy, could be maintained.

I hope you can forgive my husband and your parents. They sacrificed themselves to get you to the point you are now—with a chance to end the spread of evil in our land. Good luck. I know you'll do the right thing for Arend, your parents, Aquila, and everyone in Verngaurd.

With all my Love, Lanella"

"Are you okay, Bellae?" Lontas called out, anxiously watching the battle closing in around them. Several fire balls exploded about twenty feet from him, the rest flying off harmlessly into the sky as an Eaglian chopped off the top half of a Magician's head.

"I'm okay," Bellae said tearfully even though she was not anywhere close to it. *They could have just stayed hidden!* The injustice of their death forced her to suppress the thought that Veneficus was focusing in on the Redwoods but could not vanquish the notion that almost all of her kind, the Ainmhi Caint, had been tortured and killed because of these crystals. Her eyes blazed as she screamed for the voices to cease. *You genocide my people and then offer me temptations? That's the very definition of foolish.*

She swiftly put the newer note from Lanella under the older, yellowing one and started to read. With each word she began to cry harder. At one point, Lontas started to move forward, but Bellae put a hand up to stop him. After she read the note from her mother, she held its close and smelled, inhaling the essence of it. After kissing it, she put it back in her bag.

"Do what you're going to, kid!" an Eaglian flying overhead yelled. Bellae could feel the cardinal drops from the Eaglian's injuries pelt her as she passed above.

Nodding, Bellae started taking the crystals out. Each time she grabbed one, her eyes flashed white, and scenes played before her—sometimes of glory and riches with whispers of honeyed enticement, and other times they were scenes of destruction and death predicting the catastrophe that would befall the world if she rejected them. "I call on my ancestors, my connection to animals, the earth, and my mother to protect me."

She laid out the first four sets of crystals in a rectangular shape. While pulling out the last pair of crystals, the letters she had read fluttered out of the bag. She didn't hesitate from her task, throwing the bag aside as Lontas ran after the letters. By the time he caught them and ran back to his spot, she had put the last pair of crystals in place, inside the imaginary rectangle she had created, centered, about one foot in from the upper edge.

I willingly give up my life force and join it with the crystals in order to set them free, to set magic free! Bellae screamed, stepping into the rectangle. Lontas immediately had to shield his eyes as a wall of massive white light shot up from the five pairs of crystals encasing Bellae within the brightness. The clouds above began to swirl as the torrid wind churned. He could see her clothes fluttering and her hair dancing in a windy vortex. He hunched closer to the ground as the wind turned into a gale. The Watchers, Magicians on griffins, and Eaglians were forcibly flung away from the hill. Several of the attacking Magicians and Watchers fired towards the eddy of light and gusting wind surrounding Bellae without any effect.

The voices of the crystals rang out, dripping in feelings of satisfaction and gratification. *Deny yourself eternal life and endless contentment and suffer this…*

As the voice finished, a shock of scorching pain burned through her body. Even though it lasted a few seconds, she cried out in horror as her body shuddered in anguish. *Every atom of your being will be charred in a whirlpool of never-ending agony.*

Recovering from the initial gust, the Watchers and Magicians, understanding what she was about to do, began to fight with reckless abandon. Meanwhile, Bellae was being intermittently shocked with blistering bursts of pure pain. Her knees buckled, and her will weakened from the agony. "I don't want to do this!" she screamed. "I want to go home!"

You have no home, but you can rebuild Liberum with us! Suddenly the jolts of pain stopped, and her head was awash with enticing voices imploring her to utilize their power. *An eternity of pain or peace and prosperity for all time. Make the right choice.*

But you take more than you give! she screamed in her mind while imagining the magic-addicted, shriveled bodies of Veneficus and

Tacet-Vand, and envisioning all of her ancestors who had been tortured to death.

Fighting against the windstorm, the Watchers chanted, their cracked bodies glowed, and eyes hissed malice as they combined their magic, focusing it on the stream of white light around her, desperate to break through and get to the crystals. Her body shuddered as their magic pounded her sanctuary. She noticed Lontas screaming, "…no choice! Bellae, I know it's hard, but do what you have to, or we die and they take the crystals! You and me."

"You don't understand," Bellae sobbed. "There's insane pain, or the power of the crystals taking over more of everything that makes me, me. I can feel black tendrils twisting around my body, heart, and mind. I don't want that, but the pain…"

Her voice trailed off, and Lontas started to move forward.

"No, I can do this!" she yelled while thinking, *I'm so tired.*

Scroll 14: Time to Endure Enduring Times

Squatting, she moved her right hand towards the Seeing Crystals. They were pushing against her as a battle raged in her head as violently as the storm without. Screaming, she forced her hand down, finally squishing through their resistance. A bubble of agony encased her right arm and shoulder as a mix of burning and slicing pain gouged through skin, muscle, down to bone. She could see the flesh burn away only to heal and suffer again.

As the pain continued violently cycling through her right arm, her eyes turned white, one-fifth of the light surrounding her turned red, and Bellae's voice boomed, "The power of Seeing is in the choice! Study and meditate for the true Perception. Deception decays and destroys the giver and receiver!" Her amplified words echoed around the battlefield so powerfully Lontas and many of the combatants were knocked backwards, desperately covering their ears.

Tears and saliva dripped from her face at the torturous pain. She moved her right knee back onto the Strength Crystals, again fighting through resistance. Excruciating affliction exploded up and down her leg. Immersed in pain, it too turned white as orange and yellow joined the red light surrounding her. "Unbridled rage is Weakness confining one in a prison of hate. Humility and service for the frail is Power and Strength!" Even with his hands over his ears, Lontas' eardrums pounded. Flying creatures that had not landed were thrown about ruthlessly.

Next, her left knee struggled over the Time Crystals as the entire right side of her body perpetually healed only to be re-burnt and flayed by the light consuming it. The crystals intensified their mind-warping bargaining, increasingly desperate as she proceeded. Tears leapt out of her eyes from the savage pain only to be vaporized by the heat radiating from her. Focusing all her might, she finally forced her left knee down, and her entire left leg burst into light soaked in continually repeating affliction as green light joined the others around her.

"Time, a sacred gift, and brief foray into reality—it lets us stomp through her in the physical for only a brief moment before Death comes, crushing existence! Our tattered shred of eternity, Life, only exists within the larger fabric of the endless!" she thundered.

Bellae suddenly had to fight to stay down on the ground. She could feel the power gushing through her body while listening to a thousand whispering promises of fame and fortune, if only she would accept the power of the crystals. *The suffering can end! Transform into any being you want, any age you desire. You can change the world for good!* the voices promised while afflicting her with unspeakable pain. *End the suffering! It's not too late!*

The pain ravaging her body slackened as an image of her mother, who sacrificed herself for Bellae, was replaced by visions of generations of Ainmhi Caint. She witnessed their deaths by the tens of thousands at the hands of Veneficus as he tortured and murdered them for refusing to go along with Na Cearcaill. Shaking her head violently, she thought, *I give of myself freely. I reject your power! I avenge evil for them!* Slowly, her frame settled back onto the ground, and three-fourths of her body plunged into light-drenching agony—abused, healed, submerged in pain again. She struggled to force her left hand onto the Sacrifice

Crystal, a magnetic force shoved up against her as the voices intensified, but now turning angry, taunting her, calling her a coward. The visions flipped from grandeur to utter despair.

If you're too afraid to take on your responsibility as Supreme Master, the world will be doomed to chaos and pain! Images of war, murder, crime flashed. *Refuse us and you'll be the cause of thousands of painful deaths. The world must have magic, or cold, heartless, technology and destruction consume everyone.* Gruesome images of hideous injuries played out.

She struggled to focus on something. *Think of Lontas.* She could not see or hear him but knew he was there, willing her to succeed. Slowly, her hand began to move downwards. A shock wave blasted out as her hand touched the Sacrifice Crystals, this time blue and indigo replaced some of the silo of white around her. "Sacrifice for another is Love!" Bellae shouted. "Love builds connections and harmonizes our connectedness. Each act of warmth and affection vibrates across the net connecting us all. Hatred cracks the soul of both the Hating and Hated, destroying self and ruining the reflection of consciousness!"

Bellae had a vision of Arachne on Indra's net. She gazed at her sad expression and skin, which alternated between gashing wounds and webs of skin morphing to heal. Arachne, kind eyes glimmering, gently nodded before disappearing.

Lontas, keeping his belly close to the ground, struggled up the hill. The wind rushing from Bellae and the crystals constantly jolted against his body, trying to lift and toss him back. He could hear shouts of the warriors and magical creatures battling to get to her despite the gale. A shock wave from the crystals rushed over him. *I must be helping,* he thought. When he did not retreat, invisible hands and feet began hitting and kicking.

"Bellae, I'm here! You can do it!" he repeatedly screamed at the top of his lungs. The wind grew angrier, swirling around him ever more vigorously, trying to mute his words. Creeping on his abdomen, he was making painfully slow progress but continued yelling.

One more, she thought, seeing nothing but flashing bursts of blinding light alternating with horrifying images of death and torment.

Guessing where she had put the last pair of crystals, she tried to force her head down on top of them.

"Wait!" a child's voice screamed as she gratefully received a reprieve from the pain. "Why do you want me to die?" Suddenly, the face of Vanalia, the village girl who traveled with Bellae to the Tournament of Flags, was in front of her. "Why did you abandon us?"

"I didn't...I was trying..." Bellae stuttered before turning defiant. "You're not real." As soon as her words died down, a fresh, raging pain erupted all around Bellae's body. It felt like someone was hitting her repeatedly in addition to the blazing misery engulfing it. Several cracks around her body spoke to bones breaking.

"If you'd embraced the power of magic," Vanalia said, "you would stop war, hunger, torture, murder. Why are you letting those things continue? Why didn't you stop them from burning me and my family!"

"You could bring my daughter back from the dead and let her have another chance at life," Svika, Vanalia's father, cried out. "Your weakness is responsible for losing so many lives! Do the right thing for once, embrace the chance to cure and rescue. Save us, save the world."

Sumar, the sickly boy from the Tournament, appeared. "Why don't you want to cure me? Why do you want me to suffer?" His visage slumped, and his eyes closed as he morphed into a form full of vengeful arrows complete with streaking blood. His eyes stormed open. "You want me to suffer and die? You're weak and selfish!" Sumar and Vanalia were joined by thousands of other whispering villagers who had died at the hands of the Dark Warriors.

They're all dead. It's just another trick, Bellae told herself.

"We're a trick?" Vanalia's voice boomed with anger. "We're some sort of joke? Because we're poor, without nice clothes, we're not worth anything! Why won't you take your responsibility and protect the poor and helpless?"

Somehow, over all the noise, she was sure Lontas was yelling encouragement, and she tried to force a mental image of his face into her mind. The images of Sumar, Vanalia, their families, and the villagers wobbled, shaking violently.

Lontas! she cried out, unsure if her shouts were internal or audible.

"Bellae! I'm here!" Lontas kept yelling over and over despite the wind fighting to dampen his voice and the kicks and punches the invisible feet and fists were dishing out. After making it up the hill, he saw within the whirling brightness she was on her hands and knees. Except her head and neck, her body was encased in blindingly bright light. Looking closely, he could see alternating patches of her flesh burning to the bone before reforming to burn again, over and over, as pure agony stretched across her face. He glimpsed shadowy hands. Some were trying to lift her up, others were hitting her. He could see outlines of feet repeatedly kicking her.

"Cowards! Get me, not Bellae! I'm coming!" he screamed. For the first time in his life, he felt true rage. Unconcerned about what would happen to him, he crawled towards her.

"Lontas!" Bellae cried as the likenesses of Sumar, Vanalia, and their parents began to quake so violently they blurred. Bits of hair and flesh were flung off. The vibrating stopped to be replaced with an army of gray-boned skeletons. Their eye sockets were more pointed than round, giving them a fiendish appearance.

"You want us all to die? You'll be sorry if you put your head down. An eternity of pain awaits!" It was Vanalia's voice but made gravely and fiendish. "You think this cute little taste of pain is bad? You haven't felt anything yet."

With his eyes overflowing with tears, Lontas stuck his left hand into the towering light surrounding her. Despite the excruciating shock he said, "Let me take some of the pain for you!"

Thousands of skeletal villagers began shouting out the horrible things they were going to do to her. Without warning a hand burst through the skeletons, blowing them apart. They disappeared in Bellae's mind, and the voices stopped. *True silence can be a gift,* she thought, but it was quickly replaced with anguish as the pain cycle started again. "I can't take it anymore. I can't do it!" she screamed.

"Bellae! Do what you need to!" he yelled, howling in pain as his left hand burned in the light surrounding his friend. He could see the flesh blackening. The hands pushing her head away from the last crystals abruptly let up, focusing on him. Thousands of hands were shoving and fists hitting as he struggled to stay close. Even though only his hand was burning, he was draining some of her pain, spreading the torment across his entire shuddering body.

She quickly took advantage of the reprieve and forced her head onto the Wisdom Crystals. A massive burst of energy shot out in all directions as violet replaced the last of the white light in the tower surrounding her. Lontas was blown backwards down the hill. As he spiraled to a stop, ignoring the searing pain from his charred hand, he looked up. A colorful burst of light was shining up from the crystals towards the heavens. Reaching towards the clouds, the light started to bend over on itself, spreading out in all directions.

Bellae's body shot up into a spread-eagle posture hovering in the column of light ten feet off the ground. Her arms outstretched, she began yelling, "True Wisdom is understanding the Knowledge you possess is a tiny speck in an ocean of Ignorance. Being undaunted, dedicate your life to expand your understanding!"

Her voice was so powerful, Lontas' eardrums burst, blood oozed out of his ear canals as lightning and thunder began to rumble and strike all around the vortex of light. Bellae felt her skin explode into even more intense pain as the radiant beam around her turned to flames.

You asked for this! a voice boomed in her head. *Pain immersion!*

Scroll 15: Raining Rainbows

"I give myself to release your power!" she screamed, her voice dripping to a gurgle as pain forced its way deeper until her bones shrieked in torment. Abruptly, a deep calm settled over her. She could no longer feel the blistering pain or hear the whirling, angry wind surging around her. Looking down, she saw flaming skeletal remains on the ground, places with burnt flesh clinging futilely—her rawboned remains. *That's me?* she wondered as the crystals slowly began to shrink as light flowed out to create the tunnel surrounding her.

Time seemed to at once speed up and slow down as she relived every act of her life at lightning speed, perceiving not only how she felt, but how those around her experienced each moment. Eons of history blew by her each second, but she was somehow able to understand it all as she relived all the societies, cultures, and peoples destroyed by Veneficus over the eons. Her mind was drawn to a group of people and animals talking within a tunnel of light in front of her. They were laughing and waving. Bellae's vision narrowed on a young woman, powerfully familiar, conjuring a strikingly pleasant feeling to bubble within.

"Mom!" Bellae screamed. But in the swirling light around her, the sound was immediately swallowed. Tears of joy flowed down her cheeks. Her mother mouthed something.

"I don't understand," Bellae said.

Her mother smiled before repeating the words and motioning her into the tunnel. Again, her voice had no volume, but she could make out what she was saying, "I'm proud of you!"

Bellae sobbed harder.

"I love you," her mother mouthed.

Bellae reached frantically for her mother but could not move forward. She saw a horse, bucking in pure excitement. Bellae instantly recognized Crann, and Finn was there too, his arms outstretched. "My Inion!" he mouthed.

Bellae opened up her heart enough to let hope enter. *Could this be real?* Jumeaux appeared, wearing a big smile. Luchar arrived, no longer paralyzed, and roughed up Jumeaux's hair. Arend, Sorea, and Arquero came. Instantly, Bellae was moving forward, through the tunnel, towards her friends and family, tears streaming down her face. Abruptly, she stopped in front of her mother and father. The whirling wind was gone, as were the vortex of light and the crystals. They had been transformed into billions of tiny particles rushing up to fill the heavens.

Lontas stumbled up the hill as colorful light continued to encircle the sky. He held up his good right hand to catch the rain falling, each drop cloaked in the colors of the rainbow. Despite the pain shooting up from his blackened left hand, he smiled. "Raining rainbows...rainbows raining down. Now that's a nifty bit of magic."

Bellae moved back from her parents and looked down at the blackened remains of her physical body below—lying where the crystals had been, burnt and profoundly shattered. She spotted Lontas, and part of her wanted go back and be with him. She screamed his name, but even as he looked up, she knew he could not see or hear her.

"There's no way back," her mother said as Bellae's lifeless physical body began to rise off the hill with its skeletal arms, with blackened flesh clinging in places, outstretched.

"What happens after I go into the light?"

Her mother's face creased into a sad smile before her entire visage dissolved, but not before gently whispering, "You'll see."

"What about the darkness I kept seeing?"

"You have to find out for yourself," her mother's voice said softly.

Although no true barrier closed, Bellae could feel the doorway to return to her body slam shut. She had one choice, forward. An immense lightning bolt struck through Bellae's body and down to the ground. It was so bright and hot Lontas had to shield his eyes as he was thrown backwards again. After a few brief moments, the warmth and light were gone.

Despite his pain, he scrambled up quickly. On top of the hill, where Bellae had been, was a large and sturdy sugar maple. Its massive trunk went up to orange, yellow, and red leaves. As he moved closer, he noticed a strange mark in the bottom of the tree. Kneeling beside it, he could see a blackened area roughly the shape of his charred left hand.

A wave of exhaustion rolled over him as the colorful raindrops softly plopped through the leaves of the sugar maple to plunk faintly on his already wet skin. Sitting down with his back to the tree, a convulsion of suffering engulfed his body. Misery born from the mortality of friendship and love unleashed a lachrymal song of anguish, which flooded out of his wet eyes before dancing down his cheeks in waves of unrestrained sorrow.

A large gust of wind burst over the hill, and Lontas' eyes fluttered open. Sharp streaks of pain discharged from his left hand, making him wince. Tears squeezed from his eyes, some born from physical agony, most beckoned from the realization of what Bellae endured. His overwhelmed mind begged to delve back into the refuge of sleep.

Sometime later, he startled awake at the sound of a voice. "I'm okay, Lontas. Have a great life, and don't forget your promise to come visit me and bring animals." Lontas smiled, noticing his left hand was no longer burnt.

"Did you fix this?" he asked.

Bellae's face appeared and smiled before speaking, "It is with the icy slap of night's cruel embrace that the stone-cold reality of our existence can, if we let it, punch us in the stomach. Our lives rise and fall like the waves, and all eventually come to rest upon the shore. The best we can do is see the magic of the expedition, our tattered shred, and journey with courage."

Lontas bolted up and strained his eyes to focus on the clouds and rain, no longer colored, storming around him. The burnt remnants of his left hand howled in pain. "Oh…dreaming." After several moments of silence, he laid back down. "See you soon enough, Bellae," he whispered, beginning to sob again.

IleZuri, blood and dents decorating his armor, ran over. "You alright, child?" When Lontas did not reply, he continued, "The death of someone close always vengefully rips a part of you with it into the abyss. However, some losses, a select few deaths, shift the world beneath your feet—wrenching a mortal anchor so that everything afterwards seems a little less secure, not quite as bright, and the scenery just a little blurred." The blonde warrior knelt next to the weeping Lontas, he could not help thinking of Tacet-Vand and his betrayal, yet he also saved him from certain death in the cave to fight again.

Lontas, his soul too bruised to ever fully recover, knew that nothing would ever go back to normal. His senses would just accommodate to the new reality without his friend. He was brought back to conversations with Bellae about what any of us can truly perceive.

I guess it's time to look up from the shadows on the cave wall. This is the new reality.

Scroll 16: Epilogue: A haon The Next Morn

At sunrise the next day, Lontas woke from his fitful sleep. His left arm throbbed angrily, shooting spasms of pain to his brain. He tore his undershirt and quickly rewrapped his burnt hand, all the while trying, but unable, to shake the image of Bellae, having her entire body experience that agony over and over again. Despite the shouts of torment from his burnt flesh, he put it up next to the matching, blackened palmprint on the tree. "We did it, Bellae. We finished it…together." With the sleeve of his good arm, he wiped away his tears. Moving to stand, Bellae's notes fell out of his pocket. With his unburnt hand he quickly scooped them up.

"Hey, boy, welcome back. I thought you'd died," IleZuri said, his face looking even more exhausted and his armor further dented and scorched. "I didn't think one could sleep so soundly through such carnage. My mind told me you succumbed to a mortal's true sleep."

Lontas looked up to see several Watchers and Nishi. "Did you stand guard all night?"

"Yes, but I was not always successful." He pointed to several blackened areas on the tree. Some had gashes that seemed to be healing before their eyes. "Luckily, the tree seems to be able to defend itself, repairing against their magical assaults. I have no idea how you slept through that. Fortunately for you, I think our attackers believed your possums' play as well."

"I must have passed out. Everyone else gone?"

"Yes, even the Cavalo horses left and, to be honest, I'm not sure what to do or how long to stay," IleZuri said, absently swinging his intimidating bow in angry figure eights. "At least the rain stopped around midnight."

Lontas gazed at the creatures bobbing anxiously in the distance. "They endlessly crave power—enough for them is never sufficient—exactly why Bellae did what she did."

IleZuri nodded, unsure of what to say.

"Sorry again about Tacet-Vand."

"Thanks. In the end he redeemed himself, as was his wish. However, it's hard to believe he was once caught up in Na Cearcaill." The warrior paused. "It's easy to let past sins and grievances create new ones via their obligatory followers: hate and anger. It's okay to forgive others and yourself, whether or not other people do."

"It is hard to imagine. He seemed…so nice," Lontas said.

"Our minds tend to trim the fat of fault from our heroes, clipping their mistakes and errors to make a lean cut of what we feel our champions should be. For villains we too easily brush away any goodness, any love and kindness, but are all too happy to point out their defects and flaws, vigorously and perhaps self-righteously.

"Maybe the greatest evil is the one staring out from within and released when we let it overrule our mind and morals. Our lives are a string of moments spreading out from past actions to the future yet to be. Every person we touch echoes on to those they contact."

Lontas smiled, sad he knew so little about IleZuri, and hoping Arachne on her web could see him. "When all those strings of moments add up, we soon have a jeweled web of interconnectedness underlying the fabric of the world, of which we are just a tattered shred."

"A philosopher, I see," IleZuri said. "If we survive, I'd love to talk more." Spinning around at the howl of desperation from a Watcher, he went back to patrolling the tree while Lontas unfolded the letters. When he finished reading Lanella's note, he used his shoulders to wipe away the tears, his right hand awkwardly switching to the letter from her mother.

"Dear Bellae, It's important you understand we freely give our lives for you, for the world. My only regret is not getting to see your

beautiful face and watch you grow up. I could never speak to animals until I was pregnant. Your first gift to me! Your father and I willingly die to strike a blow at the evil one and his sinful cycle of destroying the world, building it up in a new image born from his twisted imagination. He killed most of our kind because we refused to participate in his sick plan. He gave us the chance to step out of his eternal Na Cearcaill and rule with him. Our kind could never sit by and watch the death of so many. You have a chance to end the cycle of death, but in doing so, you must freely give up your life and end our race forever, as, once you succeed, the last of us will be released from the Redwoods and the power of our people diluted and, yes, lost to time. However, we should focus on what the world shall gain, freedom. Our gift requires our ending but allows a new beginning to flower forth.

I know you're young, and this is a lot, but a small light in the darkness is worth more than a million torches in the bright midday. It's not fair to ask you to be a hero, but here it is. The world has laid before us tough choices, each burdened and blessed with opportunities. Never forget to be the light that pushes back the darkness. Even if the suns are out, never forget the power you hold within (even if the rest of the world can't see it).

I want the future to have the peace I cannot give to you. I wish the mothers of that age to spoil and nurture their children through all the phases of childhood—an opportunity I will never have. If those things come to be, then it means the evil one is dead, and the world can grow and flourish. You'll like having siblings—Gimelli and Jumeaux. Treat them like family because, in all the ways that matter, they are. Good luck on your journey for the crystals. With love greater than our lives, and more vast than the universe, your mom, Thysia, and dad, Apeiro."

She was supposed to get it before the quest, Lontas thought, again wiping away tears. A loud neigh brought him back to the present. He looked up to see a horse charging towards him. Hratt, obviously agitated, jerked his head back, signaling Lontas to get on.

Lontas took several deep breaths before tearing up the two notes, using his good hand and boots and burying them beneath the earth at the base of the sugar maple.

After struggling onto Hratt, he swore the tree shook with joy. "Come, let's go. We—"

His words were cut short. Dozens of Magicians rode hard towards him, followed by battalions of Proliators. Shrieks filled the air as griffins carrying more Magicians from the opposite direction appeared overhead. A new group of Nishi and Watchers revealed themselves.

Lontas slid off the horse. "We can't outrun them."

IleZuri walked over and sighed. "They don't seem to realize they've already lost. Power, once suckled from, is difficult to let go of."

"They don't look happy," Lontas said.

"No, no, they don't," IleZuri said. "I, however, have nothing left to lose."

Lontas shook his head. "This…this is not going to end well."

Scroll 17: Epilogue: A dó Twenty-Five Years On

Two adults—bound by marriage, lead six children—
liberated with anticipation…
and a multitude of war hounds.

Lontas stopped, peering south, watching the lightning flash passionately, followed by thunder's rage—forever doomed to always be a bit behind. Each flash stirred up bitingly painful memories of that time a quarter of a century ago. *She was forged from slaughter in fire. A quest born in blood, doomed to end in pain and death. There was always a sadness hanging over her. Was it from the past, or the future she had yet to bear? Did I do enough to help her burden?*

A gust of wind blistered against his face as he watched his family walking ahead. He looked at his wife thinking, *Can you know me when I'm alive?* and to his children, *Will you truly know what I was, much less what I have become? If such things cannot be known when I live, what will remain when my mortal fabric, my tattered shred of eternity, is gone? Will you have memories of me, and if so, how accurate will they be? No matter how much we love someone, a part of us always hides in the shadows of our private well of recollections.*

He rubbed his withered, formerly burned hand while his mind flashed back to being captured by the Proliate and Magicians after they killed IleZuri and vainly attempted to harvest magic from the tree. *They wasted much of the last precious grains of magic trying to break the tree apart. Some even ate leaves and twigs. The vapid Watchers used the final bits of their magic trying to unlock it, ignorantly turning to dust, the last of it spent.* He rubbed the roughened scars quilted across his body, courtesy of the Proliate and Magicians, vainly trying to squeeze information out of him where none existed.

Lontas was startled by the appearance of his wife. "Did you hear me?"

"I…no, no…lost in thought."

Ihana hugged him. "I knew marrying you meant being wed to your past, all of it…Bellae, the quest. Take time to remember on the anniversary of her death, but don't lose sight of our amazing present or forget our as yet unwritten future. We're almost to the Guardians of her tree."

Lontas nodded gratefully, amazed to have found someone who could love all of his scarred self, internal and external. He studied his wife's face, noting the birth of new wrinkles below her dark brown hair and webbing out from her black eyes. Despite the guilt and self-reproach he heaped upon his mind and soul, he could not deny the existence of some regret at the breadth of the shadow his friendship to Bellae and their quest cast on his current days. As wonderful as the simple joys of his life and family had been, the naked truth was that after battling magical creatures and solving unsolvable problems around the entire globe, the rest of his life could not help but to be a bit anticlimactic. *During childhood's journey, without realizing it, we leave much of our best selves behind.* It wasn't until the tear hit his hand, he realized he was crying. Memories of his time with his best friend braided together with the exhilaration of being a father and husband. For the rest of his life, they would swirl together—sometimes in competition, other times in harmony. After catching up with his children, they kept walking.

"Dad was crying…aagaaaain," Thysia, one of his daughters said. Lontas smiled, staring at the dagger around her waist that used to adorn Bellae's.

"Why do we come to this tree every year and *in winter*?" Apeiro, his tall son complained.

"Lontas, don't answer that!" Ihana said jestingly. "We've heard that tale a million times."

"I *know*, Momma, but it's always fun to hear again," Lilla-Bellae said.

"Thanks for saying that, my little beauty. You recognize this is a great story and as such needs to be told repeatedly. I hope one day, when I'm long gone, you'll bring your own kids here to honor her sacrifice. Her entire family gave their lives so we could live free from tyranny."

"This was hers?" Lilla-Bellae asked what she already knew, gently swinging the Inion medal around her neck.

"Indeed," Lontas said, smiling through the urge to cry.

"It makes me sad to hear how much you suffered—how much everyone was affected during that cursed journey," his wife commented.

"The funny thing about the toughest times in our lives is they tend to be the most memorable and endearing," Lontas said. "A metal sculptor uses fire and hammer to pound out beautiful creations. Sometimes going through something so tough can make exquisite, beautiful in their own way, memories."

"Do you miss those days?" his oldest child, Finn, asked.

"At the time we were just surviving, everything was terrifying. In many ways, I wanted it to end, but now? I'd go back in the heartbeat for a chance to see great friends, live adventure and excitement, and see so many lost to that time, forever stuck in the amber of that age."

"You guys seriously gave up unlimited magic for…a…tree?" Finn huffed.

"What…a…waste! Completely ridiculous! Who willingly gives up *magic?* You know, magic?" Apeiro added.

Lontas nodded. "I guess, from this distance it seems foolish. However, at the time many wanted that power and, sooner or later, whether starting out with good or bad intentions, corruption and depravity would have rotted through their actions. Plus, Bellae always said there would be plenty of magic, and there is."

"There are so few crystals left, and those are constantly fought over," his wife said.

"I guess I was thinking of the real magic of life: our children, the changing seasons, the rising suns, the sparkling moons and stars that provide us company on the darkest nights." He sighed as two of his sons protested.

"Are you seriously crying aaaaa-gain, Dad?" his oldest asked with annoyance.

"Sorry, Finn."

"Enough negative! Today we honor Dad, Bellae, and the League," Lontas' wife said.

"Dad, why did Friar Scelto build you that special room above the gatehouse?" Lilla-Bellae asked, with a grin to her father.

Ihana groaned but playfully winked at her husband. "I swear, you children are in cahoots to make me listen to all his stories over, and over."

"You used to like them," Lontas said with mock offense.

"Dad, how come Friar Gimelli and their kids won't be here this year?" Finn asked.

"Friar Scelto asked her to go the Proliate Islands. Even though they're coleaders, no one's more soothing than Gimelli, and the Proliators are feeling threatened since we rebuilt and built so many castles," Lontas answered. "Plus, she wanted to expose her children to travel like we had, without the war, killing, death riddles, and magical creatures, of course."

"Did I tell you kids Gimelli recited poetry to Scelto at their wedding? Did I mention what your dad did during ours?" Ihana asked. "Cried like a baby!"

Apeiro and Finn rolled their eyes, finding it hard to imagine they could be any more embarrassed by their father. Lontas was grateful they turned away after he started to sob.

Why was I crying then and now? Lontas wondered. The mystifying characteristic of tears is they do not advertise exactly what emotion gave birth to their arising. He knew his wife thought they were born of love for her, and they were, partly. However, other feelings added to the tears' creation. *If I'm honest, there's a lot of regret in them. I wish we'd never found those crystals, and when we did, I wish we'd scattered them into the bottom of the oceans. Who cares if it became someone else's problem thousands of years from now? Bellae would live.*

"The Guardians of the Tree!" Lontas' smallest daughter said cheerfully. They picked up their pace, herding the barking dogs, as the outline of warriors circling the hill came into view.

"Brother!" someone shouted from their left.

Lontas paused, the sight of a massive warrior in black armor sending a shiver down his spine. A smile quickly spread across his face at the recognition of Scelto, appearing far larger and more intimidating than even Ritari in his prime. Lontas rigidly ran forward, the cold, ageing, and perhaps the memories of the injuries all conspiring to make his legs less elastic.

"It's grand to see you," Scelto said, letting his hug linger. "Is it me, or does this anniversary come more quickly with each passing year?"

"So it would seem. How was the trip?" Lontas said.

"Grand. I saw Gimelli and the kids off from Haavi and made my way west, stopping by the Storten Flower Fields."

"You didn't head north to see Queen Hamaza?"

Scelto's face scrunched in discomfort, and his stomach lurched at the now ancient, but still poignant, dysenteric Torahammas milk memories. "Definitely not! I can't believe how big all of our kids are getting."

"Despite my best efforts, they refuse to stop growing," Lontas said, looking up to see Proliate and Southern Dwarf warriors ringing the rainbow tree. He sucked in air hard before clinching his teeth against the tears soliciting to be released at the memories this place forged.

"I know. It doesn't seem like it should be the Proliate and Southern Dwarves' turn to guard the tree on Bellae's Commemoration Day," Scelto said, thinking Lontas' reaction was related to which warriors were there this year. "Sorry, we're supposed to call them the Devout Proliate, as they worship Tallcon. More Disbelieving Proliate who refuse to swear devotion to Tallcon are being banished from the Proliate Islands every day, swelling our Knight ranks with the disillusioned. There's some concern the Disbelievers will start a civil war to be allowed to remain and fight as Proliate even though they don't accept Tallcon as god."

Lontas shook his head. "Did they not get enough of war?"

Scelto scoffed. "There's *always* another battle. With no Dark Warriors for the last twenty years, we wouldn't want to get bored."

Lontas sighed wearily and looked to his children running and playing on the open plain.

Scelto looked to the warriors surrounding the tree. "The Devout Proliate and Southern Dwarves still grumble about only letting those involved in solving the prophecy visit the tree on the anniversary of her death. Although, it really hasn't been the same since Lanella died… what, ten years ago? No relative of Sankari or Kainen has come for much longer. At least the pilgrims have thinned. I think people finally realize the Macht Crystals, and the magic they held, are gone. Still, a few with severe illnesses, some on their deathbeds, and those with great desires come to the tree for a miracle. Thankfully, there are fewer attacks on the tree now—most people having given up on 'freeing' the magic."

"But…" Lontas said, "as long as it stands, some will try. That kind of power will always bring suitors. Many accept Veneficus' misuse of magic's power, but few realize *anyone* with that much control would eventually abuse it. They fail to realize he was intent on destroying every city and culture in Verngaurd."

"Some still wonder whether Bellae should have kept the crystals for herself, or even given them to Veneficus," Scelto said.

"They don't know a fraction of the whole story or the magnitude of her sacrifice!" Lontas replied angrily, remembering her skin being flayed, burnt, and repairing over and over.

"I'm just repeating the rumors. It does seem like there are still a ton of problems."

Lontas scoffed. "There are always problems. At every time in history, there have always been, and at each point in the future, there will always be, problems. They fall into different categories, breed distinct consequences, and respond to different epithets, but are in every age."

"I didn't mean to upset you. It's just, well…twenty-five years later, people are even more disillusioned about how the prophecy ended. There's no denying all of us, even the League, expected the end to lead to more answers, to peace and prosperity. There seems to be just as much tension and friction, hunger and poverty, now as before we finished."

"The whole point is *we* get to ask the questions and *we* are allowed to discover the answers because of her sacrifice. She gave us the opportunity to make our own future. People always want easy answers instead of hard truths."

Scelto sighed. "Maybe we, as individuals and societies, weren't ready."

"Maybe we never will be. Then again, a better way to look at it is we're as ready for today as we can be, and we have to move on from here. The collective 'we' inhabiting the 'now' has to be enough."

"I get that," Scelto said. "Still, personally, I thought the ending would be…better?"

"That's the thing with painless happy endings, they're only for fairytales, as reality requires persistent, repetitive, hard work. She gave us the opportunity, the chance after stopping Veneficus' Na Cearcaill. What we make of it is up to us." Lontas paused. "I heard the Southern Dwarves are quarrelling with the Western Elves."

"They want to expand their mining into Western Elf territory after finding heavy deposits of granite and quartz in the River Horn and precious metals in the Kicsi Kapu Mountains."

"Greed is a cruel and callous master. Bellae knew that better than any of us."

"Plus, the Devout Proliate are threatening to attack the centaurs moving back to the mainland in greater numbers," Scelto said as Lontas' wife came over.

"We'll be at the tree," Ihana said, squeezing Lontas' arm. "We'll let you two chat."

The Proliate guards made several angry comments as his family and dogs slid through their barrier. Eventually, Lontas spoke, "Graveyards, and this hill is a graveyard, are filled with regret, but not of those buried—they suffer only lost opportunities. Remorse is born out of the ones visiting, arising more from self-reproach than the absence of loved ones. We think: what should, would, could I have done while the dead were alive? Did I tell them how important they were to me? Did I adequately speak of their significance and influence upon me? Friar took me to the Knight graveyard during our last Squire Battle, and I think he was trying to get me to see how important each opportunity, each relationship, each day really is."

"That was a very long time ago." Scelto sighed, thinking of the rebuilt, and much larger, Castle Liberum. "I just hope...all the sacrifice, all the loss, was worth it."

Lontas looked at his old friend. "Death may be destined to take our existence, but we are summoned to live our best lives. By we, the League, completing the prophecy and Bellae's sacrifice, we have that chance. Darkness, in the end, may be destined to extinguish all luminosity in the universe, but for the time we are allotted, we should desperately fight to spread our light."

Scelto looked at Lontas with dueling emotions of baffled misunderstanding and respect. "You, as always, are the smartest person I've ever met. Well, you'd better catch up with the family. I'll wait here so we can head back together. I've already paid my respects."

They hugged deeply, wordlessly embracing against the march of time and abhorring the fading of past memories and sacrifices. Lontas headed toward the Guardians of the Tree before pausing and looking down, understanding that once an action, like Bellae's sacrifice, is complete, the why of the time when it was committed fades to be replaced by what-ifs as the action is left dangling, stripped bare of fleshy substance for the world to scrutinize, and condemn, despite being sightless to the origins and costly price paid to achieve it. *The world forgets, or does not care for, the circumstance or motivation of why she gave herself up.*

Forcing a smile, Lontas wordlessly moved forward, squeezing through the Proliate and Southern Dwarf guards while powering through their distasteful looks. His breathing became erratic as he neared the tree towering above the plain, seemingly as out of place in the world as he always felt without Bellae. As the wind howled across the grasslands, the tree's leaves rustled a mix of encouragement and protest. He let the playful cries of his children and the barking of the dogs fade, replaced by sharp, bitter memories of the day Bellae died. Sometimes words evoke the right emotions for an experience, but not here—no words could do justice to what transpired in this place. No expressions could hold the power needed to convey her sacrifice.

"How long did the Magicians and Proliate torture you, Dad?" his son Finn asked as Lontas subconsciously rubbed the torture marks, the memories of pain breaching the surface of his consciousness with each touch.

"Untold months. It took a long time to convince them the crystals were really gone."

"Dear, those scars don't define you," Ihana said. "Remember, this is a happy time! We celebrate what you and Bellae accomplished."

"Dad, can we touch Bellae's tree now?" Lontas' son Apeiro yelled, inching closer.

After a nod from Lontas, Apeiro took off running with the war hounds. The dogs instantly began to howl and bark harmoniously to the tree.

I hope you like the dogs, my old friend, Lontas thought, unbeckoned tears again coming to his eyes. *It's nice to see you again.* He joined his wife and six children at the tree.

"Dad! Your handprint's still there!" Lilli-Bellae said.

"Is it?" Lontas said, trying to act surprised.

"I showed Bellae that I'm wearing her Inion medal!"

"I'm sure she loves that."

"Why doesn't your handprint ever move up the trunk as the tree grows?" Finn asked.

"It's just one of the mysteries of the tree," Lontas said, looking at his disfigured, formerly burned left hand. The skin was thick, scarred, and pulled tight across contracted fingers.

"I think there are more pink and purple flowers this year than last!" Lilli-Bellae declared.

"There are, indeed!" Lontas admired. "The only flowering sugar maple tree in the world."

"You say that every…single…year," Finn huffed, glancing subconsciously at the warriors staring at them. "Please don't start the Storten Flower fields story and how Bellae loved pink and purple flowers!"

"I can't wait until I'm taller," Lilli-Bellae said. "I'm going to climb to the very top!"

While his older children argued the practicality of such a climb, Lontas could not help thinking it was a cruel trick of existence that when we are young and the top of our hourglass is full, we sometimes wish to have the sands fall more quickly, to become older, not understanding the genuine consequences. Then, when the sands have run down and we near the end, we would give almost anything to fill it up again, realizing time runs faster when there is less of it left.

As his children ran around and touched the beautiful tree, he could not help thinking about what Bellae had said: of the billion ways forward, only a pitiful few avoided disastrous pitfalls for the world. Even though he knew she was talking on the tens-of-thousands-of-years scale, that fact still held power with the increasing reports of tension between the various realms.

"Daddy, tell them Bellae's tree will last forever!" Lilli-Bellae implored.

"Oh, no. The first guardian told us all that is born dies, so it shall be with this tree. Everything delivered into the world is escorted out. This tree, and our story, will eventually fade. Our time is but a tattered shred woven into the infinite story stretching out in all directions, but that also means we touch everything going backwards and forwards forever. The past runs up to us, and the future extends out from our lives and actions. That's kind of cool."

"That can't be!" Finn said. "How could anyone forget your adventure and the battles?"

"Every part of nature teaches us we, in a physical and cognitive sense, must step aside for a future we cannot yet see. Our story, as great as it is, our history, as memorable though it be to us, will dim to myth, and the myth will wither to a vague notion, before shriveling to forgotten."

Several of his younger children began to cry.

"Remember, dear, they're only kids," his wife whispered. "Not *yet* philosophers."

We were just kids when we went on the quest, Lontas thought but knew better than to fight that challenge, one he had no chance of winning. "You're right, dear. However, hold your tears for the good news. Our story will hopefully inspire you, that you shall do something great with your life and that may rouse future generations and so on. So, in that way we live on.

"The key to remember is you have to choose greatness, decide to be a good person, resolve to enjoy your time, not just on occasion, but every single moment of every solitary day. You might consider that those who focus all their life's ambitions on the outside world—praise, glory, money, vice—are the ones living in a fantasy, while those who fight the internal mental battles, ask the hard questions, search for answers, and serve others are the ones truly living. Life is an every-day, every-moment decision, each choice becomes a step, each succession of footfalls making up a journey, the sequence of journeys combining to make up your life. If goals and life were one-time decisions, the world would be full of happy people and daring heroes."

"Go run and get some energy out," his wife said, shooing the children off to play with the bounding dogs. "Someday they'll be ready for your amazing philosophy, but perhaps not yet."

Lontas nodded. "I'm trying to teach them lessons so they don't have to learn them the hard way. I don't want them to fall too hard because you can't recover from some mistakes. They're old enough to remember and begrudgingly mature enough to appreciate the lesson."

Ihana noticed her husband glancing around. "What are you looking for?"

"Huh?"

"Every year we come I notice you glancing around, like you're expecting someone."

Lontas thought about how to best answer and realized it must be hard for her, living in the quest's shadow. Taking a deep breath he said, "After the Magicians were finally…done with me, one of the first years I came back here…I saw her."

"Really?"

"I know it sounds crazy. I may have…probably was, dreaming, but it seemed real."

"Did she speak to you?"

"Briefly. She said she's in a place where there's no time and that Friar, Finn, Grym, Borb, and Crann were there. She said she met her parents as well." He paused as if reliving the event over twenty years ago. "She told me not to worry about her," Lontas explained, starting to cry. "That's Bellae, always worrying about someone else more than herself."

"What's wrong, Daddy?" Lilli-Bellae, Lontas' youngest daughter, asked upon returning.

"Nothing's wrong. These are happy tears. The girl I knew when I was your age, the one you're named after, told me I had another, even more important, mission to complete."

"Mission! Will there be dragons, swords, and magic?" she asked hopefully.

"No." He smiled. "No, it's not that kind of quest."

"Then what mission, Daddy?"

"It's one you guys are helping me with. She told me to get busy enjoying the rest of my life, for this is my beginning. Our beginning. The beginning."

Figure 14: The intricate rune Ingwaz, from the third Aett (Tyr's or Heaven's), represents the completion of our journey and, *as endings tend to do, sings forth the promise of a new beginning. One phase concludes, and we find ourselves resonating on the sword's razor edge, the tipping point of Ingwaz, swaying in the winds of time from old to new life energy after the wintery depths of a cold, and at times heartless, journey.*

There is always another evil somewhere on the horizon, always another challenge rising in the murky distance, and, unfailingly, another trial just out of sight. However, even the smallest of heroes can rise up and make a difference and, sometimes, they are the only ones who can.

There is an answer, a resolution, to every problem.
What we inherited we cannot change,
But what we bequeath to the future is truly ours to create.
Stitched within our singular mortal opportunity, our one chance to rise above oblivion and live,
Is our everything, our *tattered shred*, flapping maladroitly within the infinite eternity.
A gift, yes, but one burdened with an unforgiving time limit.
A solitary occasion, the length of which cannot be changed, purchased, stretched, bargained for, or traded. Ignorance of both the unfathomably lucky possibility that is represented in each singularity that is our lives, and the
Power of understanding this existence as *the* true, golden opportunity,
Worth more than any treasure, is an unforgivable chain of incomprehension.
Life is found in the moments, our moments, of *our* living.

There is no destination to be reached, only our unique series of actions, our life, to be carved out.

As with all things, the journey of the Far Forest Scrolls ends, but, under Rune Ingwaz, to signal the beginning of a new voyage for the characters that remain and those of you reading this now.

Life is but an elaborate, beautiful, and, mostly, eloquent cage.

Is not the innately temporary nature of the gift of life the source of its power? Its worth?

Likely, even if begrudgingly, so.

Does the length of the cage or breadth of our life within its confines change its value? Does the fact most inhabitants do not see it as an enclosure change the reality, or significance of:

Our gifted life?

Our tattered shred of eternity?

The ultimate secret?
Take each moment for the moment's sake.
Not because it will be remembered or honored in the future, not because someone else will praise you, but because it is yours to enjoy. For in the end, nothing is ultimately remembered.
The most important, tiny, almost imperceptible, second in your life is the one you are in.
However, that instant only exists as significant if you are truly *in* that instant significantly.
That being true, the greatest sins are disregarding your gifts and ignorance to the importance of cooperative ambition for every living being—for all we can achieve is all *we* can achieve.
Everything is in this moment, the one our eyes presently peer out from.
That's it.
That's the answer.
Our tattered shred of eternity is a simple, yet profound, string of experiences. The ones who live are the ones who manage to be fully in *that* moment, *the* moment, each point in time to experience love, hate, laugh, cry in each present presented. Resist the temptation of falling into the trap of reductionism. We may simply be tattered shreds within the fabric of eternity, but the substance of your forever is significant. Your life does matter, and your life's achievements, sewn with each stitch of your actions, are

everything. In the end, that is all we have, and all we shall leave behind when we cast off our mortal form: a pile of moments, memories, experiences.

Make yours good ones.

With inexpressible thanks and deepest gratitude for reading these words...

Inked from my bleeding soul.

Scrolla Croí: Unapologetic Ramblings, Rambling Unapologetically

Failures swirl, seething and boiling like quicksand within, dragging down and daring against hope and courage, and, if we let them, compress the air from life. Hindsight can be teacher or tormentor. The strain of our flaws is an optical illusion created by our own minds (often with an eye towards how "others" view us). For, there is great benefit infused within the burden, too often overshadowed by the errors' pain. Take a deep breath and release the self-punishment...

But keep the lessons.

Our existence ultimately becomes a sum of knowledge gained from rutted lessons of life and Book. That is what you, in the end, stand upon. That is ultimately how high into the

Dark of the universe you will reach in understanding.

Despite the inevitable end,

Fearlessly climb.

I hope you got lost in the pages of our story,
finding parts of yourself.
Or perhaps those you know, in the characters, while
discovering some truth of how to live.
Now, get lost in the pages of your own story and, whenever
possible, and as many times per day as feasible, garishly
flaunt happiness and jubilation to the shade wrathfully
surrounding us, circling, swirling with wolf-like hunger, its
drool glistening like stars against the blackest night.
Yes, Darkness shall overtake us,
But we shall smile until it does.
Yes, it will eventually eclipse the world,
But we shall fight to truly live in spite of it.
To love consciously is to do so knowing you are
destined to lose them.
Opening your soul up to such pain and damage is hard.
Love all the same, and do not regret the risk.

It's hard to move forward while respecting the past.
Take that next step into the future anyway.
It is difficult to hold on to hope in a world of despair.
Keep dreaming and never give up, regardless.
Evil will always be the easy choice.
Choose to be the good, nevertheless.
Destruction is an easy path—feeding its master, entropy, with greasy ease.
Decide to create and build anyway.
There will always be more knowledge to acquire.
Learn as if your life depends on it—
Building on the knowledge of those who went before, nonetheless.
Evil thrives, spite flourishes, and the mean-spirited burgeon,
Still, relate to others with compassion and humility.
Some dreams die savage, achingly painful deaths.
Dream colossally, nevertheless.
To trust is to knowingly risk that you will be betrayed and taken advantage of.
Trust anyway.
It's grim to struggle, feeling weak, against the power arrayed against us.
Continue to fight for what's right just the same.
To live consciously is to know that you will grow frail and fall into oblivion.
Consciously live with joy anyway.

To stare at your approaching death in tremulous
trepidation is to lose your life.
Wake up each morning and beam, give of yourself
blissfully to gesture rudely at the darkness,
Then smile the rest of your days.
The world expands and swirls with absolutely
brutal indifference.
This, combined with the staggering apathy of eternity
to our own existence,
Is humbling.
Despite that, with rebellious fury, we must fight
hopelessness and
Make life have meaning by,
Choosing to have a meaningful life.

As long as you, we, have breath, let us shake our fists and fight against the darkness with all the indignant fury we can muster. Build, spread light, grow. Even though we know, all of us on some level realize, the darkness, entropy, eternity, will, in the ultimate end, for us and the world, win,

Let us, with our unique, individual tattered
shreds of eternity:

Rage against the gloom.

Each day live with **temperance**.
Dedicate your life to the search of **wisdom**.
Your heart steel to **courage**.
For all within the fabric of eternity, defend **justice**.
Go now, take the first step on your adventure.
Remember, as long as you are able,
Each moment of your life is...
Your beginning,
Our beginning,
The beginning

...

www.ingramcontent.com/pod-product-compliance
Lightning Source LLC
Chambersburg PA
CBHW060540310726
48982CB00009B/1324/J

* 9 7 8 1 7 3 5 7 5 2 8 4 6 *